To Wear
the White Cloak

SHARAN NEWMAN

TOR®

A TOM DOHERTY ASSOCIATES BOOK
NEW YORK

TO WEAR THE WHITE CLOAK

Copyright © 2000 by Sharan Newman

Edited by Claire Eddy

Map by Ellisa Mitchell

A Tor Book
Published by Tom Doherty Associates, LLC
175 Fifth Avenue
New York, NY 10010

www.tor.com

Tor® is a registered trademark of Tom Doherty Associates, LLC.

ISBN: 0-812-58434-1
Library of Congress Catalog Card Number: 00-031794

First edition: October 2000
First mass market edition: January 2003

Printed in the United States of America

0 9 8 7 6 5 4 3 2 1

For Father Chrysogonus Waddell.
Scholar, monk, musician, friend.
On the 50th anniversary of his
entry into the monastic life.

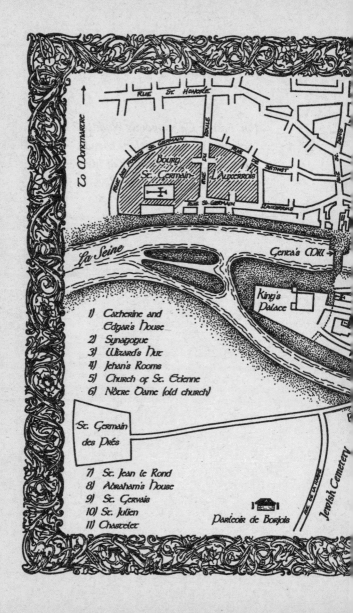

To Montmartre →

RUE ST. HONORE

RUE DES FOSSÉS ST. GERMAIN

Bourg
St. Germain
L'Auxerrois

RUE DE LA SOLLE

BETHIST

RUE ST. GERMAIN

La Seine

Genea's Mill →

King's Palace

1) Catherine and
   Edgar's House
2) Synagogue
3) Wizard's Hut
4) Jehan's Rooms
5) Church of St. Etienne
6) Nôtre Dame (old church)

St. Germain
des Près

7) St. Jean le Rond
8) Abraham's House
9) St. Gervais
10) St. Julien
11) Chastelet

Parloir de Borjois

Jewish Cemetery

RUE DE LA VIEILLE

Twelfth-century paris

To the Temple preceptory →

RUE DES LOMBARDS
RUE DE LA VERRERIE
RUE ST MARTIN

PLACE DE LA GRÈVE

RUE ST MARTIN
RUE DU MOUTON
ST GERVAIS

La Seine

Bishop's Cloister

Goat Island

Vineyards of Abraham

I wish to especially thank the following people for their help in researching this book. I would also like to thank all the people of the Mediev-l academic Internet list who answered questions and discussed historical points that I wasn't sure of. A list of their names would make this book twice as long, but I'm grateful to every one of them.

Prof. Malcolm Barber, University of Reading, for directing me to information on the Knights of the Temple and for writing his excellent study of them, *The New Knighthood,* Cambridge UP, 1994.

Dr. Betty Donoghue, for being another of my very overeducated proofreaders.

Yoram Gordon, for writing the Hebrew for me.

Prof. Susan Einbinder, University of Cincinnati, for advice on how to treat a Torah.

Dr. E. Rozanne Elder, director Cistercian Press, for instant Latin help and for permitting me to use the quote from Isaac of Stella.

Prof. Paul Hyams, Cornell University, for advice on medieval law and suggesting a background for Genta.

Prof. Jeffrey Russell, emeritus UC Santa Barbara, very much meritus with me. For wrestling with Latin at short notice and giving emotional support ditto.

Gerry Witbeck, autopsy technician, for telling me in detail the state the body would be in.

All Latin and Old French translations are mine, especially the mistakes. The only exception is the one from Isaac of Stella cited above.

Prologue

A village in Picardy. 12 kalends May (April 20), 1147; Easter Sunday; 9 Iyyar 4907.

Quae enim lues tam pestifera quis morbus tam lethalis, qui sic faciat hominem immemorem suae salutis, ridentem ac male securum appropinquare usque ad portas mortis?

Is there a plague so pestilent, an illness so deadly, that would lead a man, mindless of his health, laughing and untroubled by evil, right up to the gates of death?

—Guerric of Igny
Sermon for Pentecost

*I*t wasn't much of a fief, just a village and a keep on the edge of a marshy wood. It was one of the many new towns that had been created on recently drained lands or hacked from the forest. It had a church and even a priest now and then, little more. It wasn't on a major road, nor did it have any strategic importance. Therefore, it had largely been ignored by the great nobles and thus allowed to prosper in unobtrusive isolation. The peasants were well fed and had a bit left over after taxes and tithes. The lord of the keep, Osto, a jovial knight in his early forties, had been blessed with ambition that ended at the boundaries of his own land. His wife and only child shared his unusual complacence. But recently a summons had come from his lord that would change Osto's life forever.

This Easter afternoon everyone in the village, from the oldest inhabitant down to the newborn, whose mother could testify to the persuasive theology of the last wandering preacher, were gathered in the bailey of the keep to bid farewell to the first of their inhabitants ever to set out for the Holy Land.

"You have the hose I knitted?" Osto's wife asked worriedly. "You know how easily you get the ague when your feet are cold."

"You put them in the pack yourself, Edwina." Osto patted her cheek. "But Saint Vaast will watch out for us. And we have all of your prayers to keep us safe."

He included the whole village in his glance.

There were sentimental sniffs from some of the crowd. Lord Osto was much loved. Looking at all their familiar faces, Osto broke the gloom with a honking sneeze that startled everyone and proved that he was as much affected by the parting as any.

"Come, Bertulf!" he said loudly. "It's time we started. Remember we go in a holy cause. I know that Bertulf will distinguish himself so greatly that it will finally convince Lord Jordan to give his consent."

All eyes turned to Bertulf's son, Lambert, standing with Lord Osto's daughter, Clemence. The couple quickly moved away from each other, blushing.

Bertulf, Osto's friend and ostler as well as miller for the town, beamed with pride at his eldest, who had won both the heart of Osto's daughter and the approval of her parents. Lambert and Clemence had loved each other from childhood, and Bertulf's growing wealth from his skill at horse breeding had made him almost the equal of the knight in property.

But even a free peasant needed the permission of the local lord to marry a knight's daughter. Bertulf was determined to win that for his son by giving himself to the Knights of the Temple and fighting in the army of the faithful to wrest the holy places of the faith from the infidel Saracens. His sacrifice should prove his worth to Lord Jordon and, by extension, that of his son.

Lord Osto was also taking the cross, fulfilling his vow to join the army of King Louis of France on the coming expedition. He was proud of Bertulf's choice but had no desire to bind himself for life to a military order. His only wish was to distinguish himself without getting killed and then return home to his family.

They were taking only one servant with them, Godfrey, who had been with Osto most of his life. Having no family, Godfrey had begged to accompany his master. He stood a little way from the others, clasping his stout pilgrim's staff.

Before everyone began to cry again, Osto and Bertulf kissed their families and mounted their palfreys. Behind them on a lead was Osto's stallion, Vrieit. The horse was the pride of the town. His father had been bought at great expense at the fair in Champagne from a Jewish trader who had brought him from Spain. The Spanish stallion had then been given the best mares for three years running. The result was Vrieit, trained by Bertulf, and raised on the best local oats and marsh grass. He was larger than the palfreys by four hands' spread and rivaled any destrier in Christendom.

Everyone cheered or tried to through their tears as the three men set forth, sunlight gleaming on their untarnished mail and shields.

The great adventure had begun.

One

Paris. Thursday, The kalends May (May 1), 1147;
30 Iyyar, 4907. The feast of Saint Philip, apostle,
who had four
daughters, all prophetesses.

*Primo hoc ipsum quod cum plurimi judices viri in
Israel fuisse referantur,
de nullo illorum dicitur, quia propheta fuerit,
nisi de Debbora muliere.*

First of all, of the many male judges in Israel who are
referred to, it is said of none of them that they were
prophets, only of the woman Deborah.

—Hrabanus Maurus
Commentary on the Book of Judges

*I*t came as a shock to Catherine that the children had forgotten what their house looked like.

"Is it that one, Mama?" James pointed at every gate as they made their way through the twisty streets of Paris, toward the Grève, on the north bank of the Seine.

"No, James." Catherine patted her son's tousled curls. "Ours has the brass dragon that your father made. Remember? You lift its nose to sound the bell."

"Oh, of course," James said, his face wrinkled with the effort of imagining it.

"We've been gone over a year, Catherine," Edgar reminded his wife. "After all that time in Trier, we're lucky James and Edana can even remember how to speak French."

"We stayed too long." Catherine sighed.

She buried her face in James's hair as she fought to keep the tears from starting again. They had planned to come back in spring as soon as the roads were cleared of winter debris and the new baby was strong enough to travel. But the winter winds had carried a fever that took the month-old child between one dawn and the next.

Catherine had been sick, as well, and her grief at the death of little Heloisa had made her recovery slow. For weeks she had refused to consider returning to Paris and leaving the tiny grave alone in a foreign land. It had taken the scorn of her sister, Agnes, now married to a German lord, to recall her to the duty she owed her remaining family.

Catherine had thought that the rift between Agnes and herself had been mended when the family had come to save Agnes from being tried for murder, but marriage and security had brought back some of her sister's more unpleasant traits, among them an intolerance for emotional displays.

"You think that you're the only woman who ever lost a child?" she had told Catherine. "You have two healthy ones left. Be grateful for that and stop this moping. James and Edana need you more than the baby does. She's in Heaven now, after all."

"What do you know?" Catherine had snapped back. "You've never had children."

"I've never studied theology either, but I know it's a sin to grieve immoderately, and that's what you're doing," Agnes had replied firmly.

The fight that ensued had shaken Catherine out of her deep pain more than all the kindness of her friends could. Fury at her sister's coldness pulled her from melancholia at last. Agnes's scorn made her realize that it was time to return to life.

It was fortunate that Catherine didn't see Agnes's expression as she stormed from the room, or catch Edgar hugging Agnes in thanks. Instead, she went back to their house in town determined to prove to her sister that she wasn't being excessive in her grief.

So they had decided to come home.

Edgar was walking beside his horse, leading the way. His sister, Margaret, was riding and doing her best to keep three-year-old Edana from tumbling off in her excitement.

Catherine watched them as closely as she could while trying to keep James from jumping from his spot in front of her on the horse. She was more worried about Margaret than her own children. Edana had proven many times that she could survive a fall. Margaret was much more frail, and the trip to Germany had been hard on her in many ways.

Catherine sometimes wondered if they had been wise in bringing Edgar's sister from her home in Scotland to live with them. If her life there would have been without affection, it would also have been safer.

"Almost there!" Edgar called out. "Now, James, watch for the dragon!"

"I see it!" James cried. "There! Is that it?"

The last words were in tones of doubt that Catherine echoed.

"What's happened here?" she said. "The gate is overgrown with vines. The windows are still shuttered. It looks as if no one has been here since we left. Where's Samonie? Solomon was supposed to tell her to open the house for us."

Catherine regretted the words immediately.

"Do you think something has happened to Solomon?" Margaret asked, her voice rising in fear.

"Of course not," Catherine answered too sharply. "Solomon has been to Samarkand and back and spent most of his life wandering through pagan lands. What could happen to him between Trier and Paris?"

She tried not to think of the pilgrims and soldiers who saw no difference between killing Saracens in the Holy Land and attacking the Jews living in France. Catherine wished again that her cousin would accept baptism but knew that only a miracle could change his heart. She fell back on her reassurance to Margaret. Solomon knew how to protect himself.

"But he should be here," Margaret said. "He said he'd wait for us. What could have happened?"

"We won't find out by standing outside," Edgar said. "Come along."

He lifted his daughter from the horse, and then helped his sister down. For a moment, they clustered before the house like a troupe of beggars, then Catherine took the keys from the hook on her belt and sorted through them for the large iron one that would open the thick oak gate.

She had to use both hands to make it turn, and, when

she heard the catch click open, she and Edgar still had to push together to make it move.

The gate scraped open far enough for Edgar to enter. They heard him exclaiming at the state of the place as he tore out the encroaching vines with his one hand. At last they were able to open it wide enough to bring the horses and the pack mule in.

Catherine stopped in horror.

"What happened?" she asked. "Even the front door is boarded up. Edgar, we'll have to find someplace else to stay until the house can be aired. We can't take the children in among the foul humors. Where is Samonie? I don't understand this at all."

"Catherine LeVendeur? Is that you?"

The voice came from the road. An old woman was peering through the gateway, squinting to make them out.

"Hervice?" Catherine ran to greet their neighbor. "What's happened here? How long has the house been empty? Why is there no one here to greet us?"

"Your father was back sometime before the feast of the Nativity," Hervice answered. "He left around the time of the Purification. He told everyone he was going on a pilgrimage and that you and your husband would be along to take up his trade soon."

"But that was only four months ago!" Catherine said. "Things couldn't have got into such a state in that short time."

The old woman shook her head. "He didn't stay here, but on the Île with his Jewish friends. Odd way to start a pilgrimage, I'd say."

"Finishing his business with them, I suppose," Catherine said. She swallowed the fear and the shame that came every time she remembered that her father had actually abandoned Christianity to return to the faith of his ancestors. No one must know that he was even now on his way to join the Jewish community in Arles. It would put the whole family under suspicion, even though Catherine and her sister were both good Christians and their brother, Guillaume, had never even learned of their father's ancestry.

Hervice didn't notice her hesitation and continued her complaint. "There's been talk that he'd left a treasure behind in the house so he had the shutters nailed down and hired a guard. Sent your servants all up north to work for your brother, I think. Haven't seen the guard in weeks. Maybe he took the treasure."

"Father left nothing in the house," Catherine told her. "All of value that we didn't take to Trier, he left with my brother or the monks at Saint Denis for safe keeping."

Hervice seemed about to express her doubt about that but then looked at their tired faces.

"Fine welcome home for you anyway," she said. "Why didn't you send word? Here now, come across to my house. You can wash the dust off and have some soup and bread."

As they followed her, Edgar leaned close and whispered to Catherine, "How much gossip do you think we'll get with our soup?"

"A lot, I hope," Catherine whispered back. "How else will we find out what's been going on while we were away?"

Edgar murmured his opinion of the usefulness of kitchen talk.

"Nonsense," Catherine answered. "I'll wager Hervice knows things even the priest hasn't heard yet."

"Nor ever will," Edgar said. "But that's not the sort of news I was hoping for."

"Then just attend to the children and eat your soup," Catherine suggested. "I'll strain the truth from her tales and feed it to you later."

They settled on benches in Hervice's garden while she called a servant to bring soup.

"You'll want to slake your thirst after the journey, as well," she said. "Gilles! Fetch water for our guests!"

Edgar had been hoping for something stronger. He set down the soup bowl to take the water, ignoring the serving boy, who stared in shock at the black leather strap covering the tender skin of his left wrist where the hand used to be.

"Did a Saracen cut it off?" Gilles breathed, his eyes round.

Edgar smiled bitterly. "No, a demon in the body of a man."

"A demon!" Gilles's eyes grew even wider. "What did it look like?"

"Like my father," Edgar said bitterly. "Exactly like him."

It was clear that Gilles wanted to ask more, but Hervice ordered him sharply to stop gawking and drag out a table for their guests.

James and Edana, who had already set their bowls on the ground, fetched wooden spoons from Catherine's sack and were happily eating.

Catherine waited until the family had settled before she questioned Hervice about what had been happening in Paris over the long year they had been gone.

"Last year was a bad harvest." Hervice clucked her tongue. "Bread was dear and beggars on every corner. The wine was thin and sour. The spring has been too cold this year, as well. Not a good omen for this venture of the king's."

"We saw armed men wearing pilgrim crosses everywhere as we came through town," Catherine commented. "I thought they would have left by now."

Hervice shook her head. "I hear they're starting out any day, but it seems that the only pilgrimage anyone is making is to Paris. There are even Knights of the Temple, dozens of them, with all their squires and servants, doing God knows what. No wonder Edessa fell, if all of them are loafing about here in France!"

Catherine nodded. "I saw a group of them. I didn't realize the order had grown so. They must have come to guide the king and the emperor to the Holy Land."

"Well, I say if they're going, then they should go," Hervice snapped. "The place is overrun by men with swords. Warriors, knights, lordlings, even those who are supposed to be clerics. They say some of the knights are also monks, but I never heard of a warrior taking a vow of chastity and I have granddaughters. You give any man a sword and sooner or later someone will get run through. It's their nature."

Catherine reached a protective arm out to Margaret, who had been listening in silence. The men who had attacked her in Germany hadn't carried swords. Perhaps that was how she had survived. But what had happened to her was more brutal than a simple thrust and a quick death.

"It will be all right, *cossete*," Catherine assured her.

Margaret gave a sad smile. "Of course. We're home now."

Catherine kept her arm around Margaret as she turned back to Hervice.

"Has no one come by recently asking for us? A friend was supposed to be here when we arrived."

Hervice shrugged and yelled for Gilles to bring more water. "No one that I know of. We can ask the rest of the street. But I'd have heard of it, I think."

Catherine agreed. For some reason Solomon had been delayed. It wasn't like him, but the times were unsettled, especially for a Jewish trader, and he might have had to change his plans.

"Messages go astray," Margaret said, following her thoughts.

"They do indeed," Catherine said. "All too often. He might have sent word to Trier after we had left."

She gave her bowl to the serving boy and stood.

"Thank you, Hervice," she said. "Now we need to find a place to stay until the house can be opened and aired."

"I'm feeding a houseful now, or I'd take you in," Hervice answered, endeavoring to look regretful.

"We wouldn't think of it," Edgar told her honestly.

He took Catherine's elbow and guided her out into the street.

"So where shall we lay our tired bodies tonight?" Catherine grinned. "I agree that Hervice makes a poor hostess, but with Paris so crowded, we might not be able to find anyone better."

Margaret spoke up. "I want to stay with Willa."

They both gaped. Margaret hardly ever voiced an opinion.

"Well," Edgar began, "I'm sure Willa would be happy

to take us in. But *deorling*, she and her husband probably
don't have extra space. He's only a felt maker. Likely they
share a corner in the shop room of his master."

"I don't mind," Margaret said, never having slept surrounded by fresh felt.

Willa was the daughter of Catherine's housekeeper, Samonie, and still Margaret's best friend. A few years older
than Margaret, Willa had comforted and cared for her both
in Paris and before, in Scotland, through a dangerous, tragic
journey. Not having been brought up at a proper court,
Margaret didn't let the gaping difference in their status affect her feelings for Willa.

Edgar and Catherine, however, were all too aware of
what people would say if they arrived in Paris and lodged
with a felt maker, as well as how much their request for
shelter would disrupt Willa's husband's life.

"There are the nuns at Montmartre," Catherine suggested. "Abbess Cristina would be happy to take us in and
hear the news about Agnes."

Margaret's shoulders sagged. That would mean returning
across the fields and up the hills. Edgar bit his lip. They
were all exhausted. He didn't want his family going door
to door hunting for a night's shelter.

"James," he said. "Help me unload the tent. Edana, you
can carry the pegs if you promise not to run.

"The night is mild," he added to Catherine. "The garden
can't be so overgrown that there isn't a space to pitch the
tent. It won't hurt us to spend one more night in the open."

Catherine nodded agreement. She was as tired as the children.

"Tomorrow we can send for Samonie to come back from
Vielleteneuse and help us open the house," she decided. "If
it's too filthy and full of bad air, then we'll have to take
the children back there. Since my brother has all our servants at his keep, he shouldn't mind taking us in, as well."

"Guillaume might be better pleased if we spared him
more mouths to feed," Edgar cautioned.

"Well," Catherine considered this. "It can't be helped.

He certainly wouldn't turn us away. And I know my sister-in-law will be delighted."

That having been settled, they made their way down a passage next to the outside wall through the weeds and vines to the garden. They all stamped down an area large enough for the tent, and then Catherine ran down to the corner tavern for a pitcher of beer and cabbage pies. When she got back, Edgar was pounding in the last stake, balancing the hammer easily in one hand.

The bells for Compline were tolling by the time Catherine fell asleep. All the churches of Paris! How she had missed their individual tones! Saint Jacques, Saint Merri, Saint Magloire. From almost over their heads sounded Saint Gervais and Saint Jean le Pauvre, across the river. Then the deep notes of Nôtre Dame on the Île and farther away the bells of Saint Germain l'Auxerrois. Dozens of churches, all telling her that she was home, wishing her a good night. She snuggled into the blankets, the warmth of her family surrounding her, and felt completely happy.

It wasn't Matins yet when she awoke. There was a light glowing outside the tent. She realized at once that it wasn't from the moon. The brightness grew, not as dawn approaching, but that of someone with a torch.

"Edgar," She whispered and felt the stump of his hand against her lips. She rolled over and pushed herself to her knees and elbows to see better.

He was kneeling before the tent flap, peering through the narrow opening. His right hand held a knife. She wondered how long he had been awake, guarding them.

The light flickered over the canvas and was followed by that of another torch. Catherine held her breath, wondering if these were enemies of her father, come to burn down the house. Perhaps someone had discovered that Hubert hadn't gone on a pilgrimage to Rome. What if he hadn't been as careful as he thought in hiding his intentions?

She put her arms over the sleeping bodies of her children and prayed to Saint Genevieve to keep them safe.

There was a rattling at the boarded door and muffled

swearing. Then a voice came on a chance breeze, soft but clear.

"He said it was open last time."

The only answer to that was a growl and the sound of footsteps through the brush as the torchlight passed again, heading down to the stream.

It was several moments before Catherine could move. Beneath her arms she felt the steady breathing of Edana and James.

"Edgar!" she whispered. "What should we do? What if they come back with weapons?"

"It's nearly dawn," Edgar said quietly. "I don't think they'll risk returning tonight. Go back to sleep. I'll keep watch."

Edgar stayed at his post until the sky lightened and the bells began for Prime.

Beside him, Catherine lay still, but she couldn't return to sleep. The rest of the night her mind kept repeating that one sentence. Who had said it was open? What last time? What could those men have wanted? The mythical treasure her father was supposed to have hidden? Had someone broken in before? What about the guard that Hervice said had been left there? Why had he left his post? And where, oh where, was her cousin Solomon?

Catherine shivered. The dawn was cold.

Two

Paris, a felt maker's house on the Île de la Cité. Friday, 6 nones May (May 2), 1147. The first of Sivan, 4907. Feast of Saint Athanasius, Patriarch of Alexandria and fighter against heresiarchs.

... Bernardus de Ballolio salutem in Domino. Volo notum fieri omnibus, tam futuris quam presentibus, quod, pro dilectione Dei et salute amime mee antecessorumque meorum, fratribus militibus de Templo Solomonis XV libratas terre mee, ... Hoc donum in capitolio, quod in octavis Pasche Parisius fuit, feci, domino apostolico Eugenio presente, et ipso rege Francie, et archiepiscopo Senonensi, et Burdegalensi, et Rothomagensi, et Turonensi, et fratribus militibus Templi alba clamide indutis c xxx. ...

... Bernard of Ballieul greets you in the Lord. I wish it to be marked by all, in the future as it is now, that, for the love of God and the deliverance of my soul and those of my ancestors, I give and concede to the brothers Knights of the Temple of Solomon 15 pounds revenue of my land ... This gift was made in the Chapter meeting held on the octave of Easter in Paris, Pope Eugenius present and also the king of France and the Archbishops of Sens and Bourges and Rouen and Tournai and 130 brothers of the Temple in white cloaks....

—Charter of Paris
April 28, 1147

$\mathcal{T}$he next morning Catherine and Edgar took the children to the Île, where, down a twisty street near the river, they found Willa outside her house. She was standing in a trough up to her ankles in cold water and soap as she trod the wool to mat it. She greeted them with a startled cry.

"*Enondu!* I can't believe it!" she gasped. "Why didn't you send word you were coming? Mother would have come down and had everything ready for you."

Catherine hugged her, despite Willa's damp clothes. As she did, she noticed how much thinner the girl was.

"Solomon was supposed to have passed through Paris over a month ago," she explained. "Didn't you see him?"

Willa stepped out of the trough and lowered her skirts to cover her bare legs. She was shaking, still astonished at their sudden appearance.

"He never came here," she told Catherine. "Mother visited me last Sunday and she said nothing about a message, either. I'll send for her at once."

"We did that this morning," Edgar told her. "She should arrive by late afternoon. But Catherine and I want to start work immediately. May we leave the children here with you? Margaret will watch out for them, but things are in such a state at the house that it would be too dangerous for little ones to go unsupervised."

"Of course!" Willa smiled nervously. "But wouldn't you rather that Mother and I readied the place first? You shouldn't have to take care of such matters."

Catherine hesitated. She wasn't happy at the thought of spending the day covered with the dust and mold of a house left empty all winter, but she also worried that her father might have left behind a message or something else that might cause trouble if anyone outside the family saw it. She knew Willa and her mother could be trusted, but the state of the house and the midnight intruders had left her uneasy.

"Edgar and I can manage," she said. "As long as I know James and Edana are safe with you. Margaret will keep them out of your way, won't you, my dear?"

"I must ask Belot if it will be all right," Willa said.

She went inside for a moment. They heard voices raised in altercation, then lowered. Willa returned, smiling.

"My husband, Belot, told his master that he'll be responsible for seeing that the work is still done and the master agreed that it would be no trouble to keep the children here."

"Yes, I don't mind staying," Margaret said eagerly. "I could even help you, Willa."

Willa smiled fondly at Margaret. Then her smile faded as she noted the scar across the child's temple and down the side of her cheek. Margaret bent her head and raised her hand as if to brush the mark from her face.

Willa recovered quickly. "Well, I still think it would be better if you waited until Mother arrived, but certainly, I'd be happy to take the children. And Margaret and I have so much to tell each other. I wouldn't have known Edana! She's grown so! You don't remember me, do you, sweet?"

Edana had regarded her with suspicion until she saw Willa welcome Margaret with a hug and kiss and much fussing. Then she became jealous of the attention and demanded to be admired, too.

Although she continued to protest that Catherine and Edgar shouldn't involve themselves in menial work, Willa agreed to keep the children with her until after Vespers. After giving instructions and leaving a coin for the midday meal, Catherine and Edgar hurried back across the bridge to face the task of prying boards off the doors and nails out of the shuttered windows.

"This is going to be a long day's work," Catherine said. "Perhaps Willa was right that we should get someone else to help, at least to unboard the windows."

"There's no one in town I trust, except the clerics I studied with," Edgar answered. "And I can hardly ask them to do servants' work."

Catherine then realized that Edgar had been harboring the same fears she had about what Hubert might have left behind. The men who had come in the night had been looking for something, and she wanted to find it first. But the work was hard, and she was clumsy at it even with two hands. It was only a few minutes before she had several slivers from the rough wood stinging her fingers.

"Perhaps we should wait just until Samonie gets here with Martin?" Catherine knew the answer to that by the tightening of Edgar's jaw. He refused to admit that his missing hand posed any problem.

She didn't argue. Edgar had come so close to dying when his hand had been sliced off as he tried to stop the sword as his father raised it to strike down a serf. Every day she had to convince him anew that she didn't care that he only had one hand. That he was alive was all that mattered.

"We can certainly get into the house before they arrive," Edgar continued. "I want to know what those men were looking for last night."

"Father's fantasy 'treasure,' of course," Catherine suggested with some doubt in her voice. "What else?"

"Then why did they expect to find the house open?" Edgar countered. "Who had left it open before?"

Catherine didn't have an answer. She sighed and prepared herself to be covered in dust by the end of the day, her hands bruised and bleeding.

They decided to try getting in through the back door leading from the kitchen out to the garden. Edgar got a length of iron from the shed and, using his right hand and Catherine's left, they managed to pry the boards off the door.

"It's still locked," Catherine said as she shook the handle. "No one could have opened this since we left. Perhaps those thieves had the wrong house and we're worrying about it for nothing. I hope the keyhole hasn't rusted."

It took several tries to turn the lock and lift the bar and then a hard push before the door swung open.

Catherine looked around in dismay.

"Oh, *carissime!* It will be weeks before we can cook here again. Everything is filthy and, look, someone even left pots and bowls on the table with food still in them! I don't understand. Father wouldn't be so neglectful."

She wrinkled her nose in disgust at the smell coming from the furry masses in the bowls. Gingerly she picked them up and carried them outside.

"We'll need to dig a new midden, too," she announced when she returned. "I think the neighbors must have been throwing their refuse over the wall into ours. Edgar? Where are you?"

She went through the kitchen and up into the hall, the main room of the house, where they ate, entertained, and where the servants usually slept. Edgar was squatting before the cold hearth, poking at the ashes.

"I thought that had been swept out before we left!" Catherine said. "All that spring cleaning for nothing!"

"Someone's been here," Edgar said. "Perhaps your father came in for a few days, despite what Hervice told us."

"He wouldn't have left food lying out to spoil," Catherine said. "I can still smell it."

She sniffed and then, cautiously, drew a deeper breath. She knew that scent. It was faint, but all too familiar, like wet leaves and wine must, overlaid by something else, sickly sweet.

"Edgar?" she asked, her voice breaking in fear.

He inhaled and noticed it, too.

"Perhaps a mouse left in one of the traps?" he said hopefully.

"It's stronger over here by the stairs," Catherine quavered.

She looked up the steps, trying to will her feet to climb

them. She would not think of her father. Hubert had gone on to Arles, as he had planned. Or about Solomon. Solomon hadn't come to Paris. Everyone said so. It was a mouse in there. A very large mouse; that's what it was. Maybe even a rat.

"Catherine, wait here," Edgar said softly from behind her. "Let me check. Why don't you find a shovel so that I can carry whatever it is out to the midden?"

"Yes," Catherine said. "Very well."

But she didn't move as he went up. She heard his boots clunk over her head as he looked in the small front room, where the chests of clothes and linens were kept, and then their room at the back. Finally, he came to the door of the counting room. She heard him fumbling with the lock holding the bar over the door.

"Should I bring up the key?" she called.

"No, I'll come down for it," he answered quickly.

She held out the keyring and handed it to him before he was at the bottom.

"It's this one," she told him, separating the counting room key from the others. "The smell is stronger in there, isn't it?"

"Now, Catherine," he said firmly. "With all the parchment in there to chew on, there might be a whole nest of mice. Perhaps a cat got in and was trapped, as well."

She didn't believe him, which was why she stayed where she was. There were some things she hadn't the courage for. It made her angry with herself, but if someone she loved were lying dead above her, she wanted to be prepared before she looked on the face.

Edgar went back up. When he was out of Catherine's sight, he took off his tunic and covered his mouth and nose with it. No mouse, however big, left a smell like that. But even more disquieting to him was when he turned the key. It moved in the lock smooth as butter. The iron padlock had been oiled recently. The thought chilled him. He gave up all hope of discovering nothing more than decaying vermin inside.

There was nothing for it but to find out before Catherine

became impatient and came up to investigate.

He took a deep breath and opened the door.

"*Cristes-mæl!*" he exclaimed.

"What is it?" Catherine raced up the steps. "Not Father!"

"Catherine, don't!"

Edgar turned and tried to stop her from seeing, but Catherine craned her neck around him. She recoiled in disgust and then looked again.

"Who is that?" She asked.

"I don't know," Edgar said. "By his clothes, I'd say he's a soldier, a knight perhaps. Certainly a pilgrim."

Catherine pulled her eyes from what was left of the man's face to his mail shirt, visible under the white cloak. The dark brown of old blood had stained a cross onto the middle of his chest. There was a small cross of linen pinned to the shoulder of the cloak with an iron brooch.

Catherine studied the design on the brooch, partly to avoid looking at the remains of the man's face. It was a crude design of two knights riding one horse. Each knight held a shield. Together they held a single spear.

She turned to Edgar in confusion.

"Isn't this the symbol of the Knights of the Temple of Solomon?"

Edgar nodded. "It's very like the design on their seal and over the portal of their preceptory. This man must have been of the order."

"But what is he doing here?" Catherine wondered.

"Rotting, Catherine," Edgar said. "We have to get the body out of here right away."

"Edgar, what are we thinking of?" Catherine said.

She crossed herself and began a prayer for the dead. Hastily, Edgar joined her, both their faces raised piously to avoid looking at the still figure on the floor.

When they had finished, Edgar backed out and started to close the door behind them.

"His white cloak is also that of a Knight of the Temple," he said. "We should go to the Temple preceptory and tell them of this. Perhaps someone there will know who he was."

"How will they know?" Catherine asked.

Edgar forced himself to look at the body again. She was right. The eyes and cheeks were gone and the chin eaten away so that the man's teeth grinned at them hideously. The rest of the face and hands were black with a greenish tint, except where a gray fuzz of mold grew in patches.

Not even the one who loved him best would be able to recognize him. Edgar hoped that person would never see what the poor knight had come to.

"Perhaps he's wearing a ring or some other token that will identify him," he suggested. "But we can let his brothers of the Temple search for that. Come, my love."

"Wait. Something's odd." Catherine stepped in and knelt by the body. She swallowed hard to keep her stomach in place. Gingerly, she ran her fingers over the bloodstained cloak and tunic.

"That's strange," she said. "Edgar, come look. All this blood, but there's no tear in the material. And no stain spread out on the floor, either. Someone must have put this man's body here after he was killed."

"That is strange. But if you can't find a wound, how can we be sure how he was killed? The blood may not be his." Edgar's curiosity overcame his desire to get both of them away from this ugly death.

"Edgar, he didn't come up here to die of old age. There must be a wound someplace," Catherine said.

She looked at her husband. "Do you think we should turn him over? He might have been struck from behind."

Her face showed how little she wanted to touch the man further.

"I suppose that it might be a good idea to find out all we can, in case we're questioned," Edgar answered grudgingly. "Here, I'll do it."

He put his right hand under the body and tried to push with it and his left arm. But he couldn't get enough leverage to turn the man over.

"I'll help; it was my idea." Catherine put out her hands and stretched her neck as far away as she could. "Oh, Saint Lazarus, please don't let him squish!"

He squished.

The knight's arm flopped forward as they rolled the body but, mercifully, stayed attached. The back of the cloak was also stained but whole. When they peeled it off, though, they had no doubt about how the poor man had met his fate.

"What could make a hole that size in a mail shirt?" Catherine asked. "A spear?"

"No, more like a pointed stake, I'd say. Something about as big around as one of our tent pegs," Edgar answered. "But it may have been tipped in iron. And it would have taken great force to drive it so far into his body."

They stared at the hole in the man's back, now black except where the maggots crawled.

Catherine felt suddenly sick. She stumbled out into the hallway and threw up over the railing.

"Oh, God, the mess to clean," she moaned.

She unwrapped her scarf and wiped her mouth with the ends. Her long black braids fell loose down her back.

"*Leoffest.*" Edgar turned her about and held her.

Gratefully she inhaled the scent of his body: sweat and wool and life.

"It's strange," she babbled. "We often see corpses in this state, hanging from gibbets at the crossroads or washed down the river. I hardly notice them anymore, except to say a quick prayer for their souls. It's as if the familiarity makes them no more than part of the landscape."

Edgar patted her back. "I know. This is different. This is our home. It's been violated by the death of a stranger." He stopped in doubt. "At least I think he's a stranger."

Catherine turned her head and kissed the bottom of Edgar's chin. He bent so she could kiss his mouth. The living taste of him steadied her. Then she remembered what her own mouth must taste like. She turned her face away and closed her eyes, clinging to him until her breathing was even again.

Then she took one more deep breath and stood on her own.

"Whoever he is," she announced, "the man doesn't belong here. We need to place him in the care of his own people. Immediately."

She stopped. Her voice had begun to tremble again.

Edgar took her hand and led her back down the stairs.

"We'll go back to Willa's, wash, eat if we can and then hunt for someone in authority to report this to," he decided.

"Do you think we'll be suspected?" Catherine asked.

Edgar paused mid-stair and gaped at her. "You *are* upset!" he exclaimed. "How could we have killed a man in Paris when we've been gone for nearly a year?"

"Of course." Catherine was surprised at herself. "That was stupid of me."

Then she realized that she hadn't been thinking about herself and Edgar but about her father, who had come and gone, and Solomon, who might have been in Paris, after all. With all the fervor of the preparations for the king's expedition, there were many who felt it only right to attack the Jews at home first before the Saracens abroad. Neither Solomon nor Hubert ever announced his faith to strangers. But neither would deny it if challenged. And she doubted they would allow a challenge to go unanswered.

Yes, it was all too possible that her father or her cousin might have had a reason to be compelled to kill a soldier of Christ.

Willa was surprised to see them so soon. She had all of the children in the trough helping her stomp down the felt. When she looked up and saw their faces, she stumbled and nearly fell out into the street.

"I need to wash before I touch anyone," Catherine greeted her. "Is there a basin I can use?"

Willa stepped out at once and ran in to get water and a cloth to dry their hands with.

"In a minute, James," Edgar said, as his wet son tried to climb up his leg. "Just as soon as Mama finishes washing my hand."

Catherine dampened the cloth and rubbed it over the edges of their sleeves, as well. She had images of tiny vermin hiding in the robes of the knight's body and leaping onto her.

When Catherine had finished, she picked up Edana and let the child rub her soapy hands where she liked. Willa waited patiently for them to tell her what had upset them, but Margaret had no servile scruples.

"What's wrong?" she demanded. "Has something happened to Solomon?"

Edgar reached out to her, letting James slide back down to the ground.

"No, *deorling*," he assured her. "There's still no word from him. But we had a nasty surprise. It seems that someone has decided to use our house to dispose of a body."

"Again?" Margaret shook her head.

"Margaret!" Catherine was shocked. "No one has ever died in our house before."

"Well, from what I've heard, bodies seem to fall on you a lot," Margaret said.

"Not in years," Catherine insisted. "And your brother found this one first. Anyway, it's no one we know. What we need to do now is find someone in charge of the Knights of the Temple. It's their body we think; they can come and fetch it. Is your mother here, yet, Willa?"

"No, Mistress Catherine," Willa said. "Should I send her to the house when she arrives?"

"Goodness, no." Catherine thought a moment. "Edgar, it will be days before the house will be livable. I think that, once we've reported this, we should go back to Guillaume at Vielleteneuse. We can have Samonie arrange to have the house cleaned and aired, just as it should have been all along."

Edgar gave her an incredulous glance. "You want to go away without finding out who that man was and why he was left in our home?"

"Don't you think that the care and safety of the family is more important than some stranger who was simply dumped on us?" Catherine glared back at him.

Looking at her, Edgar realized suddenly what the real problem was. Catherine was terrified. Not for the children or themselves. There was no reason to feel that they were in danger.

But Edgar saw it in her eyes. Catherine believed that the knight had been left in their house for a purpose, not just because it was unoccupied and convenient. As much as she wanted to deny the possibility, Catherine feared that the dead man had something to do with her father, because of his apostasy. Did she really think Hubert could kill to protect his secret?

For that matter, Edgar wondered, did he?

"Catherine?" he asked.

"Not now," she answered. "Please."

She took his hand in both her own.

"Please," she repeated.

He smiled at her and squeezed her fingers in understanding.

"Very well," he said. "We have more than enough to do now."

"That we do." Catherine took a deep breath. "Willa, may we change here? I don't want to appear before the master of the Temple with cobwebs in my hair and gore from one of his men on my robes."

Willa shook her head. "Only you would have such a dilemma, Mistress," she said. "I already miss life in your household. It's so much duller being married."

Edgar and Catherine exchanged glances. Neither one of them would have ever thought their married life dull.

Accordingly they presented themselves at the gate of the Temple preceptory outside Paris that afternoon just as the bells were ringing for Nones. They had come on horseback to indicate they weren't commoners or beggars, but Catherine was nervous all the same. She had resolved to let Edgar speak for them both. When she told him that he only nodded, his expression showing his disbelief. He knew well how hard it was for Catherine to hold her tongue. This only strengthened her determination to behave for once as a proper matron.

The gate was opened by an old man in the black tunic

of a sergeant. His white hair hung in strands around his dark, weather-beaten face. Edgar's eyes widened as he realized that the man had only one arm.

"I lost this at the end of a Saracen sword, fighting for the faith," the gatekeeper said. "Gape if you want. I'm proud that I gave it for Our Lord."

"It wasn't that," Edgar said. He held up his arm to show the man the emptiness at the end of it. "I only wish my loss had been in as good a cause."

Catherine wouldn't let that stand.

"You were trying to save a man's life," she started. "That's every bit as noble as . . ."

"Yes, *carissima*," Edgar interrupted. "But it has nothing to do with our mission. We need to speak with the commander here on a matter of grave importance."

"The commander's at his prayers," the gatekeeper told them. "And you couldn't bother him in any case. He's preparing to return to the Holy Land as soon as possible on the king's business."

"Then the Marshal," Edgar insisted. "Or the chaplain. We'll wait until they've said the Office. Tell him that Edgar, son of the Lord of Wedderlie, wishes to speak with him."

He drew himself up and looked down on the sergeant with all the force of confidence coming from noble birth. Catherine watched him with admiration. Edgar hardly ever felt the need to play the lord, but when he did, he was to her mind, superb.

The gatekeeper seemed to be impressed as well, though not daunted. After all, noble birth was one requirement for entry into the Knights of the Temple. He grudgingly showed them into the gatehouse and bid them sit and wait until the service was over and he could fetch someone.

"He didn't even ask what our business was," Catherine commented, once the man had left.

"It's not his place to," Edgar said. "I wouldn't have told him if he had asked."

Catherine didn't respond to that, even though the tone was chillingly like that of Edgar's older brother, Duncan, who now held the lordship of their land in Scotland. She told herself that he must appear to the gatekeeper to be equal in rank to the knights. Otherwise, he might not let them in to see the Commander.

It was sometime after the Office had ended that they heard the door to the gatehouse open. Catherine had grown bored and was dozing on Edgar's shoulder. She sat up at once when the sergeant entered.

"You are to see the Marshal," he told them. "He will receive you in the chapter house."

"Thank you," Edgar said, and rose, offering Catherine his arm.

They followed a path that separated the knights' cloister from the stables and were led into a small room adjoining the church. A moment later a man entered, his white cloak proclaiming his noble birth. He was only a little above middle height, but he was built like a bull, with powerful arms and a thick neck. His legs were bowed from life on horseback. He seemed too big for the room. Catherine shrank back to give him space, but Edgar led her forward and bowed.

"My lord Marshal," he said. "I am Edgar of Wedderlie and this is my wife, the Lady Catherine, granddaughter of Lord Gargenaud of Boisvert, in Blois. We returned to our home in Paris yesterday after an absence of nearly a year. Although the house had been closed while we were gone, when we entered we discovered that someone had left the body of a man dressed in the manner of your Order. Murdered, we believe."

"What?" Whatever the Marshal had been expecting, it wasn't this. "One of ours? Murdered? Who? How?" he sputtered.

"We have no idea," Edgar answered. "We only ask that you send some men to claim the body of your fellow and give him a burial with such rituals as you accord your own."

"How do you know this man is one of ours?" the Marshal asked. "There's been no one missing as far as I've heard. An empty bed in the dormitory would have been noticed."

Edgar paused. Catherine forgot her promise and answered for him. Edgar hid his smile. He wasn't surprised.

"The man wore a mail shirt and the white cloak of the Knights of the Temple, with a brooch showing two knights sharing a horse," she said. Then she added, "But perhaps we were wrong, for his cloak had no red cross on the shoulder such as you wear, only a small dark one held in place by the brooch. Or is the red cross only granted to those of you in authority?"

The knight put his hand to the embroidered cross on his left shoulder almost as if caressing it.

"My mother made this at my request when I converted to the Order," he said. "But Pope Eugenius only gave us permission to carry the red cross on our cloaks a few days ago. Not all of the knights have added them, yet. Yes, the man certainly seems to have dressed as we do. What are his features?"

Catherine shivered as she remembered the distorted face.

"Time has erased his features," Edgar said. "His hair was light, though not as blond as mine. He was no longer young, I think, but I could be wrong. His size was a bit taller than you and of more slender build. Can you remember anything else, Catherine?"

She tried to recall anything beyond the torn face and gaping hole in the man's back. Something.

"He was accustomed to riding," she said suddenly.

"Meaning?" The Marshal seemed skeptical.

"He wore leather *brais*," she said slowly, thinking. "But the inside of the leg was worn the way it is when it's always rubbing against the side of a horse. That makes the leather shiny from oil and sweat. Walking causes leather to chafe and become rough, not smooth. That's why I assumed he was a knight."

The two men were silent a moment. The Marshal looked to Edgar for confirmation.

"I didn't notice," he admitted. "You can examine his clothing when you have the body retrieved. It would be best if you sent someone at once, with canvas to wrap him in. I would judge the man has been there for some time."

The Marshal went to the door and called to a guard waiting outside.

"I'm still not convinced that your inconvenient guest is a Knight of the Temple, but I shall send some of the servants to collect him," he announced. "Direct them to your home, or lead them if you will. I'll tell the commander of this. He may wish to question you himself."

"We shall be at Vielleteneuse for a few days," Catherine told him. "While the house is being cleaned. My brother, Guillaume, is castellan there. If you send a message, we can return to Paris within the day."

The Marshal agreed to this. "The body has been there a while, you say?" He rubbed his chin. "There weren't so many of us here before fourth week of Lent. We gathered all men of fighting age from the preceptories in the west to come to Paris for the pope's blessing."

"Were there many new converts?" Edgar asked.

"Several," the Marshal said. "But most were known to someone among us. All together we in Paris are one hundred thirty, by count."

"Then, my lord," Catherine told him, "someone should count again. For either you have one man missing or there was once one knight too many."

Three

The keep at Vielleteneuse, where Catherine's brother, Guillaume, is castellan. Monday, 3 nones May, (May 5), 1147; 3 Sivan 4907. Feast of Saint Hilarius of Arles, known as much for his erudition as his piety.

Impavidus profecto miles, et omni ex parte securus, qui ut corpus ferri, sic animum fidei lorica induitur. Utrisque nimirum munitus armis, nec daemonem timet, nec hominem.

Truly this dauntless knight is confident in every way, his body armored in iron, his soul in the breastplate of faith. Armed thus inside and out, he fears neither demons nor men.

—Bernard of Clairvaux
In Praise of the New Knighthood

*W*hy doesn't it surprise me, Catherine, that you would return home to find a corpse?" Guillaume gestured for the page to bring him more meat. "As a child, if you didn't trip over trouble, you always set out to find it."

"Guillaume, you've teased your sister enough," his wife, Marie, warned. "The unfortunate man's death isn't her fault. And the inconvenience has at least allowed us to have her family here for a while."

"It does seem strange to me that Edgar and I have encountered so many instances of people who have been killed," Catherine mused. "But I've decided that it must be God's will that we take an interest, for we have also been responsible for the innocent being saved from wrongful punishment."

"Including your own sister," Edgar added to him.

Guillaume shook his head. "I find it hard to see you as an emissary of divine justice. But who am I to try to understand God's intentions?"

Marie brought the conversation back to the mundane.

"We have missed you," she said to Catherine. "When your father came and told us he was going on a pilgrimage and not planning on coming home, we feared that you would elect to stay in Trier with Agnes."

Catherine broke the crust from her trencher bread and gave a piece to Edgar.

"We couldn't do that," she assured Marie. "Paris is home. Once Agnes's problems were taken care of it was only a matter of everyone being well enough to make the journey back."

"Ah, yes." Marie lowered her voice. "Poor dear Margaret. The things these foreigners are capable of! It's a miracle they didn't rape her as well. Do you think the scar will fade? You know how men are about such things."

Catherine could feel Edgar tensing beside her.

"Margaret is still a beautiful girl," she said. "If her desire is to marry, we'll have no trouble finding her a suitable husband."

"Of course," Marie nodded. "And should she choose the convent, God won't care what she looks like."

Edgar made a sudden movement that knocked over his wine cup and sent it clanging to the floor.

"Sorry," he muttered. "Very clumsy these days."

The page went running for more wine. Marie's forehead furrowed in confusion.

"Is something wrong?" she asked.

"We're just very tired, Marie," Catherine answered quickly. "The long journey and then the shock of finding that body has worn us both. Perhaps you would excuse us for the evening?"

"Of course." Marie stood and went to embrace Catherine and Edgar. "It's wonderful to have you with us. Please stay as long as you wish. You can tell the children are enjoying being together."

There was no doubt of that from the ruckus overhead, as James and Edana were making friends with their cousins. Added to the squeals of excitement was the barking of Dragon, the dog James had left behind when they went to Germany. Small enough to carry the year before, Dragon was now almost as tall as James. The boy refused to believe it was the same animal and was still looking for his puppy.

"They'll be perfectly happy sleeping like kittens, all piled together," Marie said. "Our nurse will watch them. You take the alcove between floors. No one will disturb you, I promise."

They thanked her and made their way upstairs.

∞

Edgar held back his anger until they were safely in the alcove.

"My sister is not some disfigured peasant girl!" he fumed. "How dare Marie talk about her like that!"

"Of course not." Catherine tried to take the bolster he was pounding flat. "Marie didn't mean to be cruel. You know she's very fond of all of us. She has a good heart and is truly worried about Margaret's future."

Edgar fell back on the pillows. "Isn't it enough that we should endure the stares and gibes because of my hand? Why should my poor sister have to be tormented, as well?"

There was no answer to that beyond platitudes, and Catherine had learned long ago not to offer any.

"It's not a bad scar, anyway," she temporized. "It will soon fade to almost nothing."

She finished undressing and climbed over Edgar to sleep next to the wall. He reached out to pull her close. Catherine nuzzled against him and ran her hand down his side, luxuriating in the feel of his skin.

"*Carissime?*" she whispered. "Don't you think enough time has passed by now?"

With a groan Edgar rolled away from her.

"Don't, Catherine," he begged. "You know the midwife said to wait at least a year. Another child so soon could kill you."

"I feel fine," Catherine protested. "Except for having to lie next to you instead of underneath."

Edgar sighed. "We can't risk it."

"What about the marriage debt?" Catherine countered. "I don't want to drive you to collect elsewhere."

"I'm not planning on taking a concubine," Edgar snorted. "Remember, if I hadn't met you, I would have become a priest and been celibate for life."

"The whores of Paris survive on the revenue of priests," Catherine reminded him.

"Catherine," Edgar warned her. Then he put his head back and closed his eyes. "What are you doing?"

"Just thinking of what I'm missing," she answered.

"You don't usually do that while you're thinking," he said.

"Shall I stop?"

He turned and kissed the top of her head. "Well, not . . . right away. But it isn't fair to you."

She moved closer and slid one leg over his.

"Never mind," she whispered. "I'll find something better soon, but for now this will have to do."

Early the next morning a messenger appeared at the keep.

"The commander of the Knights of the Temple in Paris wishes to speak with you," he told Edgar.

"Have they discovered the name of the man found in our home?" Edgar asked. "Was he one of your Order?"

"I wasn't told." The messenger was clearly annoyed at this. "I am to wait and escort you back with me as soon as you can be ready."

"We've only just come from Mass," Edgar said. "Come in and break the fast with us. We'll have our horses saddled and leave as soon as we've eaten."

When the man had given his horse to a groom and washed the road dust from his hands and face, he found the hall of the keep loud with debate.

"But we'd love to have them!" Marie shouted, hoisting, Mabile, her youngest, to her hip. "Who would notice three more children in this troupe?"

Edana was howling and clinging to Catherine's skirts.

"She doesn't know you!" Catherine shouted back, not because she was angry, but to be heard over the din. "She's afraid we won't come back."

Edana shrieked even more at this.

"Edgar, I'm not a child!" Margaret, normally sedate, was adding her opinion. "I want to return to Paris with you."

"Edana, wouldn't you like to stay here with your cousins!" Marie coaxed. "Evaine will let you play with her dolls."

"Mama!" Evaine, at seven, wasn't interested in sharing.

"Margaret, there's nothing for you to do in Paris." Edgar tried to draw his sister from the melee.

"Yes, there is," Margaret said. "Willa told me that my grandfather is there. She saw him in the Easter procession. I want to meet Count Thibault at last."

By some quirk of sound, Margaret's soft sentence rose above the rest of the noise and was heard clearly by all. Everyone except Edana turned to stare.

"Count Thibault?" Guillaume repeated. "Of Champagne? Your grandfather? You can't mean that Thibault. He's so powerful that he refused the throne of England."

Edgar shrugged uncomfortably. "It seems my stepmother, Margaret's mother, Adalisa, was a by-blow of the count's early years. Margaret's grandmother was of a good family, and Adalisa was acknowledged although she rarely saw her father. But no one ever told the count that he had another grandchild."

"We saw the countess last year," Margaret said. "She was kind to me. I'm sure she spoke to him. She said the count would want to know me, and I very much want to know him. So I'm going back to Paris with you."

"Saint Librare's well-soaked head!" Guillaume exclaimed. "If this is true, Edgar, why haven't you sent her to Champagne to be reared? They can give her a better chance in life than we ever could."

The messenger coughed, reminding them that a family quarrel is best not shared with strangers.

Edgar took a deep breath. "James, you and your sister will stay with Aunt Marie and Uncle Guillaume until we can all move back into our house. It should only be a few days. Margaret, you may come with us. I'll see if I can arrange a meeting with Count Thibault. Now, if the horses are ready, we must go. Kiss the children good-bye, Catherine."

To his amazement, everyone did as he ordered. Edgar felt as if he had stopped a flood with only an upraised hand. How remarkable!

He puzzled over this all through the ride into the city. His voice had never been the deciding one before, not without serious argument. Had he changed? Or had the absence of Hubert left a hole that he was supposed to fill? Edgar had often resented his father-in-law's authority, but now that he had been left in charge of everything from the business of trade to the welfare of the family, the enormity of the responsibility rushed over him. All these lives were now under his protection. What if he should fail?

Hubert's decision to leave suddenly seemed less bizarre.

The messenger led them directly to the Temple preceptory and they were ushered at once into the presence of Evrard de Barre, Master of the Knights of the Temple in France. He wasn't much older than Edgar, in his mid-thirties, perhaps. But the weight of duty and the years fighting in the Holy Land had aged him. His dark hair was streaked with grey and his face lined.

"Thank you for coming so quickly," he greeted them. "Please be seated. You are Edgar of Wedderlie, I believe?"

Edgar nodded and introduced Catherine and Margaret.

"Catherine and I found the corpse," he added. "My sister has nothing to do with this."

"Yes, of course." De Barre didn't proceed to the problem but stood and walked around his chair, tapping on the back of it as if sending a code. He then placed both hands on the wooden slats and leaned toward them.

"The body of this unfortunate was brought to our chapel yesterday," he began. "Your housekeeper supervised my men most assiduously."

Catherine hid a smile. Samonie was not impressed by rank. She also was fiercely protective of the family. She would have been sure that the body was all that de Barre's men took from the house.

"But who was this man?" Edgar asked. "And why was he left in our home?"

De Barre took his hands from the chair and raised them in a gesture of frustration.

"We don't know the answer to either of those," he admitted. "By his dress, the man was a knight of our Order, or at least intending to be, but the state of his corpse made it impossible to recognize him, and every man in Paris has been accounted for."

"There were no marks or tokens that might give him a name?" Edgar asked.

"None," de Barre said. "His mail was good quality, as was his cloak. He had no weapons or jewelry, but the murderer probably stole them."

Edgar ignored the question in the last statement. It was beneath him to deny a theft he hadn't been directly accused of.

"He had no helm, either," Catherine said. "Whoever killed him probably knew that the repair of the mail shirt would raise too many questions and so left it. But I wonder why he didn't take the cloak. It hadn't been damaged by the weapon that killed him. Blood washes out, and wool is easily mended."

She looked at the two men, neither of whom had an answer.

"By the look of him," she continued, "he must have been dead a week or more, perhaps since shortly after Easter. There was no blood on the floor or the stairs, so the body must have been hidden in another place for at least a day or two until the blood dried. Perhaps the cloak was used to wrap him in for moving. But it still would have been hard to carry such a burden far without a cart. If only we knew where he was killed."

She stopped her musing. De Barre was regarding her with a look half of amusement and half of surprise.

"Your wife has the stomach of a man," he commented to Edgar.

"Actually, somewhat stronger," Edgar said. "Except when she's pregnant."

Catherine made a face at him.

"Master Evrard." A new thought struck her. "Did all the knights come here expressly by command or was the number of one hundred thirty simply those who happened to be here on the day of the convocation?"

"We put out a call for all in the area to meet here," de Barre said. "Some will go back to the Holy Land with me now, and the others are to accompany the king and his army when it sets out later this month. The number was never exact. More may yet arrive."

"So there could have been another who came to Paris but never reported to you," Edgar said.

"Yes, of course." De Barre shrugged. "But all of our men are known by someone. If a man were expected and didn't appear, I would have been told."

He thought a moment, and then his face creased in consternation.

"Here now!" he said. "That's enough! I'm supposed to be questioning you!"

From her corner, Margaret stifled a giggle.

Catherine gave the master a look of wide-eyed innocence.

"But we know nothing, my lord," she said. "I assumed you wanted our help."

Even on short acquaintance, de Barre wasn't deceived.

"My Lady Catherine." He smiled. "I wouldn't have considered it until a few moments ago. Now, I think it possible that you and your husband might well be able to assist."

Edgar stood.

"I doubt that very much, my lord," he said. "It was simply our misfortune to own the place where your knight was found. We've been gone for several months and are ignorant of events in Paris."

The master had to look up a bit to meet Edgar's eyes. The two men faced each other unblinking. Then de Barre smiled.

"Perhaps you should find out about them," he said. "It would be only natural for you to ask about this incident. I'm sure you want to be cleared of all suspicion in the matter. You know how easily scandal erupts."

They did. Edgar turned to Catherine. He could see how much she wanted to solve this dilemma. Her face was more alive than it had been since they had lost little Heloisa. That alone decided him.

"Very well," he said. "We'll find out what we can and report to you. But we have a family whose safety is my responsibility."

"I understand." De Barre rang a bell hanging on a hook behind him. "I shall be gone soon, but this matter will be turned over to one of my most trusted men to investigate. I'll send him to you when I've told him the situation. You may bring whatever you discover to him. Any action will be on his decision."

The door behind them opened, and they realized that they had been dismissed. Once they were out in the street again, Catherine led her horse close to Edgar's. She started to ask him something.

"Not here," he answered. "When we're home."

He sank into consideration, turning over the matter in his mind, and said no more for the remainder of the way back.

At the preceptory, Master Evrard and the marshal were in council with the preceptor of the Paris house.

"Did you believe them?" The preceptor asked.

"Not entirely," de Barre answered. "They're an unusual family. I've been asking about them. The man came from Scotland to France to study and ended up marrying a merchant's daughter whose mother came from a good family in Blois that has little left in the way of land. His family is somewhat more exalted than hers, but he's the fifth son and unlikely to inherit."

"That doesn't seem unusual," the Marshal commented. "Happens all the time when boys are far from home."

"There's more," de Barre said. "Her father was in partnership for years with a Jew of Paris. There was some gossip about the strength of this Hubert's faith, although he seems to have gone on a pilgrimage now and left all his effects to his daughter and her husband."

"Seems?" the preceptor noted the stress on the word.

De Barre nodded.

"He returned just after the Nativity, they say. And, after arranging for the transfer of property to his children, he is said to have spent the rest of the time in the company of Jews."

"To close out his business dealings with them?" the preceptor suggested.

"Perhaps," de Barre said. "But perhaps there's more to these people than first meets the eye. They could be just what they say, travelers who returned to an unpleasant occurrence, their house chosen because it was empty. However, I sense that, whoever this dead man was, he has some connection to Hubert LeVendeur and his family. If he was one of our brethren, then I want to know what that connection is."

"So you want us to watch them," the preceptor said.

"Not only that," the master told him. "Encourage them to share information with you. Let them know as much as you think best of what you discover. If they're honest, they might be of help. If they aren't, then eventually they'll stumble, and we'll have them."

Catherine was amazed at the work Samonie had managed to accomplish in the short time they'd been away. The floors that had been left bare were now strewn with rushes and herbs that masked the lingering scent of death. The kitchen had been scrubbed and the fire lit. In the hall, tables and chairs had been set up, wall hangings brought out of the chests and hung. It was beginning to look like home again.

Nervously, Catherine looked up the stairs.

"I've done the sleeping chamber," Samonie told her. "And Willa and some of her friends got the children's floor ready. But we've none of us gone into that room. It gives me shudders."

Catherine agreed, but she needed to see it once more before bucket, broom and blessing made it fit for use again.

As she entered the room, Catherine wondered if the men sent to fetch the body had heard the rumors of the treasure Hubert was supposed to have left behind. The counting room would have been the most likely place to store gold coins and jewels from the East.

Everything seemed undisturbed. Only the scuff marks on the floor showed that anyone had been in the room in months. Catherine knelt and opened the lock on the book cabinet. The large account book that her father had kept since before she was born was still there, wrapped in a silk cloth. Next to it were the few books she had managed to acquire: a psalter, Macrobius, Boethius' *Arithmetic*.

At the bottom was the last present from her father, a copy of one of Master Abelard's final works, a debate on religion between a philosopher and Christian and a Jew. The Christian had won, of course, but the others had been allowed fair and reasoned arguments for their beliefs. In hindsight, she now wondered if the gift had been a sign of Hubert's intention to return to the faith of his fathers. Perhaps he had been trying to tell her for years of his decision, and she had simply not wanted to listen.

She shut the chest. No one had disturbed the books, thank the Virgin. She looked around. Nothing had been scrawled on the walls, no threat or symbol of evil. But there must be a reason the man had been left here. If the killer had only needed a place to hide the body, it might have been dumped in the hall or the woodshed. Why go to the trouble of unlocking a room and then carrying what must have been a bulky, heavy load all the way up the stairs?

Nothing in the small chamber gave her an answer. There was little more in it than the book cabinet, a table and chair and an inkpot and pen box. The walls were bare of hangings. Because of the danger of fire they never even lit a candle in here. All work was done by the light from the window.

Catherine went to look out. From the window she could see over the wall and into the garden of their neighbors, a grain merchant and his family. She should go over and speak to them, although she didn't know them well. Perhaps they had seen lights in the house in the past few weeks or noticed strangers.

Catherine sighed. If her father hadn't been so protective of his secret, they might have known the neighbors better. Unusual activity would have been noted at once and a cry raised.

"Catherine!" Margaret's voice was shrill with panic.

"What is it? I'm coming!" Catherine nearly tripped on her skirts in her hurry to get down the stairs.

"Are you hurt?" she asked as she reached the hall. "Margaret, what's wrong?"

"He's leaving tomorrow, Catherine," Margaret wailed. "For Saint-Florentin, and then back to Troyes. We have to reach him today! Catherine, what shall we do?"

"Count Thibault?" Catherine asked. "Are you sure?"

"Yes, Edgar had it from one of the merchants." Margaret started to cry. "I can't miss him, now that I know who he is. Please, help me."

"Oh, Margaret," Catherine tried to think. "We have nothing proper to wear. None of the boxes has been unpacked. We don't even know where he's staying or if he'll see us."

"We have to try, don't we?"

Looking at Margaret's tear-streaked cheeks, one rivulet running down the scar that had so horrified Marie, Catherine knew that they did.

"Very well," she said. "Where is your brother now?"

"He went out again, something about the water merchants, he said," Margaret told her.

"You know how angry he was last year when we went to see the countess without his knowledge," Catherine reminded her.

"But we can't wait for him to get back," Margaret pleaded. "You know how he is; he'll see a group of men building a house and stand and watch them for hours, forgetting everything else."

Catherine knew.

"Wait a moment," she said, calling to the housekeeper. "Samonie! Can you send Martin to find out where the count of Champagne is staying and then take a message to him that his granddaughter would like to meet him?"

She turned back to Margaret.

"We'll have to wash and see what we can find to wear that's remotely respectable. I wish the jewel box weren't still at Saint Denis. And, if Edgar comes back before Martin returns, then we must tell him where we're going. Is that understood?"

Margaret wiped her eyes and gave Catherine a joyous

smile and a hug. "Yes, I'm sure he won't try to stop me. His pride isn't that cruel."

Catherine knew the strength of Edgar's pride. Secretly she hoped they would be gone before he returned.

Thibault, count of Champagne and Blois, had been a ruler for nearly forty of his fifty-eight years. His land was five times as extensive as that governed by the king. Although, as a grandson of William the Conqueror, he could have also claimed the throne of England after the death of Henry I, he was happy to relinquish it to his younger brother, Stephen. Seeing what a mess that had become, he'd never regretted it.

In his youth he'd been somewhat profligate, causing his mother worry; but the loss of so many of his kindred in the tragedy of the White Ship had abruptly sobered him. For a time he had wanted to enter the monastery of his friend, Bernard of Clairvaux, but he had been counseled to take up his duties as a secular lord. His marriage to Mahaut of Carinthia had been happy. But he had never forgotten the child of his first love.

When Martin arrived with his message, the count was busy with representatives from Saint-Florentin, who were trying to convince him that a local lord had been dishonest with them.

"I shall decide the matter when I hear both sides," Thibault told them. "And not before."

He noticed Martin.

"Yes, boy. What do you want?" he shouted.

Martin opened his mouth but was too scared to speak. With an effort, he pushed the words out.

"My lord Count, my mistress, Catherine, daughter of Hubert LeVendeur and her sister-in-law, Lady Margaret of Wedderlie, would like permission to see you later this afternoon."

Thibault's eyes lit. Mahaut had told him of the girl's visit the previous year.

"Bring them at once!" he ordered. "The rest of you, go away. I don't want to hear any more until the trial."

So, hastily washed and combed and still in their travel garments, Catherine and Margaret appeared shortly thereafter before one of the most powerful men in the land.

He was standing in a small anteroom, quite alone. The servant who admitted them left at once, drawing the curtain behind him.

For a moment, Margaret hung back. He was so much larger and more vital than she had imagined. Not much older than Catherine's father and straighter, as a lord should be. Mastery radiated from him. His back was to the light so that she couldn't make out his face.

As she moved toward him, the sun fell on her face and she heard his gasp. Was it the deep red scar across her cheek? She knelt before him, raising her clasped hands.

"My lord Count," she whispered.

He stepped forward and put a hand beneath her chin, tilting it up. He smiled.

"You very much resemble your grandmother," he said softly. "Although she was blond, as was your mother. I never saw Adalisa after she was a child. I'm sorry for that. Is she well?"

Margaret looked up at him in panic. Catherine rescued her.

"I'm sorry, my lord," she said. "Lady Adalisa was killed by brigands in England not long ago. We brought Margaret back to France with us to keep her safe."

Count Thibault closed his eyes and crossed himself, murmuring a prayer. "My poor daughter. And is that when you were hurt, as well, Margaret?"

He touched the scar gently.

"No, my lord," Margaret said. "I was set upon, they say, by villagers in a town near Trier. They thought I was a Jewess, and I didn't have enough German to tell them who I really was. At least, that's what I was told. I have no memory of it."

Thibault set his lips in anger. He turned back to Catherine.

"I thought Abbot Bernard had put a stop to such things?" he said.

"He came to Trier after the incident, too late for Margaret," Catherine told him. "The men beat her and dragged her into a church. Because it was a holy place, they didn't violate her, but left her for dead."

"My poor child." Thibault shook his head. "And after Bernard arrived?"

"There seem to have been no more occurrences after he preached to the town," Catherine said.

"No, and now I hear that all the Jews of the area have barricaded themselves at Wolkenberg Fortress," Thibault commented. Catherine gave a start, but Thibault continued to Margaret, "Never mind, my child. The scar will fade, and I hope the memories never return. This would not have happened in my lands."

Margaret smiled. "I know, my lord. The Jews of Troyes speak very highly of you."

Thibault snorted. "Ah yes, I'd forgotten that you now live in Hubert's family. You must have met many of the Jewish traders."

"I know it may not have been proper for her to live as we do," Catherine interjected. "But there's nothing left for her in Scotland. She has a bit of dower land in the Vexin from her mother, but not enough to live from. Her brother, my husband Edgar, has agreed to take on my father's affairs in partnership with the Jew, Solomon of Paris. We have more than enough to keep Margaret. We thought it best for her to be with those who love her."

Thibault caressed Margaret's cheek again. "I agree," he said. "But you needn't worry about a dowry, Margaret. When the time comes, with my wife's permission, I shall see that you are provided for. And I want to be consulted in the matter," he added to Catherine.

Catherine bowed. "Of course, my lord Count."

Thibault smiled. "I should like to spend more time with you, but I have to settle some trivial dispute at Saint-Florentin. There are times when I wish I could bash men's heads together rather than listen to all these legal speeches."

He bent toward Margaret. "Now, I expect you to visit

me when I return to Troyes. Can you spare a farewell kiss for your grandfather?"

For answer, Margaret threw her arms about him and let him lift her and hold her close.

Thibault set her down at last and blew his nose loudly.

"Thank you for coming," he told her. "Your grandmother was a noblewoman and a good one. Our families simply had other plans for us. I'll see you again soon. May Our Lady keep you safe."

He nodded to Catherine. "Take care of her, now. She's not to be out wandering alone. The streets are full of ruffians these days."

Catherine promised. They both bowed to him again and left.

Margaret said nothing all the way home, but her eyes were shining. When they got back, they found that Edgar was home. Catherine hesitated, preparing herself for his anger, but Margaret got round it entirely. She raced in and threw herself at her brother crying, "Edgar, my grandfather is a wonderful man, and he thinks I'm beautiful!"

Over her shoulder Edgar saw Catherine. He shook his head and sighed.

"I think you're beautiful, too," he told Margaret, but it was Catherine he was looking at.

Four

The Fortress of Wolkenberg, on a hilltop in Lotharingia, near Köln. Tuesday, 2 nones May, (May 6), 1147; 4 Sivan, 4907. Feast of Saint Aurea, hermit and martyr, who charmed scorpions with her beauty.

וְיִשְׂאֶן בבי ישראל את עיניהם וידאו והבה פצירים
טועים המועבים נוסים מבלה עד

ויקשו איש מאת מנדו נוי כל מי שהיה לו מנזל
עם או מצוזה לקבלו אצלו לבא בנקרת הצורים
ולהתבא ע יעבוד

The children of Israel lifted up their eyes and saw the contemptible oppressors closing in from all around . . . Each one went to a Gentile acquaintance, anyone who owned either a castle or fortress, to accept him in the cave and hide him until the anger passed.

—Ephrahim of Bonn
Sefer Zekirah

*S*olomon ben Jacob of Paris looked down from the parapets of Wolkenberg. He had come to the hill fortress only as escort to the widow and children of an old friend. Now it was time to leave. He knew this. He had obligations to his family and to his new partner, Edgar. He shouldn't have come here at all.

And yet . . .

In the courtyard below Jewish children were playing happily. Under a tree the scholars met to argue fine points of the Talmud. Their voices rose more loudly than the children's laughter, but Solomon could hear the joy beneath the sharp tones.

The sun shone on them all.

There were no gentiles at Wolkenberg. For the first time in their lives, these Jewish families were free to be themselves without fear. No one mocked them or threw stones. No one tried to make them feel inferior or unwanted. Solomon knew this was the closest he would ever come to *Eretz Israel*. He didn't want to give it up.

"You could stay, you know."

For a moment Solomon thought the voice was a spirit answering his longings. He'd been so far into his own reflections that he hadn't heard Mina come up behind him.

"I would live here forever if I believed it would always be like this," he answered her. "But we both know it's just a temporary haven. We can't stay up here forever. There are too few of us. We need the gentiles to survive. At least for now."

"Yes, we need them, but that doesn't mean you have to live with them, Solomon." Mina's face was serious. "It worries me. You're more a part of your uncle Hubert's Christian family than you are one of us."

"I know," Solomon admitted. It worried him, too. Until the past year, he had trusted and loved his Christian relatives completely. He still loved them, but when the persecutions were at their height, he had seen the fear in Catherine's eyes, not for him, but for her children if they were thought to be Jewish, too. After poor Margaret was attacked, he felt his cousin's anxiety had been justified. Solomon still felt a stab of guilt about it. He had promised her mother that he would protect Margaret always and then the poor child had been hurt simply because she wasn't ashamed to be seen in his company.

"Solomon? Are you listening?" Mina snapped her fingers in his face. "I was saying that my cousin, Zipporah, has come of age. She's a fine woman, gentle and pious and very pretty. Her father might be persuaded to look kindly upon the match."

"Mina, not again!" Solomon gave a sigh. "Why do you want to inflict me upon these fine innocent girls? What kind of husband would I make to them?"

"A good one, I think," Mina said. "For you'd feel so sure you were a trial to your wife that you'd be twice as kind to her as any other man."

Solomon shook his head.

"Thank you, Mina, but no thank you," he said. "It's true that I've been too long among the Edomites. I don't belong in our community anymore. But I'll never belong in theirs, I promise."

Mina laughed.

"Zipporah would soon change your mind about belonging, Solomon," she said. "If you'd let her. If you wait too long, she'll be taken."

"I wish her joy." Solomon put his arm around Mina. "And I promise that when I decide I must have a good

Jewish wife, I'll let you choose her for me. But for now, I must return to Paris."

Mina pulled away from him angrily.

"What is wrong with you, Solomon ben Jacob?" she cried. "You're a grown man, now, past thirty, and it's time you started a family. I don't want to see you lost to us as your father was!"

The moment she said it, she knew she had made a terrible mistake. Solomon's expression was ice.

"What do you know about my father?" he said slowly.

Mina hung her head. "Your uncle Hubert told me before he left. He's concerned. I'm supposed to look out for you."

"I'll look out for myself, Mina," Solomon told her. "You have enough of hardship taking care of your fatherless children."

This time she met his gaze.

"Exactly," she said. "And after what the Christians did to my Simon, you still want to go live with them. Why are you so eager to spend your life among people who despise you?"

Solomon took a long time to answer. He turned from the secure contentment of the people within the fortress to the view below. He saw rivers cutting through dark forest and villages full of people who wished him and all like him swept from the earth. Then he thought of Catherine, who had risked so much for him and even more, of Margaret, the child he had promised to protect.

"Everything you say is true, Mina," His voice was soft. "But out there, amidst all those who hate me are also the people I love most. I leave for Paris tomorrow."

In Paris, Catherine could only spare a few minutes a day to be anxious about Solomon, although she did it then with great intensity. Margaret worried enough for her. Every time they heard someone at the door, her face would turn in expectation and then fall when she saw that it wasn't he.

"She loves him as a daughter," Catherine told herself, watching the disappointed slump of the girl's shoulders. "Or a favorite niece. Nothing more."

But the sadness in Margaret's eyes when no word came and Solomon failed to appear made Catherine extremely uneasy.

It was almost a relief to be forced to study the problem of the body in the counting room.

"How can we be expected to find out who killed him if we don't even know who he was?" Catherine said in exasperation. "I've spoken to all the neighbors and no one will admit to having seen or heard anything. They probably didn't. Carts come and go all the time on the Grève. I don't know where to go from here!"

Edgar blew a strand of hair from his face. His hand was occupied with trying to set up his vises again so that he could resume work. He might now be a merchant by trade, but if he couldn't turn the images in his mind into carved toys, boxes and inlaid jewelry, he would go mad. In Scotland, his family had been ashamed of his fascination with crafting objects. It was unworthy of his birth. But so was trading. If he had given up his place for Catherine's sake, it also freed him to enjoy the work he loved best.

"As soon as I'm finished here, I'll go to the Île," he promised. "There should be someone around Nôtre Dame from the old days who can tell me the news."

"But only about who is debating whom on the nature of the Trinity and which of the Masters is most popular now," Catherine reminded him. "No one there will care about the death of a Knight of the Temple. Half the scholars we know don't think they should even have been given permission to form an Order in the first place. Only Abbot Bernard's support could give them respectability."

"Well, the idea of a monk who wields a sword does seem a contradiction," Edgar answered. "But there are worldly men among the secular clerics. The canons of Nôtre Dame, for instance, keep abreast of events in town. I wish I knew if John were in Paris. He usually knows everything that's happening."

"The pope is still here in Paris," Catherine said. "Isn't John attached in some way to the papal court?"

"No, the last I heard, he was at Celle acting as secretary

to the abbot, but he's applying for a place in the curia of the Archbishop of Canterbury." Edgar grunted as he tried to tighten the vise to the table. "I never could see him as a monk. I suppose Master Adam might know where he is or . . ."

"Edgar, we could speculate all day." Catherine was becoming testy. It was hard to watch him struggle with the tools. She longed to help him, but he hated that. He let the children hold things for him, but not her.

He finally managed to attach the vise.

"You want me to go now?" he asked.

"Yes," she urged. "Tomorrow the house will be full with Marie and Guillaume bringing their four and our two. Tonight is our best chance to have a quiet discussion with a guest."

"Ah, you want me to find an informant and bring him home to dine with us," Edgar said.

"Well, of course!" Catherine nearly pushed him out the door. "Don't come home alone!"

After he had gone, Catherine went over to the worktable. The different vises were lined up, scrapes in the wood showing how often they'd been attached and with what effort. On a cloth on the bench the tools were laid out: hammers, pincers, organarium, drawplates, chisels, rasps, scorpers and files. Once he had also had a small anvil to beat out the heat-softened metal. But there were some things even Edgar had to admit one needed two good hands for.

Catherine gently brushed her fingers over the neat row of implements. She sniffed to hold back tears. Perhaps it was just because she loved him so much, but Catherine believed Edgar to be the bravest man she knew.

Samonie had prepared a pot of barley soup with early carrots and sent one of her boys to the baker's for trencher loaves. Catherine went down to the storeroom and found a small cask of Gascon wine. She sniffed the bung and decided that it was still drinkable.

The bells had rung for the end of Vespers before Edgar returned. With him was a thin man with a clerical tonsure wearing plain woolen robes. It took a moment for Catherine to recognize him.

"Maurice?" she said. "How good to see you again! You look wonderful. Are you still at Nôtre Dame?"

"Yes, I'm a subdeacon now." Maurice smiled shyly. "The food is more adequate than when I was just a student. But I shall always be grateful for the number of times you fed me in those days."

"Your conversation alone was payment enough," Catherine said. "As I'm sure it will be tonight. We've been away so long. I'm eager for a report on what's going on in Paris."

She led them into the hall and poured cups of the wine from a pitcher, then let them mix it as they wished from the water jug.

"As for news." Maurice sat and sipped his wine. "Certainly the greatest bustle involves having the pope in France and the preparations for King Louis's expedition to free Edessa. But you must know all about that."

"The world seems to be crowded with people wearing the pilgrim's cross," Edgar said. "Does Paris have time to think about anything else?"

"Well." Maurice laughed. "We have a new dean, Clement, and a new precenter, Albert, at Nôtre Dame who don't seem aware of it at all. Clement and Albert have entered into a war over the shape and tone of the music for the liturgy. They haven't come to blows, yet, but the shouting can be heard all the way to Saint Genevieve."

"I can understand fighting over the wording of the liturgy," Catherine said. "But the music?"

Maurice shrugged. "No one but those two takes it seriously. It's a change, though, from arguing over whether or not the bishop of Poitiers is a heretic."

Catherine was so astounded that she nearly dropped her cup.

"Master Gilbert!" she exclaimed. "But he's one of the most brilliant theological expositors in France, especially since Master Abelard died."

"And wasn't Abelard judged a heretic, as well?" Maurice reminded her.

"I can't believe anyone would accuse Bishop Gilbert, though," Edgar said. "Master Abelard was always offending people with his sharp tongue, but who could old Stoneface have bothered?"

"Master Peter of Lombardy, for one," Maurice answered. "And Bernard of Clairvaux."

"Oh, not again!" Catherine cried. "I was just beginning to like Abbot Bernard."

"Bishop Gilbert was at the council at Sens that condemned Master Abelard," Edgar said thoughtfully. "Abelard warned him then that accusations of heresy leap like flame from one scholar to another."

"I remember." Catherine started to say more but was interrupted by a knocking at the door.

It had barely ceased when Margaret flew out of the kitchen, where she had been helping Samonie.

"Margaret!" Catherine called after her. "What are you thinking of? Let Martin see who it is."

The girl paid no attention. They could hear her fumbling with the bar as Martin reached the door. Then there was a small sound of disappointment, and Margaret returned, followed by Martin and the new arrival.

Edgar and Catherine both leaped to their feet and ran to hug the man.

"Astrolabe!" Catherine kissed him. "How wonderful to see you. We were just talking about your father."

"Margaret!" Edgar called her back sharply. "You haven't met our guest. Astrolabe is an old friend. He's the son of Master Peter Abelard and Abbess Heloise of the Paraclete."

"I was born before she entered the convent." Astrolabe smiled at the girl.

"Astrolabe," Edgar went on, "this ill-mannered young lady is my sister, Margaret."

Blushing, Margaret bowed. "*Dex te saut*, Master Astrolabe. I apologize for not greeting you properly. Catherine has often spoken of her love for your parents and the time she spent under your mother's care at the Paraclete. Welcome."

She went into the kitchen but returned a moment later

with a wine cup for Astrolabe and a plate of dried meat
and cheese.

"Samonie says the soup is ready whenever you want it,"
she told Catherine. "Would you mind if I ate with her and
then went up to bed? I'm very tired."

The tension in her frightened Catherine.

"Of course, *ma douz*," she said. "You need to rest. Tomorrow you'll be surrounded by small children."

Margaret gave her a wan smile and left. Catherine resolved to have a serious talk with Edgar soon about his
sister's future.

"Now, Astrolabe," Edgar said when they were settled and
Maurice had been introduced. "You've been traveling more
than Pope Eugenius lately. I thought you were in Metz.
What brings you to Paris?"

"Heresy," Astrolabe answered. He drained his cup and
held it out to be refilled.

The other three gaped at him. Catherine was the first to
recover.

"*Endondu!* Whose heresy? Master Gilbert?"

It was Astrolabe's turn to gape. "The bishop? Of course
not! Who'd be fool enough to accuse him? No, it's these
Eonists. I saw them when I was home at Le Pallet visiting
my aunt. They're taking over the countryside in Brittany,
and no one seems to be able to control them."

Edgar crossed himself. "It seems like a madness lately,
almost as if people believe the Last Days have come. There
are these dualists in Germany and the Occitan, Arnoldists
in Rome. Madmen roaming the fields only need to wave
their arms to attract disciples, I swear. What do these Eonists preach?"

Astrolabe reached for the cheese. "As far as I can tell,
their leader says that he's the son of God and so his followers can do anything he wants them to. He's clearly
mad."

"He thinks he's Jesus?" Maurice couldn't take this in.

"No," Astrolabe shook his head. "He thinks he's '*eum*'
as in '*per eum*.' 'Through him' shall be judged the living

and the dead. He seems to believe that '*eum*' and '*eon*' are the same word."

Catherine blinked. "And he's built a sect on this?"

"Quite a large one; I've seen it," Astrolabe said. "There's a charisma about him. His words are empty, senseless, and yet the poor adore him. He leads them to pillage their own churches, even rob small priories of their altar cloths and candlesticks. He makes a mockery of the Mass. It is even said that they conduct orgies as a part of their services."

"Really?" The other three leaned toward him.

"But I didn't witness any," Astrolabe finished.

They leaned back.

"Where are the lords, the advocates for the monks?" Edgar wanted to know.

"That's what I don't understand." Astrolabe tapped his cup, reminding Catherine that it was empty again. "It's true that there's been confusion in the land since the death of the count, but the local lords should be concerned enough to capture this man and disperse his followers. It wouldn't take many to do it. Eon is connected to a very minor noble family, but even they are trying to convince him to stop this insanity and return to them. And yet, they do no more than that."

"But these people have destroyed property!" Catherine exclaimed. "Despoiled churches! Are they so dangerous that the knights of Brittany fear to attack them?"

"I don't know," Astrolabe nearly shouted his frustration. "It makes no sense to me. I saw no warriors among the throng that follow this man, only poor, half-starved peasants. But, since no one seems able to stop them, I've come to Paris to ask the pope to send a legate to force the barons of Brittany to do their duty."

"Do you think this bizarre heresy might spread?" Maurice asked.

"If no one counters it, why not?" Astrolabe answered. "The harvest has been bad the past two years, and there's been too much rain this spring. People are hungry and desperate. Eon gives them a fantasy of some sort, an illusion of prosperity. And, perhaps he is in league with demons who have clouded the minds of those who should speak out against him."

They all considered this. It seemed the only plausible answer.

"I wish we could blame the body in the counting room on demons." Catherine sighed.

"You have a body in your house?" Astrolabe and Maurice both blessed themselves hurriedly.

"Not anymore," Edgar hastened to assure them.

He explained what had happened. Both men were as puzzled as Catherine and Edgar.

"But if the Knights of the Temple have claimed him, it's their problem now," Maurice said.

"I wish I could believe that," Edgar answered. "Master Evrard told us that we might be of some help to him. I translate that as meaning he thinks we know more than we do."

"Anyway," Catherine added, "it's our house that's been desecrated by this. I want to know who did it and why."

"Of course you do, Catherine." Astrolabe grinned at her. "You never could pass up a puzzle."

"I know." Catherine bit her lip, thinking. Then she got up and went to the kitchen to ask Samonie to have the bread brought out and the soup poured into it.

It wasn't just the unwelcome homecoming they had received that bothered her. That was certainly upsetting. She knew she'd be scrubbing that room for months. It was more everything around them. The whole world was unsettled. People were leaving for an expedition to the Holy Land knowing no more than that they should face the east, relying on faith to get them there and back safely. Others were turning completely from all they had been taught, believing instead in new gods invented by deluded fools. Starvation threatened all around them from the barren fields and ignorant preachers were there to addle the minds of those already weakened by hunger. Bands of ruffians were attacking Jews and forcing them to baptism or death. And her own father had turned his back on the true faith, leaving his family behind. The order of the universe had been re-arranged.

Perhaps these are the end times, she thought. The world is preparing to be swept clean for the coming of Christ.

The idea made her shiver, and she scolded herself for falling prey to melancholia again.

"A good dose of valerian and chamomile before bed," she said. "That will do it."

"Do what?" Samonie stopped hacking a trough in the bread.

"Nothing," Catherine answered. "Here, I'll take the soup pot. Has Margaret gone up already?"

"Yes, and she hardly ate anything," Samonie answered. "Is the poor girl ill?"

"Just tired, I imagine," Catherine said absently.

She wrapped two kitchen cloths around her hands and lifted the pot, then walked carefully back into the hall, where Martin had set up a small table for the four of them.

The three men were laughing about something when she returned. Martin leaped forward to take the pot from her, and Catherine came and sat beside Edgar.

Her sense of foreboding vanished in the comfort of old friends. They told stories of the foibles of the masters of Paris, the debates and the legends of students now grown into bishops. It reminded Catherine of the time she and Edgar had lived in a rickety room near the great market square, just the two of them and whoever came to share their meal. It had been good to know that they could come back to her father's house to warmth and clean clothes if they needed. It had been better to have a room all to themselves with no servants and no family to overhear.

That reminded her of her present duty.

"And where are you staying, Astrolabe?" she asked.

His handsome face reddened. "Well, I had hoped, that is, Edgar mentioned, you see, all the monastic guest rooms are full with the pope here and . . ."

"I had hoped you'd stay with us." Catherine took his hand. "I swear this by the broken bones of the protomartyr.

You may stay as long as you like, or until the noise of the Vikings and Vandals drives you away."

"The what?"

"Our children and my brother's," Catherine said. "They'll arrive tomorrow. But tonight, at least, we can promise you undisturbed rest."

The moon had set and the house was dark as deadly sin when something woke Astrolabe.

He rolled over in his blankets and mumbled, "Wha'?"

Silence.

Then a rustling in the reeds on the floor.

"Rats." Astrolabe said.

He groped beneath the cot they had set up for him in the hall. After a few tries he found his boot and threw it forcefully in the direction of the noise. There was a thump, a clank, and a simultaneous high-pitched squeal. The rustling stopped.

With a satisfied sigh, Astrolabe pulled the blanket over his head and went back to sleep.

He was awakened the next morning by warm, moist breath on his face. He opened his eyes. Two little girls were standing next to the cot, peering at him curiously.

"Good morning," he said.

They both jumped back quickly, the younger one falling on her bottom.

"Mabile! Edana!" a voice called. "I told you not to go in there. The guest is still sleeping."

A woman appeared at the door. She was in her early thirties, with a gentle face. Astrolabe sat up and reached for his *brais*.

"It must be late," he apologized. "I didn't mean to inconvenience the family."

"No, we're early," Marie answered. "The children were all up before first light, so we left at sunrise. I haven't heard the bells for Tierce, yet. I'll take these naughty girls and leave you in peace. I beg your pardon for disturbing you. Girls!"

The little one, Mabile, was squatting in the corner.

Edana, who had finally mastered the chamber pot, was trying to make her cousin stop. She pulled at Mabile's hands and the two of them fell over. Edana shrieked and Marie rushed to her.

"Mabile, what did you do to her?" She picked up both children. "Edana, stop that noise. Your cousin can't have hurt you that badly."

Then Marie saw the blood pouring down Edana's leg.

"Sweet Virgin's tears! How did that happen?"

She quickly unwound her scarf and wrapped it about Edana's thigh at the same time calling for help.

Samonie ran in from the kitchen, but Astrolabe was there first.

"She's cut herself," Marie said. "It looks deep. One of the rushes must have been sharp. Can you take Mabile? I don't want her rooting around here."

Gingerly, Astrolabe picked up the little girl, holding her at arm's length. He was relieved when Samonie took her from him.

Marie was busy trying to stop both the bleeding and Edana's cries, which were escalating. Astrolabe bent over the place where she had fallen, looking for the thing that had cut her.

He found it right next to the boot he had thrown the night before. It wasn't a floor rush.

It was a knife.

Five

The hall of Catherine and Edgar's home.
Morning, Friday,
7 ides of May (May 9) 1147; 9 Sivan, 4907. Feast of
Saint Soulange, shepherd girl, who died fighting off a
noble rapist. The reason this made her a saint isn't
quite clear.

*Iam enim sitio, oteroque vorator panum in siccitate stran-
gulari, nisi clementia vestra michi vinum povideat. Hoc
utique vobis paratius est quam caelia, quae a nostratibus
[sic] usu vulgaria cervisia
nuncupatur. Ego tamen utriusque bibax sum, et non
abhorreo quicquid inebriare potest.*

But now I am thirsty and it is possible that I may choke
from the dryness of your loaves unless you, in your
mercy, give me wine, which is more available to you
than *caelia*, which we vulgarly call beer. But I will drink
both and do not disdain anything that will make
me drunk.

—John of Salisbury
Letter 33 to Peter, Abbot of Celle

*C*atherine recognized Edana's cry from upstairs. She raced down at once, pulling a long *chainse* over her head as she went.

"What is it?" she cried, scooping the child from Marie's arms.

"A knife cut," Marie said. "But it's not deep. Samonie is making up a bread-and-honey poultice."

"Oh, good. That should protect the cut," Catherine said. "All we need to do is keep her from eating the poultice. How did she come by a knife?"

Astrolabe showed it to her.

"It's a meat knife that was left among the rushes," he said. "It's not mine. The design on the handle is unfamiliar."

"It doesn't belong to the house," Catherine said after examining it. "The handle is deer horn, with a star design near the blade. Anyone recognize it? Samonie?"

"No," the woman said as she put the poultice on Edana's leg and wrapped cloth around it. "Perhaps one of Lord Guillaume's men dropped it."

"They weren't in here this morning," Astrolabe said. "At least I don't think so. But I'll ask."

As he left he passed Edgar, who had just come down, having taken time to dress and put on shoes. Catherine explained to him what had happened. With a whimper of "Papa," Edana held out her arms, sure of extra comfort. He spent a moment cuddling her and finished with a tickle as Astrolabe returned.

"None of the sergeants has seen it before," he told them. "Perhaps it was left by your father?"

He was beginning to suspect where the knife had come from, but he clung to the hope that he was wrong.

"Samonie!" Edgar called to her as she was going back to the kitchen. "The floors were bare when we got here, I remember. You just put the rushes down a day or two ago, is that right?"

"Yes, Master Edgar," she said. "There was nothing there then. I would have noticed."

"What are you thinking, *carissime*?" Catherine asked.

"Of those men who were in the garden," he answered. "They didn't find what they were looking for. Perhaps I need to set guards down by the creek at night."

"Strangers in the house?" The idea made Catherine's stomach lurch. "And none of us woke?"

Astrolabe sighed.

"I'm afraid I did," he admitted. "I thought it was a rat and only managed to come round long enough to throw a boot. There was a clank that may have been the knife dropping. Whoever it was must have been a natural thief, for I heard nothing more."

"Was anything taken?" Catherine asked.

Everyone looked around, checking chests and shelves.

"Nothing has been disturbed," Samonie told them. "Perhaps Master Astrolabe routed them with his boot."

"Edgar, do you think this was one of the men we heard when we were sleeping in the garden?" Catherine asked.

"Well, I hope so." Edgar set Edana down. "I wouldn't like to think our home has become a Jerusalem for thieves."

"But what could they be looking for?"

"It couldn't be the body." Edgar considered the question. "They must have realized we'd have found it by now. In another day the whole street would have smelled it. Yet the knight wore no valuable rings or brooches, and there was nothing in the counting room. I have no idea. But I'm posting guards in the back again until we find out."

"What is all this noise? Can't a man get any sleep in this town?"

They all looked up; Catherine's brother was scowling at them all.

"All I wanted was a little rest since we got up so early to come here. I'd forgotten how many damn churches there are in Paris," he continued. "I wake up every time they ring the hours. Marie, I know you want to shop and visit your friends, but even one night of that infernal clanging and I'll be rabid. You'd think they could at least all decide when Prime actually is."

Marie laughed at him. "You poor thing! In Vielleteneuse we have no canons at the church so the nights are tranquil. How did you ever survive growing up here?"

"I only lived in Paris until I was eight," Guillaume reminded her. "Then I went to live with my uncle. His keep in Blois was smaller even than ours, and *very* quiet."

He said this last as his children came rushing down the steps at him.

It took some time before Guillaume understood what had happened in the night. When he did, his first impulse was to pack up his family and Catherine's and set out back for Vielleteneuse.

"It's all these new people coming in," he complained. "For every honest pilgrim or soldier of Christ, there are a hundred thieves, heretics and whores."

"Not to mention the relic hawkers." Catherine sighed, momentarily distracted from the issue. "Yesterday three people tried to sell me a bramble from the Crown of Thorns. You'd think they could be more creative. I could make the whole crown myself out of the overgrowth in our garden."

"Bloodstained as well, I'd imagine." Astrolabe grinned.

"True," Catherine said. "I couldn't do it without being covered with scratches."

"Catherine," her brother interrupted, "the point is that you all should abandon the city until the army has left. It's not safe for any of you, especially Edgar's sister."

Before either Catherine or Margaret could answer, Edgar stepped in.

"Thank you, Guillaume, but if I must remain in Paris, the family stays together," he said.

Catherine nodded agreement.

"And I must stay in Paris," Edgar added. "I have to take up my new position here. Your father arranged for me to be accepted by the water merchants and the wine sellers, but I can't deal with them from the safety of your keep."

"You really intend to keep up Father's trade?" Guillaume was incredulous. "You're a nobleman! And what about Margaret? What would Count Thibault say?"

"I have no idea," Edgar answered. "But unless you have a better means for us to earn our daily bread . . . ?"

Guillaume fell silent. They all knew the revenues from his castellany weren't enough to support another family. The truth was that it had been Hubert who supplied his son with a number of the luxuries Guillaume believed his position required, such as fine hawks and tooled leather saddles.

"Master?"

It was a moment before Edgar remembered that he was now master in this house. He turned his attention to the boy in the doorway.

"What is it, Martin?"

"Two men have come to see you," the boy answered. "A Knight of the Temple and a rich cleric, by the look of him. What shall I do with them?"

It was a good question. The hall where visitors would normally be received was now crowded with family, as well as Astrolabe's bedding.

"Take them up to the counting room," Catherine suggested. "They may want to see where the body was found. The books are all locked away, so they won't be able to snoop in our accounts."

"Yes, that will have to do," Edgar said. "Show them up, Martin. And then bring two more folding chairs. Samonie, will you take some refreshment to them?"

"Of course." The housekeeper bowed to hide her smile.

She wasn't about to let the men leave without getting a good look at them.

"Tell them I'll meet with them directly," Edgar added.

"You mean 'we'll meet with them,' don't you?" Catherine asked. "I want to know what they've found out about our body, too."

"Catherine, you can't receive these men," Edgar told her. "They're from the Temple commander."

"What do you mean?" Catherine was indignant. "Aren't I the mistress here?"

"Catherine," Astrolabe interjected mildly. "No one is denying your authority. I believe Edgar was commenting on the fact that you're wearing nothing but your shift."

Catherine looked down. Her bare toes wiggled back at her.

"Oh," she said.

The men were clearly not happy about being taken up to a bare room in the middle of the house. When Edgar entered a few moments later, followed by Samonie with a tray, neither of them bothered to stand to greet him.

The cleric removed his glove to take the cup of wine. He waited until Samonie had left before he spoke.

"I am Master Durand," he said. "One of the chaplains to the brothers of the Temple of Solomon, and this is Brother Baudwin. We are here to investigate the death of one we assume to be of the Order."

Edgar bowed, ignoring their manners. "I am Edgar of Wedderlie, master of this house. Have you discovered the identity of the man, yet?"

"No," Brother Baudwin said.

Master Durand interrupted him. "His identity is still unknown. However, we expect to uncover the truth shortly."

There was a knock at the door. Martin came in, carrying another folding chair, followed by Catherine, who was now decently covered.

"My wife, Catherine, daughter of Hubert LeVendeur," Edgar said.

Still the men stayed seated. Catherine raised her eyebrows.

"Welcome to our home," she said too smoothly. "Martin, please set my chair next to Edgar's."

She smiled at the men in a way that put Edgar immediately on his guard. "Would you like a poppyseed cake?"

She offered them the tray. Brother Baudwin took one and stuffed it quickly into his mouth, leaving crumbs in his beard.

"Now, how may we help you?" Catherine smiled again.

Brother Baudwin looked to Master Durand, who returned the smile and muttered in Latin to the knight, "These two should pose no problem. I'll soon know if they're lying."

Baudwin seemed not to understand, but Catherine did. Her eyes widened in surprise and anger. She opened her mouth to respond. Quickly Edgar took a cake and gave it to her, with a warning look.

"Really, my dear." Master Durand leaned forward with a patronizing expression. "This is a nasty business and nothing you need trouble yourself about."

This was too much. Catherine dropped the mask.

"Having spent the past two days scrubbing the blood and ichor from this room, as well as killing the maggots, I have already been troubled. Now I want to know who this man was and why he was left here."

The chaplain looked at her sharply and then to Edgar. Catherine was aware of his outrage and didn't care.

"Master Durand?" she prompted.

Both men straightened. Brother Baudwin finished brushing out the crumbs with his fingers.

"We were sent here to ask you that," he answered for them both. "Commander Evrard isn't satisfied with your explanation of the discovery of the body."

"Really?" Edgar stood. "I find that as amazing as the fact that you've managed to offend both me and my wife in the initial moments of your visit."

He went to the door and opened it.

"Martin!" he called. "Our guests are leaving."

Baudwin and Durand both got to their feet but not to depart.

"How dare you refuse to answer to us!" Durand said, trying to pull himself up to meet Edgar's eyes. He was several inches too short. "We'll have you taken to the Temple for questioning!"

Behind him Catherine laughed.

"You're not in Antioch or Jerusalem, Master Durand," she said. "You can't drag citizens of Paris from their homes. The king would have something to say about that."

Durand snorted. "I'm sure the king would respect the wishes of the commander of the Temple, especially since he's relying on us to guide him to the Holy Land."

Edgar had had enough.

"We shall be happy to test your hypothesis, Master Durand." He held the door open. "I assure you that respect is something I expect to both give and receive in my dealings with others. When you are prepared to offer it, my wife and I will give you our full attention and aid."

Brother Baudwin turned bright red, and Catherine feared he would choke on the second cake he had picked up as he was leaving. She moved behind him and tried to edge him out. One corpse to clean up after had been quite enough.

Neither of the emissaries said another word as they stomped down the stairs and out into the courtyard. Master Durand turned as they passed through the front gate.

"You'll regret this!" he warned.

Edgar shook his head.

"Weak, very weak," he commented. "I've received much better threats from simple knights. Until next time, *Dex vos saut.*"

He shut the door and leaned against it, exhaling in relief.

Catherine hugged him in glee.

"I love it when you act the haughty lord!" she exclaimed. "Except when you do it to me."

She tweaked his nose.

"That, *ma dame*, is taking a dreadful liberty!" he said,

and pinioned her with his left arm while he tickled her rib cage.

"Edgar! Stop!" She laughed.

There was a tug on her skirts. Still laughing, she looked down into James's reproachful eyes.

"Mama, Papa," he said. "You shouldn't play without me."

They both began laughing again, wounding their son's budding pride. Catherine lifted him, and they held him between them, tickling until he started to hiccough.

Edgar patted his back. "There, there, son. Hold your nose and count back from ten. Now you see what happens when you play grown-up games."

His face grew serious as he looked at Catherine.

"I only hope that isn't what you and I are doing. Master Durand could well be a powerful enemy."

"Better that than think him our friend," Catherine answered. "He's not a man to trust. You heard what he said to Brother Baudwin. He wants to blame us for the death. It's simpler than investigating and perhaps finding something he doesn't want to know."

"Or for others to discover something Durand already knows." Gently Edgar set James down. "There's only one thing to do, isn't there?"

Catherine nodded. "We have to find out first."

Edgar saw that the mysterious knife was locked safely away in the spice box in the kitchen and spent the afternoon, once he had finished his business with the head of the water merchants' association, hiring a couple of men to patrol outside the house from Compline to dawn. He accomplished this by going from one tavern to another until he found a friend who knew someone who knew someone who had a friend who knew of a man who had been one of the king's guards until an unfortunate incident with a lady had left him with only one eye. This man had a brother, just arrived from the country, and they were looking for honest work and didn't mind staying awake through the night.

Nothing to it.

Edgar was congratulating himself over a bowl of new beer when he heard his name called.

"Maurice!" he greeted the cleric standing at the door. "Come, sit with me. Have something to drink. How are things at the Cathedral? Have your precentor and chanter come to blows, yet?"

"Not since last night." Maurice filled his bowl from the beer pitcher. "But our music is suffering from the animosity."

He sat a moment in silence, rocking the bowl in his palms.

Edgar refilled his bowl. "The lack of melodiousness in your choir upsets you that much?" he asked, noting Maurice's distraction.

Maurice came out of his reverie. "That? No, of course not," he said. "I was thinking about something I heard this morning. There's talk of calling a meeting to make the bishop of Poitiers answer questions as to the orthodoxy of his teaching."

"Really?" Edgar raised an eyebrow. "And who, besides perhaps Master Peter of Lombardy, could possibly understand his answer? I never made much sense from the subtlety of Master Gilbert's lectures."

"To my mind that is certainly the problem," Maurice answered. "Master Gilbert is so subtle that someone not so gifted in theology could easily misinterpret his words."

"And end up by assuming himself to be the son of God?" Edgar laughed.

Maurice joined him. "Perhaps not that radical a conclusion." He sipped from his bowl. "You know, I think I may have seen some of those followers of that Eon or *Eum* near Nôtre Dame this morning. I hadn't paid them much mind before, but there's a clutch of beggars who, I swear, are wearing ragged silk and linen with bits of fine embroidery still showing."

"That's strange," Edgar said. "Astrolabe gave me to understand that this heresy was confined to Brittany."

"Well, these people may have been given worn altar cloths as charity," Maurice said. "I suppose I assumed they were Eonists because the one crying alms had a Breton accent."

He shrugged. The world was full of bizarre heresies. Most of them vanished quickly with a few well-placed sermons.

Edgar was spinning his bowl of beer, watching the residue settle on the rim like seaweed on the beach. He looked up to find Maurice watching him with amusement.

"Sorry," he said. "I was worrying about that dead man left in our house. It seems no one at the Temple can name him."

"You said his face was eaten away," Maurice replied. "Why should it be odd that no one recognizes him?"

"Maurice, wouldn't you be able to identify me, even if my face were gone?" Edgar asked.

"Of course, by your . . ." Maurice stopped suddenly.

"My hand, yes," Edgar finished for him. "But apart from that?"

Maurice pursed his lips. "Yes, I could at least guess, by your hair and form."

"Exactly," Edgar said. "The knights are all noblemen, and they tend to join the order in groups of friends. Many know each other anyway. They've fought beside or even against one another over the years. This man would have had to come from far away for no one to know him."

"You think he may not have been a member of the Order?" Maurice asked. "If so, then why was he wearing their white cloak?"

Edgar had no answer to that.

When Catherine had convinced her brother that they would not go back with him, then he insisted, despite protests from his wife and oldest daughter, on leaving at once.

"Catherine and Edgar seem to enjoy danger," Guillaume stated. "I prefer to face it knowing that my family are on the other side of a motte behind thick walls. Come along, Marie, Evaine, we'll return soon enough. I'm sure the commander of the Temple will have everything solved in a few days."

Catherine refrained from answering that, if Master Evrard's investigators had their way, the case would be resolved even more quickly. She just nodded.

Marie understood her expression. Taking Catherine aside, she made one more plea.

"Let me take your little ones back with us," she begged. "Look at what's happened to Edana already."

Catherine wavered, then shook her head. "Accidents happen everywhere. Don't you worry about Gervase every day?"

Marie pressed her lips together. Catherine realized that she had used an unfair tactic. Guillaume and Marie's first child was now nine and had recently been sent to Vermandois for fostering and training. It was a coup on Guillaume's part to have his son under the protection of the count, a great lord and cousin to the king, even though at the moment he was under a decree of excommunication. But, reasoned Guillaume, if the king didn't mind that, why should they? This did not help Marie's grief at sending her young son away.

"If you change your mind," Marie answered finally, "we'll always take them in."

"Thank you." Catherine hugged her. "It's a comfort to know you'll be there if we need a refuge."

Still it was with relief that she waved them all out. The house, she reflected, was too small for four extra children. Before they had left for Trier, Edgar had been planning an addition on the back. She should remind him of it once things settled down.

If they ever did.

At the moment the house was as peaceful as it was likely to get. Edana was napping on the blankets that had yet to be put away. Astrolabe had left for the day. Samonie and her son were busy in the kitchen. She could hear James with them. But where was Margaret?

Catherine checked upstairs first, but all the rooms were empty. Then, stopping to be sure Edana still slept, she went into the kitchen, where Samonie was chopping early lettuce and carrot tops to add to a fish sauce for dinner. The two boys had cleared a space on the floor for a game of conkers.

"Samonie, have you seen Margaret?" she asked. "Did she go to visit Willa?"

"I don't think so," Samonie answered. "She knows Willa is busy today. She didn't go out this way."

"Yes, she did, Mother." Martin looked up from the game. "Just before Lord Guillaume's family left."

"Why didn't you tell me?" Samonie turned on him. "I'm sorry, Catherine."

"She's fourteen, Samonie," Catherine said. "She doesn't need watching like a baby. There's no reason for Martin to have reported it."

Nonetheless, she was worried. The last time Margaret had gone missing, she had nearly died.

"I think I'll just go to the market and see if she's there," Catherine decided. "Would you boys take the conkers into the hall in case Edana wakes?"

They didn't dare grumble. Even James sensed that Catherine was worried.

Catherine hurried down the street hoping that she could find Margaret before Edgar returned home. She had told Samonie that Margaret was old enough to look out for herself, but she didn't believe it and feared that Edgar would blame her if anything more happened to his sister. But Catherine would blame herself even more.

She asked at all the places she thought Margaret might stroll to: the ribbon makers, the leather workers, the seller of embroidery thread. No one had seen a young woman with red-gold hair and a scar along the side of her face.

Catherine was beginning to panic when she caught a glimpse of a red braid swinging amidst the crowd. She pushed her way through and found Margaret heading in her direction on the arm of Abraham the vintner.

"Margaret!" she cried, gathering the girl into her arms. "What were you thinking of? Why didn't you tell me where you were going?"

She looked at Abraham. "Thank you for bringing her back. Where was she?"

The old man guided them to a quiet side street before he answered.

"She came to my door," he said. "Unescorted."

He gave them both a stern look.

"Margaret, why bother Master Abraham?" Catherine hadn't even realized Margaret knew the man.

Margaret sniffed back tears. She knew she'd been foolish.

"I had to go, Catherine," she said in a wobbling voice. "We've heard nothing, but I thought some one of his people might have had a message."

Catherine finally understood. "Oh, *ma cossette*, if there had been word of Solomon in the Jewish community, they would have told us instantly."

Abraham patted her shoulder. "Of course we would. But, Catherine, you must make her understand that it's not safe for her to come to our homes without you or Edgar."

"She should know that already," Catherine said. "But I'll explain again. Thank you, Master Abraham."

The vintner bowed and turned back toward his home, ignoring the dirty looks some of the people in the street gave him.

Catherine let the lecture wait until they reached the house. She paused only to be sure everything was quiet, and then she bundled Margaret upstairs and sat her on the bed.

"You should be whipped for doing something so stupid," she began, fear making her harsh. "Your brother will be furious."

But the stricken look on Margaret's pale face was too much for her. Catherine relented and sat down next to her.

"My dear, after what happened to you in Germany my stomach freezes if I can't find you," she said.

Margaret leaned against her shoulder. "I know. I was frightened to go. But I had to find out. Why aren't you worried about Solomon? What if those people who listened to the false monk in Köln come for him, too?"

"I am worried about him," Catherine admitted. "But only

a little. Solomon has spent most of his life among strangers. He knows how to protect himself."

She didn't add that, for the most part, the greatest danger to Solomon in the past had not been from anti-Jewish mobs but from the relatives of attractive young women he had encountered.

"There are a hundred reasons for him not being here when we arrived," she continued. "All of them perfectly natural. He might have learned of a wonderful opportunity for trade and decided to follow that."

Margaret wasn't convinced.

"There's another thing." Catherine hated to mention it. Margaret should have understood without being told. "Abraham was not only concerned for you, but for himself and his community. If you had been noted going into his house, he could be accused of trying to proselytize and, if you were hurt, all the Jews might be accused."

Margaret's eyes grew round with fear. "I didn't think it was like that here," she said. "Remember, there are no Jews in Scotland. I've had to learn so much since I came to France."

Catherine squeezed her hand. "I know, and the fact that Solomon is my cousin is somewhat confusing, I'm sure. We trust you with the secret. But with that trust there are responsibilities."

Margaret sighed. "I'll remember."

"Good." Catherine got up. "Now, while the chaos in the house has abated for a while, will you help me with a more pressing problem?"

"Of course." Margaret was relieved that the lecture seemed to be over.

"It's the matter of the body in the counting room," she said as she led Margaret back down the hallway. "If we can't find out who he was, we should at least try to learn why he was left with us."

"How can I help? I don't know what to look for," Margaret said.

"I don't either," Catherine answered. "But this is the only room in the house that has its own lock. When we got here, the lock had been freshly oiled. Samonie told me she didn't do it. The only thing I can think of is that someone knew about this room and went to the trouble of bringing oil so that he could pick the lock or to make a key turn more easily."

"Does that mean it's someone we know?" Margaret sounded fearful again.

"Not necessarily." Catherine was speaking more to herself. "The house was empty for several weeks. If someone wanted to steal the supposed 'treasure,' then he surely would have expected it to be locked away."

They entered the counting room. There were still crumbs on the floor from the cakes they had given Brother Baudwin and Master Durand. Rushes weren't allowed in the room, no more than lamps. Hubert had had an exaggerated nervousness about books and fire.

Catherine went over to the book cabinet and examined the lock.

"That's odd," she said. "This one hasn't been tampered with, that I can tell. *Avoi*, look Margaret. Do you see any scratches or oil?"

Margaret bent to study the lock. "No, it's even a bit rusty."

"Now why do you think someone would go to all the trouble of breaking into the house, into this room, and not try to open the one place where something valuable might be kept?" Catherine tapped her fingers on the wood in irritation.

"They were looking for something big?" Margaret guessed.

"Bigger than the book cabinet?" Catherine couldn't imagine what that might be.

Margaret shrugged. "I was just guessing."

"Well, your guess is as good as anyone's," Catherine assured her. "I don't even have that much."

Below they heard the gate opening. Margaret looked up in anticipation.

"It's just Edgar coming home," Catherine said. "I wonder how his talk with the wine sellers went?"

Then they heard voices. Catherine couldn't make them out, but Margaret did. She was out the door and flying down the stairs so quickly that she missed the last three steps, throwing herself in a leap upon Solomon.

"Sweeting! You nearly knocked me down." Solomon caught and held her. "Is that any way to . . ."

He realized that Margaret was sobbing hysterically.

"Margaret, what's wrong? What's happened?" he tried to pull the damp hair from her face.

"I thought they'd killed you!" she managed to say. "I thought you'd gone and died and left me behind! Solomon, Solomon, promise me you won't die without me!"

"Of course, Margaret," he said. "Or not at all, if you prefer."

He patted her back as the sobs diminished to gasps for breath and quieter tears. As Catherine came down, he mouthed a question at her.

"What's wrong?"

Catherine eased Margaret away from him and hugged her cousin, whispering sternly as she did.

"Solomon, we need to talk."

Six

Paris, the home of Edgar and Catherine, Sunday 2 Ides May, (May 11), 1147: 10 Sivan, 4907. Feast of Saint Antimius, priest and prophet, who was saved by an angel from drowning in the Tiber, only to have his head cut off.

Et idcirco quæ in peccato originali est culpa . . . ad utrumque tamen tota redundat: in illam quidem quia peccavit in istum, quia peccanti consensit et peccatum illius consentiendo suum fecit.

Therefore, as to whom [Adam or Eve] is more guilty of original sin . . . it fills them both to the brim; she because she committed the sin, he because he agreed to the sin and allowed her to sin by consenting to it.

—Hugh of Saint Victor
De Sacramentis Christianæ Fidei
Book I, Part VII

*I*t was long past sunset. The last of the spring twilight had faded but Catherine, Edgar and Solomon still sat in the hall, sipping their wine and edging around the topic most on their minds.

Finally, Solomon put down his cup. He could barely see the faces of the others in the flickering lamplight.

"Do you want me to leave?" he asked abruptly.

"Of course not," Edgar's answer came quickly, with a firmness that satisfied Solomon of his sincerity.

Catherine took longer before she replied.

"You're needed here." She spoke slowly, unsure of how to give her suggestion without hurting her cousin. "You and Edgar must show that you can trade as dependably as Father and Uncle Eliazar did, if we're to live. But it might be a good idea if Margaret were sent away for a time. Either to my brother or, if they'll accept her, to the court of Count Thibault and Countess Mahaut at Troyes."

Both men stared at her in horror.

"How can you even think of such a thing!" Edgar exclaimed. "After what she's been through, to exile her as if she'd committed some grave sin!"

"You want to punish her for being fond of me?" Solomon was outraged.

Catherine stood up and went over to the cold hearth, kicking at the rushes to release her own feelings. She turned back and faced Solomon and Edgar. It was easier to explain things when she could look down into their faces.

"It's exactly because Margaret has endured so much that I feel she should be somewhere else," she said quietly. "Between the damage to her body and to her spirit, her humors are terribly unbalanced. Apart from the attack, dear Lord, she watched her mother murdered!"

Solomon winced. Catherine looked on him with pity. She knew how he blamed himself for not being able to save Adalisa. She would not have mentioned it but for the seriousness of the problem.

"I know very little about the scars Margaret bears in her heart or how best to heal them, but I do believe that she needs some place quiet to become whole again," she finished.

"Well, *I* think she needs to be with those who love her most," Solomon said.

"You certainly don't believe that anyone would find peace at Vielleteneuse," Edgar argued. "The children alone make the place as chaotic as a battlefield. And with preparations for the count's son to go with the king to the Holy Land, the court of Champagne is no better. You saw for yourself that Thibault and Mahaut are constantly involved in adjudicating some dispute or other. A court is no place for my sister."

Catherine rooted among the rushes with her toe for a moment. Both men had reasonable rejoinders to her proposition, but she still sensed that it was imperative that Margaret not be around Solomon until she was calmer and better able to understand the impossibility of her desires. She remembered how, at fourteen, she had fancied herself terribly fond of her uncle Roger. Three years at the convent of the Paraclete had given her time to realize how foolish that was.

"Of course!" she exclaimed. "What better place for Margaret to compose her mind, as well as be educated for whatever position she'll have in her life. Mother Heloise will take her in, just as she did me."

"What?" Solomon rose to protest. "No, not a convent! Not even that one."

"I'm not suggesting she take the veil," Catherine said.

"She's too young, in any case. Mother Heloise won't let any woman make final vows before she's eighteen. Margaret could join the students there. You must admit there's no better place for her to improve her Latin."

"Why should she?" Edgar wasn't convinced. "She reads both French and English well enough. There's no call for her to study Latin unless she wishes to enter the Church."

Solomon was standing, too. "That I would never tolerate," he said. "I promised her mother to care for her, not . . ."

He was abruptly interrupted.

"I don't suppose any of you have considered that I might have an opinion in this."

All three jumped as if lightning had struck the room.

"Margaret!" Catherine cried. "We thought you were asleep."

"Obviously," Margaret answered. Her lip trembled, and she bit it to steady herself. "I know that my worry for Solomon may have seemed excessive to you." She took a deep breath. "Perhaps it caused my melancholic humor to influence my behavior. But that is no excuse for you deciding my future without consulting me."

"Margaret, we would never . . ." Edgar started.

"I was only thinking of your welfare," Catherine said.

"It's my duty . . ." Solomon tried to explain.

Margaret just looked at them sadly.

"I do love you, Solomon," she said. "Perhaps, as you say, my devotion is only as that of a daughter. I don't know. I haven't much knowledge of filial affection. You always seemed to care for me more than my own father ever did. Do you wonder that I return your kindness?"

Edgar had to agree with that. His father and Margaret's had seen his children only as possessions. He was generally indifferent to them unless they opposed him. Edgar had vowed when James was born that he would never treat his son as Waldeve had treated him.

"None of us has denied Solomon the right your mother entrusted to him. Your welfare matters to all of us," Edgar explained. "But, Margaret, you aren't a child anymore, and you must understand why we're concerned."

Margaret's hand went to the scar on her cheek. "Yes, I do. Catherine reminded me not long ago. But when we're all home together, I forget that Solomon is an 'infidel who must be shunned.' "

Solomon smiled tenderly at her. "I am grateful for that, my dear. I sometimes forget that you all are 'idolators to be scorned.' "

He sighed and held out his hand. "Come sit with us, then. Do you want some wine? I know that you're of an age to be consulted. But you're still weak from all you've suffered. Catherine may be right. It would be better if you could be somewhere peaceful to regain your strength."

Catherine was suddenly overwhelmed with sadness. Perhaps her humors needed assistance, too.

"Look around us, Margaret." She stretched her arm out, as if to include the whole of Paris. "The streets are full of warriors and pilgrims eager for glory, their swords hungry for blood. In the countryside people are starving, and mad heretics roam unchecked. Not a stone's throw from here civilized scholars want to condemn a bishop for a point of theology so precise only ten people in the world can grasp the subtlety of it. And we're under suspicion of having murdered a total stranger and locked him in our counting room. Why would you want to stay in this cauldron of wickedness?"

Catherine seemed on the edge of hysteria, herself. Edgar got up, put his arm around her waist and kissed her temple. Catherine buried her face in his tunic.

"It isn't only Margaret who needs a respite, *carissima*," he said to her. "Perhaps you should take the children and all of you pay a visit to the Paraclete."

"And leave you here to face those men from the Temple?" Catherine exclaimed. "I would never do that!"

"That's how I feel, Catherine," Margaret added. "I know I've been unsettled lately, but now that Solomon's back, I already feel much better. I want to help you. Please, don't send me away."

The other three looked at Margaret. The lamplight gave

her pale skin and auburn hair a glow like ivory and flame. That and her tranquil dignity made her look like some otherworldly apparition that a word might dispel.

Solomon shook his head, astonished to feel tears on his cheeks. He took a draught of his wine, letting the cup hide his face.

"Edgar?" Margaret reached out to him.

Edgar released Catherine and took his sister in his arms. "I'm not our father," he whispered. "I won't force you, only beg you to consider my advice."

Catherine sat down next to Solomon. She took his chin and turned his face away from Margaret's to hers. The pain she saw in him struck her deeply. The matter wasn't settled. She realized that he understood his own feelings even less than Margaret did hers. Catherine vowed to stay watchful of them both lest it end in worse than tears.

The next day was clear with a southern wind that promised summer. All of Paris seemed to take a deep breath and move more slowly. Benches were set up outside the taverns, and shops lowered their shutters to use as counters to display their wares. The street of the drapers was festooned with fluttering ribbons, feathers and sparkling glass and bead ornaments.

Catherine barely glanced at them as she made her way to the *rue des juives*. The night before, lying next to Edgar, she had made up her mind, but the decision didn't rest easily. She feared that what she contemplated was a sin. The theologians weren't completely certain on the matter. She only hoped that, if it were, one day, far into the future, she might feel enough contrition to repent.

She knocked at the door, trying to look as if she had a perfectly innocent reason for her visit. She had brought a basket of early greens from her garden as a gift.

The maid who opened the door smiled at her in a kindly fashion, but Catherine was so sure that her mission was written on her face that she drew back and stumbled over her words.

"My ... my name is Catherine, daughter of Hubert

LeVendeur," she said. "That is, Johanna and Eliazar who used to live nearby, they're . . . they're friends of mine. Johanna once told me . . . um . . . I mean, is Rebecca at home?"

"I believe so," the maid said. "I'll go see. Would you wait here in the court?"

She stepped back to let Catherine pass through the dark hallway and out into the inner yard. Gratefully, Catherine perched on the side of a copper washtub and tried to collect herself.

"Catherine!" Rebecca came out almost at once. "I haven't seen you since Johanna left for Troyes! How delightful! How are your children? Please, have some cider and cake."

She had brought out a pair of folding stools, and the maid set them up before leaving to fetch the cider.

Catherine felt herself blushing at the welcome. "I'm happy to see you, as well. We've only just returned to Paris. I know Solomon and Edgar will be coming by soon to discuss buying wines with your husband, but"—she bit her lip—"I must confess that I wanted to see you alone. Long ago, Johanna said something that made me think perhaps you could help me."

She paused and looked down. "My last birth was a hard one and the baby too weak to survive the winter and the midwife said . . ."

Rebecca put her hand over Catherine's.

"Don't be ashamed, my dear." She smiled. "You're not the first Christian woman who's come to me for instruction. Why don't we have something to eat and drink? Tell me what news you have from dear Johanna. Then we'll go up to my room, and I'll show you what you need to do."

The conversation of the night before had been a forceful reminder to Solomon and Edgar that they were now responsible for the survival of the family. They were up in the storage room making an inventory of goods when Martin announced the visitor.

"A man from Flanders, by his accent," the boy said.

"Says he bought a horse from you once. He's waiting in the hall."

"Remind me to have Catherine explain to Martin about getting the names of our visitors," Edgar said, as they went down.

"I'd also like him to find out if they want to complain about a bad bargain or make a new one," Solomon answered. "I want to know in advance if I'll need to defend myself."

The man waiting for them didn't seem belligerent. He was older and shorter than either of them, his brown hair, what was left of it, greying. He rose as they entered and gave them a nervous smile.

"You may not remember me," he addressed Solomon. "I'm Bertulf, of Picardy. Several years ago my lord Osto and I bought a horse from you and your former partners at the fair in Troyes."

"Yes, you do seem familiar," Solomon squinted to see him better. "It was a Spanish bay, wasn't it?"

"Yes, a fine animal. We bred him to our lowland mares, and the results were excellent." Bertulf paused.

Solomon waited.

"You wish us to find you another horse?" Edgar asked. "Or sell one for you?"

"Oh, no, no, not at all!" The visitor seemed unsure of what to do next.

"Then why have you come to see us?" Edgar prompted. "What may we do for you?"

In some embarrassment, Bertulf opened the purse at his belt and took out a silver brooch.

"Lord Osto and I came to Paris to join the king's army; that is, Lord Osto did. I have other plans. In any case, we had thought ourselves well prepared for the journey," he explained. "But many places would not feed or house us unless we paid, even though we are pilgrims. And Paris is so much more expensive than I remembered. So."

He held the brooch out for Edgar to examine.

"I see." Edgar held the piece in the light. "We don't take objects as pledges, you understand. We're not usurers. If

you wish to sell it, I can give you only fifteen pennies of
Paris. The silver is light, the design crude and scratched.
You might do better taking it elsewhere."

He looked at Solomon, who nodded agreement. Edgar
then handed the brooch back to Bertulf.

"I'm sorry we can't give you more," he said.

Edgar meant what he said. Bertulf's plight touched him
deeply. The man was clearly worn. His troubles weighed
on him so that Edgar could almost see them pressing him
down. How did Bertulf expect to survive the trip to the
Holy Land?

"You and your lord have a place to stay, don't you?" he
found himself asking.

"Oh, yes, of course," Bertulf said. "Fifteen pennies will
keep us until the king sets out, I'm sure."

He gave Edgar back the brooch. Solomon stared, wondering why he was buying such a shoddy piece of work.
Edgar shrugged. Later, when Catherine found the notation
in the record book, it was listed as "alms for Jerusalem."

"Just a moment, then," he told Bertulf. "I'll get the
money."

He went upstairs to the counting room, where the box
that held the coins for daily use was kept. Bertulf started
to follow him, but Solomon stepped in his path and, taking
his arm, guided him back to the center of the hall.

The door to the kitchen opened and Samonie appeared,
balancing a basket of newly washed linen. When she saw
them, she started and dropped her load, sending it tumbling
onto the rushes.

"*Damedeu!*" she exclaimed as she bent to pick up the
wet clothes and shake the bits of herb from them. "I didn't
know anyone was here."

Solomon hurried over to help her. "*Dant* Bertulf was just
leaving, Samonie. As soon as Edgar pays him. Are these
going to the roof to dry?"

She nodded.

"I'll take the basket," Solomon continued. "Perhaps you
could give our guest some bread and soup before he goes."

She glared at Bertulf, who cringed, but she didn't dare protest.

"He can have what's left in the pot," she said. "Come with me *Dant* Bertulf."

She went back into the kitchen. Bertulf followed at a safe distance.

Solomon carried the basket up the stairs, stopping to call out to Edgar.

Edgar came out of the counting room. He grinned at Solomon.

"We're taking in washing, now?" He laughed. "Have you no faith in my trading skills?"

"Not if every bargain you make is like this one," Solomon answered. "No, this time I don't grudge the man his pennies, even though I have no interest in giving charity to these pilgrim knights of yours. But Bertulf is so pathetic that I can only pity him. He must mean to leave his bones at Antioch."

"Yes, he's a strange man to be a warrior," Edgar said. "It may be that his lord commanded Bertulf to accompany him, and the poor man had no choice but to go."

"I'd have picked a squire more fit," Solomon commented as he continued up to the roof.

Edgar considered this as he went down to the hall. He heard voices coming from the kitchen, but when he opened the door they stopped. Samonie was ladling soup over a crust from the previous night's supper. She seemed angry. That puzzled Edgar. Normally Samonie was happy to share what they had with others.

"Here are your pennies, Bertulf," he said as he put the coins on the table. "The king should leave any day now, so I'm sure you'll have no more difficulties. If you do, come to me before you decide to join the beggars in the parvis of Nôtre Dame."

"Yes, thank you." Bertulf put the money in his purse without even counting it. "Very kind, thank you."

He took the crust from Samonie without waiting for the soup to soak in and, spilling as he went, he hurried through the hall and back out into the street.

Edgar stared after him.

"That Bertulf is a strange pilgrim," he commented. "But there was no reason for you to treat him rudely, Samonie."

"I have reason." Samonie then snapped her mouth shut. Edgar knew she would say no more.

He sighed. "It's nothing to me. By the way, you've left the door to the spice cabinet open. Lock it, please, in case any other 'pilgrims' come by for charity."

Solomon returned, having passed Bertulf in the hall. He broke a corner from a hunk of cheese and shook his head.

"That man has something on his conscience," he said.

Samonie grunted and pointedly began wrapping the rest of the cheese. Edgar looked at her quizzically.

"What is the matter with you?" he asked. "What is your reason for disliking Bertulf? Is there something wrong with that man? Do you know something about him that you should tell us? Do you think he stole the brooch he sold me?"

"No, my lord," Samonie answered. "I have no doubt it was his. This Bertulf seemed harmless enough. I've nothing against him. I'm just out of sorts today. Perhaps it's the moon."

Edgar accepted that. Catherine had a problematic relationship with the moon, as well.

"You do remember Bertulf from Troyes, don't you Solomon?"

Solomon chewed reflectively. "Oh, yes. I couldn't recall the name of the buyer, but I remember the horse well enough. The man's face was familiar. He and another bought the bay together. They said at the time that they were going to breed him."

"That's all right, then." Edgar took a deep breath. "Then let's return to the storeroom. We need to organize it according to a system of our own. Hubert's makes no sense to me. I know he said there was a box of saffron in there somewhere, and one of the water merchants told me he had a buyer for it. But we have to unearth it today, or he'll find a vendor elsewhere."

They left the room. Samonie heard their boots clomping

above her. Carefully, she put the cheese back in the pantry. Then she made herself a chamomile tisane and sat sipping it until she stopped trembling and the tears dried.

As she walked home, Catherine felt as if everyone were looking at her and knew what she had hidden under the kerchief in her basket. Desperation had driven her to it, she told herself. There was no other course. She was determined to carry the plan through, but she wouldn't feel sanguine about it until she was safe at home with the thing locked in the box under their bed far away from prying eyes.

Her heart almost stopped when she came around the corner from the bridge to the house and ran into a hunched-over man rushing the other way. She barely glanced at him or heard his apologies; she was so terrified that the basket would spill.

Bertulf had a vague impression of having bumped into something, but he was as preoccupied as Catherine. Without looking back, he hurried on to the tavern by the river where Godfrey was waiting.

"Did you get it?" he asked before Bertulf had sat.

Bertulf nodded and signaled for a pitcher of beer.

"She gave it to me right away, once we were alone," he said after taking a long gulp. "I stuck it up my sleeve. You should have gone, you know. I'm not meant for this sort of subterfuge."

"You had seen them before. I couldn't have convinced them so well. Did they recognize you?" the other man asked.

"Not really," Bertulf said. "The Jew knew he'd sold me a horse, but didn't know my name. It's a good thing Hubert has left. I never could have faced him and lied."

"Old Hubert would have helped us," Godfrey said. "He understood how the world works. This son-in-law, his father's a lord in Scotland, they say. The high nobility, they look at things differently. They can't be trusted, even on oath. What's wrong?"

Bertulf had suddenly stood up and was patting himself

all over, turning out his sleeves and shaking his belt.

"It's not here!" he cried. "I know I had it. I must have dropped it in the street!"

"Calm yourself, Master!" Godfrey pulled Bertulf back onto the bench. "It doesn't matter. As long as it's no longer in the house. No one will ask where it came from if they pick it up from the gutter."

Bertulf saw the sense in that and cursed himself for drawing the attention of the others in the tavern. Of course it didn't matter. As long as no one connected it with him. He finished his beer and sighed.

"Now we have to present ourselves at the preceptory of the Knights of the Temple. That frightens me even more. Oh, Godfrey, what have we set in motion?"

Godfrey put his arm on Bertulf's shoulder. "We're following the original plan; that's all. It's what he would have wanted. You honor his memory with your sacrifice."

Bertulf lifted his chin. "I give it gladly for my child and my descendants," he said. "If only I knew that it wouldn't be in vain."

Edgar looked at the object in Catherine's hand as if he expected it to leap at him.

"What is that thing?" he asked. "And why have you brought it to bed?"

Now that the time had come for explantions, Catherine's courage faltered. Only the scent of Edgar's skin so near kept her from abandoning her plan. Another night of this would drive her mad.

"It's called a *mokh*," she said. "Aunt Johanna told me about it after our first child was stillborn."

She stopped. After all this time the memory still hurt. Edgar caressed her cheek. The grief was his, too.

"I told her then that I didn't need any such things," Catherine went on. "But the past few months have made me change my mind. In my mind I went over all the issues the Fathers of the Church raised, and there seems to be a question as to how bad it is to use this. After all, it's to save us from a greater sin."

Edgar gingerly poked at the spongelike object. It had a long cord sewn onto it, rather like a tail.

"I'm afraid to ask what one does with it," he said.

She explained.

Edgar realized that his reaction wasn't so much guilt as disgust. What would it feel like?

"What if it gets stuck?" he asked.

"I tie the cord around my leg," Catherine said. "Rebecca told me how. Edgar, it's either this or we both go insane. Unless you want me to risk another pregnancy now."

"No! Of course not." The thought of listening to her cry out in the agony of childbirth, fearing all the while that this time she would die, was terrifying. Edgar knew that bringing forth children in pain was the curse placed on Eve, but when it happened to Catherine all he could think of was that it was all his fault.

"Isn't there any other way?"

"I know of herbs and potions one can use," Catherine admitted. "But they're dangerous. They can cause a woman to become barren or even die. This simply prevents the seed from planting itself in the womb."

Edgar grimaced. That was what they'd been doing already. He supposed this wasn't any different except that Catherine could enjoy it, too.

"Very well," he decided. "We'll try it. But I don't know. Maybe I won't be able to."

Catherine moved closer to him. "Beloved," she whispered, "that's one problem I never even considered."

It was well past dawn when Catherine awoke. Edgar was already up. She could hear him downstairs coaxing Edana to stay on her stool while she ate her bread. She smiled. She felt wonderful. After some internal conversation, she decided that she had been right; the sin of preventing conception wasn't nearly as bad as denying the marriage debt.

Removing the *mokh* wasn't as pleasant as putting it in, but Catherine managed it and slipped it back in the basket, meaning to rinse it in cold water when she emptied the chamber pot. As she pushed the basket back under the bed, it fell over and something clanked.

She leaned over and saw a knife caught in the folds of the scarf. She picked it up.

"That's strange," she said. "How did that get in here? I thought Samonie had put it away in the kitchen."

She pulled a *bliaut* over her shift and went down to greet her family.

"Edgar, isn't this the knife that cut Edana?" she asked, holding it out to him.

Edana stood on the stool and pulled at the bandage.

"Yes, sweeting." Catherine picked her up. "You're much better. We'll look at it later. I thought Papa told you to finish eating before jumping around."

Edgar examined the handle. "It looks the same," he said. "There's a star pattern etched here like the other. Why?"

Catherine told him. "I don't see how it could have fallen into the basket. I picked the greens on my way out yesterday. I was nowhere near the kitchen. Samonie!"

The housekeeper's head appeared around the door.

"Do you still have the knife that Astrolabe found?" Edgar asked.

"It was on the counter," Samonie answered. "I was using it to slice cheese. But I didn't see it after that Bertulf left yesterday. I suspect him of making off with it. Fine thanks for your charity."

"You mustn't condemn him, Samonie," Catherine said. "I found it upstairs."

"What?" Samonie stared at the knife.

Catherine shook her head. "Perhaps one of the children took it and dropped it in the basket. Were one of you playing with this?"

Both James and Edana denied touching the knife, and neither was good at lying.

Catherine fretted over it all morning. What was bothering her the most was that the knife had been in the basket with the *mokh*. Could it be some sort of warning? Perhaps her interpretation of the theology on the duties of marriage had been too facile. What if the knife had not been put there through human intervention?

It was an odd sort of way for a Sign to be manifested, but what did she know of the Ineffable?

Catherine shivered. That worried her more than the dead knight. She wasn't going to be easy in her mind until this mystery was solved.

Seven

The chapel of the Knights of the Temple of Solomon, Paris preceptory. Tuesday, 3 ides of May (May 13), 1147; 11 Sivan, 4907. Feast of Saint Servais, Bishop of Tongres, on whose tomb it never snows.

Si aucun chevalier seculier, ou autre home, se veaut departir de la masse de perdition, et abandonier cest siecle, et eslire la vostre comunal vie, ne vos assentez mie tantost a lui recevoir . . . Esprovés l'esperit se il vient de Dieu.

If a secular knight or any other man wishes to leave the expanse of perdition and abandon this world and choose your common life [of the Temple], you shouldn't agree to admit him at once . . . test his spirit to see if it inclines to God.

—Rule of the Order of the Temple, Part 55

*B*ertulf and Godfrey rode to the gate of the preceptory, Vrieit on a lead behind them. The sun of the day
before had been covered by thick clouds, and a mist hung
around them, making their beards glisten and their noses
red.

"Should we both dismount?" Bertulf wondered aloud.
"Knights are supposed to be humble."

"They also have to be nobly born," Godfrey said. "You
stay where you are, and I'll knock. No, even better. You
get on Vrieit. Show them what you have to offer."

"Yes, that might be better." Bertulf got off the palfrey.
"Here, shouldn't we move a bit away until we get him
saddled?"

They moved into the shelter of a shed that had been left
open and empty. Quickly, they unwrapped the fine leather
saddle and the bridle with its iron bit. The blanket was of
English wool, woven in their own village. Bertulf felt a
pang as he remembered how the weavers had given it to
him as their contribution to defeating the Saracens. He
brushed away a tear. He mustn't even dream of ever seeing
his home again.

As they were working they were startled by the creak of
the gate and a pounding of hooves. Both men looked out
from their hiding place. The formidable wooden gates were
wide-open. A procession was leaving the Temple. Dozens
of knights in shining white cloaks, followed by others in
brown and black. It seemed as though all the soldiers of

Christ were setting forth. As they passed, the sun broke through the mist; and Bertulf crossed himself in awe. The knights shone like angels going to battle Satan. He almost thought he saw the Archangel Michael at their head, brandishing the sword he had used to kill the dragon.

Godfrey nudged him.

"Is there anyone among them who might know us?"

Bertulf turned to him with wide eyes. "I . . . I don't know," he said. "I was so dazzled by their glory, I forgot they were just men. Oh, Godfrey! What were we thinking of? We're country people, horse breeders. We were only trained to fight off bandits and *ribaux*, not an army. Why would they want us?"

"You're blinded by the white cloaks," Godfrey said as he rechecked the girth. "Under them they're human like us, and most of them have reasons far worse than yours for joining the brethren. You've heard that one can lift an excommunication by pledging oneself to the Temple?"

"You can? When was that enacted?" Bertulf was shocked.

"Not long ago," Godfrey said. "They must be in desperate need of men who can fight." He finished fastening the last buckle. "There, now you're ready to face the brothers."

"Wonderful," Bertulf said sadly. Then he brightened. "With any luck, we just saw all of them leave."

Coming from the market, Catherine was caught on the wrong side of the road when the knights went across the Grand Pont on their way to the bishop's palace on the Ile. The men in their white cloaks, most now adorned with the red cross of pilgrimage, made a stirring sight, and the citizens of Paris lined the street to see them pass. They were accompanied by their sergeants, men not of the knightly class but warriors all the same. These wore black cloaks on which the red crosses front and back were equally impressive. Behind them, the squires in a variety of browns were less impressive. The troop together was an army in itself. The way everyone cheered one would think that Edessa was already freed from Saracen rule.

Catherine had to admit that she couldn't imagine a force strong enough to resist these warriors. When one added the armies of the king of France and the Holy Roman Emperor, they would certainly sweep through the Holy Land in a wave of righteousness that would put the sacred places of Our Lord's life forever in the hands of the faithful.

Catherine crossed herself and murmured a prayer for their success. She could see in the faces of those around her that to them these were heroes as great as any who ever rode with Charlemagne or Arthur.

Who would want to kill such a man? What could be gained by the death of one who had renounced his patrimony, family and friends to become a soldier of Christ?

As she made her way through the crowd and back to the house, Catherine mused on the problem. The men sent to investigate the death had not reappeared. Perhaps they had found their answers elsewhere. So much was happening now that the loss of a man known to no one might not seem very important. Even she had had little time to spend searching for the answers. Most of her day was taken up with children, the house, and helping Solomon and Edgar in their efforts to organize the goods and plan the next trading journey.

But at the back of her mind it was always there. Not just the fear that the body had been left with them as some sort of warning, but that some poor soul had died without the last rites. His family could offer no prayers for him; they likely had no idea he was dead. Somewhere a woman might be waiting for word, watching the road every day in the hope of seeing him again. And somewhere a murderer was walking around free.

Catherine resolved not to let obligations to her family cause her to ignore the stranger who, even in death, was still in their midst. She pushed open the gate to their house and stepped back into family turmoil.

"*Deorling!*" Edgar greeted her. "We can't find the bundle of silk ribbons that your father brought back from Marseille last year. Do you know what happened to them?"

"They were all sold at Provins," she answered as she

took her basket of cheese and vegetables out to Samonie.

Solomon's head appeared over the railing. "Did we sell all the amber beads that I bought in Hungary, as well?"

"No," she called back. "They're in the iron box we left at Saint Denis. Must you have them today?"

The head vanished, so she presumed the need wasn't urgent.

"Mama, Mama!" Edana was at her skirts, almost tripping her. "James broke my doll again."

"Your father will glue it." Catherine patted her cheek. "Come along. You can help me gather some greens to have with the cheese-and-turnip pie tonight."

"Lady Catherine." Martin picked up Edana and carried her as they went into the kitchen. "There was a man here earlier. He said he wanted to speak with you. I told him Master Edgar was at home, but he didn't want to see him."

"Did he give you his name?" Catherine asked. "Edana, if you pull Martin's hair, he'll drop you."

"He wouldn't say," Martin complained as he loosened the child's fingers from his hair. "And I *did* ask him. He was familar, though; I think he's been here before, a long time ago. He wore a mail shirt."

"Well then, we can rule out the clerics we know," Catherine said. "What did he look like?"

"Taller than me, but not so tall as Master Edgar," Martin answered quickly. "Dark, although his hair was running to grey and his face lined. He wasn't as old as Master Hubert though, I think."

Catherine stopped so abruptly that Martin ran into her, causing Edana to grab at her neck, tearing Catherine's *bliaut*.

"It's all right, sweeting," she said absently. "Don't howl so."

The description of the man sent chills through her. It couldn't be. Why would he have returned to Paris? And, even more, why would he come to see her?

And yet, if the man had been Jehan, it would explain a lot of things, including the body. He hated her family passionately. He had long hoped to marry Catherine's sister

Agnes, but that had been thwarted when Agnes had found a better match. But he had resented Edgar and Catherine for years before that. Through a series of misadventures, mostly of his own making, his life had gone awry, and he blamed them for every piece of ill luck that had come to him. He had vowed to destroy the family altogether. And Catherine feared that he knew enough about them to be able to do it.

But Jehan was supposed to have gone on the expedition to the Holy Land in the army of Emperor Conrad. He should be far away by now.

The knot in the pit of her stomach told Catherine that he might be all too close.

Her hand tightened on the handle of the basket. She took a deep breath to calm herself. There was no point in becoming frightened until she knew for sure.

"Does my husband know about this visitor?" she asked Martin.

"Oh." He grimaced. "I forgot to tell him. Mother sent me on an errand and . . ."

"Good," Catherine said. "We won't bother him with this. Did the man say when he'd return?"

"Tomorrow, after None," Martin was relieved that his lapse wasn't serious. Doorkeeper was a new task for him, and he had a hard time remembering all the rules.

"Good," Catherine said. "Solomon and Edgar should be gone by then."

Margaret was helping Samonie chop the turnips. They were the last of the winter store and withered to the texture of oak. The force needed on the cleaver sent pieces flying across the room.

Catherine handed over the basket and took Edana from Martin. "Samonie, would you like to take Margaret and the children and go see Willa tomorrow afternoon?"

"I thought we were going to clean out the root cellar," Samonie said. "You've been after me all week to make time for that."

"Oh, yes," Catherine said. "Oh well, we've all summer

to do it. Let's wait until it's so hot that spending a day underground sounds pleasant."

Samonie shrugged, but her eyes were suspicious. She'd known Catherine too long not to doubt this sudden change of plans.

"Please, Samonie," Margaret said. "We'll help Willa with the felt. Edana likes the splashing."

"I don't mind," Samonie answered, looking at Catherine. "You're mistress here."

She nodded to Catherine, who smiled thanks. Both of them knew who really kept the household functioning.

"Martin will stay here in case I need anything done," Catherine added. "With all of you gone, I may have the quiet I need to make some sense out of the lists Solomon and Edgar have been making. They've written and rubbed out things so often that the wax looks like a chicken has been scratching at the tablets."

That settled, Catherine let herself relax. Nothing would happen until the next day. Perhaps her fears were nonsense and the man was simply a friend of her father's who had come by to pay his respects to the family.

She firmly ignored the warning voice in her head.

The evening was calm. They ate in the garden, sharing the pie with the guards when they arrived. Edgar was beginning to think of dismissing them. There'd been no more trouble, and he paid the men three pennies a night just to sit by the stream and fish. Now that Solomon was there, the two of them could keep watch.

As they were finishing Astrolabe appeared with a pitcher of fresh beer flavored with early strawberries. Soon after James and Edana fell asleep on their parents' laps.

"Are you staying the night?" Catherine asked Astrolabe.

"If I might," he answered. "Maurice found a bed for me yesterday, but it's been taken tonight by some messenger from Rome."

"Is the situation there any better?" Edgar asked.

"Not enough to allow Pope Eugenius to return," Astrolabe said. "The dissenters have resurrected the Senate, they say, and mean to found a new Republic."

"Amazing," Edgar commented. "And Arnold of Brescia is leading them. Who would have believed when he studied here that he could do such things?"

"I remember the discussions he would have with my father," Astrolabe said. "Poor Arnold wanted to reform all of Christendom. Father suggested that he start with himself."

Catherine joined the laughter. The intensity of the monk from Brescia had always frightened her a little. Arnold didn't have the humor that saved Abelard from total pomposity.

"I saw the Knights of the Temple ride through town today," she mentioned. "With their *gonfanons* waving and in full armor. Does that mean the king is finally setting out?"

"I think it was just another convocation," Astrolabe told them. "But the rumors are that they'll be leaving soon. All the groups are to convene at Metz."

Catherine sighed. "I wish they'd hurry. The streets are always crowded, and bread is dear with so many needing to be fed."

"It may be worse if the weather this summer is as dry as last," Edgar said. "I fear the famine may spread east."

"Following the army." Astrolabe chewed his lip. "My mother would laugh at me, but I see too many signs that God may not be in favor of this expedition."

Solomon had not joined the conversation so far, but now he put down his cup, stretched and yawned.

"Now you're saying what we knew all along," he told Astrolabe. "Why should the Holy One care if the Christians or the Saracens have Jerusalem? I certainly don't. If anything, the Ishmaelites are easier to do business with. Now, before you all start trying to convert me again, I'm taking myself to bed. Shall I drop James and Edana into theirs as I go?"

Catherine handed her burden over to him. "You'll have to wake her enough to put her on the chamber pot first."

"I'll come with you." Edgar let James flop over his left shoulder.

They took care of the domestic chores and came back down. Before they went outside Solomon stopped Edgar.

"I've been waiting for a moment alone with you," he said. "Abraham came to me today. He says a man was at the synagogue this morning asking for news of Hubert."

"A Jew?"

Solomon shook his head. "Abraham didn't know him. But the man seemed to know more than he should. He wanted to know where Hubert had really gone."

"Saint Oswald's holy head!" Edgar exclaimed. Then he lowered his voice. "No one would tell, would they?"

Solomon grimaced. "I don't think so. Isaac the draper is no friend of Hubert's, but he hates the Edomites even more. Who do you think it was?"

"I don't know." Edgar chewed one end of his moustache, a sure sign of perturbation. "I wonder if the men Master Evrard sent to investigate the body have decided to look into Hubert's past."

"He was long gone when that man was killed," Solomon assured him.

"I hope so."

Edgar was cut off by the entrance of the rest of the family, who had decided it was time for all of them to go to bed. Soon the house was silent.

The moon was just setting when there was a cry from the garden. One of the guards had caught a fish.

Evrard de Barre was the commander of the Temple preceptory in France. But, with the participation of King Louis in this new expedition, his duties had increased tenfold. He had to find as many men as possible, some to go with the king and others to prepare the way for him. His new responsibilities only added to the obligation placed on him by Louis to go ahead of his army and negotiate with the emperor in Constantinople. Bertulf and Godfrey had not expected to be given an audience with him. Both of them were nervous in his presence. Bertulf, especially, was certain he would stumble over his words and appear a fool.

The commander sensed their discomfort and smiled on them.

"I understand you've come to join the brethren," he said. "From Picardy, are you? And the horse you brought is apparently magnificent. There's been talk of nothing else since you arrived."

"Thank you, my lord," Bertulf answered. "I bred him myself from a Spanish destrier belonging to my lord, Osto. But he is mine alone."

"You have your lord's permission to leave your land and join us?" Evrard asked.

Bertulf stood straighter. "I do, though I don't need it. I'm a free man of the village. I hold the mill and twenty *arpents* of land clear of all duties except the tithe. My wife is dead, and I've given my son, Lambert, my property. I reserved only my sword and Vrieit, the best of my horses."

The commander turned to Godfrey. "And you? Do you come to us of your own free will? Or are you simply this man's servant?"

"I am here to attend my master, who gave me a place at his table and in his home." Godfrey licked his lips. "But I come willingly in order to serve Our Lord by defending and protecting His pilgrims."

"Well said." Evrard tried once again to put these men at their ease. "Because of our great need, the time of probation has been shortened. You may stay with us one week, observing how we live, learning our rule and reciting the Office in the chapel with us. At the end of that time, you will be asked the questions and, if you agree to abide by our statutes, you may join us."

Bertulf let out a sigh of relief.

"However," Evrard continued, "our life is a hard one. We take the same vows of poverty, chastity and obedience as any monk. As you watch us, remember this. You'll be asked to fight for no booty but the glory of Christ, and then, when you are more worn than you can imagine, to wake at night and pray. You must set your minds on God alone and ignore the needs and desires of your body. You must understand totally that your reward will not come in this life."

He let his eyes meet Bertulf's. The man looked back at him with bleak despair. It unsettled the master. He wondered what sins Bertulf was here to expiate. Perhaps this was one of those who saw the only hope for salvation in martyrdom. Well, the knights who were driven by desperate fear for the fate of their souls were often the best. This man was older, too, which meant they might be able to count on him to keep a cool head in battle. And if his horse were any indication, he would be a valuable addition to the sergeants. He might even rise to be undermarshal, in charge of the stables. Evrard hoped that Bertulf wouldn't be driven to expiate his sins too recklessly. He sighed. Anyone could die for the Faith. It was much harder to find people willing to live for it.

"Very well," he said. "Galdino, would you take these men to the draper to be fitted out?" He turned back to Bertulf and Godfrey. "We supply anything you might be lacking, but if you decide not to remain with us, the articles must be returned."

The two men seemed relieved to be dismissed from his presence. Evrard rubbed his forehead. Even as the hours of sunlight lengthened each day, more tasks came to fill them. He longed for a day to spend sleeping. He knew it was Satan's way of tempting him, but it was hard not to give in.

There was a tap at the door.

Evrard straightened. "Enter."

The knight Baudwin and the priest, Durand, came in on the heels of the man assigned to announce them. Evrard greeted them. Once the pleasantries had been accomplished he asked for their report.

"The body has still not been identified," Durand said. "We're beginning to wonder if the man was a member of the Order at all."

"He had a cloak of our issue, didn't he?" Evrard asked.

Durand raised his hands in a gesture of doubt. "It appears to be," he admitted. "But a white wool cloak isn't impossible to find elsewhere. And, if he's none of ours, we can turn the matter over to the bishop. He's responsible for the investigation of deaths in the city."

"What about the people who own the house where he was found?" Evrard asked.

"Haughty and stiff-necked as Jews," Durand answered.

Brother Baudwin nodded agreement. "It's always like that when noblemen have to turn to trade. This Englishman Edgar made a most improvident marriage. I'm amazed his family allowed it."

"Do you think they killed the man and are trying for some reason to put the blame on us?" Evrard was perplexed by the whole situation.

Baudwin grimaced. "I'd like that to be the case, but everyone says they didn't arrive until the day before the body was discovered, and he'd obviously been dead some time. But I think they know more than they're telling us. These people have some strange friends."

"Very well," Evrard said. "Continue your investigation for now. Try not to be too obvious about it, though. I've learned that Abbot Suger is their protector, and his power stretches far these days."

The two men rose and left.

When they were out in the street again, Durand turned to Baudwin.

"We must work harder," he insisted. "Those people are hiding something. Perhaps they're heretics or worse. I see no point in going all the way to Jerusalem to defeat infidels only to come home to find that that sort have taken over."

Baudwin agreed. "English! Their king is sending hardly anyone to the Holy Land. Too busy trying to hold on to his crown. This Edgar could even be a spy."

Durand thought about that. "For the English?"

Baudwin shrugged. "Or the Jews. He's not what he should be, I know that."

"Then," Durand stated, "it's our duty to find out what he is."

∞

Unconscious of the suspicions of Durand and Baudwin, Edgar was most concerned with the need to feed his family. The reserve that Hubert had left them wouldn't last another winter. He was so preoccupied with the meetings before him that day that he didn't notice how tense Catherine was.

"We'll see Archer and then talk with Abraham," he told her. "Spices will be hard to come by this winter, they think. I have to see about getting more now. Then there's a meeting of the water merchants. We won't be back until Vespers."

"Good," she said. "I mean, we'll keep some pie warm for you."

She kissed him quickly, then hurried Samonie and the children out, as well. That left her alone with Martin.

"I'm going to the counting room," she told him. "If that man returns, take him to the hall and then come get me."

"Should I give him some wine?" Martin asked.

Catherine hesitated. "Yes. I won't be thought lacking in hospitality, no matter who comes to my door."

"Cakes, too?"

"Yes, cakes, too." Catherine laughed. "Such generosity may confuse him enough that he'll forget the purpose of his visit."

She then set about making sense of the notes and numbers scrawled any which way on the wax tablets Edgar and Solomon carried to record transactions before recording them on parchment.

It didn't help that the warm weather caused the wax to soften and blur. But it was a task that Catherine had been charged with since she could hold a stylus. It was her facility with numbers that had caused her father to let her progress to learning to read, first in French and then Latin. But it was her mother who was overjoyed when Catherine desired to join the convent. And it was her mother whose heart had been broken when she left.

"Concentrate!" she told herself. "Is that IX barrels of wine or LX? It must be nine. Where would they store sixty?"

Soon she was involved enough in her work that neither

the past nor the future could torment her. When the knock came at the door, she was so startled that she blotted the page.

"Mistress?" Martin's face appeared around the door. "He's back. I offered him wine and cakes, but he refused them."

"Oh, dear." Catherine's heart sank. "I'll come right down. Be sure you stand just outside the door in case I need you, Martin."

Her hands were icy. Perhaps she should have told Edgar. Yet, if she faced Jehan alone, he would probably only shout at her. If Edgar or Solomon encountered him, she knew blood would be shed. Catherine rubbed her hands on her skirts, lifted her chin and entered the hall.

Jehan hadn't even condescended to take a seat. He was in mail and helm, with his pilgrim cross sewn prominently on his overtunic. He was perspiring freely but whether from his constant anger or the heat, Catherine couldn't tell.

One look at him and she did know that manners would be wasted.

"What have you come for?" she greeted him. "I thought you'd be halfway to Jerusalem by now."

"I'm sure you wish me halfway to Hell," Jehan answered.

Catherine couldn't deny that. She waited out of his reach.

"No. Thanks to you and your sister, I couldn't find a place in Emperor Conrad's army." He spat each word at her like venom.

"We had nothing to do with your idiotic actions!" Catherine retaliated. "You nearly got Agnes killed, camping at her gate, offering to prove her innocence in combat! Everyone thought she'd murdered her husband to be free to marry you! It's not our fault if you ended by appearing to be a fool!"

"If you hadn't shown up, I would have saved her!" Jehan roared. "It was you who made me look foolish. You and that apostate father of yours!"

"Mistress?" Martin's timid voice came from the doorway.

"It's all right, Martin," Catherine told him, glad that Jehan now knew she wasn't completely alone in the house.

Catherine flinched inwardly at his last accusation and prayed no sign of it showed in her expression.

"I don't know what you mean," she said. "You were born a fool, and my father is even now on a pilgrimage to worship at the shrines of the saints for the health of his soul."

Jehan smiled. It was the ugliest thing Catherine had ever seen.

"Is that so?" His grin widened. "Well, I've decided to change the direction of my pilgrimage. The king of Spain is accomplishing more than these dawdling knights of the north. When he takes a city, he keeps it. I thought I'd offer my services to him. On the way, I plan to stop at Arles. There must be a saint there that I should pay my respects to."

"I wish you a good journey," Catherine said calmly. Inside she was panicking. How had he learned that her father had gone to Arles?

She turned to call for Martin to see him out. In a movement too quick to see, Jehan caught her wrist, gripping it so tightly that her fingers went numb.

"Don't pretend with me, you *engineuse*!" He pulled her against him and growled in her ear. "I know what you are and what Hubert is. I can destroy all of you."

Catherine tried to pull away from him without showing how frightened she was.

"That's what you've always wanted," she said. "So, if you think you know so much, why haven't you denounced us already?"

He grabbed her other wrist, twisting her arm back. Catherine fought the urge to scream for Martin to run for help. She had to know what proof Jehan had.

"The time isn't right," he said. "You'd weave your sorcery on the judges, spin words around them until they were addled with a jumble of Latin. But I will trap you, and I want you to know it. I want you to wake up every morning wondering if this is the day when I destroy you and yours."

Catherine exhaled in relief, despite the pain in her arm.

He had nothing solid to attack them with, only guesses and hate.

"I shall add you to my morning prayers, Jehan," she tried to overcome the shaking in her voice, "that you might soon win a martyr's crown, as you deserve. If you only came to threaten me one more time before you leave, then you've accomplished your mission. I suggest you leave before my husband returns."

"Your husband," he snorted. "A cripple who couldn't use a sword even when he had two hands. No, I came to do more than warn you of your impending fate. My journey will be more costly than I had expected. The months I spent in my efforts to save your sister drained my resources. You owe me, Catherine. I need enough to get me to Spain."

She should have known. He wasn't asking her to buy his silence. That would make him no more than a tradesman. He was demanding what he felt was his due. That had always been his worst trait. All his misfortunes were of Catherine's making. And for that she owed him reparation.

He let go his hold on her. She stepped back, rubbing the bruised wrist. She lifted her chin and glared at him defiantly.

"You want me to pay you to leave me alone," she spoke with scorn. "Why should I? Your hints and rumors can't hurt me or my family. We're good Christians and respected members of the community. No one will believe your lies."

"Oh, yes they will," Jehan said with confidence. "Hints and rumors are what people believe most readily. But, in return for the cost of my journey, I'll give you time to repent before I show Bishop Theobald my proofs of your apostasy."

It was so like Jehan to prefer slow torture to a quick kill. Catherine had once pitied him. Now her only feeling was loathing and a deep desire to be rid of him forever. She wanted to ask him if he had been the one who murdered the knight, but, if he didn't know about it, then that would be just one more thing he'd add to his list of their crimes.

Reluctantly, she made her decision.

"Martin!" she called. "Will you bring my jewelry box?"

She hunted through her keys for the small one that opened the box, thereby avoiding Jehan's eyes.

"I have a gold chain that belonged to my mother," she said. "I shall give it to you, in memory of the services you once performed for my grandfather and father, before you went mad, and as alms for the good of my soul."

Martin came in carrying the box. It was not very big. Most of the jewelry had been taken by Agnes as her dowry. Edgar had carved the box for her, and she treasured it far more than the few pieces inside.

She took out the chain and handed it to Jehan, draping it over his outstretched palm.

"Go to Spain," she said. "Earn a fief there and make a better life. There's nothing for you here."

Jehan dropped the chain into his purse.

"I may well find honor in Spain," he said. "But there will always be something for me here."

He took no leave, but walked to the door, his spurs scraping the wood floor and catching bits of straw and herbs as he went. Catherine didn't move as he opened the door. Martin, who had been listening in the passage, immediately led him to the gate.

The boy returned to find Catherine sitting on a folding chair by the hearth. She was trembling.

"Shall I get you some wine, Mistress?" he asked.

"Yes, please, Martin." She pulled her sleeve over the hurt wrist, wondering how she could explain the marks to Edgar. "Martin!" she called after him. "I'd like you not to mention our visitor to anyone. He's going away for a long time, perhaps forever. There's no point in worrying the others."

Martin nodded and went to get the wine. He would obey Catherine's instructions for now, but in his heart he feared that it wasn't the last they would see of Jehan.

Eight

A few moments later

Pervenit ad nos quosdam judeorum ad christianam fidem conversos, denuo, instigante diabolo, ac judaismum fuisse reversos; guod quoniam ad ignominiam nominis Christi ac christiane religionis contemptum vehementer pertinere congnovimus, tante presumpcionis injuriam regii terrore precepti inhibendam esse decrevimus. Statuimus igitur et regia auctoritate sanctimus, ut quicumque decinceps judeorum, per baptismi gratiam in Christo renati, ad sue vetustatis errorem revolare presumpserint, in toto regno nostro remanere non audeant, et si capi poterint, vel capitali dampnentur judicio, vel membrorum porcione multentur.

It has come to our attention that certain Jews, having converted to the Christian faith, deny it at the prompting of the devil and have returned to judaism. And we have become aware that this is a disgrace to the name of Christ and that they are strongly contemptuous of the Christian religion. Such great presumption being hurtful to the realm we issue a decree to prohibit it. Therefore we decree and we sanction by the authority of the king, that whosoever of the Jews, successively having been re-born in Christ through the grace of baptism, should presume to return to the ancient error, may not dare remain anywhere in our kingdom, and should they be captured, either be condemned to death by law or be punished by being torn limb from limb.

—Edict of Louis VII, 1144

Catherine took the wine Martin brought her and carried it up to the counting room. She found that the blot had dried on the page, so she scraped it off, rubbed the spot clean with a bear tooth and redid the numbers. She tried to concentrate on the rest of the records, but her mind refused to focus on them. All she could see was Jehan's sneer.

Once he had just been one of many knights without a fief, fighting in tournaments and private feuds, carrying messages for her grandfather or Abbot Suger, guarding the goods that her father transported. Then, one incident at a time, he had grown to be her private demon. The hatred he bore for her and Edgar had assumed the posture of some epic nemesis. He carried resentment with him like an aura that made his very appearance sinister. Catherine had long believed him insane. Now she wondered if he might not also be possessed.

Was his malevolence so great that he would kill a man and try to put the blame on them?

Oh, yes.

Catherine shivered and downed the last of the wine.

Edgar and Solomon were having their own problems. Abraham the vintner had told them that the casks they had sent him hadn't been properly scoured and would have to be purified again before he could use them. The buyer had found someone else to sell him saffron. Now they were in the middle of a shouting match at the Water Merchants'

Hall, the *Parleoir de Borjois*. It was a huge building with an inner courtyard supported by marble columns. It had been built so long ago that no one knew who had made it or why. But the merchants had it now, and they found the court a fine place to debate.

The provost was doing his best to maintain order.

"My good men!" he shouted over the din. "The king has only proposed that we increase the tolls for goods coming from Normandy and England. He wants the surplus to be used to buy grain to store in case this year's harvest is as bad as the last. Then the poor won't starve this winter."

"The king is starving the poor through his Jerusalem tithe!" a voice called back. "Why should we pay for his folly?"

There were mutters of agreement.

"Do you want people saying that you got rich through provisioning the army of Our Lord?" the provost pled.

"They'll say it whether we do or not," another merchant complained.

The muttering grew to shouting again.

Solomon and Edgar stood in the back under the portico, watching the debate.

"I shouldn't be here today," Solomon said. "The king will get his way, as usual, and the merchants will need someone to blame."

Solomon wasn't a member of the water merchants. One had to be Christian to swear the oath all of them took when they entered. But Jewish traders often attended the meetings, and usually no one questioned their presence.

"You can't go," Edgar told him. "I don't know these people the way you do. Until I learn whom to trust, what their weaknesses are, how they bargain, you have to make sure they don't try to cheat us."

"You can't trust any of them," Solomon said. "Their weaknesses are greed and their own distrust of each other, and they all want to buy low, sell high and be the only one allowed to trade in some commodity. Now you have all the knowledge I hold."

"What was I thinking of?" Edgar sighed. "I know less

of the art of exchange than James. These men can tell me anything, and I'll be as trusting as a lamb, and as easily slaughtered."

"No, you won't," Solomon reassured him. "They can't pass off shoddy goods on you. You know the look of real amethyst and amber. You know when something is well made and, even though you know nothing about the quality of wool, your English accent will make them believe that you must."

Edgar considered the men around him. He knew some of them already. They were the upper echelon of those who traded in Paris. Only the water merchants were permitted to take boats up the Seine beyond Mantes and unload them in the city. Most of them specialized in only one kind of goods: leather, wine, beef and pork, salt or furs. They were fiercely protective of their rights and monopolies.

Hubert had won their trust by dealing in a variety of items that complemented their goods without infringing on their trade. He brought fine wine from Clos du Val, but only in small amounts for the table of the bishop and the king. He brought unset jewels and rare spices from Spain and the East and amber from Russia. And he used his contacts with the rich abbeys and the court to secure commissions for his fellow merchants of the guild.

But Hubert was gone now. Would his old affiliations carry over to his son-in-law, a foreigner not born to the trade?

As he worried over this, one of the other merchants caught his eye and started toward him. Edgar straightened and prepared himself for anything.

"Edgar!" the man greeted him with a smile. "Good to see you back!"

Quickly Edgar nudged Solomon, who stretched out his hand to the man.

"Archer! We're glad to be back," Solomon said. "Edgar and I are impressed with the growth of the association in the year we've been gone."

"Ah, Solomon, yes, well." Archer hesitated. "The king's expedition has been good for trade, so far."

It was clear that he wanted to speak to Edgar alone. Solomon took pity on him and excused himself.

"I'll be at the Blue Boar when you finish," he whispered to Edgar.

Archer heaved a great sigh when Solomon had gone.

"Sorry," he said. "I never know what to say to them. Solomon seems almost a Christian, and his uncle Eliazar was a decent man, but you hear so many things . . ."

Edgar stared at him, waiting.

"Yes, well," Archer started again. "You know Genta, don't you? A very respectable woman, raised at court. She has several mills and ovens in the suburbs of Paris."

Edgar nodded, more to encourage the man to continue than from any memory of the woman.

"So, it seems that she's decided to donate some property to the Knights of the Temple next Thursday. There will be a ceremony, of course. She tells me the king and dowager queen will be there," Archer looked to see if Edgar were suitably impressed. "Afterward, there will be a feast. She asked me if you and your wife would care to attend."

Edgar was surprised. In the time they had lived in Paris with Hubert, no one had asked them to any festivities. It hadn't occured to him that anyone would. What had changed?

"Thank you," he told Archer. "Please tell Mistress Genta that, unless my wife knows of other plans, we would be happy to celebrate her gift to the Temple."

"And, of course, your sister is most welcome, too," Archer added.

Edgar froze. Archer licked his lips nervously. So that was how it was. Edgar wondered how many people had learned of Margaret's ancestry.

"My sister has been ill," he said. "We shall have to decide if she's well enough for an evening out."

"Genta has hired musicians and a dancing bear," Archer coaxed.

Edgar forced a smile. "I'm sure Margaret would enjoy that if her health permits. I'll send word to Genta when we've discussed the matter."

He gave a curt nod and left the *Parleoir*.

All the way to the tavern he was muttering to himself. His face was so angry that a beggar with her hand out scuttled across the road to avoid him.

Solomon wisely waited until Edgar had sat, drained a wine cup and refilled it before asking what was wrong.

"I don't suppose your indignation is over the fact that Archer is uneasy around Jews." He gave Edgar a wry smile.

"You would make anyone uneasy," Edgar answered. "Including other Jews."

Solomon shrugged his admission of the fact. Edgar took a deep breath to calm himself. The tavern was windowless. The only light came through the open door, dim in the late afternoon and often blotted by passersby. It was hard to see who else was there, but Edgar peered into the gloom and found no one he knew. He lifted the cup again.

"*Wæs hael*," he said without much enthusiam.

"*Drinc hael*!" Solomon raised his beer. "Now are you going to tell me what's making you so angry, or just drink yourself under the table?"

Edgar explained about the invitation. In this case he felt Solomon would understand his feelings better than Catherine would. He was sure of it when he saw his own anger reflected in his friend's expression.

"Margaret shouldn't have to associate with people like that," he said. "She's not in trade."

"Archer said Queen Adelaide would be there," Edgar considered. "Perhaps even Louis and Queen Eleanor. They are certainly fit for Margaret to meet."

Solomon snorted in disgust. Edgar laughed.

"Anyone would think you were the girl's grandmother!" he said. "When did you become a prude?"

"When I promised to care for Margaret." Solomon didn't share the laugh.

"Well, I agree with you, although not for the same reasons," Edgar said. "I don't want her used by those who wish to reach Count Thibault. And I don't want people speculating about how she came by her scars."

Solomon nodded grimly.

"Then we won't mention this at home?" he asked.

"Not tell Catherine?" Edgar stared. "Are you mad?"

Solomon sighed. "At least not Margaret," he conceded.

Catherine jumped when she heard the steps in the court-yard. Then Edgar's voice called out to her, and she felt such relief that she ran to him and embraced him as if he'd been gone a week.

"*Carissima!*" he exclaimed, returning her affection with joy. "Does this mean the children are out?"

The noise from the hall dispelled that hope.

"Don't you want to have your family about you?" she teased.

"Not every minute," he whispered. "Can we send them to bed early?"

Catherine smiled at him. With a twinge, Solomon turned away. It was a source of both wonder and pain to him that they could still look at each other like that after so many years together.

Catherine led them into the hall, where James and Edana were racing around the room shrieking at some imaginary monster. Margaret sat by the window, well out of the way, with her embroidery on her lap. Martin was trying to set up the tables for the evening meal without much success.

"James!" Catherine said sharply. "Edana! Come here and greet your papa like children and not wild animals."

Edana stopped at once and ran to him, her arms out to be held. James made one more circuit of the room, and then trotted over. He stopped in front of Edgar, put one hand over his heart and bowed.

"God save you, Papa," he said. "Did you have a good day?"

Catherine's lips twitched. She and Margaret had been training him for days on this.

With no trace of humor, Edgar acknowledged his son's obeisance. "God save you, as well, James. My day was satisfactory. I hope to learn from your mother that you have been dutiful and not led your little sister into misdeeds."

James looked up at Edgar with exasperation. "Papa, you know Edana won't do anything I say!"

"Just like her mother." Edgar gave Edana a squeeze. She giggled and patted his cheek, confident of her power to turn away his wrath should she ever deserve it.

"All is well here?" Edgar looked at Catherine. "Those men from the Temple haven't returned?"

"No, it's been very quiet," Catherine answered.

Jehan, she hoped, would be gone soon. Edgar need never know he had tried to beset them again.

It wasn't until after sunset, when Edgar and Catherine were sitting in the garden savoring the twilight, that they could finally talk. Margaret had gone up to bed when the children did, and Solomon was out visiting Abraham the vintner. They sat for a while without talking, listening to the sounds of the city around them: singing from students in the street; the jingle of the bells around the necks of the pigs as they were gathered and penned for the night; shouting from a nearby house as a woman berated her servants; a wine cryer calling out the latest arrival of casks from Burgundy.

The noises were so familiar to Catherine that she sensed them only as a sign that all was well and she was where she belonged. It was a moment before she paid attention to what Edgar was saying about the invitation.

"Genta!" she whined, when she caught the name. "Oh, Edgar, I know all about her feasts. Father and Mother had to go to them and then Agnes, after Mother had entered the convent. Do we have to go?"

"Yes," Edgar answered. "I think we do. If we're to survive in this business, we can't be seen to be haughty or secretive. If we don't go, people will say we thought ourselves too good to mingle with other merchants."

"But it isn't that," Catherine protested. "Everything Genta does is so pretentious. There will be eight or ten courses, not counting the sweets, and way too much wine. And we'll have to hear about each dish and how rare the ingredients are and how it's not like when she was at court but she does her humble best. She simpers, Edgar. You can't imagine how awful it is!"

Edgar chuckled at that. "Yes I can, *leoffest*. I've met women of her sort before. Why was she raised at court? Is she a bastard of the old king?"

"I don't know," Catherine said in annoyance. "No, I remember now. Her father was the old king's physician. She's getting a dancing bear, too, isn't she? They smell so. I always sneeze. And we'll have to endure the whispers, the gossip about us, even without Margaret."

"Ah, yes; about Catherine, the woman who ran away from the convent to marry a poor student?" Edgar grinned.

"Or of Edgar, the Scottish lord who abandoned his prospects in the Church for a merchant's daughter," Catherine suggested with a smile. "We've both behaved scandalously. No wonder people stare. Must we endure an evening like that?"

"Not if you don't wish to," Edgar said slowly. "Of course, the reason for this extravagance is for Genta to celebrate her gifts to the Temple of Solomon. I suppose a number of the knights will be there. Perhaps even the master."

Catherine sat up.

"Why didn't you say so?" she chided. "Of course we'll go. A week from today, you say? Samonie will have to start tomorrow on my *bliaut*. The best one needs airing and mending. We need to go to Saint Denis and retrieve the box of jewelry we left with the abbot."

Edgar smiled. "I'm glad to know your interest is caught. I feared you'd forgotten about discovering the story behind the poor man in the counting room."

"How could I?" Catherine moved closer to him. The evening was growing cool. She nuzzled against his shoulder until he put his arm around her. "I feel him every time I enter the room. He wants us to help him."

Edgar peered through the shadows to make out her face. "Are you serious?" he asked. In his family, if someone said he saw a ghost, he was taken at his word.

Catherine laughed. "Not the way you mean. I'm only

reminded of the fact that he was left for us. We have a duty to the dead, for they can no longer speak for themselves. It's not just the danger to us if the truth is never found. His family must not even know that he's dead. No one has said a Mass for him, except the ones we ordered. I keep thinking about how his soul must be so lonely, with no one to pray for his release from Purgatory."

Edgar laid his cheek against her head. "My dear, if I were gone on a long journey, perhaps never to return, would you pray for me, not knowing whether I walked the earth or lay beneath it?"

Catherine tried to swallow the terror that rose in her at the very thought. "Every moment," she breathed. "With every bit of my being. My whole life would be nothing but a prayer for your safety and your return."

She choked on the last word, and Edgar bit his lip to keep tears from his own voice.

"So what makes you think that this poor man doesn't have someone who loves him just as much, praying for him as fervently as you would for me?" he said.

Catherine turned her face up to his.

"I can only hope that there is no such person," she answered. "I would never wish such loss upon anyone. This deep a love is worth any price, but still I pity anyone who must pay it."

The only answer to that was to hold her close.

They sat together until the darkness was complete, the trees shielding them from the stars until they were roused by the sound of Solomon swearing as he tripped over a toy horse James had left in the hall. Edgar kissed Catherine's nose to bestir her and took her up to bed.

In the chill dawn a man and woman approached the north gate of Paris. They were riding a knobbly mule that was one misstep from the tannery. As the bells began ringing for Prime, the gate creaked open. A line of carts loaded with firewood, spring vegetables and cheese moved slowly into the city. They had arrived the night before to be the first at the markets that day. The mule wove between them, the riders too tired to guide it well.

"Watch it!" one of the carters shouted. "Keep that animal away from my lettuce or I'll have its skin!"

The man roused himself to tug on the reins. The woman looked up at the man on the cart, startled. He stared down into a pair of brown eyes and a delicate, frightened face. The carter pulled off his cap.

"Excuse me, lady," he began. Then his eyes narrowed. "Here, what are you up to?"

The woman lowered her veil and the man urged the sluggish mule forward. The carter looked after them a moment. Runaway, he thought. Maybe from a convent. Could be a reward in that. Then he shook his head. More likely just trouble. If the lords couldn't keep their daughters under control, it was no concern of his.

"Are you sure this friend of our fathers will take us in?" Lambert said as they entered the city.

"He must," Clemence answered. "I heard Father telling Mother that Hubert LeVendeur was the most honest merchant in Paris."

Lambert was still worried. The burden of her safety weighed on him. They had almost used up the coins they had brought. He had had no idea how many tolls there were between Picardy and Paris.

"Honest is one thing," he muttered. "But generous is quite another. We look like beggars enough now. I think we should find a bathhouse first."

"Oh, yes!" Clemence agreed. "I haven't washed my hair in two weeks, and the rest of me aches in every part."

"Also," Lambert added, "I can't think of a better place to discover how to get to the home of Master LeVendeur."

At home, Catherine was caught up in preparing for the evening out. Edgar had been sent to Saint Denis for the jewelry box and to ask Simon the silversmith to make her a new pair of earrings set with some lapis stones that Solomon had bought the year before.

They had both agreed that Margaret should not go with

them. Catherine had anticipated rebellion on Margaret's part, but the girl accepted the decision with obvious relief.

"I don't know what to say to people," she explained. "In Germany I could pretend I didn't understand. Here I might have to find polite answers to their prying."

"Very wise of you." Catherine smiled. "I wish I could stay home, as well. But, since I must go, will you help me get ready? Edgar wants me to dazzle."

Margaret laughed. "We could sew bits of the silver wire Edgar uses into your *bliaut* so that they reflect the light."

"That would be impressive," Catherine agreed. "I'll let Edgar decide just how radiant he thinks I should be. Why don't you and I go to the street of the drapers today and find material to edge my old silk *chainse*? And ribbons, I think, for you and Edana."

They left shortly after, with a list of articles that Samonie needed, as well.

Having the care of the house and the children kept Samonie busy and so, when someone sounded the bell at the front gate she called out to Martin to tell whoever it was that no one was home.

Martin hurried to answer, reciting in his head the things he'd been told to ask of visitors. He knew he'd forget something.

He slid the board in the gate open so that he could see who was waiting.

In front of the gate was a young man in a plain wool tunic and leather *brais*. Behind him was a woman, heavily veiled, seated on a mule.

"Is this the home of Hubert, merchant of Paris?" the man asked.

Martin thought. "Well, it was," he said. "But Master Hubert's gone off on a trip for the good of his soul. Only God knows if he'll ever return."

The man's shoulders sagged.

"Master Hubert had a partner," he said. "A Jew. Where can we find him?"

"Oh, Master Eliazar lives in Troyes now," Martin told them.

The woman gave a moan. The man bit his lip in frustration.

"Is there anyone here we can talk with?" he asked.

Remembering his mother's command, Martin shook his head.

"No one's here," he told them. "Come back later."

He shut the grille with a clap.

Clemence took Lambert's arm. "What can we do now?" she asked, trying to remain calm.

Lambert thought for a moment, then came to a decision.

"I shall take you to the nuns at Montmartre," he said. "They'll look after you, give you food and a bed while I try to find someone who can help us."

"But, Lambert," Clemence protested, "we don't even know if our fathers came to Paris at all. They may well have both joined Count Thierry in Germany. Your father could have decided to wait to join the Temple until he reaches Jerusalem."

Lambert stopped and took her hands.

"What else can we do, beloved?" he said quietly. "Go home? There's no hope there. Surely someone in this city will know where our fathers have gone. And, if not, then we must take our case to someone else who can help us."

"Well," Clemence considered, "the pope may still be nearby."

"Possibly, if it comes to that," Lambert said. "But I was thinking more of Abbot Bernard. They say he can work miracles, and at this moment that's what we need."

A milk pedlar shouted at them for blocking the road. Lambert led the mule under the eaves of a small church.

That gave Clemence time to think.

"It would be best if my father could be found," she answered. "He'd set everything right in a moment. But, failing that, the support of the Church might be useful. Or the king."

Lambert put his arms about her waist and laid his head against her breast.

"It might turn out," he said slowly, "that you'll be asked to marry someone else."

"No." She ran her fingers through his light brown hair. "Father wants two things equally, for you to inherit his castellany and for Lord Jordan never to have control of it. Even if we can't find him, everyone in the village will confirm this."

"If only your mother hadn't died so suddenly," Lambert said. "I never would have brought you with me."

"You couldn't have stopped me." Clemence smiled sadly. "And, as long as I'm with you, you can be sure Lord Jordan hasn't tried to force me to marry anyone else."

"He can't now." Lambert touched the ring on her hand.

"He would try to have our marriage annulled," Clemence said practically. "No, we made the right choice. Now all that remains is to find our fathers and tell them what has been happening at home."

Gently, she pushed Lambert away, conscious that passersby were gaping at them.

"I would rather stay with you in Paris," Clemence continued. "But until you find us shelter together, I'll seek refuge with the nuns. The abbess may well be able to advise us. I have heard of her wisdom and kindness."

Mournfully, they made their weary way up the hill to the convent of Montmartre, site of martyrdom of Saint Denis. Lambert was overwhelmed with the enormity of their task and his responsibility to protect Clemence. He had yet to learn the depth of her determination or of her fear.

Nine

Paris, the preceptory of the Temple. Saturday 16 kalends June, (May 17), 1147; 15 Sivan, 4907. Feast of Saint Montan of Lotharingia, who regained his sight by bathing his eyes in the breast milk of the mother of Saint Remi.

Notum itaque fatio ego, nomine Genta . . . quod pro remedio anime mee, predecessorumque meorum, et pro anima nobilissimi Francorum regis, venerandeque memorie Ludovici, qui me benignitate regia enutrivit, molendinum quendam Paris in sub magno ponte, quem ab Archerio, filio Savarici, comparaveram, militibus Templi Ierosolimitani, ipso Archerio et uxore sua concedentibus, in manu Ebrardi de Barris, post decessum meum . . . donavi.

Let it be known that I, Genta, make this gift for the good of my soul and for the soul of the most noble King of France of revered memory, Louis, who very kindly raised me at court, I donate a certain mill in Paris under the Grand Pont, the one that I have prepared with Archer, son of Savaric, to the knights of the temple of Jerusalem, the same Archer and his wife having agreed to give it into the hand of Evrard de Barre, after my death.

$\mathcal{M}$aster Evrard was no more excited about attending a feast than Catherine was. The donations Genta was making were so tied with restrictions that the knights would get little more than a part of the tithe for years. The mill would be theirs at her death, but she was still a young woman, and he was bitterly sure she would long out- live him.

Nevertheless, he had sent his acceptance. Genta was known to be a favorite of the dowager queen, Adelaide. And, now that Adelaide had achieved the enviable position of widow to the king, as well as subsequent happiness with a second husband of her own choosing, she was known for her generosity. She had the profits from whole villages at her disposal.

Evrard turned his mind to more important matters. This desire of Queen Eleanor's to accompany her husband on his pilgrimage was becoming a serious problem. If she had been content to travel as a simple pilgrim, Evrard would have praised her piety. But the woman was outfitting herself as an "Amazon," presumably to do battle with the infidel. And now the other ladies of the court were following her example. There had been no word as to whether they would have their right breasts amputated to facilitate the use of a bow. More likely, Evrard feared, they would decide to take their hunting hawks and loose them to bring down Saracens.

The Temple master felt bile rise to his throat again. His

stomach had been sour for days. There was too much to
do. He could no longer concentrate on his prayers. As he
recited his *Pater Noster*, his thoughts dwelt not on the hope
of Heaven but the number of men he could arm. His waking
hours were spent on minutiae, reports of problems and nonsense like this dinner.

So when word came that Brother Baudwin and Master
Durand wished to confer with him, Evrard was not of a
disposition to commiserate with their problems.

"Commander, we have had no luck in finding out who
this man was," Brother Baudwin began. "I'm of the opinion
that he had nothing to do with us. Anyone can wear a white
cloak."

"And the brooch?" Evrard asked. "How many wear our
symbol? If he wasn't a Knight of the Temple, then he was
posing as one. That should concern us as well."

Master Durand was tapping his foot impatiently. Evrard
looked pointedly at his boot.

"You disagree with me, Father Durand?" he asked.

The boot stopped in mid-tap.

"I propose another possibility, Commander," Durand
said smoothly. "What if these people found a dead man in
their home, perhaps someone they knew? What if they also
knew who had killed him? In the state the body was in, it
would have been difficult for them to dispose of it without
someone seeing."

"Yes, that's what I think!" Brother Baudwin interrupted.
"They dressed the corpse as a knight and laid the problem
on us!"

Master Durand gave him a glance that would have shriv-
eled a more sensitive man. Baudwin smiled proudly and
went on.

"The man, Edgar, does metalwork, even though he has
only one hand. Why, I don't know. They're a strange family as we've told you. Anyway, he could have made up a
brooch easily enough."

"As the body continued to rot over his head?" Evrard
raised his eyebrows.

"He might have had the brooch already," Master Durand

suggested. "As a gift for another knight or even to sell."

Evrard looked at the men. His glance strayed to the window. He realized with surprise that spring had come. The trees were misty with new leaves. He could hear the bleating of lambs from the field nearby. It only reminded him of how much there was to do before the king set out.

And yet he couldn't let this death be ignored. If the man was one of their own, then he must be honored and his family notified. If he wasn't, then they must find out why the Order had been used so shamefully.

He had to know before he left. The Knights of the Temple of Solomon in Jerusalem were heroes now when the Saracen threat was imminent and so many needed their protection. But there were too many in Christendom who distrusted the idea of a knight in the service of God. The order could afford no scandal.

"Your speculations are all very well," he told the men. "But I need proof before accusing these people. Bring me someone who saw the body being carried into the house. Discover where it came from. Find a reason for this Edgar to have involved us at all. Is he working for those who would see the Order disbanded? We have only a few weeks before the army sets out. The matter must be settled by then. Do you understand?"

They did, although neither man looked happy about it.

"We've questioned everyone on the street," Master Durand protested. "And many of the merchants who knew Hubert LeVendeur. No one knows anything."

"Or perhaps no one will tell you anything," Evrard said. "Most people prefer pleading ignorance to becoming involved in a murder. You need to be more subtle in your investigation. Get some of the sergeants who aren't known in town to go to the taverns in the guise of pilgrims. Let them listen to the gossip, dropping a word from time to time to guide it."

"That takes the skill of a spy," Master Durand said. "Where will we find such men among the soldiers?"

Evrard sighed. "There are several hundred sergeants in

Paris at the moment. Among them you must be able to find two or three with the requisite skills."

He pressed his hand to his stomach. The fire within was raging.

"I'm sure you want to begin at once," he told the men. "You may leave."

Once outside, Brother Baudwin turned to Master Durand.

"To find the right men will take all the time the commander has given us!" he exclaimed. "It's an impossible task!"

Master Durand pursed his lips. His eyes narrowed. Brother Baudwin knew the signs. The cleric was planning something. Respectful of the workings of a learned mind, Baudwin said no more.

By the time they had reached the main dormitory for the sergeants, Durand had created a plan. Baudwin could tell by the satisfied sniff and thin smile.

"So, what do we do?" Baudwin asked.

"We find the most recent arrivals from the most remote place," Master Durand answered. "We give them their instructions and send them out to loiter in the taverns, as half the pilgrims in Paris do anyway. Then, if they fail, we put the blame on them."

Baudwin felt as if he just been given full pardon for all his sins. He grinned in relief.

"I'll ask the draper who he oufitted last," he told Durand. "How many do we need?"

"Two should be enough," Durand told him. "Make sure they come from outside France. I don't want them recognized."

"That shouldn't be a problem," Baudwin said. "Shall I have them sent to you for instructions?"

Master Durand nodded. "Tomorrow, after Mass. They can start in the afternoon as soon as the taverns open."

"Where's Solomon?" Margaret asked.

"He's spending Saturday with Abraham," Catherine told her. "He said he felt the need to observe the Sabbath. I hope he isn't getting sick. He won't be home until after sundown."

Margaret went back to the paper she was copying onto a tablet. Every few moments, she'd mutter in annoyance, rub out a letter and start again. Catherine finally left the mending and came to see what was so difficult for her.

"It's my old *alef-bet*!" she said. "Where did you find it?"

"In the chest with your shifts," Margaret said. "You were going to cut one down for me."

"Yes, although you've grown so, I think a belt will be enough to keep it from dragging on the floor," Catherine said. "But why are you copying the letters?"

"I wanted to learn to read Hebrew," Margaret told her. There was a hint of defiance in her voice. "I thought it might be useful."

"All knowledge is useful," Catherine quoted. "I learned Hebrew letters because my father used them as numbers for his accounts. I meant to continue the study when I was at the Paraclete, to be able to read the Pentateuch in the original, but I was never very good at it. Still, you don't need to bother with such things; we don't expect you to be our clerk."

"Perhaps I'll enter a convent one day," Margaret said. "Then I can be of use in making translations."

Catherine had been thinking of other matters, but now she focused all her attention on Margaret.

"I didn't realize that you had felt called to the religious life," she said.

"I don't at the moment," Margaret answered. "But I might, and it's good to be prepared."

Catherine sat down next to her.

"Margaret, dear," she said, "this interest doesn't have anything to do with Solomon, does it?"

"Of course not," Margaret said, but her cheeks flushed. "Except in that in learning the *Hebraica veritas* I might be better able to make him see the error of his beliefs so that he comes to the true Faith."

"Good luck to you," Catherine said. "I've been trying for years. But he won't be won by logic; he doesn't believe logically. Jewish is what he is, more than his religion. If he converted, he wouldn't be Solomon anymore."

She thought that idea would bother Margaret, but the girl only nodded.

"I know that." She went back to the tablet.

A moment later another thought struck her.

"Catherine, is it a sin to care about Solomon?"

"I don't see how it could be," Catherine answered carefully. "I talked both with Master Abelard and Mother Heloise about this. Solomon is a good man, even if he persists in denying the truth of the Incarnation. Master Abelard felt it would be more of a sin to abandon him. Perhaps one day our love and our prayers will cause his eyes to open to the truth."

The tension in Margaret's face relaxed. She smiled.

"He told me that preaching would never change his heart," she said. "But perhaps praying will. And since he won't hear me, he won't be vexed by it, either."

Satisfied, she folded the paper and went to put it with the writing material, in the counting room.

Catherine returned to her work, unsettled by the conversation. Solomon had talked with Margaret about his feelings for her and reported that she had told him that her regard for him was what was proper for a ward to her guardian. He had convinced himself there was nothing more than that. But he was also spending more time away from the house, to Catherine's sorrow, even though she felt it was best.

As Margaret metamorphosed into a woman, Catherine felt herself more bewildered by her sister-in-law. Of course Margaret had suffered more than Catherine ever had. But there was something so self-contained about her. When the impropriety of her behavior toward Solomon had been explained, she had accepted it without a murmur and adapted accordingly.

Catherine wished she believed that the inward change had been as dutiful.

∞

Shortly after sundown Solomon thanked his hosts and rose to leave.

"Rebecca, your home always fills me with peace," he said.

"I'm glad, Solomon," his hostess answered. "But I would be happier if you told me it filled you with piety."

For once, Solomon didn't laugh. "I wish that came to me as easily as to you and Abraham." He sighed.

Rebecca held out her hand to him.

"If you lived according to *halakah*, my dear friend, then piety would follow. How can you hear the Holy One, blessed be He, when you're surrounded by the voices of idolaters?"

The sadness in Solomon's eyes distressed her. Rebecca believed that there was great passion in him. But for what, she wasn't sure.

"In Wolkenburg, I thought it would be easy for me to follow the law, to pray each morning with my heart," Solomon told her. "I was happy there. To wake each day and know that I need not pretend to be something I despise. To know that there was nothing impure on the table. It should have been heaven."

"It sounds so to me," Abraham added.

"But I felt useless," Solomon said. "I'm no scholar or craftsman. Discussion of tractates puts me to sleep."

"Only a few are gifted in study." Abraham smiled. "You have other skills."

"Yes, I know how to survive among the Edomites," Solomon answered. "In a place where there are none, I am unecessary."

"You judge yourself too meagerly." Rebecca handed him his cloak and kissed his cheek. "Someday you'll learn that."

Abraham stood. "I'll walk with you," he said. "I need to move after that meal or it will never shift."

They didn't speak until they were almost to the bridge. The sound of the mill wheels steadily turning made it unlikely that any would overhear them.

"There was a man asking after your uncle yesterday," Abraham said. "He acted as if he knew that Hubert wasn't on a pilgrimage. Seemed to be sure that some of us would know where he really was. His guesses were too close to the truth."

Solomon leaned closer. "What did this man look like?"

"I don't have to describe him," Abraham said. "It was that knight who used to carry messages for Hubert and Eliazar to Abbot Suger. You must know him, too."

It was as if a horse had kicked Solomon in the center of his stomach.

"Jehan," he forced out. "I thought he was long gone."

"He wore the cross on his tunic," Abraham said. "If it was genuine, then he should leave when the king does. Don't worry; no one was eager to chat with him."

Solomon chewed at the corner of his lip. "What did he want, just to find Hubert?"

Abraham shook his head. "I don't think so. He seemed more to be gloating over some knowledge. Then he hasn't tried to speak to Hubert's daughter?"

"No," Solomon said. "She would have told me. At least, I think she would."

It occurred to him that Catherine knew well that both he and Edgar would be glad of an excuse to thrash Jehan. It would be like her to try to avoid this.

"He's mad, you know," he told Abraham. "He was always a cold-blooded bastard, who inflicted pain with joy, but now he seems to live for nothing else. His hatred of Hubert's family has destroyed any sense of honor he might once have had."

"Then may the Merciful One keep him from your path," Abraham said. "At least now you know to be watchful."

Solomon grasped his friend's hand. "Don't worry. I'm never anything else. Good night, Abraham."

"*Leila tov*, Solomon."

The spring twilight was long and it hadn't gone completely dark as Solomon crossed the bridge and made his way back to the Grève. Despite his assurances to Abraham, he could feel a wariness at the back of his neck and between his shoulder blades, as if tensing for the prick of a knife.

There were still people about, students on their way to

the brothels, men coming home from the taverns or their stalls at the Halles. In the gathering gloom, each one seemed about to leap at him.

As he reached the gate with the dragon knocker, Solomon laughed at himself for his nervousness. There was enough to worry about without imagining attacks from lunatics on the streets of Paris.

As he knocked for Martin to let him in, a hand fell on his shoulder.

Solomon whipped around at once, his knife half-unsheathed.

The canon, Maurice, jumped back, terrified.

Swiftly, Solomon slid the knife back into the sheath.

"Forgive me, Maurice," he gasped. "I didn't know it was you."

"I shouldn't have come up on you so quietly," the canon told him. "I was hoping to catch Edgar before he went to bed. I'm not normally out this late, myself. You had every right to think me a brigand."

At this moment, the grate slid open and Martin's brown eyes shown in the light of the lamp he carried.

"Solomon?" he asked.

"Yes, Martin, with Maurice. Is Edgar still downstairs?"

"He and Catherine and Margaret are all in the garden," Martin told them as he opened the gate. "The night is so mild, no one wants to go in. Should I fetch another pitcher of wine?"

"Oh, no," Maurice said.

"Certainly," Solomon told him. "And cups for both of us."

As they came out into the garden, Margaret immediately moved from her bench to sit next to Catherine. Inwardly, Solomon winced. Once she would have demanded that he sit with her. He wished they'd never spoken to her. The feelings she had for him would have faded with maturity, he had no doubt.

"How wonderful to see you, Maurice!" Edgar exclaimed. "What brings you out so close to Compline?"

"A favor, I'm afraid," Maurice answered, taking the wine cup with a nod of thanks.

"Anything," Edgar said.

Maurice licked his lips. "I don't like to bother you on something so trivial. But the dean was in such a state about it that I promised I'd try."

He pulled a gold chain from the purse at his belt. One of the links was twisted and broken.

"He didn't want to take it to the goldsmith for the Cathedral," Maurice explained. "The damage was done in anger, and the chain belongs to the precentor. I'm afraid the dean was so upset about the singing of the liturgy that he snatched the chain from the precenter's neck and stamped on it."

"Goodness!" Catherine said. "What did the bishop say to that?"

Maurice twisted the chain in his hands as he spoke. "Well, Bishop Theobald is already so angry with both men that he said any more disturbances would result in neither one being allowed to arrange the music, no matter who caused it. That's why I'm here. I like both of them and wish to help make peace between them."

Edgar took the chain and went over to the lamp to examine it.

"This should only take a few minutes," he said. "Solomon, would you hold the link over the coals for me to soften it while I get my tools?"

"I can help," Maurice said, standing.

Catherine gestured for him to sit again. "Solomon knows what to do. It will be quicker if you let them. Now, other than this vicious feud in the choir, what other news do you have?"

"The roof that Stephen Garlande put on Nôtre Dame is leaking," Maurice commented. "My spot in the choir is just under one of the drips. I don't suppose that's of terrible concern to you, though, with the Knights of the Temple questioning people about you."

"What!" Catherine sat up straight, spilling the bowl of

early strawberries in her lap. "They were asking about us at Nôtre Dame?"

"I presumed it was about that body left here," Maurice said as he helped her pick up the berries. "They didn't speak to me, but I heard about it from one of the canons. Apparently Master Peter the Lombard remembered your association with Abelard and that your husband had been a student of Bishop Gilbert."

"What has that to do with anything?" Catherine brushed at her skirts, rubbing the juice into the material. "And Edgar didn't study with Gilbert de la Porée. I was the one who attended his lectures, when I could."

Maurice rubbed his stained hands on his robe. "I don't think Master Peter cares anything for a dead knight. Right now everything he hears sooner or later refers to the promulgation of what he sees is Bishop Gilbert's heresy."

"And this is what he told Master Durand and Brother Baudwin?" Catherine was trying to decide if this would hurt them or merely confuse the investigators.

"Perhaps not," Maurice admitted. "I only learned of it through the usual gossip, because my friend was aware that I knew you. Master Peter may only have said he knew nothing about Edgar except that he had once been a student. I didn't mean to upset you."

"No, don't be sorry," Catherine said. "I would much rather learn what's being said of us. How else can we be prepared to answer any questions the men from the Temple may have?"

"So you don't know any more about your unwanted visitor?" Maurice asked.

"Nothing," Catherine said. "It's as if he didn't exist until he appeared in our counting room. I don't understand it."

They fell into silence then. Maurice fidgeted on his bench. Catherine realized he was worried about getting back to the Cathedral by Compline.

"Margaret," she said, "could you go see how much longer your brother will be? Margaret?"

"I think she's fallen asleep," Maurice said. "I'll go see."

As he rose, Edgar and Solomon returned. The chain was

hanging over Edgar's left arm. He let it fall into Maurice's hands.

"It was a simple matter to twist the metal back to the original shape," Edgar told him. "There are scratches that would take longer to smooth out. I could do it if you left it here until Monday."

"No, this is excellent." Maurice held up the chain and examined it in the light. "Both the dean and the preceptor owe you their profound thanks, and I shall see that they pay you."

"No need," Edgar said. "Tell them that I did it in the hope that they will come to a reconciliation and together offer a Mass for me and my family."

Maurice grinned. "You're asking for a miracle, Edgar. But I'll tell them. I fear that at the moment any Mass they assisted at would be most discordant. Actually, I can attest to it."

He thanked them again and left. Catherine yawned.

"Edgar, help me get Margaret awake enough to go up to bed," she said.

"Don't wake her," Solomon said. "She's deep asleep. I'll take her up."

Before they could protest, he scooped Margaret off the bench where she lay curled. She did no more than murmur as he carried her up the stairs.

Just as he reached the door to the room she shared with the children, Margaret stirred, nuzzling against his shoulder, her arm around his neck. She was less than half-awake but the trust implied by the gesture made him stop a moment, swallowing hard before he went in and laid her gently on the bed.

He met Catherine coming up the stair.

"Thank you," she said. "I'll take off her shoes and belt. She can sleep in her *bliaut* tonight. Good night, Solomon." She kissed his cheek and continued up.

Edgar was putting his tools away when Solomon entered the hall.

"There's still wine in the pitcher," he commented.

"Enough for two, I'd say. Or one who wants to sit and think."

"Shall I leave half for you?" Solomon asked.

"No, I'm exhausted," Edgar said. "Don't forget to bar the door when you come in."

He went up stairs.

Catherine was waiting for him. "This state of affairs isn't good for either of them," she said without preamble.

Edgar got in beside her and turned so that she could rest her cheek against his back with her arm around him. He sighed in contentment. Then he considered her statement.

"Yes," he said at last. "It may be that a year at the Paraclete would be just what Margaret needs. But it will be hard to let her go."

Catherine didn't answer, just kissed the nape of his neck and snuggled closer.

Solomon finished the wine and sat out in the garden until the first streaks of dawn shot into the sky.

In a stable on the outskirts of town, Lambert huddled under his blanket, grateful that the nuns of Montmartre had accepted Clemence as a guest for the night. There was no other place in all of Paris suitable for her. And she had been spared hours of growing despair. He had been asking everywhere, all day. Even at the Temple preceptory no one had seen or even heard of Lord Osto. Everyone he asked about Hubert knew only that he had gone. It was beginning to appear that they had made the journey for nothing. Both their fathers might be as far as Germany by now.

What was he to do? At home he understood how things worked, from repairing the mill to breeding horses to negotiating with the men who came to collect the various tithes and duties. Here he felt like a green stripling, easily flattened.

Perhaps he and Clemence should have stayed in their own village. The whole town had attended their marriage, and everyone knew it was what their families had most desired. But even if the daughter of a lord were so foolish as to marry the son of a miller, it was rare that she would be allowed to come into her inheritance. Without Lord Osto's support or the blessing of some great noble, they would be lucky only to be turned out of the castle.

He was roused from his nightmares at dawn by the ostler who had taken pity on him and not charged for a place in the straw. But the charity ended there, and Lambert was sent out into the streets with the suggestion that he go to the canons of Nôtre Dame for alms.

"Only get there early," the man told him. "The lines are longer every day. The winter wheat rotted in the fields, and between our own poor and the pilgrims swarming, there's not enough for all."

The glare the man gave him suggested to Lambert that strangers such as he would do well to leave and not burden the citizens of Paris further.

He didn't go to the Cathedral. The shame of begging for his food was too great. The bells of Paris were calling the faithful to Sunday Mass. Most people were going about their business, though, preparing for the opening of the shops in the afternoon or recovering from a night in the tavern.

It was too early to go fetch Clemence, Lambert realized. She owed the nuns attendance at services in return for their kindness. He wandered aimlessly through the streets, trying to ignore the smell of fresh pastry. The few coins he had left were to care for his wife.

He was standing in the *rue des Juifs*, looking wistfully at a boy feeding a sausage to his dog, when a man stopped and asked his name.

"Lambert, of Picardy," he said.

"Are you the one who's been asking about Hubert LeVendeur?" the man asked.

Lambert wasn't sure about answering. The man was half a head taller than he, with a face weathered by time, adversity and something else that made Lambert want to cross himself. His hair and beard were streaked with white. Still, his clothes were good, and he wore the cross of the pilgrim.

"Yes," he admitted at last.

"What's he done to you?" the man's eyes were avid for information.

Lambert stepped back. "Nothing," he said. "I only sought information from him about my father who, like you, has set out to free Edessa from the infidel."

"Why would Hubert know about him?"

"They had done business together," Lambert explained. "My father was raising horses with Lord Osto. They bought a Spanish destrier from Hubert and his partner and sold them some of the foals each year thereafter. My father told me they were going to Paris to make some arrangements with Hubert about future trade before leaving for the Holy land."

"I see." The man stared at him for a moment. "But Hubert supposedly left Paris months ago."

Lambert ignored the qualification. "So everyone tells me," he said sadly. "I've had to assume that my father is also long gone."

"I wouldn't be so certain." The stranger laid a hand on Lambert's shoulder. "Have you also heard that when Hubert's daughter arrived home from a journey she found that the house had been shut but that *someone* had left the body of a murdered knight of the Temple inside."

"How sad," Lambert said. "But Lord Osto had no intention of becoming a member of the Knights of the Temple, sir. My father planned to offer them his services, but he wasn't a nobleman and would only have become a sergeant or even lower servant. He isn't a warrior."

"Anyone can wear mail," the man said. "And his skill won't be tested if he's already dead. You say your father came to Paris to find Hubert and no one has seen him since. Don't you think you should at least ask about the man found in his house?"

Lambert was young, frightened, overwhelmed by his responsibility to Clemence and the people of their village. He didn't believe that this poor dead man could be his father, but even the hint of it was enough to make his heart constrict.

"Yes, thank you," he said. "Do you know where they took the body?"

"Oh yes." The man smiled. "I'll take you there, myself. But first we should break our fast, don't you think, Lambert? I fancy a meat pie. Will you share it with me?"

The prospect of food decided him. The man bought a hot pie and broke it in two, giving Lambert half.

"Now all we need is beer." He laughed. "Don't worry, young Lambert. We'll find out what Hubert LeVendeur did to your father, and I'll see that he's avenged. Count yourself lucky that you've come under the protection of Jehan of Blois."

Ten

Sunday afternoon, 15 kalends June (May 18), 1147;
16 Sivan, 4907. Feast of Saint Theodote, tavern keeper
and martyr.

Marie as piés Nostre Seignor plora
Lava les bien, terst et oinst et baisa,
Et tout ses pechiés Jhesus le pardona . . .
Ma douce Dame Marie, le barnesse,
Veés con m'ame est orde et pecerresse . . .
Se ne m'aïes, Dame, qui m'aidera?

Mary you have washed the feet
of Our Lord with your tears,
wiped, anointed and kissed them.
And Jesus pardoned all your sins . . .
My sweet Lady Mary, the woman of ill-repute
You see how my soul is stained and sinful . . .
If you don't help me, Lady, who will?

—Anonymous (but definitely a woman)
Prayer to Mary Magdalene

*B*ertulf and Godfrey were alarmed when the summons came for them to present themselves before Master Durand. They hurried across the courtyard to the chapter at once.

"Do you think we've been discovered?" Godfrey asked.

"I don't see how," Bertulf answered. "Perhaps we've already managed to break one of the rules. Do I appear too proud?"

"You've made no mistakes that I could see," Godfrey said. "And no man would call you proud."

They waited nervously until told to enter by Brother Baudwin.

"It's nothing to worry about," he whispered, seeing their expressions as they passed him. "I wouldn't mind an assignment like this, myself."

Seated at a table facing the door, Master Durand considered the men standing stiffly before him.

"I understand you're both new to the Order?" he asked. "Therefore, you haven't been initiated into the brotherhood, nor have you yet taken any permanent vows."

"That is correct, sir," Bertulf answered. "But we both intend to become full members of the Temple as soon as it is permitted."

Durand waved his hand dismissively.

"I have no doubt that you will," he said. "Or I wouldn't set you this task."

He could feel the curiosity. But Durand had another question.

"You're strangers to Paris?" he asked. "You have no friends or family in the city?"

A fraction of a hesitation.

"No," Bertulf said. "We have no connection to Paris at all."

Master Durand nodded.

"Good. It would be embarrassing for us if you were recognized," he explained. "We have a problem that requires secrecy and tact."

He explained what he wanted them to do. As he did, Godfrey's eyes widened. He looked sideways at Bertulf, who gave him a nudge with his toe, warning him to say nothing.

"Do you understand?" Master Durand finished.

"Yes, sir," Bertulf said. "We've only to keep our ears open and occasionally ask a question. Godfrey and I can do that."

"Master," Godfrey spoke for the first time, "we will need something in hand to buy beer with."

Bertulf seemed annoyed by his request.

"Quite right," Brother Baudwin said. "We hold everything in common so you assuredly kept nothing back for yourselves when you arrived. You shall have a few sous from the common purse. Don't drink it all in the first tavern, mind you. We need you to have your heads clear."

The two men bowed and left. When they had gone Durand lifted his eyebrows at Baudwin.

"Those two were the best you could find?"

Outside, Godfrey was breathing as if he'd just been chased by wolves across an open field.

"Can you imagine!" he exclaimed. "What are we going to do?"

Bertulf put a hand on his shoulder. "What we've been ordered to do," he said. "We can't be blamed if there's no information to be found."

"I don't like it, Master," Godfrey said. "Perhaps it would be better if we told the truth."

"We couldn't tell all of it in any case," Bertulf reminded

him. "It would ruin everything. Now we also have a real chance of finding the murderer. And I want to be the one to do it, before Master Durand, in any case."

"You don't like that cleric, do you?"

"I don't like the way he looks at me." Bertulf clenched his fists. "As if I were a horse he didn't believe could be trained."

"Ah, well, that's the way these men are." Godfrey was philosophical. "They think nothing has a use if it can't read Latin. He likely feels the same way about that Brother Baudwin."

Catherine spent the afternoon composing a letter to Abbess Heloise for Astrolabe to take to the Paraclete the next time he went there to see her. She told herself that there was no point in asking Margaret to go to the convent if all the places for students were taken. However, down deep she knew that she wanted to postpone bringing the subject up for as long as possible.

She rolled up the parchment, tied it with a ribbon and sealed the ends of the ribbon with wax. Then she went down to see what trouble her family had managed to get into.

The hall was empty and eerily quiet. No children, no servants, no clanging of dishes from the kitchen. It was unnatural.

Catherine passed through to the kichen and then to the back, where the summer oven was hot from bread baking. Still she saw no one.

"Samonie!" she called. "Margaret!"

"Down here, Mistress!" Samonie's voice wafted up from the little orchard by the stream at the bottom of the garden.

Catherine went down to join them.

Samonie, with Edana attached to her belt by a long cord, was picking mint to use in a sauce for dinner. Margaret was helping James to climb the low branches of the apple tree.

"Careful not to knock the blossoms off," Catherine warned. "Or no apple tarts next winter."

"Did you need me for something, Mistress?" Samonie asked as she worked.

"No, I just wanted to count noses," Catherine admitted.

She took another look at Samonie. The woman seemed tired today, lines of weariness tightening her mouth and eyes.

"You've been working too hard," Catherine told her. "I shouldn't ask you to take care of the children along with your other duties. I'll ask Edgar tonight about finding a nurse for the little ones."

"They're no trouble," Samonie said. She gave a tug on the cord to pull Edana away from the river. "The last thing we need is another person in the house!"

The ferocity of her response startled Catherine.

"Very well. If you're sure," she said. "I don't want to overburden you."

The anger drained from Samonie. She gave Catherine a wry smile.

"You have never overburdened me with work, Mistress," she told Catherine. "My family and I owe you much. Should I need help with the children, I will let you know. Unless," she added, "you feel I'm lax in my care of them."

"No, of course not," Catherine answered. "Since everything is in order here, I'll just return to my work."

But she didn't feel that everything was in order. Samonie had been withdrawn and irritable ever since they had returned. What was the matter? Was she worried about Willa and her new husband? Had someone threatened her? Could she possibly know something about the dead knight? If so, why didn't she tell them? Samonie knew all their secrets; Catherine had thought they knew all hers. What would be so awful that she couldn't share it?

Her mind full of dark speculation, Catherine tried to settle into finishing the hemming of a new *bliaut* for Margaret to wear over the hand-me-down shift. Even the simple stitch was too much for her to concentrate on. After she had stabbed her finger the third time, she gave it up.

Wandering aimlessly through the house, she wound up in the upstairs storage room where Edgar and Solomon kept the smaller, more valuable items of their merchandise. Inside were a number of caskets and barrels stuffed with straw to protect the goods. It had never occured to Catherine in her father's day to ask why this room had no lock and the counting room did. Of course all the containers were sealed or chained shut, but it was strange that Hubert had felt his records to be more precious than his possessions.

Catherine sat down on one of the boxes, heedless of the dust. Alone there, among the things he had left them, she missed her father as much as if he were dead. Of course, having reverted to Judaism, he was worse than dead. She knew he could never safely return to Paris.

"Papa," she whispered, "how could you abandon us? Without you, everything is falling apart. I never realized how much you took care of me."

She was settling in to a good, steady fit of tears when a thumping from below warned her that Edgar was back. She stood up, wiping her face on her sleeve.

"I'm up here!" she called. "I'll be right down."

Edgar didn't wait for her. He came bounding up the steps, two at a time. He met her on the landing and took hold of her, as if to lift her. It was only when his empty arm touched her that he remembered. A shadow crossed his face, then he hugged her and grinned.

"Solomon and I have a commission!" he announced. "Abbot Suger has sent word that he needs good English wool for blankets for the king's journey. He wants us to negotiate for them with the wool merchants. The profit from that and what we expect to take in at the *Lendit* this year should keep us through next winter."

It wasn't until she saw the relief in his eyes that Catherine realized how worried he had been.

"That's wonderful, *carissime!*" She kissed him. "I'm so proud of you!

"Does that mean you'll have to go back to England?" she added with less enthusiasm.

"Don't worry, we'll go no farther than Flanders and not until the end of the summer," Edgar said. "The abbot will

send the blankets after the army, to catch up with the king
before the winter rains in the Holy Land."

"How nice to have something to celebrate," Catherine
said, as they went down to join the rest of the family.

Clemence had no occasion to rejoice. She was very grateful
to the sisters at Montmartre for their care of her. She knew
that Paris was a dangerous city just now with so many
strangers in it. She was very lucky to have a bed. Clemence
knew all this and appreciated her good fortune, but all she
wanted was for Lambert to come back and tell her what
was happening.

"Would you like to help us distribute alms?" one of the
nuns asked, seeing her sitting alone.

"Yes, of course," Clemence answered dutifully.

She followed the nun to the refectory, where they were
given baskets of broken loaves, some soaked in sauce from
the last meal.

"Don't give more than one piece to anyone," the nun
told her. "Unless it's very small. It's dreadful to send people away only partially fed, but Abbess Cristina says that's
better than having to turn some away with nothing at all."

"I understand," Clemence said.

But when she saw the crowd of people, so many of them
with children, Clemence wasn't sure she could obey the
rules. The men frightened her, unkempt, unshaven and with
a look of being one step from savagery. Some of them
snatched at the bread and began eating without even saying
a blessing. The children had eyes too large for their faces.
Most were barefoot and had open sores on their legs and
faces.

"Are they lepers?" Clemence whispered, pulling back a
little.

"Probably not," the nun next to her said. "It's mostly
insect bites or scratches. We try to look for those with the
spotted sickness or other illnesses that children pass to each
other. But usually the beggars notice it themselves and
drive the truly diseased away."

"What happens to them?" Clemence asked in horror.

"Some are tended to at the monasteries; most die or re-cover, as God wills." The nun's tired face showed how much she would have liked to save all who came to them.

Clemence finished distributing the contents of her basket. They had poor at home in Picardy, of course. But they were the town's poor. The monks at Saint Omer put by grain every year against famine, and she didn't think anyone had ever starved, not in her memory.

There were still people waiting for alms.

"I'm sorry," the nun told them. "This is all we have to spare today. Come back tomorrow. Or try Saint Genevieve. The monks there have more than we do."

No one even protested. They simply turned from the gate and started back down the hill. Clemence noticed how many leaned on sticks or had to be carried by others.

"Sister," she asked, "do I eat food that you would nor-mally give to the poor?"

"Of course not," the woman answered. "The bread you left last night went to them. You might say you added to the gift."

Clemence was slightly comforted. She was just begin-ning to realize how sheltered her life had been. Her village was prosperous, so much so that Lambert's father was much richer in gold and property than her own, even though Osto was the castellan and Bertulf merely a miller.

The nun was speaking to her.

"I beg your pardon," Clemence said. "What was that?"

"I just wondered what brings you and your husband to Paris," she repeated. "Is he going to join the king on his pilgrimage?"

"Oh no!" Clemence was terrified at the thought. "It's our fathers who are going. They left together some weeks ago. But not long after, my mother died suddenly. We came to find my father, Lord Osto, and tell him. He left the care of the village to her, and now there's no one left but me. If Father doesn't return, Lord Jordan will give the castellany to someone else, and I'll have no home."

"You poor child!" The nun patted her hand. "I'll pray for the soul of your mother, shall I?"

"Yes, thank you," Clemence said.

"But you shouldn't have come yourselves to find him," the nun continued. "Why didn't you send one of your men or ask your lord to do so?"

"There was no one who could be spared," Clemence told her.

She hurried back to her room. Her answer sounded flimsy even to herself, and she wondered if the sister thought so, too. It didn't seem wise to say that it wasn't safe for her to stay behind. It was possible that the nuns of Montmartre, noblewomen themselves, wouldn't approve of her decision.

If Lambert didn't come for her soon, Clemence vowed that she would go find him, whatever the risk.

Bertulf and Godfrey were sitting on a bench outside the Blue Boar, watching a circle of men playing a complicated game with dice and round wooden counters. Neither one knew the rules and so didn't join in the suspense felt by other observers.

"Do you think we've been here long enough?" Godfrey asked.

"We've another few hours of daylight," Bertulf answered. "We have to be back for Compline, but I doubt Master Durand will be happy to see us much before."

"I still don't understand what we're doing," Godfrey complained. "The murderer must have left Paris by now. And, as for the rest, we could tell Master Durand most of what he wants to know now."

"No, the man is still here," Bertulf said. "I'm sure of it. He has no reason to leave. He knows we couldn't see his face that night. What he doesn't realize is that I heard him speak before he attacked us. Master Durand has given us the perfect opportunity. We shall go from tavern to tavern until I hear that voice."

"And then?" Godfrey asked.

"And then I will dispense justice," Bertulf answered.

Godfrey hoped no one saw his friend's face at that moment. It would be the end of their deception, and of their dreams.

Early Monday morning, Samonie slipped out of the house, carrying a bag. She made her way to her daughter's home, knowing that they would be up at first light to prepare the wool for the day's work.

Willa was already spreading the matted wool as Belot poured water into the trough. She greeted Samonie with a kiss.

"What are you doing here so early, Mother?" she asked.

"I need a favor of you, *ma fillote*," Samonie said, holding up the bag. "A man will come by for this later today. His name is Bertulf. He's somewhat older than I am, and his hair, what remains of it, is brown streaked with grey. His accent is that of Picardy. He'll ask for you by name. Give this bag to him and no other."

Willa took the bag gingerly, as if she expected it to snap at her.

"What is it?" she asked.

"Food and a few other things I promised him," Samonie answered.

"Why couldn't he come to Master Edgar's?" Belot put down the water bucket to stare at the bag suspiciously.

"Because I'll be in and out today, and he might miss me," Samonie answered. "You'll not be going anywhere, will you?"

"Not with all this to do," Belot grunted. "Felt hats for every pilgrim in Paris, it seems! By the time King Louis sets out I may have enough to rent a place and open my own shop."

"That's wonderful! I'm proud of you both," Samonie smiled. But as she did, she also noted how red and callused her daughter's hands and feet had become and how young Belot was already getting a stoop from carrying the heavy water buckets.

"Well, I must be getting back before the porridge boils over," she said. "Good-bye, my dears. Take care of yourselves."

The streets were crowded as Samonie made her way back to the Grève. Pilgrims, mountebanks, monks, beggars, citizens of Paris trying to earn their daily bread. Every now

and then someone important came through, with guards
moving ahead to clear the way for them. The beggars tried
to get as close as was permitted, for occasionally a flurry
of small coins was tossed to them from the noble riding by.

Catherine was already down when Samonie returned.

"Good morning," she smiled. "I was hoping you'd gone
out for some early strawberries to have with the porridge."

Samonie showed her empty hands.

"I couldn't find any," she said. "The Île is full of people
today. I'm surprised some aren't pushed off the edge into
the river."

"No matter." Catherine stirred the barley to keep it from
forming hard blocks in the broth. "Honey will do. Perhaps
you can see if Margaret needs help dressing the children."

Samonie went at once.

Catherine continued stirring the porridge, staring into the
pot as if the answers to all her questions could be revealed
there. But the future was as murky as the congealing barley.

Secrets. Did all families have so many? Sometimes Catherine wanted to shout all of hers from the spire of Nôtre
Dame, simply to be rid of the solid shadows that kept her
from leading an uncomplicated life. They surrounded her
and pressed against her throat, choking her when she
wanted to speak. And now Samonie had secrets from her,
too.

It was such a beautiful morning. Why did her heart feel
made of lead?

On the other side of the river, in a small room over a bridle
maker's shop, Lambert was feeling much the same way.

"Are you sure we're talking about the same man?" he
asked Jehan. "How could my father have been so misled?
He always spoke of Hubert LeVendeur with the utmost
respect."

"Don't blame your father," Jehan told him. "Better men
than he have been totally ensorceled by Hubert and his
family. He drove my friend Roger to his death and his own
wife, Madeleine, to madness. I had prayed that his daughter, Agnes, would escape him, for her eyes were not de-

ceived by his wickedness. But only last year he managed
to have her sold into marriage in Germany so that now only
I remain to stand against him."

Lambert tried to put together all he had been told the
night before. It was a lot to take in at once.

"I thought you said Hubert was gone," he said. "That's
what the boy at his house told us."

"They say he's gone." Jehan's voice lowered. "But I believe he still lurks in Paris, perhaps in the lairs of the Jews,
perhaps in secret rooms in his own home. He may even
have mastered the trick of becoming invisible and be listening to us at this very moment."

Lambert shivered and moved farther away from his new
friend. It all sounded like nonsense. Christian converts returning to the Jewish faith like dogs to their vomit; plots
to infiltrate the court and the abbey of Saint Denis with
infidels; A family of heretics and magicians out to destroy
all of Christendom, if Jehan were to be believed.

It sounded impossible. But in the past few weeks Lambert had seen and heard so many things he had never
thought possible before. And both his father and Lord Osto
were missing, along with the faithful Godfrey. No one else
had been able to tell him anything. Could this peculiar man
be the only one with the truth?

He wanted to discuss it with Clemence.

"I understand the need for haste," he told Jehan. "But I
must inform my wife of what is happening. She'll be worried."

"It will upset her more if she knows that you are going
to face these monsters in their den," Jehan answered.

Lambert's eyes widened. "I am?"

"You must. They don't know you. You can gain admit-
tance to the house, find out their intentions." Jehan chewed
on a fingernail as he formulated his plan.

"Why would they tell me?" Lambert wasn't sure this
direct approach was the best one. "And what could I ask
them, 'Begging your pardon, did you happen to kill a castellan from Picardy anytime recently?' I don't think I'd be
very good as a spy."

"Wait! Do you have a cross about your person?" Jehan asked abruptly.

Lambert pulled out a small iron one on a chain around his neck.

"Good, that will protect you doubly." Jehan smiled happily. "The cross for Our Lord's guidance and iron to frighten away the demons."

Lambert stood and edged toward the door.

"Please, I really don't think I can do this," he started.

Jehan's muscular right arm fell on his shoulder and sat him back down.

"You shake like a heifer when she's just seen the bull," he sneered. "Are you a man or not? You came to Paris to find what happened to your father. I believe he was snared by these devils in human form. Isn't it your duty to confront them? Perhaps they still hold him alive but in constant torture. What would he say if he knew you lacked the *pendons* to rescue him?"

A vision of his father's face appeared in Lambert's mind. Bertulf was laughing at him, as he had in the days when he had been teaching Lambert to ride. Then the face changed to one of horror and pain.

This Jehan might well be mad, but Lambert knew that he couldn't turn his back on the only possibility he had been given.

"Very well." He sighed. "I'll return to the house at once. Tell me what I should say to them."

Jehan's arm lifted from his shoulder. The knight grinned down at him.

"Don't worry, friend," he laughed. "I won't let you enter the hell mouth unprotected."

This promise did not reassure Lambert at all.

Catherine had just finished dressing when the deputation of her neighbors arrived at the door. Martin let the women in and set up chairs for them in the hall before he went to tell her of her unexpected guests.

"Hersende is downstairs," he said, his nose wrinkling in distaste. "And *Domina* Luca, the baker's wife, is with her.

Also, *Dominae* Alesia, Eremberga and Richilde."

"Sweet Virgin!" Catherine exclaimed. "Whatever do they want?"

"I don't know, Mistress," Martin said. "Should I have asked them?"

"No, no. Just have your mother offer them some wine and sweets and tell them I'll be down in a moment,"

Catherine rummaged on her dressing table for a hand mirror. None of those women had been inside her house since Agnes had moved out over five years ago. Catherine had a sick feeling that they hadn't come to welcome her home.

She forced herself to smile and appear relaxed as she entered the hall. Samonie was pouring the wine and Catherine noted that all the women except Hersende had accepted a cup.

"Welcome!" Catherine said. "God save you all. I'm delighted to see you here."

Hersende stood. "A blessing on the house and all within," she said quickly and with no warmth.

"Thank you," Catherine said before she could continue. "May I offer you some *gastelet*? Luca and her husband make them so well."

Luca smiled nervously. The other women each took one of the small cakes from the platter Martin offered. Catherine took one, as well, and seated herself between the others and the door.

"I regret that I've been unable to offer you our hospitality before," she told them. "I've been most remiss since our return from my sister's wedding. Please forgive me."

Hersende put down her cake and brushed the crumbs to the floor.

"Catherine, we've come not to chastise you for not entertaining your neighbors, but because some very disturbing information has reached us."

The other women all nodded solemnly.

"We believe that it's nothing but slander, of course," Luca added. "But you know how the appearance of scandal can have the same results as the truth of it."

"I know this all too well, Luca," Catherine said. "I'm grateful for your bringing me word of this. Who is defaming us and what do they say?"

Luca twisted the end of her sleeve in her hand. "Rumor has no face, Catherine," she said. "But it is whispered that your father's departure was much later than he had intended. And that he is not on his way to Rome."

"Really?" Catherine's hands were icy. "Where do they say he has gone?"

"Into Spain," *Domina* Richilde spoke up. "They say he's gone to Cordoba to study the wizardry of the Jews and Saracens and that, to gain entry into their circle, he had to bring them the blood of a Christian knight."

Catherine's jaw dropped.

"What!"

Hersende defended the statement. "Well, there were lights in the house long after Hubert told me he was leaving, and then there was that man you found dead."

"Lights in the house?" Catherine said. "Why didn't you mention this when we asked you before?"

"I didn't remember then," Hersende muttered. "But you must admit it doesn't look good. Especially since Hubert spent so much time with Jews. You still have one of them in and out of the house as if he owned it."

"He does own part of it," Catherine stood. "Solomon is partners with my husband, as his uncle and my father were partners, as his grandfather and my grandfather were partners in Rouen. Our families have been trading together for almost a hundred years, and no one has ever questioned our fidelity to Our Lord or accused us of such nonsense as wizardry!"

Except one man.

Catherine blinked as the thought hit her. Only one man had ever insisted that she was an enchantress or that Hubert gained his wealth through sorcery.

Perhaps Jehan had not left Paris after all.

"Thank you for coming, my friends." She swallowed. "I believe I know who has started this evil calumny. He's someone who feels himself wronged by my father. This man has threatened all of us, including my poor children. He wears the cross of a pilgrim, but there is nothing in his heart but hatred."

Richilde put her hand to her mouth. "Catherine, you should have told us! What if my Agneta were playing with James and this beast found them! I'm not going to let my child near here until this man is caught."

"I'm sure he wouldn't . . ." Catherine tried to calm her, but the other women were adding their opinions. And, in honesty, what could she tell them? She wasn't sure their children would be safe from Jehan. She didn't know what atrocities he was capable of, goaded as he was by the demon within.

"Please!" she tried again.

"Someone should tell the provost!" Hersende shouted. "He should have his men out looking for this monster."

"Our children need protection from such men!" Luca agreed. "Paris is overrun with them now, all because Louis has decided to take an army to Jerusalem."

"And leave good citizens at the mercy of villains!" Eremberga stated angrily. "As well as tithing us to pay for his folly!"

"There's wickedness and heresy enough right here!" Richilde added. "He has no business going so far. He should first silence those street preachers who say we should give all we have to the poor, or they'll take it from us."

Catherine stared in awed fascination as the women leaped from anger at her to blaming the men in power for causing their fears. They seemed to have forgotten why they had come. All were on their feet, speaking at once. Luca, now close to the end of a pregnancy, was in tears.

Samonie came rushing in, sure that Catherine was being attacked. Instead she found Richilde and Eremberga arguing about whose husband should go to the provost, Alesia and Catherine patting Luca's back and urging her to lie down and, on one side, Hersende sitting next to the table, pouring herself another cup of wine.

"Saint Jerome's naked dancers!" Samonie exclaimed. "Mistress, what should I do?"

Catherine gave her a look of confused panic. "I don't know." She waved her hands helplessly.

"What is going on?"

The voice from the doorway was deceptively soft, but carried authority. It penetrated the clamor and, as one, the women stopped and turned to see Margaret.

She stood quietly, her vibrant red hair in plaits on her shoulders. Her clothes were no better than those of the others. Yet she radiated an air of authority that Catherine felt could only come from knowing she was born into the nobility. Margaret didn't know that she possessed such an air. It was as natural to her as it was to Edgar, who had learned to put on the manner of a merchant only with difficulty.

"Is there something I can do to help?" Margaret asked.

Richilde smoothed her skirts and gave a tiny bow. "I'm sorry you were disturbed, my lady," she said. "It's nothing. We'll be going now. Thank you for the refreshments, Catherine, dear."

Catherine felt as if she had just stumbled in and out of one of those antipodean countries that scholars speculated about, where people walked around upside down. As the visitors filed past Margaret, who smiled at them all in bewilderment, Catherine understood that the gossip on the street had not only been about Hubert. Each of the women knew that Margaret was not only the daughter of a Scottish lord, but the granddaughter of a count.

When they had gone, Margaret came over to help Catherine and Samonie pick up the cups and put away the chairs.

"Are they going to visit us often?" she asked.

Catherine shivered. "I don't think so, *ma douz*. In fact, I wouldn't be surprised to find charms hung at all the windows on the street, to protect the neighbors from us."

Margaret thought about this. "Do you think we could get one of our own to keep away unwanted company? Only put it at the back of the house. I'm afraid of the men who come to the garden at night."

"What?"

Catherine sat with a thump on the last chair. Perhaps instead of sending Margaret to the Paraclete, she should go herself. She felt in dire need of a calm place to think.

Eleven

Paris, Tuesday, 13 kalends June (May 20), 1147; 18 Sivan, 4907. Feast of Saint Plantilla, noble Roman, who was baptized by Saint Peter, dipped her veil in the blood of Saint Paul and still managed to die a natural death.

Et multi quidem signati sunt ipso loco, ceteros autem ad opus simul provocavimus, ut qui ex christianis necdum signati sunt ad viam Ierosolimitanam . . .

And there are many signs in that same place, and to others likewise we had preached the task before us, so that who among Christians are not yet marked for the road to Jerusalem.

—Bernard of Clairvaux
Letter 457

*E*dgar received all of Catherine's news with alarm.

"I don't know what worries me more," he said, running his hand through his hair. "That people are lurking near our home by night, or that all the women of the Grève seem to think my sister is nearly a countess."

"Would you prefer they thought her a serving girl?" Catherine countered. "Both of you are too wellborn for my family. Margaret has made no public renunciation of her birthright, as you did. Now that the count has acknowledged her as his granddaughter, she should be allowed to accept the benefits his recognition gives her."

"I wish I believed they were benefits." Edgar rubbed his forehead. "Very well. Perhaps that problem can wait a while longer. First, these midnight prowlers. I'll have to get the guards back and this time not let them bring fishing nets."

They were sitting in the garden. The roses were starting to bloom. The air was full of perfume and the humming of bees. Catherine had fresh mint mixed with the honey in her porridge. She took a bite, then prepared herself to confess that Jehan had also been to the house.

At first Edgar could only glare at her, stupefied at her actions.

"You met him alone!" he finally shouted.

"Martin was there." She looked up at him quickly, then concentrated on her porridge bowl.

"Martin! And what could he do?"

"Run for help?" Catherine suggested.

"While Jehan strangled you," Edgar said. "Which I'm sorely tempted to do myself. How could you have been so stupid?"

"Edgar, I've known Jehan most of my life," Catherine protested. "He doesn't want to kill me; he wants to humiliate me . . . us."

"A fine excuse for clearing the house, just as if he was your lover," Edgar snorted.

"Edgar!" Catherine stood. The porridge spilled onto her skirt and stuck. "How can you even think that?"

"Catherine, right now I'm so angry I don't know what to think." Edgar's voice lowered.

Catherine felt as if she'd just been dropped into an icy stream. His anger had passed into the cold depths that terrified her, all the more because it was so rare for her to be the object of it.

"I know I should have mentioned that Jehan was coming," she said as steadily as she could. "But I thought he'd go away at once. All these *trufeors* made such a fuss about how eager they were to set off for the Holy Land. But none of them seem to be in a hurry to leave!"

"Catherine." Only Edgar's lips moved.

"You shouldn't be bothered with Jehan, Edgar!" she went on. "He's already half in Hell. When I look at him I can see the demons behind his eyes. No one of any sense would pay attention to him."

"You pity him, don't you?" Edgar shook his head in amazement. "After all he's done."

"Edgar, he has nothing." Catherine looked up at him, pleading.

Edgar took her hands. "Catherine, he deserves nothing."

Catherine nodded. "I suppose I should leave him to God. If he comes again, I'll send for the priest."

"No." Edgar didn't raise his voice. He didn't have to. "You'll send for me. But first you'll bar the doors and take the children to the cellar to hide until I say it's safe. We've underestimated his wickedness too often. Now he must be treated as the savage he is! Don't you ever see him alone again!"

She gave a small cry as his grip tightened.

He looked down in surprise. "Catherine, your hands are freezing!"

"I was frightened," she said quietly.

"Of me?" he asked. "But I'm only angry because I'm afraid of what he might have done to you, to our children. I love you."

"I know." Catherine caressed his cheek with her numb fingers. "That's the worst of his evil; the way it rubs its filth off on us."

"It will wash." He tried to smile, but settled for kissing her nose. "And as for Margaret, I don't believe she cares what the people on the street think of her. She behaves the same way to everyone."

"Just so they don't start asking her to petition the count for favors," Catherine said darkly. "Then they'll find out just how much of a lowborn fishwife *I* am."

Edgar got up and stretched. He felt as though he had spent the last few minutes wrestling with the devil. "I'm meeting Archer at the *Parleoir* just after Nones, and I want to be there before the bells stop. These merchants have to find out that I'm as serious as they are about the trade."

As they went in, they met Martin coming for them.

"There's a man to see you," he said. "He was here a few days ago, asking for Master Hubert."

"Why didn't you tell us?" Edgar asked in alarm.

"I didn't know you wanted me to." Martin sighed; there were so many rules to remember! "I told him then that Master Hubert was gone and so he and the lady left, too."

He went to the gate and returned a moment later with Lambert. The young man's eyes darted from side to side as if wishing he could see behind his back. His left hand clutched something on a chain around his neck. He was so obviously terrified that Catherine's first impulse was to sit him down and get him a bowl of hot milk and valerian.

"My name is Lambert," he began. His right hand moved in a sign Catherine knew well.

"Greetings, Lambert," Edgar said. Catherine could tell that he was still not under control of his temper. "Why do you feel you must ward off the Devil in our home?"

Lambert's hand froze. "Sorry." He thought quickly. "I'm a stranger in Paris. I find myself unable to judge the honesty of people here."

Edgar nodded. "I have the same problem. Would you care to sit and tell us the reason for your visit?"

"Martin said that you came last week and asked for my father," Catherine said. "He's gone on pilgrimage, but . . ."

Lambert started violently at her words. Catherine wondered if he was afflicted with Saint Vitus. She smiled, trying to reassure him.

It had enough effect that he consented to sit and take a cup of wine.

"Master Hubert traded in horses from Spain with my father, and Lord Osto, our castellan," Lambert managed to explain. "They were supposed to have come to Paris, where my father planned to join the brethren of the Temple. Lord Osto's wife died suddenly, and he's needed urgently at home before his lord gives his castellany to another."

"I'm very sorry," Catherine said, puzzled. "I don't believe anyone by that name has been here. . . . oh, 'to join the Temple,' of course!"

Lambert nodded. "At the Temple preceptory they knew nothing of Lord Osto or my father. But then I learned of the man you found here."

"We have no knowledge about the poor man," Edgar said. "The body was much decayed, I'm afraid. He seemed to be of middle height, with light hair, greying. He could be anyone."

"I saw the cloak and brooch the man was wearing," Lambert said, "and they were unfamiliar to me. Lord Osto had dark hair, but there wasn't . . . isn't much left of it. And there would have been no reason for him to be dressed as a Knight of the Temple. It was a forlorn hope that you could help, but Master Hubert was my only connection. Lord Osto knew no one else in Paris."

There was a clatter on the stairs, and James bolted into

the room, waving a wooden lance, followed by the new puppy his uncle Guillaume had just sent him.

Lambert tried to grab his cross and wave his hands at the same time. His wine cup crashed to the floor.

"James!" Edgar said. "If you and the dog can't behave better than that, you can both sleep in the shed."

The idea seemed to please James, but not the scowl his father was giving him. His face crumpled into tears.

Catherine lifted him up and wiped his face.

"We have a guest, James," she said. "You know better than to behave so."

She set him down. James dropped the lance and put his hand over his heart, bowing and reciting the greeting he had been taught.

Lambert nodded back, seeming to forget the response. James glared at him.

"You're supposed to say, 'God save all here,' " he whispered loudly.

"Oh, James!" Catherine hid her face in her scarf and tried to stifle her giggles.

Edgar was not so amused. "You may now go upstairs and wait with your sister and your aunt until we send for you."

James slunk back up as Catherine tried to apologize.

"It's quite all right," Lambert told her. "Children are the same everywhere."

But there was confusion on his face. This was a family of demons?

"While we are most concerned with discovering the identity of the man so rudely left with us," Edgar continued as if the interruption hadn't ocurred, "my partner and I would be happy to ask among our acquaintances for word of your father and Lord Osto. Where can we reach you?"

Lambert stammered his reply. "I have n . . . no f . . . f . . . fixed place." He took a breath. "I'll return tomorrow, if you'll permit."

"Fine," Edgar said. "This time leave a message with the boy at the door if we aren't in."

Lambert thanked them and stumbled out.

Catherine turned to Edgar.

"What a strange man! I don't feel right letting him wander about alone. Perhaps we should ask Maurice if he can have refuge at the hospice of Nôtre Dame."

Edgar shook his head. "He's young and ignorant of the ways of the city, but older than I was when I came here. He'll be back tomorrow, and you can feed him if it makes you feel better."

The bells began tolling None.

"*Cristes flæschama!*" Edgar swore. "I'm going to be late."

He gave her a lopsided kiss and ran out.

Lambert had gone out of the house at a run. As he reached the Petit Pont his steps slowed. He rubbed the sweat from his face, glad to feel that he hadn't sprouted fur or donkey's ears. All his limbs were still attached. He faced a nearby corner and felt cautiously beneath his tunic. Yes, everything was where it belonged.

Jehan had warned him that these demons would try to lull him by showing fair faces. But Lambert couldn't get a sense of enchantment about them. Catherine and Edgar weren't that attractive. He sensed no urge compelling him to worship at their feet. Neither had invited him to a moonlit carousal. And the child was very much like the little boys in his village, only somewhat more obedient.

But that could be part of their trickery. Perhaps to work the greatest evil one had to appear most ordinary.

Lambert started across the bridge to find Jehan. He had promised to report at once. But after that, he was going to Clemence. Knowing she was safe with the nuns was comforting, but he wanted her to be safe with him. Fulfilling her father's desire that the two of them keep his castellany didn't seem half as important at the moment as finding a place with a bed big enough for them both.

The bells for Nones woke Bertulf. Owing to the late nights they were being forced to keep and the fact they had not yet taken vows, he and Godfrey were given special permission to sleep well into the morning.

Bertulf pulled himself up and immediatly regretted it. Beer in Paris wasn't like beer in Flanders. They made it sweeter here, and after a few bowls, his mouth felt glazed with honey and herbs. This morning his whole head felt that way.

Perhaps this hadn't been such a good plan, after all.

Godfrey's snoring hadn't changed even through the ringing. Bertulf kicked his cot as he went by to the water basin. Godfrey moaned and pulled the blanket over his head.

"Master, I have a confession to make," he announced as he lowered the covers and squinted at the sunlight. "God never intended me to be a toper."

Bertulf smiled.

"Ah, I thought it was my age." He splashed cold water over his face and beard. "Now I know it was Providence. Thank you, Godfrey."

"Must we do this again?" Godfrey tried getting up.

"We could try drinking more slowly," Bertulf suggested.

"I think I might try spilling it all," Godfrey answered. "The way my hands shake, it shouldn't be difficult."

They emerged into the courtyard, hoping that they hadn't missed the morning meal. No sooner had their faces appeared round the doorway than they heard a voice calling for them.

"You two! Over here!" Brother Baudwin shouted. "Master Durand is waiting for your report."

"Saint Paul's bouncing skull!" Godfrey groaned. "He'll be lucky if I don't spew the report all over his boots."

Master Durand's expression was stern enough to control even Godfrey's willful stomach.

"You've discovered nothing?" He raised his eyebrows in a manner more daunting than a raised sword.

"With all that's happening in Paris," Bertulf explained, "there's no interest in the death of a stranger."

Durand pursed his lips. "Perhaps you haven't been paying close enough attention." He leaned forward, fixing them with his glare.

"Master Durand," Bertulf said with a touch of anger, "despite broad hints from us, no one has mentioned a dead knight of the Temple found in a merchant's house."

"Did you think of asking if this Hubert LeVendeur had been seen with a *live* brother?" Durand was barely containing his scorn.

"We did," Bertulf answered to Durand's chagrin. "Those who knew the merchant told us that he didn't trade with the Temple, but sought out materials for Abbot Suger to adorn his church with, or rare spices and suchlike for the count of Champagne."

"An unusual sort of trader, who has no specific commodity," Durand commented.

Beside him, Brother Baudwin seemed perplexed. "Don't the other merchants keep him from trafficking in their wares?"

Bertulf shrugged. "Apparently not. The man arranged for transport and buyers in distant lands. He was willing to work with Jews. He took less trade from the merchants of Paris than he sent their way. They found him useful as an intermediary."

"So all you have discovered is that no one has any complaint against this man, who has now become a holy pilgrim?" Durand asked.

Godfrey finally spoke up, seeing that Bertulf refused to give information that might be injurious to Hubert.

"There are those who resented him," he said. "Some who felt he was too friendly with the Jews. Others muttered that he must have used trickery and deception to manage so many lucky bargains."

"But there was no proof, no specific case," Bertulf added quickly. "Only tavern gossip. All wealthy men have enemies among those not as successful."

Master Durand sighed. "That is all too true."

He tapped his fingers on the table, considering the problem.

"Very well," he decided. "Another day or two, no more. Search out information in the marketplace. Ask the traders coming in for the Lendit. Perhaps one of them knows of some dealings this Hubert LeVendeur had with the brethren of the Temple in Spain or the Aquitaine. There must be some connection, or the body wouldn't have been in his home!"

"The Lendit?" Bertulf asked.

"It's a plain north of the city," Baudwin explained. "Between here and Saint Denis. There are two fairs held there, one starting on Saint Barnabas's Day and ending just before the Eve of Saint John's. They're already preparing the ground to build the booths."

"The fur and spice merchants would have dealt with this Hubert, as well as the vellum and parchment makers," Durand added, "if he had commissions from both the count and the abbot. Seek these men out. Some live in Paris, others have already arrived to negotiate with the monks for the best site at the fair."

"Perhaps the draper has need of more boot leather or material for clothing," Brother Baudwin suggested. "These two can do him a service while they work for us. I understand that the king plans to leave before the fair begins. We go with him and so will need our goods beforehand."

Master Durand seemed surprised at the intelligence of the idea. After a moment's consideration, he gave his approval.

"You take them, Baudwin," he ordered. "I have more important things to attend to."

Outside, all three men took deep breaths, as if the air inside Master Durand's room had been too stale to support life.

Baudwin led them to the supply rooms where a number of other sergeants and servants were hard at work. The draper was happy to give Bertulf and Godfrey some errands to perform. They left shortly after with a tablet listing the items that they were to find.

"This is better than the tavern," Godfrey said as they rode into the city. "But I wish I'd had a day to let my stomach recover."

"We don't have any more days," Bertulf told him. "Soon we'll be asked to take the oath of the Temple and, if we haven't found the murderer by then, what am I going to do?"

The *Parleoir* was busier than ever. While the merchants were as worried as their wives about the damage the king's tithe would do to their profits, most hoped that the extra business would make up for it.

Archer wasn't so sure. He was a miller, who belonged to the water merchants by virtue of the fact that his mills, along with the one he leased from Genta, were all on the Seine, two under the *Grand Pont*. He had a strong interest in the transport of grain into and out of the city and owned several boats that docked within the limits of the merchants' purview.

"The army the king is collecting is undisciplined," he complained to Edgar. "They'll spread out over the countryside, trampling and devouring all in their path. At least when it's two lords fighting each other, there's usually someone to protest to. What will I grind into flour if the fields are destroyed? The harvests are bad enough as it is."

Edgar gave a gesture of helpless sympathy. He had no idea whom one went to if the king's men caused the damage. Solomon came to his rescue.

"Abbot Suger has been named regent," he told Archer. "Apply to him if there's a shortage of grain. If Paris has no bread, he'll find it hard to control the citizens."

"Of course!" Archer said.

Solomon could see the man's mind working and knew the exact moment Archer remembered that the link to Abbot Suger was Edgar, who had inherited Hubert's account with Saint Denis.

Archer smiled in a way that managed to include them both without showing any real friendship for Solomon.

"Perhaps the next time you have an audience with the abbot, I might come with you to make just that point." His eyes were those of a hopeful puppy.

Edgar looked at Solomon. "We might be able to arrange a meeting," he told Archer.

"Fine, fine." Archer didn't seem as pleased as Edgar had expected.

"Was there something else?" he asked.

Archer scratched at the side of his beard. "Well, it's my wife." He sighed. "Richilde went to visit your wife yesterday."

"So I heard," Edgar started angrily.

"Yes, yes," Archer raised his hands in placation. "They seem to have sorted things out. But I understand that you've had some trouble. If thieves and madmen are roaming the *Grève* by night, we should all be alert to the danger."

"In these times, there are thieves and madmen everywhere," Edgar said. "I've arranged for men to guard my property. I suggest you do the same."

Archer looked as though he wanted to protest. They were interrupted at that moment by Hugo, the money changer, who had come to the *Parleoir* especially to see Archer, he said, as he pulled the miller away.

Solomon waited in silence while Edgar struggled to control his temper.

"This is what I must spend the rest of my life associating with?" He grimaced.

"He's no worse than the men of the king's court, or the bishop's, for that matter," Solomon reminded him. "You might have spent your life rubbing shoulders with priests instead of sharing your bed with Catherine."

Edgar gave a snort of laughter.

"You do have a way of making me see the advantage of my decision," he said.

"And you probably wouldn't have me to cheer your gloom," Solomon added.

He grinned at Edgar, daring him to respond.

Edgar knew better. Instead he suggested a trencher of lamb stew and a bowl of beer. Solomon had no argument with that.

In the small attic room, Jehan was at the same moment staring at Lambert in horror.

"You let that woman give you wine!" he shouted. "Saint

Lucy's loosened eyes, man! Have you no sense! Didn't I warn you?"

"I didn't drink it." Lambert tried to push himself farther back, but Jehan loomed closer.

Until now, Lambert had always thought "blazing eyes" a fanciful description by the *jongleurs*. Now he knew what they meant.

"The child startled me, and I dropped the cup before I took even one sip," he explained.

"Well, thank the Virgin that happened," Jehan said. "Or you might have fallen under their persuasion and even now be committing horrible acts of blasphemy."

Lambert crossed himself.

"I remembered your warnings," he insisted. "I was praying the whole time I was in the house. But the visit was to no purpose. The description of the man was nothing like Lord Osto. Perhaps he never went to see them."

"I'm sure he did." Jehan paced the tiny room, his boots thumping wrathfully. Below, a man shouted at him to stop the racket. Jehan stomped with greater fury.

"Catherine LeVendeur and her husband are capable of the most wicked treachery and deceit." He fixed Lambert with his terrible eyes. "Why should she tell you the true appearance of this man they killed? She's hoping the knights will bury his memory along with his body."

"Perhaps, but what can I do about it?" Lambert said. "I've no proof that Lord Osto and my father even came to Paris. No one reports having seen them here."

Jehan reached over and grabbed the young man by the strings of his tunic.

"What kind of men do they grow in the north?" he growled. "You mewl like a lamb that's lost its mother. You need proof? Well, I tell you it's in that house. All you have to do is find it. Now, are you going to go back to that wife of yours and tell her you've failed?"

"Uggleger . . . argle!" Lambert choked.

Jehan released the strings. Lambert coughed until he could breathe normally again.

"I only asked for your advice." He coughed again.

"Return to the house," Jehan ordered. "Pretend to make friends with Catherine and Edgar. Tell them you know no one in Paris; all the things you told me. That should be easy for you. But you must also stay on your guard. Lull them into speaking in front of you without caution. And, no matter what, don't trust them!"

"How can I avoid taking hospitality from them?" Lambert asked. "If I'm to feign friendship."

That gave Jehan pause. "Hmmm, you'll need to find something else to counter enchantments and prevent poisoning."

"Come with me," he said suddenly. "I know of someone who can help us."

They clattered down the stairs and out into the crowded street.

"Follow closely," Jehan spoke softly in Lambert's ear. "I mean to follow an indirect path, to confuse anyone who might be spying on us."

Although the sun was warm on his back, Lambert shivered.

Jehan led him through the narrow streets, up and down, doubling back often almost to the river. They circled around the Jews' cemetery and past rows of vines covered with leaves and the promise of wine. They stumbled over bits of masonry from ancient buildings and once cut through a small church. Finally, Jehan stopped at a low door on a narrow street off the *rue de la Bucherie*. The house was built on the bank of the Biévre, one of the streams flowing into the Seine.

Jehan knocked softly. After a few moments, the board over the grille moved a fraction. Lambert thought he had a glimpse of a rheumy eye peering at them. Then there was the sound of a bolt being drawn, and the door opened only enough to let them enter.

Lambert found himself in a room not much higher than the door. Both he and Jehan were forced to stoop. It was dark, smoky and stifling. The only light filtered in from a slot cut in the wall on the far side. It was some moments before Lambert could make out the person they were visiting. He thought it was male, but very short. The house was the right size for its owner.

"So," the man said, squinting at Jehan. "Back, are you? The charms I gave you must have worked, or you wouldn't have returned alive."

Jehan snorted. "Well enough, for what they were," he said. "But I survived through my own strength. This boy needs something to protect him in a stronghold of evil."

Lambert could only make out the movement of a head in the gloom. He knew that he was being examined.

"In case they try to poison or ensorcel me," he explained to the man.

"Of course." Their host turned and began to rummage in a box next to the wall. He pulled out several small bags and laid them on a bench.

"These should work," he told them. "I'll have to mix them. Artemisia, holly, some ground rowan leaves, a few other things. Wear it in a sack around your neck. Breathe into it if you start to feel dazed. A pinch in a wine cup will dilute the effect of most poisons."

He worked as he spoke. Lambert had no idea how he could measure and grind the herbs in so little light. What if the man mixed the wrong amounts?

"Now as to your payment," Jehan said.

The man interrupted him. "Three *deniers* of Paris. I don't bargain, if you recall."

Lambert's heart sank. "I don't have that much."

"I do." Jehan went into the bag at his belt. "Just remember, if the boy dies, so do you."

This threat gave Lambert no comfort. As they emerged into the sunshine, his only desire was to see Clemence again before he infiltrated the demons' lair.

Catherine was going through the jewelry box. Her sister, Agnes, had taken most of it to Germany as her dowry. Now that she had given her mother's chain, most of the pieces left were ones Edgar had made. She held up a silver brooch, a sample of his first efforts at shaping metal. A true craftsman would have thrown it back in the crucible, but Catherine treasured it.

She sighed as she lifted a tangle of silver and gold chains. Beneath them lay a pair of gold earrings, with garnets laid into them. Yes, those might do, if she could only find the pendant that went with them.

Despite her protestations that it would be a dull gathering, Catherine was nervous. She had no doubt that Edgar would behave perfectly. And he was pleasant to look at in more eyes than hers. He might be too fair for some tastes, but she knew there were plenty of women who watched him admiringly.

Alone in her room, Catherine had to admit that it was her own behavior she doubted. Her mother or sister had always taken care of the social duties. They had excused Catherine as one who was intended for the convent as well as one who was most likely to tip over a tray of sweets or trip over the dogs in the homes of others. As a consequence, Catherine now realized that she had little experience in being a merchant's wife.

She was sure she would offend someone or embarrass Edgar. It might be better if Margaret went instead. She was the one everyone wanted to meet.

Samonie was calling her. Catherine took out the earrings, closed and locked the box. She tried to lock up her doubts, as well.

The housekeeper was waiting impatiently at the foot of the stairs. Next to her stood Martin. The boy's tunic was muddy and torn. His face was scratched and one eye was swollen shut.

"Holy Mother!" Catherine exclaimed. "What happened to you?"

"He was attacked by a *ribaudaille*!" Samonie said angrily. "A band of robbers right in the middle of Paris."

"Mother, they didn't rob me," Martin contradicted her. "And I know who they were. Most were from the students who rent from Archer and Richilde. The others live nearby."

"But why?" Catherine said. "What did they want from you?"

"Nothing," Martin said. "We just got into an argument, and I came out the worse for it."

"Tell her the truth, Martin," Samonie said. "She should know."

Martin glared at his mother. "It was nothing but words, Mistress."

"Martin." Catherine came closer to him. She saw that his lip was cut and swollen, as well. "Have you been defending our honor?"

Martin looked down. "They said it about all of us. Mother, as well. That you were murderers and Master Hubert had gone on a pilgrimage to Hell and that no one would work in a household like ours except whores and their bastards that no one else would take in."

Catherine set her lips tightly. "I see. They did seem to cover everything, didn't they?"

Samonie hid her face in her hands. Martin put his arm around her.

"Mother, don't cry," he pled. "I don't care. I don't believe any of it. It's my father who was the bastard, for using you. He's the only one I blame. If I knew who he was, I'd challenge him."

Samonie wiped her eyes and tried to smile.

"You're a good, brave son," she said. "I'm proud of you. Now come to the kitchen and let me wash those cuts."

Martin looked to Catherine.

"I agree," she said. "Thank you for standing up for us all. It grieves me greatly that you should be so tormented. I'll do what I can to see that it never happens again."

She went slowly back up the stairs. Matters had gone too far. They had lived in too much secrecy, shut off from their neighbors. It was time to face the world. Even if it meant enduring Genta's simpering and her dancing bears.

Twelve

Montmartre, the Convent of Saint Genevieve, Thursday morning, 11 kalends June (May 22), 1147; 20 Sivan, 4907. Feast of Saint Julie, virgin of Carthage, enslaved by the Vandals, but free in her faith. Martyred shortly thereafter.

Hoc inspectanti divini plasmatis hostis
Invidie patrie, non esse valebat amori
Unde sibi ingeniti livoris fomite moto . . .

Seeing this, the Father of Envy,
The enemy of divine creation
Had no desire to love it
And thus he fired the tinder of his inborn spite . . .

—Gilo of Paris
Historia Vie Hierosolimitane
Book VI, lines 150–152

$\mathcal{Y}$ou mustn't worry about me, Clemence," Lambert urged. "You see, I'm well protected against the snares of evil."

Clemence surveyed the collection of crosses, charms and herbs hung around his neck.

"My dearest," she said gently, "if these people are so wicked, why not bring them to the attention of the bishop and let him deal with them?"

"Because they are far too clever for that." Lambert had been thoroughly advised by Jehan. "They even have disciples among the canons of Nôtre Dame."

Clemence's eyes widened. "How horrible! But, if *that* is so, then what chance have you?"

Lambert explained once more about the efficacy of the charms.

Clemence was quiet for a moment. Then she looked at Lambert with an expression that, even after less than a month of marriage, he was learning to fear.

"If your amulets and herbs protect you," she told him, "they can shield me, as well. We shall face these demons together; my prayers added to yours."

"Clemence, no! It's far too dangerous."

"You just told me it wouldn't be, Lambert. How can it be safe for you and not for me?" She took his hands. "Do you doubt the sincerity of my faith?"

"These tokens will only save us from magic and sorcery," Lambert countered. "What if we're attacked with knives or cudgels?"

"Then there will be two of us to fight them off." Clemence let go his hands and began packing her bag as if the matter were decided.

"But, I can't let you," Lambert said with little hope. "What would your father say?"

"We won't know until we find him," Clemence answered, her chin trembling. "And I'm out of patience with waiting here with the sisters, my hands folded in resignation. Mother would never have done so."

Now a tear did escape, and Lambert knew he had lost the battle. Deep down, he was relieved that she would be with him when next he faced Edgar and Catherine. He was young enough to believe that love was the strongest weapon against evil. His love for Clemence was too powerful for any demon to pierce.

So, well armed, they set out.

Surveying the scene in the children's room, Edgar would have believed that elves had come in during the night and left a shambles.

Samonie and Margaret were hemming a border on Catherine's new *bliaut*, a rose silk embroidered with vines. Catherine stood on a stool, trying to balance so that the edges would be even.

"I could just wrap the extra length to hang over my belt without all this torment," she complained. "My foot's gone to sleep."

"No, you can't," Margaret said firmly. "I've observed the ladies of the court, and they all wear loose chains for belts that have to be held up by loops. No one shortens her skirt by folding anymore. You don't want to be out of fashion, do you?"

"Heaven forbid," Catherine said. "The street has enough gossip about us already. Edgar! Get that away from Edana!"

The child had got into the makeup box and was happily spreading kohl over her cheeks.

"Will you be long at this?" Edgar asked as he took the

stick of kohl from his daughter, and then lifted her, screaming in anger, to his hip.

"Edgar, to make the proper impression, I shall be all day
getting ready," Catherine said. "Once I'm sewn into my
sleeves, Samonie still has to arrange my hair."

"Why? Won't it be covered?" Edgar asked.

Margaret looked at him with pity.

"Brother, you don't understand fashion," she said.

"Nor do I want to," Edgar said. "I hope you don't intend
me to wear those idiotic shoes that need hooks on the toes
fastening them to the hose to keep one from tripping, because I won't do it."

He turned his attention to the squirming bundle under his
arm. "Edana, that's enough. I'm taking you down to wash
this stuff off you. Stop wiggling."

"Your good boots will be enough," Catherine told him.
"Samonie has laid out your shift, tunic and hose. Wear the
belt of black leather with the silver trim."

Edgar left the room before any more orders could be
flung at him. He had to admit that when Catherine decided
to do a thing, she did it properly.

He was busy in the kitchen wiping the sticky black kohl
from Edana and onto a good table napkin he had found
when Martin came in to announce the visitors.

"It's that man who was here before," the boy said. "And
this time the lady is with him. Shall I fetch Mistress Catherine?"

"Godeherre!" Edgar swore. "No, she's half-stitched right
now. Cut up some cheese and bread for them while I make
myself presentable. You too, little imp!" he added to Edana.

Martin found a wooden platter and cut a hunk of cheese
and another of bread. He looked around for a smaller knife
for the guests to use and picked up the first one he saw.
Then, as Edgar quickly washed, he brought the platter in
and set it on the table in front of Lambert and Clemence.

"Master Edgar will join you in a moment," he said with
dignity. "May I bring you some beer, as well?"

Clemence smiled. "Water please, or cider, if you have
it."

"Certainly, my lady," Martin bowed and left the room.

Lambert surveyed the block of cheese.

"I suspect the mistress of the house isn't here," Clemence said. "We mustn't hurt the boy's feelings. Cut me a piece and break off a corner of the bread, if you can. It doesn't look appealing enough to be enchanted."

Lambert picked up the knife and sliced the cheese. He gave a piece to Clemence. Then he stared at the knife, and his eyes grew wide with horror.

"Beloved, what is it?" Clemence dropped the cheese on the floor as she rushed over to him.

"Look!" Lambert held up the knife. "Jehan was right! He wasn't imagining the danger. This is your father's knife!"

"Let me see!" Clemence snatched it from him. "It does look like it, but . . ."

"The star on the handle, right where one's thumb would rest, see?" Lambert pointed. "He used to joke that the meat was so tough he would be branded for life with that star."

Clemence closed her eyes. He was right. Ralf, the smith, had made two of them, one for each of her parents. She had her mother's with her.

"How could they have come by this?" she whispered.

"Only one way." Lambert put his arm around her. "Lord Osto wouldn't have given it away; it's not fine enough for a present. Everyone here has lied to us. Our fathers were here, at least yours was."

Clemence bit her lips. Once she asked the question, she knew there would be no turning back.

"You believe that Father was the knight whose body was found here, don't you?"

"I fear so, my dearest," Lambert said softly. "Even though the description doesn't match. We must be on our guard. We're surrounded by evil, just as Jehan warned."

At that moment, Edgar came from the kitchen. Instead of getting the kohl off, he had managed only to get streaks on his own face as Edana rubbed against him. He held her sideways under his arm, her face and hands striped black and white with smears. She was now crowing in delight, enjoying the ride.

Clemence took one look at them and screamed. Lambert could only gape. He took his wife's hand and pulled her out of the house as fast as he could.

Edgar put Edana down and followed them to the door.

"Hallo?" he called after them. "Are you all right?"

He shut the door, shaking his head. What strange people! The customs in Picardy must be very different from Paris.

Lambert and Clemence ran until they were stopped by the river. They stood on the pathway overlooking the bank, panting until they could speak.

"What was that thing?" Clemence gasped.

"It was just as Jehan warned, a *nuiton*, a creature of evil," Lambert answered. "You see how the man carried it like a pet. Some of its wickedness had even rubbed off onto him!"

Clemence had caught her breath now and was trying to retrieve her wits. She had been startled by the apparition so soon after recognizing her father's knife. The sight wasn't clear in her mind anymore.

"I'm not certain of that," she said. "I wish I hadn't panicked. We had all that protection with us. We should have stayed and demanded an explanation from that man. Was he the master of the house?"

Lambert was beginning to feel foolish, although any good Christian knew that running from the Devil was the wisest course. But in Paris he was surrounded by pilgrims who were preparing to face not only evil, but cold steel and a hot desert. He should have been brave enough to stand firm.

"Yes, that was Edgar," Lambert admitted. "Do you think we should go back?"

"Not today," Clemence said. "I couldn't face them after running off like that. My mind is in such turmoil that I'd muddle a simple *Ave Maria* and leave myself open to their sorcery."

"Do you believe me now?" he asked.

Clemence put her hands on his shoulders and looked up at him.

"I know you would never lie to me," she said. "But I

don't think either one of us has the truth. And, if that truth is that my father has been killed, either by his old friend, Hubert, or by someone of that family, then we must prove it, no matter what the cost to us."

Lambert had momentarily forgotten that the reason he had brought Clemence all this way, subjecting her to untold dangers, was the fear that she might be forced into another marriage while he was gone. But if it was proved that Lord Osto had died, then it was certain a new castellan would be chosen. And it wasn't likely to be he.

"I agree," he said with regret. "Your father must have justice. Perhaps it's time we went to someone in authority to report our suspicions. Jehan says that these people have tendrils stretched everywhere in the city, but there must be some honest person they haven't yet corrupted."

"The bishop?" Clemence suggested. "Or perhaps the brothers of the Temple. Your father was going to join them, after all. Mine may have decided to do so, as well. Perhaps he bought the white cloak and the brooch you told me about here in Paris."

"But I've been to the preceptory," Lambert said. "No one there knew of him."

"You asked at that house about the description of the body," Clemence said. "Did you also ask at the Temple? If both of them say the man was fair, then we know it wasn't Father."

"True, I didn't ask." Lambert thought a moment. "And, if it was your father, then what has happened to mine? And to Godfrey? If Lord Osto had been killed, they would both have come home at once, wouldn't they?"

"Of course!" Clemence sighed in relief. Then another thought sent her into despair again. "Unless they were all slain, and only Father's body has been found."

Lambert leaned against the stone wall separating them from the river.

"I don't know what to do, Clemence," he admitted. "The only person who has offered to help us is Jehan, and so far, he's been right. He said there would be proof in the house, and we both saw the knife. That shows they had some contact with Lord Osto, at the very least. I should have taken it with us."

"No, then how could we prove we'd found it there?" Clemence said. "Perhaps the Knights of the Temple would be a good place to start. The commander could get the provost to send his men to search the house. But it must be done quickly before they realize what we know and destroy the knife."

Her decisiveness sent new courage flowing into Lambert.

"We'll go now," he said, taking her hand. "This very minute. We'll find the truth, no matter what."

On the other side of the river, Bertulf and Godfrey were seated under a chestnut tree drinking a bowl of cider.

"Not as good as what we get at home," Godfrey pronounced.

"I suppose they don't even make proper cider in Jerusalem," Bertulf said glumly. "I can't fancy using dates or oranges or other foreign fruit. Drink up; who knows if we'll ever have more."

Godfrey drained the bowl. He looked around. They were on the higher ground south of the river, and, between the buildings, he could see the vineyards that belonged half to the Jew, Abraham, and half to the canons of Saint Victor. He could hear geese honking as they were driven up the road for market. It was a fair enough land, but he missed his own village. He had vowed to follow his master even into the jaws of hell, but his heart would always remain in Picardy.

"When can we end this pretense of trying to discover what we already know?" he asked Bertulf.

"Soon, I hope," Bertulf answered. "The army will be leaving and with it, the Knights of the Temple. I've made a decision, Godfrey and I want you to honor it."

"Anything, Master." Godfrey sat up straight, his hand over his heart.

"I don't want you to take the oath to the Temple with me," Bertulf said. "No, don't protest. Such a promise should only be made freely and in deep faith. I cannot order you to come with me or hold you to a vow of loyalty. It's too great a sacrifice."

"I wish to make it," Godfrey insisted.

Bertulf smiled. "No, you don't. And I have a task for you that is just as important. I want you to return home."

Godfrey's face suffused with joy, though he quickly tried to hide it.

"But, Master . . ." he began.

Bertulf continued. "You must go to Lord Jordan and tell him that Lord Osto and his friend Bertulf have renounced the things of this world to join the brethren of the Temple of Solomon and protect the pilgrims in the Holy Land. Tell him also that it is our wish that Lambert and Clemence be married and that the castellany be managed by Lambert until their oldest son comes of age."

"He won't like it," Godfrey said.

"It's the final request of ones who have gone to seek martyrdom," Bertulf answered. "Father Mikel and all the men of the village will swear this was our intent. Lambert may not be nobly born, but he has good sense and understands what needs to be done. What he doesn't know, Clemence can teach him."

"The son of a miller as castellan." Godfrey shook his head. "You're asking a great deal."

"That's why you must be there to insist," Bertulf said. "Will you go? If you don't, then all this will have been for nothing."

Godfrey stood, then knelt before Bertulf, placing his hands together and raising them.

"I will, my lord," he swore.

Bertulf bowed his head. His tears trickled through his beard and fell upon the cross sewn onto his black cloak.

Edgar spent quite a while with Edana in the garden, alternately soaping and pouring water over her. Fortunately, the day was warm, and she enjoyed it. When he finally had her clean, dried and dressed, he went back up to Catherine to tell her of their strange visitors.

"Well, it does sound as though the two of you looked

like trolls rising from the earth," Catherine said. "And, if
the woman was anything like this Lambert, she would be
easily unsettled. They probably both need a tonic to calm
their humors."

"I didn't see her clearly, but at first, I thought it was your
sister come to visit." Edgar deposited Edana on the children's bed. All the excitement had worn her out, and she
had fallen asleep on his shoulder.

Catherine stared at him. She was now in her *chainse*,
being sewn into a pair of tight sleeves over which the
hemmed *bliaut* would fit.

"Agnes?" she said in disbelief. "We may have made
peace but I know she's much happier having hundreds of
miles between us. It couldn't have been."

"Of course not," Edgar said. "But there is a resemblance.
I wonder who she was."

"From the impression you made, I doubt we'll ever find
out," Catherine said. "Ow!"

"I'm sorry, Catherine," Margaret told her, as she wiped
the blood off the needle. "But you should stop moving
about so. When is Solomon coming?"

"Solomon?" Edgar asked.

Catherine tried to talk without moving her arms.

"He and Astrolabe are coming to entertain the children
while we're gone tonight," she told him. "It was their idea,
so don't scowl so. I don't think they have much faith in
the guards."

"I don't like using our friends as nursemaids," Edgar
said.

"Samonie doesn't mind the extra work in feeding them,"
Catherine said. "You should be grateful for their concern."

Edgar continued grumbling as he put on the long hose,
chainse and loose tunic. He added rings with various
stones, and a gold chain. He wondered sardonically if he
should pin a brooch on the leather patch covering his
stump. Finally, he called for Martin to help fasten the belt
and pull his boots on. There were so many minor tasks that
had become impossible since he had lost his hand. Having
to get help for them only increased his ill temper.

Just after Vespers Martin came back to tell him that the horse had been brought around. Edgar called to Catherine to hurry.

She came down the stairs carefully, trying not to slip in her soft leather-and-silk shoes. Her hair had been woven into plaits with ribbons that hung down her back below her headdress. The long loose sleeves of the *bliaut* had been pleated with a hot iron. Along with the garnet earrings and pendant, she wore bracelets, rings and the ivory cross Edgar had carved for her before their marriage. The kohl had been applied delicately around her eyes in a way that emphasized their vivid blue.

Catherine stopped at the bottom of the steps, waiting for his comment.

"*Carissima*! I believe you're nervous." He laughed. "You're unusually pale."

"It's the powder," she explained. "Am I all right?"

"Oh, yes," he said. "More than that. You'll outshine every woman in the room."

Catherine relaxed. "I know better than that, but I don't want you to be ashamed of me."

His answer would have been more forceful if Catherine hadn't pushed him away so as not to ruin hours of work.

"Have Astrolabe and Solomon arrived?" she asked.

"They're in the hall, being lions for James to stalk," Edgar said. "Neither seems to feel that our absence will spoil the evening."

Catherine grimaced. "I'm sure they'll enjoy it more than we will."

She went in to pay her respects.

Solomon was on his hands and knees, roaring at James, who was waving a wooden sword at him. When he saw Catherine, Solomon stood so quickly that he got a whack in the shins as James lunged.

"Catherine! You look absolutely enchanting!" he said in surprise. "You'll have King Louis forgetting all about Eleanor."

"Not likely," Catherine laughed. "Everyone knows he's

besotted with her. Have you two nothing better to do than spend an evening in children's games?"

Astrolabe grinned. "An indifferent Jew and the son of a heretic? We don't have many invitations to court."

"Genta would have nothing to do with me in any case," Solomon said as he continued to fend off James's attack.

"Why not?" Catherine asked. "Did you try to seduce her?"

Solomon gave a rude snort. "That one! Never. No, she's rabidly against Jews. Her parents were converts, and she's passed her life trying to distance herself from us."

"Really? I'd never heard that," Catherine said. "Are you sure?"

"Abraham knew Genta's family," Solomon said. "Her mother married a Lombard convert, Obizon, who was the old king's physician. She converted then. Of course her family said *Kaddish* for her, although they always hoped she'd return to them. Genta makes a point of not even walking by houses where Jews live."

"Catherine!" Edgar called. "We have to leave."

"Thank you, Solomon, for telling me," Catherine said. "At least I'll know not to send her your regards."

After they had left, Samonie reminded Margaret that she was now responsible for the welfare of their guests.

"As soon as Edana wakes, bring her down and join them," she said. "You might even rouse her now. With this much sleep in the daytime, the child will be up with the owls tonight."

With some effort, Margaret got Edana up and brought her down to the hall along with a comb to try to smooth the little girl's tangled curls.

Both men greeted Margaret with delight.

"Catherine has given me a letter for the Paraclete," Astrolabe said. "I understand you wish to study with my mother."

Margaret nodded as she sat down with Edana on her lap and started the task.

"Only for a year or two," she said. "Catherine made me

understand that I should be prepared to be a lady with her own court, if my grandfather decides to assist in finding me a husband."

Her face was hidden behind Edana's head so neither man could see her expression when she said this.

"I know my mother will be glad to have you," Astrolabe said. "And two of my cousins are nuns there, as well. Both of them are very kind and gentle. They'll see that you aren't lonely."

Margaret continued combing, occasionally jerking Edana's head back as a snarl refused to give. No one spoke for a while, except Edana, who protested loudly and tried to get away. Finally, Margaret finished and let the child free, whereupon Edana went straight for Astrolabe, who was picking at a dish of almonds.

Margaret looked directly at Solomon for the first time that evening. It startled him how much she had matured in the past few months.

"I miss my mother," she said simply.

"I do, too," Solomon answered. "Every day. If only I had been stronger, or quicker . . . I should have saved her."

"I wasn't reproaching you," Margaret said. "More apologizing for my behavior in recent days. Catherine tries, but she doesn't understand some things the way my mother did, especially about preparing to be a proper wife."

"If you mean seemly," Astrolabe commented. "This isn't the house to learn that. Despite her splendor tonight, Catherine will never adhere to rules. But if you mean honorable, I can't think of a better home to be in."

Margaret smiled, the scar on her cheek creasing. "I know that. It's only that I thought when we got back to Paris, everything would be much calmer. Instead our lives are as unsettled as ever."

"That seems to be our fate," Solomon agreed. "You know I don't like the idea of you going to a convent; but if you must, I'd rather the Paraclete than any. You'll learn all the things you seem to think are necessary, and they won't encourage you to take the veil unless that's what you desire most."

Margaret rubbed her cheek. "It may be the best choice. Perhaps no one but Our Lord would want me now."

Solomon dug his nails hard into his palms to keep from reaching out and taking her into his lap to comfort as he had when her mother died. She might not understand his intent. He had a sudden fear that he wasn't sure about it, himself.

Astrolabe broke the tension.

"Nonsense!" he said. "First of all, your beauty is obvious, as well as your breeding. And, secondly, the scar will fade with time and be only a line of white, hardly noticeable. Now, shall I go down to the kitchen and tell Samonie we're ready to eat?"

"Of course." Margaret was the hostess again. "I'll get the pitcher, soap and towel for our hands. Martin always spills."

Bertulf and Godfrey had returned to the Temple preceptory for Vespers. They found the courtyard bustling with people. Sedan chairs were lined up on one side and a number of horses were being held by squires and stableboys.

"What's happening?" Godfrey asked one. "Are we setting out at last?"

"I don't know about that," the boy said. "My master is here to witness a gift to the Temple, that's all I was told."

"In that case we should make ourselves scarce," Bertulf suggested to Godfrey. "I don't want to spend the evening as part of some procession or listening to speeches."

"Yes, I think I'd rather clean out the stables than that," Godfrey agreed.

The stableboy watched them as they crossed the courtyard and went into one of the buildings. Then he forgot all about them. He'd heard the king was going to be there tonight. He wondered if the pope would come, as well. Then his mind turned to the more important matter of whether or not anyone would remember to feed him.

Lambert and Clemence were taken aback by all the activity.

"Something's happening tonight," Clemence said, "perhaps we should come back in the morning."

"What if this means they're leaving the city?" Lambert worried.

"Then why are all the women here?" Clemence asked. "They're dressed for a banquet, not to wave farewell."

This puzzled Lambert, as well. They stood by the gate out of the way of the horses and sedan chairs entering the preceptory. Clemence became very excited when a party rode up, the lady in a chair and other women riding pillion behind knights, many of whom wore pilgrims' crosses on their tunics.

"Look at how fine their clothes are!" she said. "Do you think one of the men is the king?"

"I have no idea," Lambert said.

There was a man standing near them, observing the spectacle. He overheard the question.

"No, that's his mother, Queen Adelaide," he told them. "With her second husband and her maids."

"Do you know why they're here?" Clemence asked.

"No idea," the man said. "But the queen doesn't go out much, so it must be something important."

Lambert turned to Clemence. "We should go. I'm sure we won't be allowed in tonight."

Clemence nodded. "Could we wait a bit longer, though, in case the king comes? I've never seen a king."

"He's just a man," Lambert said, not willing to admit that he was curious, as well. "But we can stay a little while longer."

Clemence asked the other watcher, "Do you know what the king looks like? Will you point him out to us?"

"That's him." The man gestured. "The thin blond in the center of those riders."

Clemence looked. Louis, king of France, wasn't much older than she was, a man in his mid-twenties. His fair hair hung down to his shoulders under the velvet cap he wore. She was disappointed that he wasn't wearing a crown. She studied his face as he rode by. His countenance was serious and, although he smiled and waved at the people standing by the road, Clemence had the feeling that he didn't see them. His mind was somewhere far away, Jerusalem, perhaps.

"Queen Eleanor isn't with him?" she asked.

"No, she and her mother-in-law don't get along that well," the man said with an air of one who knew all the doings of the court. "They hardly ever appear together."

Clemence was about to ask another question when Lambert grabbed her hand and pulled her back into the shelter of the preceptory wall.

"Look!" he told her. "Over there. Careful! They might see us."

Clemence craned her neck to see around the helpful man. Just behind the king was another group of people. Among them was a man with one hand. On the horse behind him rode a woman in a rose *bliaut* over a deep blue *chainse*.

"What beautiful clothes," she breathed. "I think the *bliaut* is pure silk. She must be very rich."

"Never mind the clothes," Lambert whispered in her ear. "Don't you recognize them? That's Hubert LeVendeur's daughter, Catherine, and her husband. He was the one with the demon this afternoon."

"Really? He looks much better now," Clemence said.

"Darling," Lambert said, "do you understand what this means? They not only have friends at the bishop's court, but here, as well. Their influence stretches all the way to the king."

Clemence tore her eyes from the ladies' attire. "Then we can't risk telling Master Barre what we know. Oh, Lambert, where can we look to find help?"

"Only to Jehan," Lambert said. "Where he and I are staying isn't fit for you. I'm taking you back to Montmartre for now. Then I'm going to report to Jehan at once and ask him what we should do next!"

Thirteen

Paris, the chapel of the Temple perceptory. That same evening.

Prandia cum cena sic sat fiunt opulenta
fercula post multa, post pocula tam numerosa
limpha datur, modicum residetur dum biberetur.

Thus the dinner and banquet were overly abundant
After many courses, after just as many cups
clear wine is given; they linger a while as they drink.

—Ruodlieb, 11, 105–107

$\mathcal{M}$y feet are freezing," Catherine whispered. "I should have known Genta would insist on a Mass before the donation."

"Would you rather a Mass or the bears?" Edgar whispered back.

"At least I can sit in warmth to watch the bears," Catherine grumbled.

Then she swiftly crossed herself and murmured an apology to Christ for disdaining His offering.

She and Edgar were standing toward the back of the chapel, now crowded with members of the Temple, the water merchants and courtiers. They made a strange mix, with the Knights of the Temple appearing the least genteel in their mail and white cloaks with no other ornamentation. All the others were festooned with fine mantles and jewelry.

Catherine kept her toes wiggling in her thin shoes through which she could feel the cold stone floor. At last the service ended. Then the donation was read out and signed by the witnesses. The knights cleared a path to enable Queen Adelaide and her maids, King Louis and his men, Genta and Master Evrard to proceed out. At last the rest of the guests were permitted to leave.

"Don't try walking across the courtyard in those silly shoes," Edgar told Catherine. "I'll get the horse and come back for you. Stand here by the *perron*."

Dutifully, Catherine waited by the stone block used for riders to stand on while mounting their horses. She looked around at the rest of the company. The king had already left, but William, his butler, was talking with the queen, who had had the forethought to bring a rug to lay over the mud so that her feet were warm and dry while her chair was being brought to her.

Archer's wife, Richilde, bowed to her from the other side of the yard, as she listened to Thierry Galeran, one of the courtiers. It was clear that Richilde wanted Catherine to notice that she also had friends in high places.

Catherine was regretting being there at all, when a voice greeted her. The man was standing directly behind her. She jumped when he spoke, nearly landing in the mud, herself.

"*Dex vos saut*," he said. "Lady Catherine."

"Good evening, Master Durand," Catherine said. "I noticed you at Mass. I hope you're keeping well."

Durand lifted his eyebrows. "Do you? Thank you. It surprises me that you're here."

"Really?" Catherine raised her eyebrows back at him. "My husband and I have been eager for your report on the unfortunate knight. Have you discovered his identity?"

"Not yet," Durand answered. "When I do, you and your husband will be among the first to know."

He smiled thinly and continued on his way. Catherine shivered. She devoutly hoped he wouldn't be at the banquet at Genta's.

Edgar soon returned, and they followed the procession to the suburb of Les Champeaux, where Genta had set up a large tent for the banquet. Outside, guests were being entertained by jugglers, tumblers and a fire-eater. From inside came the sound of musicians and the clink of dishes.

"Want to wager what side of the salt we'll be placed at?" Edgar said as he helped Catherine dismount.

"If Margaret were with you, we'd probably have a salt cellar all to ourselves," Catherine answered. "But as it's only me, I suspect we'll be at the foot and never see the seasoning at all."

Catherine was mistaken. They were placed at a side table above the saltcellar but only just. She and Edgar were given a silver *escuelle* to eat from and put the remainder of bread or meat bones in. A servant handed out silver spoons. Another pair came around with soap, water, basin and a towel for them to wash their hands.

Then the bread was broken and sent around the table and the courses began to be carried in.

"Where did she get all this meat at this time of year?" Catherine said in wonder as platters went by piled high with smoked pork, fowl and game.

First they were given eels in saffron sauce, then chicken in cumin and garlic, then an assortment of vegetables with lentils and every fresh herb that grew in France, Catherine thought. Then the pork was sliced and handed out. After that there was quail roasted with its own eggs, and a swan. Servants circled constantly to fill the wine cups or replace napkins as they became too greasy to use.

Catherine was already queasy when the washing water was brought around again and the *escuelle* removed before the sweets and the raisin wine were served.

"We'll have no chance to talk with Master Evrard," she muttered to Edgar. "We're trapped in our place, and if I even smell more food, I'm going to throw up."

"Breathe deeply," Edgar advised. "I knew we would have little chance to gossip. But we can observe."

"I suppose," Catherine said, as she signaled for more water to mix with the wine. "All I see are a lot of people in fine clothes that are rapidly becoming stained."

Edgar smiled. "*Carissima*, I know you prefer student debates to the feasts of the nobility, and I agree. But try to put aside your intolerance and notice what Genta is accomplishing tonight."

Catherine gave the cup to Edgar to sip from and tried to follow his suggestion. What did he want her to see?

At the high table, Genta sat with Queen Adelaide and her husband, Roger, at her right. On her left was Master Evrard, looking about as uncomfortable as Catherine felt. There were other members of the court on either side of them. Interspersed among the courtiers were Archer and Richilde and Giselbert Engania, or Trickster, who was now master in the enamelers' guild. His nickname, however, came from his youth when he had earned a few *maille* on the side from making dice that could be counted on to fall as they were told.

It did seem an unusual combination for the high table. The nobility, of course, but why the tradesmen? And, as she looked around the room, she wondered why, other than Knights of the Temple, there were no clergy?

"What is Genta doing?" she asked Edgar. "There's no one from the king's court except the butler. Louis didn't even come to Champeaux after the donation. There's no one from the bishop's court or any of the monasteries. And Queen Adelaide is sending bits from her dish to a common guildsman."

"Well, it might be that these are the only people Genta knows," Edgar said. "But I think she's telling us something."

Catherine tried to think what it might be.

"Well, it can't be that she's a heretic, or she wouldn't be associated with the Temple." She took the cup from Edgar. "The lower tables are almost all guild masters, merchants, the wealthy of the city."

"Right, and Genta counts herself among them," Edgar prompted.

"Edgar why don't you just tell me your conclusions," Catherine said. "I've had too much wine and food to think."

"Very well," Edgar said. "I think she wants us to know that she has power. The gift to the Temple was nothing, but it's a way to remind the rest of us that she has a connection to Jerusalem and those who guard it. In the coming months much of our business will depend on the success of the army. Will the king bankrupt us or bring home booty as well as glory? Genta may be deciding to traffic in information."

"And by associating the gift with Queen Adelaide and the memory of old King Louis, she reminds us that she has the protection of the king, as well," Catherine finished. "So everyone here is silently calculating what she can do for them and what they'll have to pay for it."

"Exactly." Edgar wiped some gravy from her cheek.

"Your deductive skills aren't as impaired as you think."

"But why were we invited?" Catherine wasn't satisfied. "Is it just because she hoped Margaret would come, too?"

"That I don't know," Edgar admitted. "I'm hoping that at some point in the evening it will be revealed. Look, the bears are being led in."

Catherine didn't need to look. The smell of bear, mixed with lamp oil, meat and a hundred bodies was too much for her.

"Edgar, I've got to get out of here at once." She stood. "I hope Genta thought to arrange for privies. No," she added as he rose. "I can go alone. You've held my head enough times."

Her lips pressed together and the napkin held over her mouth and nose, Catherine hurried out of the tent.

Outside, there were attendants ready to point the way to a row of curtained cubicles. Catherine went into one, only to find nothing but a folding stool with a hole in the seat set over a bucket. The smell from that was worse than the bears. She slipped out the other side and made her way into a wooded area nearby.

Away from the crush of people, she leaned against one of the trees, taking slow breaths of sweet air. She began to feel better but was unsure of what would happen if she moved.

It was nearly dark. The wood was full of shadows and the reflections of the flicker of the torches around the tent. Mist was beginning to creep along the ground. Behind her, the darkness seemed populated by unearthly beings. Catherine stepped out of the concealment of the trees, closer to the light. A few feet away from her, one of the shadows moved.

Edgar enjoyed the dancing bears. They stumbled about with an odd dignity that reminded him of his uncle Æthelræd. The trainers gave them stemmed goblets that they took in both paws to drink from. Then one put its paws on the other one's shoulders, and they marched in step around the tent and out.

It wasn't until the minstrels had returned to sing an interminable lay that had something vaguely to do with Charlemagne but was mostly a series of verses detailing one single combat after another between Christian and Saracen knights that Edgar realized Catherine had been gone an unusually long time. Her stomach had always been sensitive, and several pregnancies had only increased the problem, so her nausea hadn't worried him. The fear crossed his mind that perhaps the *mokh* hadn't been as effective as they had been told. No, he realized, the unaccustomed rich food was enough of an excuse.

He waited a few more minutes. Then, since the minstrels showed no sign of coming to a close, he got up.

Outside he met Giselbert Engania.

"Edgar!" the man said. "Quite a feast, isn't it?"

"Too much for me, Trickster," Edgar said. "I've no head for so much wine anymore."

"And I thought the English were famous drinkers!" Giselbert commented. "I noticed that Catherine decided to leave early, but I assumed you'd stay the course."

"What?" Edgar gave Giselbert full attention. "Catherine only went out for some air."

"From the back of a horse?"

Edgar's hand caught Giselbert's arm. "When did you see her?" he demanded.

"Not long ago," Giselbert told him. "I went out to relieve myself and saw Catherine come out of the woods with a man."

He paused there, for effect, but Edgar's face had turned to stone.

"And?" Edgar said.

"The man was leading a horse. He mounted and pulled Catherine up behind him. They rode off toward Paris."

"You didn't try to stop him?" Edgar said. "Or call out to her?"

Giselbert shrugged. "Why should I? She didn't seem in trouble. It wasn't my business."

"Are you certain it was Catherine? The woods are dark."

"The torchlight shone on her face clear enough," Gisel-

bert insisted. "Her scarf had slipped back, so I could make
out her features easily."

"The man, what did he look like?" Edgar's hold on Giselbert's arm tightened.

"He wore a felt hat; I didn't see his face," Giselbert said.
"He wasn't dressed for the banquet, more like a squire. I
assumed he was a friend of hers."

Edgar didn't like the emphasis the Trickster put on the
word *friend*. But he was too worried to be distracted by it.

"Dressed like a messenger, perhaps?" Edgar said.

"I suppose," Giselbert answered. "But if there was a message, why didn't the man ask for you in the tent? You
needn't pretend with me, Edgar. It's not that unusual. She
probably thought she'd be back before you missed her."

He didn't have time to feel relief when Edgar let go of
his arm because the next moment Edgar's fist crashed into
his jaw, sending him sprawling to the ground.

"You idiot!" Edgar shouted. "She's been abducted and
you did nothing to save her!"

"Don't be so blind, Edgar." Giselbert struggled to get up.
"She didn't call for help."

"Get out of my way," Edgar shoved him down again.
"Here, you! Bring my horse at once!" He called to a passing
servant. "No, never mind. I'll get him myself."

Giselbert sat on the grass, rubbing his jaw.

"You're the one whose slackbrained, Edgar! Or you'd
know when you'd been cuckolded!" he yelled.

"*Or poes aler au lagon!*" Edgar screamed back.

As he watched Edgar gallop by, Giselbert was helped to
his feet by the servant.

"You'll be in hell long before I will!" he shouted.

Edgar was too far away to hear.

The darkness soon forced him to slow to a walk. The path
was uneven and hard to follow. He was close enough to
Paris to make the ride in less than an hour in daylight. But
from all he could see, he might have been at the edge of
the world with no other soul within a day's journey. He
cursed himself for not having stopped long enough to take

a lantern. But there hadn't been time to spare.

What could have possessed Catherine to go off like that without telling him? Edgar couldn't think of a reason dire enough. Trickster must have been mistaken. Either the man who took her had forced her in some way, or, and now he slowed even more, the woman he saw hadn't been Catherine.

Should he go back? What would she think if she returned to the banquet only to find him gone and the only person to witness his departure a man whom he had just knocked down and consigned to perdition?

As he dithered, Edgar heard the sound of a horse approaching from the opposite direction. He cursed himself again, realizing that he was out in the middle of the forest, in the middle of the night, dressed in gold and jewels, with only a meat knife to protect himself and his only hand needed to guide the horse.

The glow of a lantern shone as the rider came around a curve in the pathway. Edgar waited. Usually brigands don't carry light.

The other rider came closer.

"Edgar?"

Edgar blinked. He couldn't make out the face behind the light.

"Astrolabe? Is that you?"

"Thank the Virgin I found you!" Astrolabe answered.

"What's going on?" Edgar's worry for Catherine expanded. "Are the children all right? Have you seen Catherine?"

"They're all fine, but you must come with me at once," Astrolabe answered as he turned to lead Edgar home.

"Tell me what happened," Edgar said.

Astrolabe twisted in his saddle. "It started just after dark, when the guards came to the door to say that someone had tried to get into the garden but that they'd chased him off."

"Did they know who it was?"

"They weren't close enough to him to make out the face," Astrolabe continued. "But, not long after, Abraham's son, Joel, came with a message for Solomon. Solomon became very agitated. At first, I assumed there had been more trouble between the Jews and the pilgrims. Joel told him to come at once. Solomon asked me to stay and promised to send word as soon as he could."

"But what about Catherine?" Edgar demanded.

"I'm coming to that," Astrolabe told him. "I went back and helped Samonie and Margaret put the little ones to bed. Margaret was sure Solomon had gone out to get himself killed. It took some time to calm her. Then Joel returned, this time with a message from Catherine that I was to go and find you at Les Champeaux and bring you to Abraham's house at once. Of course Margaret believed all her terrors had come true. I had to assure her that I'd return as soon as I'd taken you there with a full report, or I believe she would have insisted on going to Abraham's herself."

This recital had Edgar's head spinning. In part he was still concerned that something terrible had happened, but he was also growing angry. Catherine shouldn't have been so thoughtless. Whatever it was, she should have come for him before leaving. He had no doubt that Giselbert Trickster was now regaling the party with the tale of how Edgar had gone chasing off after his adulterous wife.

"Who is watching over my children and my sister?" he asked sharply.

"Samonie and Martin are staying up until we return, and the guards are now at both doors," Astrolabe answered. "They'll be safe. Any possible danger is at Abraham's, and since Catherine is there . . ."

"Yes, we must hurry," Edgar urged. "Hold the lantern out more. I'll follow you."

Soon houses began to appear from the darkness, first a few and then in clusters and finally they were back in the city, entering north of the main gate. A beggar trying to sleep against a wall pulled his feet in as they passed, and a pair of drunken young men tried to snatch the reins of Edgar's horse. He kicked them off with an oath.

The *rue des Juifs* was silent as they rode down it to Abraham's home. The dull thud of the horses' hooves in the mud echoed in the narrow passageway. Edgar had the sense that behind the shuttered windows everyone sat alert, ready to defend themselves or flee from an imminent assault.

They arrived at the house. Before Edgar could raise the knocker, the door opened. Joel came out and took the reins as they dismounted.

"Go upstairs," he whispered. "I'll see to your horses."

As they went up the steps the door at the top opened and Catherine came out. In two bounds Edgar was beside her, not sure if he wanted to kiss or shake her. She solved the problem by throwing herself into his arms and sobbing.

"I'm sorry," she said when she could speak. "I had to come. Solomon was afraid that if he came into the banquet for us, there would be too many questions. I didn't dare wait."

"Catherine, *I* have questions," Edgar said. "What, by the holy face of Lucca, is going on here?"

"He couldn't reach us," Catherine sniffled. "One of our guards threw a rock at him. He barely made it to Abraham's. He's hurt and in such danger. What are we going to do?"

Solomon came out on the landing, his face grave.

"I apologize, Edgar," he said. "Come in. He wants to talk to you."

Edgar followed him into the hall. At one side of the room a brazier had been lit, even though the night was warm. Near it a bed had been made up, and in it a man was lying, his head wrapped in a bandage. He gaunt face was hidden by a thick black beard liberally streaked with grey and it was a moment before Edgar realized who he was looking at.

"Hubert!" he cried. "What are you doing back home? Jesus' tears, man, don't you know that if they find you here, you'll be killed?"

Fourteen

The house of Abraham, the Vintner, sometime before Matins, Friday, 10 kalends June (May 23), 1147; 21 Sivan, 4907. Feast of Saint Bobo knight of Provence, who conquered and converted Saracen pirates.

. . . et ut fieri solet quod morbus obliquii ab uno serpat in omnes . . .

. . . and, thus it is common that the malady of evil talk creeps from one person to another and then to all . . .

—William of Malmesbury
Gesta Regum Anglorum
Book II, Part 201

Catherine went to sit on the floor beside the bed. She took her father's hand.

"Edgar is right," she said. "We would have found a way to come see you in Arles eventually. You shouldn't have taken such a risk in returning to Paris."

Hubert squeezed her hand. "I had to come, my dear, but not for you. I know you would all be safer if I never went near you again."

His voice was weak. Edgar guessed that the blow the rock had struck wasn't the cause of his frailty. Hubert looked to him like the hermits of the forests who survive on nothing but roots and rainwater. He had the pallor of a man who never so much as smells red meat.

"You would be safe forever if you truly came back to us," Catherine said wistfully.

Hubert sighed and loosed his hand from hers.

"That cannot be, my precious child," he said. "No matter how much I love you, it's only since I have returned to the faith of my ancestors that I've found peace. I've so many years to atone for, so many things to learn."

"They don't seem to have agreed with you, Hubert," Edgar said. "Have you been ill?"

"No, not at all." Hubert gave a wan smile. "But from the way my clothes hang on me, I don't blame you for thinking it. I occupy myself so fully with my studies that I forget to eat, sometimes even to sleep. I feel as if a whole world were being shown to me, and I want to see as much as I can before I die."

Rebecca entered the room, followed by a servant with a tray.

"You've all had a shock," she announced. "I've made up a *tisane* to restore you. Husband, have you given Chaim a chance to explain why he's here?"

It was a moment before Catherine remembered that Chaim was her father's original name, before he had been taken by a Christian family and baptized.

"I was just coming to it, Rebecca," Hubert said. "I've let myself wander far from the matter at hand."

"No wonder, with that bump on the head," Rebecca said as she poured the cups of hot spiced wine. "Imagine being attacked outside your own house!"

"As for that," Hubert said, as Edgar began to apologize. "I'm glad you had the sense to hire guards. With all the evil roaming the streets these days, you need more protection than a few prayers and rowan branches at the windows."

"I'm not fool enough to let charms be my family's sole defense. But you speak as if there were a specific evil, Hubert," Edgar said. "What is so threatening that you'd risk your life to warn us of it?"

"Nothing that would endanger you," Hubert said. "There was something I had to leave behind last winter. Now I've found a safe place to put it. There was no one I could trust to send to retrieve it."

Catherine couldn't accept the idea. "You don't mean that there is a treasure in the house, after all?" she said. "I told everyone that it was only a rumor."

Hubert grimaced. "I'm sure no one believed you. Everyone thinks merchants hoard gold and jewels. But no one has given you trouble, have they? Is that why you have the guards?"

"Not precisely," Edgar hedged. "But why didn't you warn us long ago? The house was broken into before we got back from Germany. We thought nothing had been taken, but perhaps this treasure of yours has been stolen."

"It can't have been!" Hubert cried. "I hid it in the counting room and locked both the chest and the door."

Hubert struggled to sit, but Catherine pushed him back down.

"I've been all over the counting room," she told him, "And found nothing there. And, unless you left a dead Temple knight along with your treasure, someone else was in there."

"A what?" Hubert did sit up this time, closing his eyes at the abrupt pain in his head.

"Catherine!" Rebecca scolded her. "Think what you're saying! Chaim, drink this and calm yourself."

She moved Catherine away from the bed and bent over Hubert with the tisane. He sipped a little, then pushed it away. His heart was racing and his hands numb with dread.

"What were the Knights of the Temple doing in our house?" he said. "Of all people!"

"Hubert, we didn't let them in," Edgar told him. He proceeded to explain their discovery.

"And we still have no idea who the man was," he finished. "We thought it might be a Lord Osto, but . . ."

"Osto? The Picard? What would he have been doing dressed as a brother of the Temple?" Hubert's head was spinning. He had only been gone a few months, and it seemed that all he had left behind was in chaos.

"I don't know," Edgar said. "A man came looking for Osto, but said our description of the body didn't match. The knight was a man of about your age, I'd guess, or a little younger, with blond hair going to grey."

"Not Osto, then," Hubert said. "He hasn't had any hair to speak of since I've known him. But this makes no sense." He pulled the blanket off and swung his legs over the bed. "I have to get home and see this for myself."

He was overpowered by the others in a moment.

"Chaim! It's the middle of the night," Abraham reminded him. "You'll stay with us, all of you, until dawn. At this hour only thieves, drunks and monks are abroad. Do you want to be challenged by the watch?"

"Catherine and I need to get back to the children," Edgar

said. "We'll risk the ruffians. Astrolabe, will you come with us or stay?"

"I'll come," Astrolabe said. "The three of us on horseback should intimidate even the watch."

Hubert was still resisting those who were trying to keep him in bed. At the mention of the children, he stopped struggling.

"My grandchildren? They haven't been harmed by this, have they?" he asked. "And poor Margaret! She's suffered enough for us."

"The children were fine when we left, Father," Catherine said. "But what you tell us, or rather, *won't* tell us, makes me uneasy about being away from them."

"Yes, I would like to see them again." Hubert sighed. "I never even learned if the new one is a boy or a girl."

Catherine winced. "The baby died, Father, in the winter. It was a girl."

Hubert fell back onto the pillow, his eyes closed.

"I am so sorry," he said softly. "I know well, that no matter how many survive, the ones taken from us leave an ache that lasts forever."

"Yes," Edgar said. His voice was harsh. It was a subject he didn't want to discuss. "We'll return to see you early tomorrow, Hubert. If you tell us what we're looking for and where you left it, we can give you a report then."

Hubert rubbed his forehead, dislodging the bandage. "Yes, very well. It's a wooden box, the length of my arm and about two handsbreath in width and depth. I nailed it shut. I put it in the chest with the false bottom."

Catherine stared at him. "And which one is that?"

"I showed you years ago," Hubert said, then paused, rubbing his head. "Or maybe it was your mother. The one that holds the books. Surely you noticed how shallow it is inside?"

Catherine felt exceedingly stupid. She had noticed, but it had never occurred to her to ask why. If thieves had searched the chest, she knew they would have seen the false bottom at once.

"We'll look there as soon as we get back," she promised. "And bring you the box in the morning."

Solomon saw them to the gate.

"Try not to be angry with him, Catherine," he said.

Catherine bit her lip. Edgar answered for her.

"He's put our family into danger and made it impossible to clear ourselves of suspicion because of the need to protect him." He spoke quietly but with great intensity. "We have every right to be furious."

"I know," Solomon said. "And he does, too. He'll never find the peace he seeks unless you forgive him."

"A man who abandons his family and the true God needs more forgiveness than I can provide," Edgar said.

He turned away and, using his loop, pulled himself clumsily onto his horse.

Catherine gave Solomon a pleading look as Astrolabe helped her to mount the horse behind Edgar.

"Let's not speak of it tonight," she begged. "We need time."

Catherine held tightly to Edgar as they made their way through the dark streets and over the bridge, where they were challenged by a startled guard but quickly permitted to pass. Edgar's tone brooked no opposition. Catherine could feel the anger in every muscle. Her own feelings were so confused that she couldn't sort them out. She had longed terribly to see her father again, but he had changed so much that now he seemed a stranger.

Hubert's leaving had made it difficult for them. She knew how hard Edgar fought his own nature every time he dealt on equal terms with the merchants and craftsmen of Paris. They both hated lying about Hubert's "pilgrimage." They had only done so for the sake of love.

Why hadn't he told them about the treasure before he left? Why couldn't he have trusted them with the knowledge of what it was. Had her father been taking church plate or relics in trade? Was there something else that would prove he had always been Jewish? How could they defend themselves without knowing that much? What if

intruders had ransacked the house and found this thing?
What they had found was bad enough. Why, she cried in
her heart, why couldn't he have remained a Christian for
their sakes, if not his own?

Hubert was having many of the same thoughts lying in
Abraham's house, instead of the one he had spent his whole
adult life in on the Grève. He had felt the accusation in his
daughter's tone, hidden beneath her concern for him. It
wasn't even hidden in Edgar. He didn't blame his son-in-
law for his anger. The protection of the family was the most
important thing, and Hubert knew he had jeopardized that.

"I should have left it there," he muttered. "Perhaps it
never would have been found."

"That's right," Abraham said. "And it would have been
lost to us forever. You're doing a brave thing, Chaim."

Hubert turned his face to the wall.

"I doubt that my daughter would agree with you," he
said. "But thank you, old friend, and good night."

Solomon had taken his drink over to a corner of the room
and settled down on a pile of cushions. They assumed he
was asleep, but his eyes were bright in the glow of the
brazier, and he didn't doze off until after the first roosters
had welcomed the dawn.

"Edgar, I'm not going to bed until we've checked the book
chest," Catherine said, as he waited for Astrolabe to help
her down.

"Hush, Catherine, you'll wake the house," Edgar said.
"Do you want all the neighbors to hear?"

"Oh, dear!" She said no more until they were inside.

"Catherine! Edgar! Is he all right?"

They looked up. There at the top of the stairs sat Margaret, her braids undone and her hair flowing loose so that
she seemed surrounded by an auburn curtain. Her eyes were
puffy from tears and wakefulness. Catherine ran up to her
at once.

"Oh, *preciocissma*!" she said as she took the girl in her
arms. "Did no one tell you? Solomon is fine. Nothing has

happened to him. Were you waiting all this time?"

"Didn't the messenger I sent tell you there was no need for concern?" Astrolabe asked. "He did come, didn't he?"

Margaret sniffed and nodded. "I thought you were just trying to keep me from worrying and coming over to see for myself."

"Yes, we were." Edgar came up the steps and sat on her other side. "But only because there was nothing you needed to fret about. And now look at you, *deorling*, you don't even have slippers on. Is Samonie in the children's room?"

"I'm here." Samonie's voice came from the landing above. "James and Edana are sound asleep; Martin, too, poor boy. And I'd like to go to my bed now, as well."

She came down the stairs, still holding the poker she had kept to hand all night to fight off villains.

Edgar couldn't help but smile.

"Thank you, Samonie," he said. "You've defended the castle bravely. Sleep all you need to. Catherine and I will get up with the children tomorrow."

Catherine moaned and yawned but nodded agreement.

"Thank you, Master," Samonie said. "But it is tomorrow. I'll put the barley on to soften before I sleep. Master Astrolabe, there's water to wash in the hall and a bed made up for you."

"I'm forever in your debt," Astrolabe said, and vanished into the hall.

Edgar took Margaret by the elbow and led her up to her bed. Catherine followed to check on the children before she snatched whatever rest she could before they awoke.

Once Margaret had been settled, Catherine headed for the counting room, but Edgar stopped her.

"It will wait, *leoffest*," he said. "We've had a harrowing evening, and we both need sleep. No one will take Hubert's treasure before morning."

Catherine was almost falling down with fatigue. Edgar closed his eyes and rubbed his forehead.

"But Edgar!" Catherine couldn't believe him. "How can you think of sleeping?"

"I'm exhausted," he said. "And so are you. Your father

has caused us enough trouble for one night."

She felt shaky and ill from too much food, wine, fear and shock. She didn't even have the energy to cry, much less argue. They went into their bed chamber. As they took off their elegant, stained banquet clothes, she shook her head at their condition. She'd never wear those shoes again. Then, just as she got into bed, she brightened.

"At least," she murmured into the back of Edgar's neck, "I didn't have to sit through those damn dancing bears."

They thought they would be awakened by the happy squeals of their progeny jumping onto the bed. However, soon after daybreak and the opening of the city gates there was a pounding on their door.

Catherine barely opened her eyes as she heard Martin trudging down to see who was disturbing them, but Edgar was alert at once and was throwing his tunic over his head and pulling on his *brais* before they heard the creak of the hinges and Martin's querulous voice demanding to know who wanted them so early.

Edgar was down the stairs before Martin even started climbing them.

"What is it?" he demanded.

"Some servant of the Lady Genta's." Martin shook his head. "Old poke nose wants to know if everything's all right, as you left her gathering so suddenly."

"Origen's lost genitals!" Edgar swore. "As if we didn't have enough. Go on up and tell Catherine not to worry. I'll deal with this."

He opened the door wide to reveal a smirking young man, still dressed as if for a feast. The servant bowed.

"Greetings, Lord Edgar." He smiled. "Mistress Genta sends her regards and asks if she can be of any service to you."

Edgar regarded him as if he were a particularly repellent form of slug.

"Thank Genta for her concern and assure her that we are all fine," he said. "The dinner, while sumptuous, disagreed with my wife. Of course my first care was to see her home safely. Give your mistress our apologies."

The man started to say more, but Edgar had endured enough and shut the door.

He went back up to find Catherine in her shift in the counting room, taking books out of the chest.

"What did the man want?"

Edgar told her.

"Wonderful," she said. "Now I'm an adulteress with no manners and a bad stomach."

"You don't seem terribly upset about your ruined reputation," Edgar said.

"I'm more interested in this. I checked on Edana and James," she assured him, as she saw him look up toward the children's room. "They're playing quietly so as not to wake Margaret. It was their own idea. I don't question miracles. Now." She got the last book out and bent into the chest. "Look! How could I have been so stupid all these years?"

The bottom of the chest was not only several inches higher than the outside edge, but the board wasn't even nailed down, only held in place by a wedge underneath. It was a simple matter to lift it.

"How long do you think he's been hiding this?" Edgar asked.

"Maybe all my life," Catherine said. "What could it be?"

The box they had revealed gave no indication of its contents. Edgar lifted it out with a grunt. It was heavier than he had guessed. Catherine caught it before it slipped from his hand.

There was no rattle. Whatever lay inside was either the same size as the box or well padded.

"Can't we get something to pry it open?" Catherine suggested.

"No," Edgar said. "It's best to take it directly to your father." He saw her consternation. "I know. I'm afire with curiosity myself, but we might damage whatever it is. And, if we're caught with it, it's better to be genuinely ignorant of the contents."

"Do you think it's something forbidden?" she asked, staring at the uncommunicative wood.

"Yes," he said. "Or it would have been sent with the other valuables to your brother or to Saint Denis."

Catherine looked at the roughly made box. It hadn't been scarred by infernal flames eating their way out. There was no feel of the supernatural about it. Yet her father had never told her of its existence and had put them all at risk by coming back from Arles to retrieve it.

"Edgar, if I don't find out what's inside this box, I'm going to go mad."

Her consternation was so great that Edgar was forced to laugh. She seemed like a small child deprived of a present.

"Very well, Pandora," he said. "I'll get a canvas bag to wrap it in and we'll take it to Abraham as soon as Samonie is awake."

Catherine had forgotten her promise to let the woman make up the sleep she had lost on their account. She made a face and got to her feet.

"Very well," she said. "I'll get James and Edana dressed and fed. Perhaps we'll make so much noise, unintentionally of course, that Samonie won't be able to stay abed but get up to see what's going on."

Thus cheered, she went back up to see what noiseless disorder the children had managed to make.

Edgar did try to be quiet as he crossed the hall to the stairs down to the kitchen, but Astrolabe was already up and gone. Surprised, Edgar went on down to find his friend stirring the barley broth for the morning meal.

"I heard the scraping in the counting room," he greeted Edgar. "Did you find the hidden treasure?"

"We found something," Edgar said. "At least the thieves didn't take it."

"Do you think anyone was looking for it?" Astrolabe asked. "I had the impression that most people thought Hubert had a cache of jewels or rare spices. From the way he spoke last night, I don't think that's what he was hiding."

Edgar threw himself down on a bench in exasperation.

"Astrolabe, I haven't known what was happening in or

around this house since we came home," he complained. "The past three weeks have been nothing but one inexplicable event after another. I'm beginning to think that there never was a body in the house, just a phantasm left by Satan to lead us into disaster."

Astrolabe continued stirring.

"Well," he said after a moment's reflection, "you know I'm not a scholar like my parents or you and Catherine. But I'd say the Devil works more often through people of weak faith rather than confronting the righteous directly. It would be easier for him to use a real body murdered by some poor damned soul than to fabricate one from æther. There, I got up most of the bits stuck to the bottom of the pan. Shall we eat?"

Clemence had not taken kindly to being brought back to the care of the nuns on Montmartre.

"Why can't I come with you to see this Jehan?" she had asked.

Lambert had spent most of the trip up the hill explaining to her why the place they were staying wasn't proper for her. She hadn't believed him, but since he was so earnest about it, she had finally acquiesced.

Now she was sorry. Out there, all sorts of things were happening that could affect her life. All this talk about a body that might be her father. Didn't Lambert realize what that meant? He thought only about the possibility that the two of them might be parted and she coerced into another marriage. That would be terrible, but not as bad as losing both her mother and her father within the space of a month.

She couldn't wait patiently. She didn't want to wait at all.

Her inner turmoil was not evident to the nun who came and asked her help with the alms again.

Clemence opened her mouth to snap a refusal. Then she thought of her mother and followed obediently, offering this sacrifice for the peace of her soul.

There were other women staying at Montmartre. Some of them had been among the party at the Temple the day

before. Clemence wanted to ask them about it but was
afraid of their taking too great an interest in her. Fortunately, they didn't seem to care who listened to their gossip
as they shoved broken loaves at the poor.

"The spoons were all marked, you know," one said.
"And the butler had his eye out for anyone trying to slip
away without giving theirs back."

"Too bad you missed your chance." Another laughed. "I
rather enjoyed myself. Genta doesn't stint with the sauces.
Everything spiced so that you wouldn't know what meat it
was. I'd like the use of her spice box during Lent. I can
only think of so many ways to make eggs and fish."

"I thought it was overdone," a third woman said. "Not
the meat, everything. Genta tries too hard. She knows we
wouldn't have anything to do with her if it weren't for the
old queen's patronage."

"Why not?" Clemence asked, forgetting herself.

The three women turned to stare at her, and she blushed
in embarrassment.

The third speaker, an attractive woman with large green
eyes and rosy cheeks, smiled at her.

"If you're going to stay in Paris dear, you should know."
She let her voice drop slightly. "Genta's really a Jew at
heart. Her parents had her baptized, since they were at
court, but no one really trusts her."

Clemence nodded politely, puzzled. She hadn't ever met
a Jew that she knew of, but her father had dealt with them
and never said anything bad. They were infidels, of course,
but she'd never heard they were untrustworthy.

She wished she were home.

The women went on with their critique of the evening.
The entertainment had been too long, especially the poet.
The pages hadn't circulated often enough with the soap and
water.

"And that poor woman who ran out sick," said one. "I'd
have sent a servant after her at once, to attend to her."

"Didn't you hear?" the green-eyed woman smirked. "She
wasn't ill at all. Giselbert Trickster saw her leaving with

another man. Her husband ran out after her, spewing flames, he told me."

"Are you certain?" the other asked. "She looked positively bilious to me. And you know how Giselbert likes to joke."

Clemence lost interest then.

Despite the amount of clatter Catherine made, Samonie didn't wake until the afternoon. A short time later, Catherine and Edgar set out for Abraham's house. Edgar carried the heavy box in a bag over his shoulder.

"I'm not leaving without seeing what's in it," Catherine said. "I don't care how dangerous Father thinks it is. I'll be consumed by curiousity for the rest of my life, otherwise."

"He owes us that," Edgar agreed.

When they got to Abraham's, they found a number of men and women standing by the gate. They were trying to appear as if they had all just happened to meet there and stopped for a chat. But the eagerness in their faces as they saw Edgar and Catherine ride up was unmistakable.

"Good day, Isaac, Bella, Yehiel," Catherine said to those she recognized. "How nice to see you again."

She stayed close to Edgar as they approached the door, which was opened at once. No one made a move toward them. They only looked on with reverence. It made Catherine acutely uncomfortable. Edgar also felt as if he were carrying some holy relic. He began to cross himself and stopped only just in time to avoid offending those watching. But it made no sense. What could be so holy to Jews? Solomon had often scoffed at the Christian reverence of the bones of the saints.

Joel barely glanced at them as they entered. He reached out to take the box from Edgar.

"No, thank you," Edgar said. "I'm bringing this to Hubert myself."

Joel shook his head. "You shouldn't be there when it's opened. You're idolaters."

Catherine reached out to take his hand. "We'll be respectful, I promise," she said. "Perhaps there will be a miracle and we'll convert."

"Very funny. That this has survived is enough of a miracle for me," Joel said, but he didn't try to stop them from entering the room.

They came into the hall to find Hubert sitting up in bed. Abraham stood beside him. Both were wearing velvet caps. Abraham and Joel were in their best clothing, reserved for holy days. Edgar swung the bag from his back and handed it to Abraham.

It seemed incongruous to Catherine to see the finely-dressed men kneeling on the floor with crowbars, prying up the nails from a crude wooden box. She came closer as the lid rose but Rebecca held her back.

"No, Catherine," she said gently. "This isn't something for a Christian woman to touch. Even we would not open it without covering our hands first."

The box was open now. Abraham let out a long sigh of pleasure.

"The leather is still soft," he said as he lifted the object in his arms. "You've kept it well."

"Will someone tell me what this thing is?" Edgar asked with impatience.

For answer Abraham gently unwrapped the leather casing to reveal a scroll rolled onto two bobbins topped with gold finials. He laid his gloved hands on the cover but did not try to open it.

"It's a Torah," Joel told them. "Very old, from before the time of Saadia Gaon. It was brought to France by Isaac, the emissary of Charlemagne to Haroun el-Rashid, the ruler of Baghdad. On his way back, Isaac stopped in Jerusalem and was given this for the brethren of Ashkenaz. We thought it had been destroyed when the Edomites pillaged our homes in Rouen."

"My father left it with Gervase, the Christian who adopted me," Hubert explained. "He was a friend of my father's and had promised to guard his possessions. I found it among his things when he died. Gervase had kept his oath and never opened the box. I didn't know then what it was, but I brought it to Paris with me and showed it to my brother Eliazar. He thought it would be best kept hidden until a time of less uncertainty."

Catherine craned her neck to see better. She wondered if any woman was allowed to touch the Torah. Perhaps it was something like the shrine of Saint Cuthbert in Durham, where the saint refused to allow even devout women near his tomb.

Edgar also stood back. "But Hubert, this is still a very unsettled time for Jews," he said. "Why reveal it now?"

"Joel and I are taking it back to Arles with me," Hubert said. "I realize now that all times are uncertain and, if this is to survive, I couldn't leave it in a place where it might be found, stolen or, worse, burned. Now you see why I was always so fearful of fire in the counting room. The responsibility weighed on me even more as I began uncovering the mysteries of the words of the Holy One. I had thought about sending it back to Rouen, but not with the war in Normandy. We are going to give this to the community of scholars in Arles to keep in the synagogue. They will guard it safely in a vault of stone."

Catherine hadn't heard Solomon enter the room. When his arm went around her shoulders she turned to him and smiled.

"You don't have to stand apart from it," she told him. "It's your holy book."

"And yours," he reminded her. "I'm not worthy to touch it. My sinful hands would turn black and shrivel to cinders."

Catherine looked away. Solomon rarely voiced such deep belief. His pain at his own failings hurt her as much as his refusal to become Christian. She squeezed the hand resting on her shoulder.

Having assured himself that the scroll was still intact, Abraham took a length of silk from Rebecca and wrapped it carefully again before putting it into the leather bag.

"Do you understand now why I couldn't send anyone to do this for me?" Hubert asked them. "Three hundred fifty years our family has been the guardians of the Torah."

"I understand that you felt the obligation was yours alone," Edgar admitted. "But you might have trusted us more."

Hubert sank down onto the pillows.

"It wasn't trust I lacked," he explained. "I didn't want the burden put on you."

Catherine had been thinking.

"Father, you're sure that you told no one that you had this book?" she asked. "Never?"

"Your mother knew," Hubert said. "I felt I had to tell her, but she was so horrified, I'm sure she told no one."

"I wonder," Catherine said. "What if she had hinted something, say to her brother, Roger? And what if he had long ago confided it to his comrade in arms."

"Jehan!" Edgar exclaimed.

"Jehan," Hubert echoed. "But he's long gone to fight Saracens."

"Not yet. He's in Paris now," Catherine said. "And I fear he's seeking evidence of something in our house that will finally give him the chance to destroy us all. This may be it."

Fifteen

That same afternoon, at a tavern near Montmartre.

יִשְׂדָאֵל חֶוֹדָה רֵאלוֹהִים אָחֵז הֵם

Israel, Torah and God are one.

—*The Zohar*
Vol III, 4b

*J*ehan was not as angry with his failure as Lambert had feared.

"You couldn't have known how far their tendrils reach," he said, mixing beer into his soup to cool it. "But now you must realize how difficult it will be to bring these monsters to justice."

"If we could only find a way to have someone in authority discover Lord Osto's knife in their house." Lambert munched sadly on a gristly sausage.

"That's the difficulty with these people," Jehan agreed. "I've thought so many times that I had them, but they slip out of the noose like phantoms."

He took a long gulp of beer. "It's up to us. If we could only get into the counting room. I'm certain it holds the answer."

"That must be the most secure room in the house," Lambert said. "Lord Osto used his to hold valuables for half the village, and it was always locked and barred. Only he and his wife had the keys."

Jehan waved away that problem.

"Locks are easily picked, if one has time enough and the trick of it," Jehan confided. "It's getting into the house and past the spells that guard the treasure that can be troublesome."

Lambert was confused. "What sorcery could they have that would defeat men of true faith? Our Lady and Saint Omer shield me, I know."

Jehan's lined face creased in a grin.

"The very thing!" he exclaimed. "I've waited long for a man of your conviction to aid me in my efforts. With certainty like yours, none of their enchantments can touch you."

"But your faith must be at least as strong as mine," Lambert said. "You've even taken the cross."

"Of course," Jehan replied smoothly. "But my face is well-known to them. When I appear they are instantly on guard. However, if you could overcome your repugnance at being in a house where demons lurk and are even carried about like pets, you could be the one to help me obliterate them once and for always."

"Tell me what to do," Lambert said. "I promise not to fail you."

His fervor brought Jehan close to tears. It had been so long since he had a companion to share the burden. Excitedly, he sketched out the plan.

By that afternoon all Catherine wanted to do was fall face-down onto her bed and cry herself to sleep. But Samonie had been waiting for them to return so that she could go get the pork pies from the baker for their dinner. James and Edana were more energetic than usual, racing around the house and tripping in the rushes. Edgar had work to do making arrangements if they were to have anything to trade at the Lendit, so Catherine was, by elimination, the nurse-maid.

The day was threatening rain but the ground in the back garden was still dry, and so she took her lively children out. She started them rolling a ball back and forth, but they wanted her to join the game. Margaret came out to help, but she was as tired as Catherine.

"Thank you for telling me why you went out so hurriedly," she told Catherine as she kicked the ball toward James. "I hate it when you don't trust me with your secrets."

"I always trust you, *ma douz*," Catherine said as she lifted Edana to keep her from being knocked over. "But not all secrets are mine to share. Anyway, the scroll is out of our hands now. If it had been found here, we would have had no explanation, since my father didn't trust me with all his secrets, either. It was wrong of him. I can't protect him, or us, if I don't know where a threat might come from."

They continued a while with the game. James preferred to run after the ball and carry it back so that he could aim it directly at them from close proximity. Catherine threw it nearly to the creek so that he would be some time getting it. While they waited, she sat with Edana in her lap.

"Solomon didn't come back with you," Margaret commented.

"I'm sure he will, soon," Catherine said. "I suppose he has much to discuss with my father."

The sadness in her voice told Margaret not to venture further. Faith, instead of being a bulwark, had become a fence keeping Hubert and Solomon from them. It made Margaret angry. Why didn't God simply make the Truth so manifest that no one could doubt it? Then there would be no more Jews or pagans or Saracens. Of course, she thought as she remembered her family in Scotland, Christians could always find reasons to fight each other. On the whole, it all seemed very bad organization on the part of Heaven. She supposed that was part of being Ineffable.

"Don't sigh so, dear." Catherine smiled at her. "It will be all right soon. Father will go back to Arles. Solomon will stay with us again, until he has to go to trade for more goods. But he'll come back. He always does."

Samonie returned with the dinner, and Catherine gratefully took everyone in to eat. This was a night when she intended to be in bed long before Compline rang.

Edgar had been busy with Martin, replacing the false bottom in the chest and this time fastening it down tightly.

"You should put something else in it," Martin suggested.

"Why?" Edgar asked, bemused. Martin hardly ever gave an opinion about anything except the distressing number of visitors they received.

"Because if I were a thief and found a box with a hiding

place and nothing in it, I'd be suspicious," Martin explained. "I'd think the treasure was someplace else and go on hunting."

"That's excellent logic," Edgar said. "We need to put something in that has value but that we can prove was come by honestly. Can you think of anything?"

Martin was surprised to be asked. He rubbed his chin as he thought.

"What about the boxes of amber that Master Solomon brought back from Russia?" he suggested.

"Yes, that will do well," Edgar agreed. "We won't be needing them until the autumn, when the English and Irish traders come. Very good, Martin."

The boy beamed. Edgar watched him as he deftly handled the hammer and nails, whistling a tavern song between his teeth.

"Martin," he asked abruptly. "How old are you now?"

"I'll be fifteen on Michaelmas," the boy answered.

"That old! I didn't realize how you'd grown while we were away." Edgar rubbed his chin, noting that he needed to visit the barber soon. "Now that your sister is married and your little brother a stableboy at Vielleteneuse, have you thought what you want to do? I could buy an apprenticeship for you with the carpenters, if you like."

Martin dropped the hammer.

"No, Master Edgar, I don't!" he said with passion. "I want to stay here and be appentice to you and Master Solomon."

"Us?" Edgar was taken aback. "Doing what?"

"Whatever you need," Martin said. "Carry messages, help organize the goods, be your squire when you go on journeys. I want to see the world outside of France. I want to go to Spain and England and even Constantinople. I know I could be useful. Just give me a chance!"

The intensity of the boy's plea surprised Edgar. Martin had seemed to him to be a rather doltish boy, a bit sullen even. Now his whole face was alight with desire and intelligence. Edgar unexpectedly found himself wondering who Martin's father was. He knew that Samonie had been

a maid of all work in Troyes, and part of that work had
been to accommodate the men of the castle as well as visitors. It was possible that she didn't even know herself who
had planted Martin in her.

"That is something I'll have to consider and discuss with
Solomon," he said. "I make no promises."

"But you will think about it?" Martin begged.

Edgar nodded. Martin could hardly contain his excitement as he gathered up the tools and went to tell his mother.

Although he was as tired as everyone else, Edgar stayed
up until past sundown, checking all the bars on the doors
and the shutters on the ground-floor windows. He strolled
down to the garden to be sure the guards were staying
watchful. Then he checked the locks again.

He'd passed through exaustion into a kind of otherworldly focus, where everything he looked at seemed somehow clearer and yet not quite real. He laughed at himself.
Without trying, he had reached the level that others attained
only through days of fasting and deprivation.

Once he would have worked off his tension by picking
up a piece of wood and whittling at it until a shape appeared or he lost interest. Now he would have to prepare
his vises and get someone to help him set them up before
he could even begin.

Edgar stared down at his left wrist. In his present state
he almost believed that he saw his hand there, whole again.
He blinked, and the image vanished. They had told him
that the hand had been buried in a box by the church at
Hexham where the accident had occurred. He never could
reconcile the knowledge that while he still lived, breathed
and aged, a part of himself had already rotted and was part
of the earth.

Perhaps, he thought in a flash of understanding, that was
how his grief at the loss of baby Heloisa differed from
Catherine's.

He shivered, although the night was mild. The humors
of the air were causing him to be fanciful.

Later, he slid into bed, trying not to wake Catherine. She

lay curled up facing the wall, one hand beneath her cheek, one of her long braids coming undone. Edgar was tempted to unravel it the rest of the way, as he had once, years ago when he first realized that he loved her.

But his tiredness finally overcame him, and he contented himself with curling against her, his chin resting on the top of her sleeping cap. After all, there was always the morning.

Solomon was trying to adjust to the change in his practical uncle, Hubert. It seemed that, when he had sloughed off the pretense of being a Christian, another man had emerged.

Rebecca had just finished lighting the Sabbath candles. Abraham had gone to the synagogue. Hubert had wanted to go with him, but the others had convinced him that he shouldn't take the risk of being recognized. Solomon had declined to go.

"There will be plenty without me," he said. "Paris always has enough for a *minyan*. I'll stay with Uncle Hu . . . uh . . . Chaim."

Abraham gave him a look of disgust but at a glance from Rebecca didn't pursue the question.

After he had gone, Hubert smiled at Solomon.

"It's good to be here," he said. "Without having to pretend. You see before you a man made whole."

Solomon didn't doubt it. In the warm glow of the Sabbath candles, Hubert's face was beatific.

"You didn't mind then," he asked. "Returning to *cheder* at your age?"

Hubert laughed. "It felt strange at first, to be sitting with the young boys. But I already knew my *aleph-bet*, and the rest came quickly. Now the men I study with are only a third my age. They're kind to me and welcome me like a traveler from a distant land who has sought sanctuary."

"As you are, Chaim," Rebecca said.

Solomon thought he understood. Part of him was envious. He longed for the freedom to do as he liked. He had barely begun learning the secrets of the Talmud when he went to work, picking up the art of trading from his uncles.

He had passed his whole life traveling, seeking out rare goods, bargaining to get the best price without causing resentment in the seller.

He had seen so much that made no sense to him. There were so many questions that ate at him. Like Margaret, he was perplexed by the randomness of fate. If the Holy One had left the answers for man to find, they had to be in His books. Solomon was often tempted to give up his life in France and devote the rest of his days to searching the texts until he found an explanation that satisfied him. Then he thought of those he would be leaving behind and knew he couldn't abandon them.

"But, Uncle," he said, "didn't you realize that your story of going on pilgrimage would be doubted when you spent all the time before you left here, instead of with the priests? You've left Catherine and Edgar with a host of problems."

"I left them the house, goods and money enough to live on for a time and my blessing," Hubert said. "Perhaps I would have worried more if I'd known that Jehan hadn't gone to the Holy Land with Emperor Conrad but was back in Paris. But I did all I could and left my affairs in much better order than many a man does."

"Did no one else have keys to the house or counting room?" Solomon asked, letting Hubert's defense stand for the moment.

"I gave Samonie a house key, but only Catherine and I could get into the counting room," Hubert said.

"But someone did," Solomon said. "The question is, was the body left there to incriminate you or to hide it so the men who killed him would have time to escape?"

"I can think of safer places to hide a body," Rebecca commented.

"So can I," Hubert said. "And you say nothing was taken. It does seem as if someone knew that my daughter and son-in-law wouldn't simply dispose of it quietly but report the death."

Solomon hadn't considered that. "Perhaps they were hoping that Catherine and Edgar would bury the man without ceremony to avoid just the scandal that they've been subjected to."

"It surprises me that anyone expects to discover his identity," Rebecca said. "Paris is full of foreigners these days. With the eagerness of so many of them to fight, I wouldn't be surprised to learn of a hundred such unknown corpses."

"No, it is strange," Hubert said. "Few men set out alone on an expedition. If not friends, he would have had traveling companions, someone willing, for the gift of a cloak or pair of boots, to tell his family of his death."

"The matter may never be explained," Solomon said. "And while the brethren of the Temple may give up the investigation, the gossip will always remain. The street's full of it already, and you know how that can affect business."

Hubert scratched at the bandage on his head. "You know, there are days that I wish I'd never let Catherine come home from the convent," he said. "It seems that since then there's been one crisis after another."

"Oh, really? For ten years?" Solomon said. "You think their god is punishing you for not making your daughter a nun? Hubert, I think you lived as one of them for too long. You've caught their superstitions."

Hubert laughed ruefully. "It's hard not to see a divine hand at work in things we don't understand."

"Of course it is," Rebecca got up from the table. "Because there is a divine hand. If we didn't hold to that, we'd all die of despair. And I don't intend to. Now, Abraham will be back soon and we'll have a nice Sabbath cup of wine before we eat. Both of you are far too melancholic."

The rain that had threatened all day Friday broke loose Saturday morning with thunder and lightning that was a harbinger of summer. Lambert pulled the hood of his woolen cloak over his face as he skidded down the hill from Montmartre. In his haste he slipped and fell more than once, sliding into passersby, causing them to drop their bundles and swear at him. By the time he reached Jehan, he was covered with mud as well as more odorous detritus from the streets.

Jehan wrinkled his nose at him.

"What did you do, roll in all the shit in Paris?" he asked as he backed away.

"Sorry," Lambert said. "I have to tell you though. Clemence is missing!"

"Your wife?" Jehan still kept his distance, but took his fingers from his nose to answer. "How could she be? Did the nuns turn her out?"

"They told me she left after morning prayers," Lambert said. "She said she was coming to find me. But how could she? I never told her where we were staying."

"Did the sisters mention any message she might have received from you?" Jehan asked.

"But I sent none."

"Lambert, anyone can bring a message and say it's from you," Jehan said. "You obviously don't have a devious mind."

Lambert sighed. He didn't.

"What should we do?" he asked. "How can we find her? By the sacred corpse of Saint Omer, if those people have hurt her, I'll . . ."

"I'm sure you will," Jehan tried to calm him. "I'll help you. But before we go to the provost and have his men confront them, we must be certain of what happened. The nuns said she left alone? Could she be trying to reach you?"

"Of course." Lambert tried to stop shivering. He didn't notice that he was soaked through. "But she only knew your name, and there are Jehans everywhere. Where could she start?"

"The same place we will," Jehan decided. "We'll ask at the stalls and the inns from Montmartre across the Île and out the Orleans road if we must. You told me she was beautiful. Someone will have noticed her."

He didn't add that there were many in town who would do more than notice a young girl, lost and alone. Lambert was agitated enough. He found himself hoping, for more reasons than one, that Edgar and Catherine had Clemence.

It also occurred to him that she had provided them the perfect excuse for getting into the house on the Grève and searching it without the inhabitants being able to stop them. There was no need to search for long before bringing in the provost.

"Don't worry," he told Lambert. "We'll find her. But first I think you'd better change your clothes. You won't get close enough to anyone to ask about her as long as you're smelling like that."

That morning Catherine was thinking of the peace of the convent with nostalgia. The rain had driven everyone into the hall. Edgar had set up his tools in one corner and was showing Martin how to tell real gold wire from gilt. Margaret and James were trying to teach his puppy to sit on command. Edana was fiddling with the edge of one of the wall hangings on some task known only to herself. Samonie had brought in the sewing, and she and Catherine were trying to decide what could be mended and what made into rags.

"We could use more soft rags," Catherine commented as she sorted.

"With three women in the house, I'd say so," Samonie agreed. "Willa could use some, too, although she hasn't mentioned it lately. I wonder if she's expecting. Fancy, me a grandmother!"

"I can't imagine it," Catherine said. "But I don't remember either of mine. You don't look as if the idea pleases you."

"No, it isn't that." Samonie came out of her reverie. "I was thinking of something else. Nothing that matters."

The yapping of the puppy made conversation impossible for the next few minutes. James had grown bored with training it, and the two were running in circles, the puppy jumping for an old strip of leather James was holding just out of his reach.

"James, stop that at once," Edgar shouted. "Before he bites you."

It was too late. In snapping at the leather, the puppy had

got James's fingers as well. The boy cried out in pain and surprise. Catherine spilled her sewing basket as she rushed over to him.

"Is it bad?" Margaret asked at her elbow. "I'm sorry, I should have stopped him at once."

Catherine examinded the fingers. Edgar knelt beside her, his pale face ashen.

"It's all right," Catherine said, more to reassure Edgar than her son. "It was just a nip. Look the skin isn't even broken. James, you shouldn't tease your dog."

James saw that he wasn't going to get any more sympathy, so he stopped crying.

Samonie was on her hands and knees trying to find all the cards of thread and needles among the rushes.

"We need to sweep these out and change them," she grumbled. "Get some straw with fresh herbs. A family that spills like this one can't leave the rushes a whole month."

Catherine realized she was right. One more tedious task. She hated the trouble of sweeping out the rooms and filtering the garbage from lost pieces of toys or other salvagables.

She was distracted from this concern by a crow of delight from near the ceiling. Catherine whirled around and gasped. They had been so preoccupied by James and the puppy that they had forgotten to keep an eye on Edana. Somehow the child had managed to reach the top of the wall hanging and was now dangling from the rod holding it. At the moment she was too proud of her accomplishment to be afraid, but in another instant she would realize that the only way down was to fall.

Edgar ran up at once and reached out to her. He was tall enough that his hand nearly reached her leg.

"Edana," he ordered. "Jump to Papa."

Smiling, she let go and fell. Catherine let out her breath, Edgar turned around with Edana in his arm.

"If one more thing happens today," he said sternly as he put her down, "I'm going to . . ." He thought. He didn't know what he would do, but he did know that he was on the edge of something drastic. "I'm going to be very angry," he finished.

Margaret shrank from him, hearing an echo of her father's voice in his. Waldeve didn't threaten, he acted. So far she hadn't seen his violence in Edgar but now she was afraid. She bent over and took Edana by the hand.

"Let's go up to our room and see if we can find your doll," she suggested. "Maybe we can make a *chainse* for her from Mama's scraps."

Edana was oblivious to the tension in the room. She smiled and hopped out at Margaret's side.

Edgar looked around. Everyone was staring at him, as if he had been the one causing all the commotion. Even the puppy seemed fearful, cringing in James's lap. That angered him as much as the chaos.

"What's the matter with you all?" he shouted. "I just want a quiet afternoon and some peace to work in!"

"So do we all, Edgar," Catherine said softly.

"Good," he snapped, going to his table to sit down. "Then let's have no more excitement today."

It was inevitable that at that moment there would be a crash of thunder followed by a pounding at the gate. Edgar dropped his pincers and swore.

"Martin, see who that is," he said. "Tell them to enter at their own risk."

"Yes, Master."

Edgar looked at Catherine, who rose and came to kiss his forehead.

"Having a family seemed a lovely idea before the children were born, didn't it?" she murmured.

He looked up at her and smiled. "Most days it still does," he said. "God, what it must be like at your brother's, with all their own and the fosterlings, as well! I should be grateful."

Martin wasn't sure that Edgar was joking. He hoped the visitor was a friend. Astrolabe was supposed to be staying with the canons of Nôtre Dame until Monday, but perhaps he'd come back for something. That would be safe. He slid open the grille and looked out.

Before him stood a bedraggled figure in a long muddy cloak. He couldn't see the face, but the hands appeared feminine, scratched and dirty. He was about to tell the woman to go to Saint Merri for alms when he took another look.

The cloak was mud-splotched, but not ragged. The weave was good and the pattern complicated. The hands were scratched but not callused or gnarled by work. If this was a beggar, then she hadn't been at it long.

"God save you, Lady. Who are you and whom do you seek?" he asked. Catherine had taught him what to say, and, for a wonder, he remembered.

"I'm Clemence, daughter of Lord Osto of Picardy," the girl said. "I'm looking for my husband, but no one will help me find him and, even if you're all demons, I've no place else to go except back to Montmartre and I don't think you're demons, even though Lambert says so and maybe it wasn't an imp that the man had and there may be a perfectly good reason for you to be cutting your bread with Father's knife, so will you please let me in because I'm wet and cold and starving and there's a man across the road who's been following me for ages and I don't like the look of him."

She lifted up her hood then, and Martin was captured in her pleading eyes and delicate face. With no more hesitation, he opened the door and let her come in.

Sixteen

Paris, a wet Saturday. 9 Kalends June (May 24), 1146; 24 Sivan 4907. Feast of Saint Manahen, milk brother of Herod the great, converted by Saint Luke.

> *Douce amie o le vis cler,*
> *or ne vous ai u quester*
> *ainc Diu ne fist ce regné*
> *ne par terre ne par mer,*
> *se t 'i quidoie trover,*
> *ne t 'i quesisce.*

> Sweet love, of bright countenance
> I don't know where to seek you
> But God has created no kingdom
> on land or sea,
> that I would not search through
> If I could find you there.

—Aucassin and Nicolette (35)

$\mathcal{B}$efore allowing him to begin his search, Jehan took Lambert to wash.

They followed the cry, *"li bain sont chaut!"* until they came to a bathhouse. The hot tubs were full of people because of the damp weather, so they were forced to wait until the attendent called their names.

As they sat there, a young woman in a yellow *bliaut* came up to them with a smile. Lambert's first thought was that she must be freezing; her *chainse* was so loosely laced that he could see her bare skin all the way from under her arms to her thighs.

"Would you be wanting some company in your tub?" she asked. "I can scrub all those places you find hard to reach."

Jehan was about to ask her price when Lambert spoke up with indignation.

"What are you thinking of, *jael*?" he said. "Can't you see that this man has taken the cross? Have you no care for his soul, and your own?"

Instead of being chastened, the woman was amused. She gave Lambert a gentle slap on the cheek.

"Just in from the country, are you lad?" She laughed. "In that case I can do both of you for a special price, only for warriors of Christ."

"Never mind the boy," Jehan told her. "You spotted him for a rustic. He's easily affronted, and I humor him. We'll need none of your aid today. But I think I'll be more than ready for a good scrubbing before setting out to fight Saracens. I'll return then and look for you."

"I be waiting with my scrubbing brush." The woman smiled at Jehan and caressed his cheek.

When she had gone, Lambert shivered.

"Don't worry, boy," Jehan said. "We'll soon have you warm and dry."

"I'm not cold," Lambert answered. "That woman made me uneasy."

"That whore?" Jehan laughed. "Are you so much a monk as that? I pity your wife, then."

"Couldn't you feel it?" Lambert asked in wonder. "Her lips smiled and her words were merry, but her eyes were full of hate."

Jehan looked at Lambert with new respect. Perhaps the boy wasn't such an innocent as he appeared. It might be wise to pay more attention when telling him things. It wouldn't do if Lambert started thinking for himself.

At the Temple preceptory Bertulf and Godfrey were in their room after dinner and as content as they had been since the terrible night when their comrade had been killed.

"That was the best wine I've ever drunk," Godfrey said. "And the finest game pie. Do you think the knights feed their men that well all the time?"

Bertulf half opened his eyes. He had been dozing on the pillows that a servant had forgotten to store. "No, Godfrey," he said. "I think we got such a meal only because the pope was eating with us."

Godfrey's jaw dropped. "He was? Which one was Pope Eugenius? I only saw the bishop and a few of the white monks!"

"Eugenius used to be a white monk," Bertulf explained. "Back when he was called Bernardo. It suits him to forgo the regalia of his office sometimes. Especially when his old mentor, the abbot of Clairvaux, is present."

"Bernard was there, too?" Godfrey felt like an idiot. "The most important men in Christendom, and I didn't even recognize them! No wonder everyone was deferring to the monks. I couldn't understand it."

"And no wonder they ate less than anyone else." Bertulf chuckled. "Master Evrard would have done better feeding them beans and lettuce with water to drink. Poor Brother Baudwin! I could see how torn he was between making a good impression and filling his belly. He must have been in agony!"

Godfrey sank back onto his pillows, confounded by what he had witnessed all unknowing.

"Master," he stated, "we must end this pretense before we lose our lives and our souls."

"I know, Godfrey, I know." Bertulf sighed. "But I see no other path for me than to carry out the plan as best I can. Our dream must not be lost because I lack courage to see it through."

"And what shall I tell your wife when I return home?" Godfrey asked with concern.

Bertulf closed his eyes. "That I charge her to maintain our property, to guide Clemence and Lambert in their duties and to pray for me."

Godfrey had been grateful that his duty lay back in Picardy. Now, thinking of those he would have to face there, he wasn't so sure.

Clemence had followed Martin into the house like Saint Perpetua entering the coliseum, peering right and left as if expecting the bears and gladiators to attack any moment.

Instead of a den of heretics, she had found two women working on their sewing and a little boy on the floor with a puppy. The only ominous sight was the one-handed man at a workbench by the window, fashioning some strange object from wood and wire.

She tried to keep Martin from taking her wet cloak, but he was determined to prove his worth as all-round servant and pulled it from her grasp.

"Hang it by the kitchen fire to dry," Catherine told him. "Good afternoon," she greeted Clemence. "Who are you and what brings you to us on such an inclement day?"

She was puzzled when their visitor began to back toward the door, smiling uneasily.

"Edgar?" she asked. "Martin didn't say the girl was a mute, did he? GOOD AFTERNOON!" she said to Clemence again, grinning brightly.

Edgar got up from his worktable and approached Clemence, who continued backing away until she hit the wall.

"Weren't you here a day or two ago?" he asked, squinting to see her more clearly. "Yes, with that poor madman. Is there no one looking out for the two of you?"

Clemence's response to that was to burst into a flood of tears. Edgar turned to Catherine and Samonie with a helpless gesture.

Catherine got up at once, spilling the threads again. She came and put her arm around Clemence.

"Please, *douz amie*!" she begged. "Compose yourself. Samonie, is there any spiced cider on hand? Could you fetch a bowl for our guest? Now"—she guided Clemence to a stool and sat her down—"tell us all about it, if you're able."

Between sobs, Clemence managed to get most of the story out.

"I left the convent this morning," she finished. "I hated it that Lambert wouldn't tell me what was going on. He wouldn't let me stay with him and his friend. This man told him you were sorcerers and in league with the Devil, but I thought even facing Satan would be better than the constant torture of waiting."

She wiped her nose with her damp sleeve. Catherine handed her a clean cloth. Clemence sniffed and thanked her.

"So you came here even though you feared we would hurt you," Catherine said. "That was very brave."

"That was very foolish," Edgar said, frowning. "What do you think your husband will do when he finds you've gone?"

Catherine grimaced. She knew Edgar was speaking from experience.

Clemence looked up at him with her brown eyes wide in supplication.

"I thought I could find him," she said. "But the city is bigger than I believed, and the only place I could find my way to was here. I'm not even sure how to return to Montmartre."

She was so pathetic that Edgar gave in.

"Well, since you have no other guardian at hand," he said, "we'll see to you for now. When you've eaten and your clothes are dry, I'll take you back to the convent. Then I'll try to find your husband for you. Now who is the 'friend' of his who believes us to be so wicked?"

"I've never seen him." Clemence sniffed again. "When we came to Paris, we asked everywhere for Master Hubert, and this Jehan was the only one who would help us."

"Jehan!" Catherine and Edgar cried together. "*Cristesblud!*" Edgar added. They both instantly crossed themselves.

"Clemence, my dear," Catherine said in horror, "if this is the same man we know, then Lambert has fallen in with a lunatic, possessed by a demon of hate!"

"Are you certain?" Clemence's fear dried her tears. "There are many men with that name. Lambert told me he's a knight and he wears the cross of a pilgrim."

"There are indeed many Jehans," Edgar agreed. "But only one who would slander us so. He's an old enemy of ours, who we hoped had vanished forever into Spain with his cross and sword. Catherine is right; his wits are sadly warped, although he may still seem sane to those who don't know the truth behind his wild tales."

"Then we must find them at once." Clemence rose to go. "Before he does something to Lambert!"

"Hush, now," Catherine said. "You say your husband is helping Jehan. As long as he does, then he's in no bodily danger. You should return to Montmartre in case he comes back looking for you. Then you can tell him not to trust his friend. Jehan won't help the two of you find your fathers. Is there no one else you can go to?"

"Only Master Hubert. We came to this house in the first

place because he and my father were friends," Clemence explained. "Father said they would stop with him when they arrived in Paris and before they went to the Temple knights. Lambert's father was to join, if they would have him."

"They never came here," Catherine said. "Father hasn't seen them."

Clemence looked up quickly. "How do you know?" she asked.

"I mean, he left before you say they came here." Catherine hurried to cover her mistake. "Father's been gone since before Lent."

At that moment Samonie came back with the spiced cider and the information that Clemence's cloak was steaming nicely. Clemence took the drink with thanks for Samonie and a worried glance at Catherine, who was inwardly cursing her own stupidity.

"As soon as the rain lets up, I'll send Martin for my horse," Edgar said. "Or did you ride here?"

"We have a mule," Clemence told him, "But I left him with the sisters. The journey here almost finished the poor beast."

"Fine, then I'll take you back to attend to him," Edgar said.

Catherine could tell that his temper was fraying once more. He had had little sleep and much worry the past few days.

As if to emphasize this, there was a flash of lightning followed immediately by the crash of thunder and hard upon it the rush of footsteps as Margaret ran down the stairs, carrying Edana.

"The oak tree in back by the stream is ablaze," she gasped. "The lightning struck it as I watched. It was like a giant flaming finger!"

In her arms, Edana sucked her thumb in a state of unusual quiet.

"It's a sign," Clemence breathed.

"It certainly is," Edgar said shortly. "Martin! Run and get Pagan, Archer and Giselbert! Tell them to put out the alarm. We have to make sure the fire doesn't spread."

"The roofs should be well drenched," Catherine said, more to herself than for Clemence. "But the wind is fierce, and sparks could blow anywhere. Margaret, will you run to Hervice and ask for the loan of a bucket and her servants? Here, give me the baby."

Samonie had already run to get their buckets and was out in the back garden with Edgar. Catherine watched them from the doorway, hoping that the neighbors would arrive before the branch hanging over the fence and above the merchant's grain shed cracked and fell. The shed was thatch and wood and would certainly collapse from the weight of the branch whether it caught fire or not.

Edgar realized that if the branch were cut farther down toward the trunk, where the fire hadn't yet reached, it could be levered to fall back into their property. He also knew that he couldn't manage the ladder and saw himself.

Clemence scurried into a corner out of the way, as Martin returned leading men who carried ladders, buckets already splashing with rainwater, saws and pruning hooks.

Catherine stepped aside to let them out into the garden.

"Trickster!" Edgar called, spotting Giselbert. "Bring that ladder over here. I think we can contain this if we hurry."

Catherine was watching the activity when she heard a squeal from the hall.

"What is it?" she cried as she ran back in.

She found Margaret and Clemence holding a man by his belt as he struggled to free himself without hurting them.

"Archer!" Catherine said in surprise. "Margaret, why are you hanging on to Archer?"

"He was trying to go upstairs," Margaret said. "I saw him as I came back with the bucket. He thought everyone had gone outside."

"I was going to see if the fire had caught on any of the trees by the house," Archer explained, pushing the girls' arms away and trying to regain his dignity.

"We've nothing growing close by," Catherine said. "The danger is more to our neighbors than to us. All the others are in the back. Perhaps you could help them."

Archer gave a curt nod and followed Catherine out.

"You saw him, didn't you?" Margaret asked Clemence. "He was looking for something to steal, I'm sure of it."

"I didn't see him," Clemence said. "I only heard you cry out and came to help you."

"Well, I saw him, and he was sneaking," Margaret said. "People don't sneak when they're trying to help. Oh, and thank you, whoever you are."

By the time the rain and the neighbors managed to leave the oak only a smoldering ruin, everyone was soaked and bedraggled. Samonie opened a wine cask and handed cups around, with Martin refilling them as necessary. The men thanked her and tracked mud and soot back through the hall as they left.

Samonie surveyed the mess.

"I did say the rushes needed changing anyway," she said.

Edgar came in, his face as black as the first time Clemence had seen him, when it was smeared with kohl.

"God spare me another such day!" he exclaimed. "Are we all accounted for?"

"Yes, *carissime*," Catherine said, trying to find a clean spot on his face to kiss. "Actually, we've one extra."

She indicated Clemence, back in the corner, looking tired and confused.

"It's nearly dark," Catherine continued. "We'll have to keep her here for the night."

Clemence overheard her. "Oh, no!" she exclaimed. "Lambert will be frantic!"

"There's nothing for it," Edgar told her. "Montmartre is too far to go in the dark, especially in this weather. Lambert should know that you'd have sense enough to find a safe place to stay."

He looked at Clemence. It struck him that she was about the same age Catherine had been when they met and with the same look about her, as if the world hadn't so much as breathed upon her yet. If Lambert were any kind of man at all, he'd be more than frantic by now. Edgar felt a great pity for him.

Samonie could be heard down in the kitchen, clanging
pans. Catherine looked at Edgar.

"Perhaps you could go down there to wash," she suggested. "Instead of having Samonie bring the soap and water to you."

Edgar listened. The clanging had an angry tone to it.

"We should think about bringing in another servant," he
said. "Especially if we have any more days like this."

"I'm so sorry," Clemence said to Catherine after he had
left. "I've just added to your problems."

"Of course not," Catherine assured her. "You may even
be the answer to some of them. If Jehan is now suborning
strangers to assist in his plans to harm us, then it's well
past time for him to be stopped."

Sometime later they were all relatively clean, the rushes
swept to one side of the hall and a dinner assembled. Catherine and Edgar stood at either end of the table and gave
thanks that the fire had not caused any serious damage.

They had just sat down when the knocker sounded again.
Before Edgar could do more than swear, Catherine got up.

"I'll see who it is," she said. "Perhaps someone left a
bucket behind."

She pulled back the grill and looked out.

"Oh, Solomon," she said. "I didn't think you'd be back
tonight."

"I heard that there were fires on the Grève and I came
to be sure you were all right."

He followed her in.

"By the smell of it, something was burning nearby," he
said. "Hubert was worried, too, by the way."

"Hush." Catherine looked to see if Clemence had overheard. "We're fine, Solomon, just very tired. Here, you can
share the loaf with Margaret. The children are already
asleep."

"Thank you," Solomon said.

He started to sit next to Margaret, then noticed Clemence. He glanced at Edgar, who waved his hand in resignation.

"Our guest for the night," he nodded toward Clemence.

"May the Lord protect you," he said as he straightened. "My Lady . . . ?"

His look was full of admiration. Margaret suddenly had trouble swallowing her bread.

"This is Clemence, Solomon," Catherine said. "She was caught out in the storm. She'll be sleeping with Margaret tonight. I'll explain everything in the morning. Please."

Edgar noted Margaret's stricken expression and bent over his own loaf, groping around in the sauce for a bit of meat. He prayed sincerely that this day was finally ended.

As soon as the Sabbath was over, Hubert started packing his bags.

"What are you doing, Chaim?" Abraham asked.

"The sooner I've gone, the safer it will be for everyone," Hubert said. "Including you."

"What about your daughter and her family?" Rebecca said sharply. "Don't you think you owe them more?"

Hubert responded with equal annoyance. "The best thing I can do for them is vanish. Now that the Torah is out of the house, there's nothing left that can make them appear to be apostates."

"I suppose not," Rebecca said. "Certainly the *mokh* wouldn't . . ."

Hubert gaped at her. "Catherine is using a *mokh*? Why?"

"Because the midwife told her another child so soon could kill her," Rebecca answered. "And from what she told me of her last delivery, I agree."

"And that *mesfaë* son-in-law of mine can't control himself for her sake?" Hubert exclaimed. "Some Christian!"

Rebecca laughed. "You haven't rid yourself of all their attitudes, yet, Chaim. My impression was that it was Catherine who was fed up with abstinence, not Edgar."

Hubert found that thought somewhat unpalatable.

"Well, it doesn't matter," he said. "Even if someone found the *mokh*, they wouldn't know what it was."

Rebecca laughed again, shaking her head at him.

"I could name you a dozen of your neighbors who would

spot it at once for what it was," she said. "Do you think
Catherine is the only Christian woman who has come to
me for instruction? And they talk with each other. How
else would Catherine have known what to ask me for? I
think that when you shed your old life, you lost your common sense!"

Hubert went on with his packing.

"Nevertheless," he stated, "my presence is dangerous to
them and to you. I'm leaving at dawn."

"Alone?" Abraham asked. "With no guard? How far do
you think you would get before you were relieved of everything you have, from the Torah to your boots and *brais*?"

"I've traveled these roads most of my life," Hubert said.
"I know how to avoid brigands."

"What you carry is too precious to risk, Chaim," Abraham said. "There's a party of traders leaving at the beginning of next week. You and Joel won't be noticed among
them."

"And until then?" Hubert asked. "Must I remain in hiding like some criminal?"

"To the Edomites, that's what you are," Rebecca reminded him. "And I don't consider my home exactly a vile
dungeon."

Hubert hastened to placate her, saying that he wanted no
better refuge.

"You can pass the time studying," Abraham said. "Rabbi
Jacob has loaned us some of his grandfather's tractates to
copy. Rabbi Isaac explains the meaning of the Bible carefully and clearly. It's just what you need before going on
to the Talmud."

Hubert agreed with little enthusiasm. The subject interested him greatly, but he wasn't sure Rabbi Isaac's commentary would be enough to overwhelm the feeling of
dread that had been growing in him ever since his return
to Paris.

Lambert had passed a fruitless night, asking for Clemence
at every church, convent and respectable inn. He'd even
tried the Temple preceptory. The doorkeeper there had

turned him away rudely, with the statement that no woman would ever be allowed past him after dark and precious few before then.

"Where could she have vanished to?" Lambert lamented to Jehan.

"The time has certainly come to fear the worst," Jehan shook his head. "We can only assume she's been taken by the demons."

"I prayed we'd find her anywhere else!" His heart was pounding so fiercely that he could barely form the words. "And now we've wasted so much time! What might they be doing to her? We must go to the provost at once."

"I'm reconsidering that," Jehan said. "The guards have no weapons that will harm demons. Has Clemence any protection of her own?"

"She wears a cross of her mother's that has an ampule embedded in it that holds one of the tears of the Virgin," he reminded himself. "Caught in a vial by Saint John at the foot of the Cross."

"Well," Jehan threw up his hands, banishing all doubt, "if you had told me that at the first, I would have reassured you at once. Whom Our Lady protects needs no earthly guard."

Lambert was comforted enough by this to be able to sit quietly while Jehan explained his rescue plan.

"The moon is entering the last quarter and, if we're lucky, there will be clouds tomorrow night, as well, making the street dark."

He sat on the deep windowsill and kicked his heels against the wall. It occurred to Lambert that he had never seen Jehan completely still. The man even tossed in his sleep.

"It should be no problem to evade their guards," Jehan was saying. He stopped. "Are you attending to me, boy?"

Lambert jerked his attention back. "Yes, we evade the guards. How do we get around the sleeping household? Don't we have to go through the hall to reach the steps to the counting room? Surely the servants sleep there."

"No, the woman and her son sleep in an alcove in the

kitchen," Jehan explained. "We'll have to be careful there. But the hall should be empty unless there's a guest."

"And if there is?" Lambert said after a moment. He was trying to keep his mind off Clemence's peril, but it wasn't working.

"If there is, don't worry," Jehan smiled in anticipation. "I'll take care of it."

The smile should have alerted Lambert, but he was too worried about Clemence to notice.

"Must I go back to Montmartre?" Clemence said the next morning. "Is there no one else who could take me in?"

They had finished morning prayers and broken their fast. Edgar had sent for the horse and was in a hurry to take Clemence back and get to the *Parleoir* in time to discuss some Spanish leather with the man who supplied the king's soldiers with tack. Clemence sat at the table with Edana in her lap. Edgar shook his head. It seemed that Margaret and Edana between them had totally allayed Clemence's fears. He hoped the girl wasn't always so trusting.

"There really isn't any other safe place for you," Catherine said. "With Lambert believing Jehan's lies, it would be better if he didn't find you here."

"Yes." Clemence spoke slowly. "He might believe that you've bewitched me. Perhaps you have." She hugged Edana. "But if so, then I find enchantment very pleasant. I only wish you would tell me how Father's . . ."

"Catherine," Margaret interrupted, struck by a new idea, "I know Clemence isn't used to rough quarters, but the felt maker has decided to rent a room on his second floor, just until the pilgrim army leaves. His wife doesn't much like the idea of soldiers or students there. She'd be pleased to have a wellborn lady stay with them, and I think could be persuaded to bring her meals up so Clemence needn't go out. And Willa would be right there to see that she's well taken care of."

"Oh, that would be wonderful!" Clemence exclaimed. "And when I find him, Lambert could join me and not have to room with Jehan anymore. But what about . . ."

"That would be a blessing," Catherine said doubtfully, not hearing the last words. "Edgar?"

She could tell that Edgar wasn't pleased with this. Clemence would perforce still be under their protection until she was safely bestowed on either the nuns or her husband.

Edgar pulled at his chin, bending his mouth into an exaggerated frown. The three women stared up at him, four if one counted Edana. Blue, brown and light green eyes pled with him to agree. He decided to accept defeat.

"Very well," he muttered. "If the room is decent and hasn't already been promised, I'll take Clemence there instead of to the nuns."

"Thank you, my lord, thank you." Clemence slid Edana to the floor and knelt before him. "I'm forever in your debt."

"That's no matter," Edgar answered, embarrassed. "Margaret, do you know how much the price of the room is?"

There was a swift change in Clemence's expression.

"Price?" she repeated. "Of course. I hadn't thought of that. I'm afraid I have nothing to pay with, unless you'll take my necklace as a pledge."

She began to unhook it. Edgar closed his eyes and hit his forehead. Not even Catherine had been this naive.

"I'll settle later with your husband." He sighed. "Or your father. For now, let's simply find you a place that will suit you."

And, he said to himself, where you'll be off my conscience.

He could have sworn he'd said nothing aloud, but Catherine's look told him she knew exactly what he was thinking.

Seventeen

The courtyard of the Temple preceptory, Paris. Monday,
7 kalends June (May 26), 1147; 25 Sivan, 4907. Feast of
Saint Augustine, not the one who confessed; the other
one, the first Archbishop of Canterbury.

*Sensus vero rationalis in tribus existere dignoscitur, in-
genio videlicet, ratione, memoria; quae in animalium
capite distinctis, et ordinatis cellulis, ancipite, sincipite,
occipite vigere et exercere
propria creduntur officia.*

Rational understanding is usually spoken of as including
the threefold faculty of discernment, reason and memory.
It is considered that in the heads of animals these three
faculties occupy each a particular section, in the order of
front, middle and back of the head where each exercises
its particular function.

—Isaac of Stella
Sermon for Septuagesima Sunday

*T*he ground was beginning to crust and dry from the storm of the previous Saturday. Bertulf and Godfrey had taken Vrieit out in the sun to brush and groom him. He glistened under their attentions, and his strong muscles were well defined beneath his coat.

"I never thought when he was born that Vrieit would be the one we took into battle," Bertulf said sadly. "I had hoped to sell him to a great lord who would ride him only in jousts."

"We trained him for what he'll do best," Godfrey said as he sponged stable mud from Vrieit's legs. "I feel better knowing he'll be with you. He won't panic at the first smell of blood."

"Yes, it's good to know my horse is braver than I," Bertulf said.

"You won't know that until you face the enemy," Godfrey said. "But I believe you have as much courage as any man I know, my lord."

"Hush," Bertulf said. "Here comes Father Durand. He'll want to know if we've made any progress, I suppose."

Both men bowed as the priest came up to them. He greeted them politely but, instead of asking about the investigation, his interest seemed to be totally taken up with Vrieit.

"A fine animal," he commented, walking around the horse without taking his eyes off him. "How did you two come by him?"

"We bred him ourselves," Bertulf answered. "From a Spanish stallion. Took years to produce him. He's sturdy as a Norman pony but faster and, as you can see, larger, but still small enough to mount without a *perron*, if necessary."

Durand whipped around. "*You* bred him?" he asked. "And where did you get the money to buy this stallion, to begin with? What right have you to own a horse like this? He's clearly a mount for a nobleman, not a miller."

Bertulf was dumbfounded. He opened his mouth to ask what business it was of the priest's, who should ride nothing but a mare or gelding. Godfrey sensed trouble and answered quickly.

"We did indeed breed him," he insisted. "With my lord, Osto. When Master Bertulf made it known that he was going to join the Knights of the Temple, Lord Osto would have him ride no horse but Vrieit. No other was worthy."

Durand still seemed suspicious.

"A most generous gift. See that you treat him as he deserves," he said. "And now, about the matter of our dead comrade?"

Both men felt their hearts sink. They had tried to make Durand understand that the search for the man's identity was hopeless, but he refused to allow them to quit. For the next several minutes, they were forced to listen to a detailed explanation of what they must do next.

"Remember, this is not just the death of one man," he told them, "He represents one less soldier that we shall have to protect Jerusalem and the pilgrim roads. Whoever killed him has also cost the lives of those he would have saved."

"We wish for nothing more than that his murderer be brought to justice," Bertulf said. "But without knowing who he was, it's impossible."

Durand couldn't seem to tear his eyes from Vrieit. Now he turned to face Bertulf. "I've just remembered. There was a man here the other day, looking for a Lord Osto. We described the body to him, and he said it didn't match. But it is odd to me that someone would be looking for your lord, when you say he's still at home in Picardy."

"We didn't say that," Bertulf replied. "He's gone to Reims to meet with the count of Flanders and wait for King Louis."

"Ah, you saw him on his way?" Durand lifted one eyebrow. "Should the young man return, I'll pass the information to him."

Finally, Durand left to torment some other servant of the Temple.

Godfrey was concerned.

"Who would be looking for Lord Osto?" he fretted. "And not Bertulf and me, as well."

"I don't know," Bertulf said. "But it unsettles me. Perhaps it's time to admit that Osto is dead."

"What will happen to our village, then?" Godfrey asked. "At least as long as there was a chance of his returning, Lady Edwina could perform the duty. Now Lord Jordan is sure to give the keep to one of his men."

"Edwina won't let him."

"She'll only have dower rights," Godfrey said. "Perhaps you should have let Clemence and Lambert marry before we left, although even that might not have been enough, but it would have made it harder to give Clemence and her inheritance to someone else."

Bertulf ran both hands through what was left of his hair.

"Perhaps we should never have attempted such a wild scheme at all." He sighed. "In the panic of the moment, I didn't think it through. But here we are, and any way I foresee our stepping seems to land us even more deeply in trouble."

"Or something just as sticky," Godfrey sadly agreed.

Edgar and Catherine conferred with the felt maker and his wife, who were awed to be hosts to someone like Clemence.

"Will she bring her own bedding?" the wife, Bodille, asked. "I've nothing fine enough. And dishes?"

"I'll see that she's supplied with furnishings suitable to her station," Catherine said. "The main thing is that she be guarded from danger and the sort of people who are all too common in Paris now."

"Don't worry about that," the felt maker said. "We have children of our own and apprentices. Between the heretics and the soldiers, it's not safe to venture out even in the midst of day. We'll see that she's never unaccompanied in the streets."

Clemence wasn't quite as thrilled by that promise as Catherine and Edgar were. She didn't relish being cooped up in this tiny house for the next few days. But it had been her choice, she reminded herself. And, when Lambert did come, these people would give them one bed, something the nuns would not.

And the only important thing now, she reminded herself, was to find Lambert and rescue him from the madman. If, she considered again, he was a madman. She liked Catherine, Edgar and their family. But she knew the Devil hides behind fair faces and manners. And there was still the mystery of how her father's knife had come to be in their house. Somehow, every time she started to ask, they had changed the subject. There must be a way to find out without causing them to become wary of her. There might be an innocent reason, although she could think of none.

If only she could be sure! Without Lambert, there was no one else to trust, no one to turn to. Clemence realized that Catherine was still talking.

"Edgar has sent a messenger to the portress at Montmartre," Catherine continued. "If your husband comes looking for you there, she'll direct him to the felt maker."

"And I'll ask at the *Parleoir* whether anyone has run across him, as well," Edgar said. "I know what he looks like. It's possible he went to one of the other merchants seeking news of Hubert."

They left Clemence only after she vowed not to leave the house without a proper escort, even if Lambert came for her.

"May I come visit Margaret later?" Clemence asked, a plan forming in her head.

"Of course," Catherine said. "I'll send Martin and one of the guards for you."

As they left the house, Catherine and Edgar both felt as if they had aged in the night. Suddenly, they seemed to have more obligations than they could handle. Each had a wistful, if guilty, longing to be unencumbered once more.

"Will you be all right, going home alone?" Edgar asked as he kissed her good-bye in the *parvis* of Nôtre Dame.

"I'm not a sweet young country rose." Catherine laughed. "I know what sort of people to avoid."

"See that you do, *leoffest*," Edgar said with mock severity.

Once he had gone, Catherine dawdled along the streets of the Île, spending some time looking at the stalls of goods set up in the open space in front of the Cathedral. Near the wall of the canons' cloister there was a group of boys and young men listening to one of the masters lecture. She went nearer to hear what the lesson was, but was disappointed to find it an elementary class in arithmetic. It seemed a hundred years since she had sat like that, off to one side, absorbing the teachings of Master Abelard, Robert of Meulan, Gilbert de la Porée, Adam de Petit Pont and so many others. The debates had been lively and exciting. Now Master Abelard was dead, Master Gilbert was bishop of Poitiers. Master Adam was growing old. She didn't know the new teachers, many of whom seemed as young as she.

In a side street a man dressed in patched *brais* and a ragged tunic pleaded with passersby to return to the life of the apostles, give up their goods to the poor and trust to God for their sustenance. He had gathered a small group around him, but most people avoided looking at him or jeered as they went by. Catherine hurried on, feeling uncomfortable with the earnestness in the young man's demeanor. She knew that unless he advocated taking goods from the rich or despoiling the churches as they had done in Rome and other places, no one in authority would trouble the fervent reformer to get a license to preach from the bishop, but no one was likely to act upon his suggestions, either.

As she made her way to the bridge, Catherine was tempted to stop at Abraham's to see her father. It was true that he had seemed to cast them off along with Christianity, but she couldn't stop loving him. How dangerous could it be to drop by for a few minutes?

She had just made up her mind to go and had even turned her steps back when she saw a familiar shape from the corner of her eye. Quickly, she ducked behind a stack of pewter dishes outside a shop and peeked around them in the hope that she had been mistaken.

No, it was Jehan.

Her first impulse was to throw herself at him, kicking and pounding. The intense anger that surged through her had been building for years. Just once she'd like to give way to the need to hurt him for all he'd done to them. She was stopped only by the knowledge that he was strong enough to shake her off like a hound would a playful kitten. She couldn't hurt him, but he could kill her with a blow.

There seemed to be no one with him. Catherine looked around for Lambert, but there was no young man in the vicinity, only a little girl sitting on a barrel enjoying the shaft of sunlight that fell between the eaves overhanging the street on either side. Farther down some women were chatting at the communal well.

So, what was Jehan up to?

Catherine knew that whatever it was, she should find out about it. Now, how could she follow him without being recognized? She already had her head covered, the black braids tucked out of sight. Perhaps if she bent a bit to hide her face and walked with a limp. She tried that. After a moment she decided she ought not to make the lameness too exaggerated, or she would soon lose him in the twisty streets.

She hoped he was returning to the room he shared with Lambert. Then Edgar and his friends could go later and extricate the young man. But as she followed, she noticed that Jehan was heading away from the area where one could rent rooms we crossed the river and went down along the bank, where poor people made shift with crude huts and lean-tos that were washed away each year in the spring tides.

She found it hard to keep her footing on the marshy path, especially since she had to duck behind a bush or low wall every few moments. She caught her scarf on one bramble and nearly lost Jehan as she struggled to free it.

Finally, he turned down a narrow trail, hardly wide enough for one. Catherine stopped in time to see him knock at the door of a building that seemed to have grown like a mushroom by the river, a confusion of boards, stone and moss. She jumped back as the door opened and so didn't see who answered. When she looked again, Jehan was gone.

While she was standing on the path considering what to do next, she was startled to hear someone call her name.

"Catherine? Have you come to consult the wizard?"

Once she had pushed her heart down from her throat, Catherine smiled.

"The wizard, Maurice?" she said. "Is that who lives there? It looks like a sorcerer's hut, now that I consider it. No, I was just . . . uh, hunting for early berries. What brings you this way?"

Maurice smiled back at her.

"I'm coming home from Saint Victor," he said. "I spent the morning among their books, but now I have to get back to my duties as a new subdeacon. Your basket is empty. You had no success?"

"No, it's too early, I guess," she took his arm, almost dragging him back up the path and to the Petit Pont.

"What were you saying about a wizard?" she asked casually. "Is it just because the house is so tumbledown?"

"No, it's really more of a joke," Maurice said. "The old man who lives there is harmless. He's been trying for years to contact a demon that will do his bidding, but without success. Some of the students come to him for love potions and such, but they never work. He's been there so long, he's almost as much a part of student life as Master Adam on the bridge. I'm surprised you've never heard of him.

Edgar must have. He's a source of much humor among the students."

"So the bishop doesn't mind his doings?" Catherine asked, wondering why Edgar had said nothing of him before. Could he have once wanted a love potion?

"None of them has so far," Maurice said. "Someday we might get a bishop who thinks he's dangerous, but, as I said, at the moment he's more of an example of the futility of dabbling in magic."

Catherine wondered if Jehan knew he was consulting an inept sorcerer.

They had reached the gate of the cloister of Nôtre Dame.

"Do you want me to escort you to your home?" Maurice asked.

Catherine rejected his offer, knowing that he would still have work to do after taking the extra time for her.

"I hope you'll be able to visit us soon, though," she said. "We miss you now that you've become so busy. I'd like to learn more about what you've been reading."

"Come to Vespers someday," Maurice offered. "And I'll come back with you. Clement and Albert are working together on the liturgy this week, and the result is true magic, if you'll excuse my saying so. But who knows how long it will last?"

Catherine rushed back to the house, hoping that she would get there before Edgar. She wanted to share the information with him but didn't know how without admitting that she had taken a risk in going after Jehan. She wondered if she could fit Maurice into the story to make it seem that he had been with her the whole time without actually saying so.

"Samonie!" she called as she came in. "I'm sorry I'm late. Have the children behaved? Samonie?"

She slipped out of her wooden-soled outside shoes and went through the hall and down to the kitchen.

"Samonie? Margaret! Where have you got to now?"

It seemed that people were always wandering off without telling her.

"Catherine?" Margaret's voice came from far upstairs.

Catherine trudged back up to the children's room, where she found everyone just waking from their afternoon naps.

"Is something wrong?" Samonie's face appeared at the top of the second landing. She was yawning.

"No," Catherine said, feeling foolish about her moment of alarm. "I didn't realize how late it was. Did you all have a good morning?"

"Quiet," Samonie answered. "That, in itself, made it good. Did Clemence balk when she saw how felt makers live?"

"She seemed grateful for their kindness and flattered by how obsequious they were," Catherine told her. "I don't think she's used to being treated like nobility."

"Those country castellans with only a village or two don't live much better than their peasants," Samonie observed. "Still, I'm surprised Clemence's parents let her marry a miller's son. Do you think she was telling the truth?"

"Why would they be hunting for her father if he hadn't approved the marriage?" Catherine asked.

Samonie had come downstairs, and they moved into the hall, newly strewn with fresh rushes and herbs. Samonie picked up one of Edana's toys, thoroughly chewed by the new puppy.

"They might not be hunting for him at all," she suggested to Catherine. "What if it's a ruse? Perhaps they know he's dead and want to be sure suspicion doesn't fall on them?"

"Nonsense!" Catherine said. "For that, all they had to do was stay in Picardy."

"And if they weren't in Picardy when the man died, but Paris, wouldn't they need a reason?" Samonie responded.

"Oh, Samonie!" Catherine put her hands to her temples. "I never considered that possibility. I thought the worst thing about this death was finding the poor man's body. But all this confusion and suspicion is horrible. Won't it be ironic if the man had nothing to do with us or the Temple but was simply left here because the house was empty?"

Samonie gave a thin smile. "I'm sure we'd all have a good laugh about it."

She then went back to her housework, leaving Catherine
to ponder what she should do next and if there were anyone
outside of her family whom she could trust.

Lambert stood in a space between the buildings on the
Grand Pont, staring forlornly into the water rushing below.
The creaking of the mills below the bridge almost drowned
out the cries of the pedlars. But there was only one voice
he wanted to hear, and he would have picked it out through
any other sound.

It had been a mistake ever to let himself be parted from
Clemence. He was responsible for her welfare. He de-
pended on her counsel. Without her he was lost and baffled
by all that was happening. Now Jehan proposed they com-
mit an act that he could be hanged for. The knight insisted
that it was necessary in the fight against evil and that they
might never find Clemence otherwise. He also reminded
Lambert that the wizard had given them protection, in case
the saints should fail them.

But why should the saints abandon him if he were la-
boring on the side of God?

He was so sunk in gloom that he nearly fell into the river
when a man with a bucket pushed him roughly aside.

"Out of the way!" the man ordered. "This spot is for
taking a quick piss, not lounging."

The bucket was already full of night soil, and the man
seemed perfectly happy to dump it on Lambert if he
couldn't get to the river.

By the position of the sun, Lambert realized that Jehan
was probably at their room, waiting for him. He finished
crossing the bridge and slowly made his way out of the
light and down the side street to the bridle makers. Despite
Jehan's friendship and encouragement, Lambert wished
with all his heart that he had someone, anyone, else to turn
to.

"You'd think Catherine would at least come back to see
how I was," Hubert grumbled to Solomon.

"You told her it wouldn't be wise, remember?" Solomon

said. "She has enough to worry about. Your reappearance has only added to their problems."

"I hate leaving them with this new trouble," Hubert continued. "I'm sure that body is Jehan's doing. I'd suspect him of anything that caused us trouble."

"I can't think of anyone else," Solomon admitted. "And Catherine would be happy to agree. But we have no proof. It would give me pleasure to see him swinging at the crossroads. I swear Edgar would pull the rope."

Edgar's name diverted Hubert.

"What do you think of him as a partner?" he asked. "Will he be of help to you or another burden?"

"Honestly, I'm not sure yet," Solomon answered. "He has an inborn contempt for merchants and traders that he's finding hard to overcome. But he has a good knowledge of the wares, and he can talk with the abbots and lords as an equal; something we could never do."

"Does he take good care of Catherine?" Hubert prodded.

Solomon laughed. "Can anyone? My cousin needs half of Heaven to keep her safe. But you've seen them together enough to know that no one would better tolerate her quirks. He does love her, you know."

Hubert grudgingly conceded that. But he had never really been able to understand Edgar and had the lingering fear that one day he would disavow his wife and children and return to Scotland.

"I'm going mad staying in the house," he blurted out. "Abraham and Rebecca are wonderful to me, but to be home and not be able to walk the streets, not to see my grandchildren . . ."

He got up from his chair and went to the window, peering through the crack in the shutter to the sunlit world outside. Solomon shook his head at him.

"That's the price you must pay," he said. "You should have known better than to return at all. I would have brought you the *Torah*. Are you sure you aren't regretting your decision?"

"Not my decision." Hubert turned back to him. "But the world that casts me out because of it. You're right. I came back partly because I wanted to make sure everyone was doing well. I wanted to hold James and Edana in my arms again before they forgot me."

"Don't contemplate it," Solomon warned. "Catherine has decided they can never know the truth. For them, you've gone on a pilgrimage. When years pass and you don't return, she'll tell the children that you've gone to Heaven with all your sins forgiven."

Hubert slumped against the wall. "This is my punishment, for not returning to the True Faith at once, isn't it?"

"How should I know, Uncle?" Solomon was losing patience. "But for the sake of everyone you care about, including me, you must stay hidden until you can leave Paris safely. And you must promise that you'll never come back."

Hubert gave no answer. He turned his face back to the sliver of light, all that he could see of the world he had left.

Edgar arrived at the *Parleoir* to be enthusiastically greeted by Archer and Giselbert.

"We thought you might not be here today," Giselbert explained.

"Why not?" Edgar asked, looking over their heads for the leather buyer he had come to see.

"Those men from the Temple were here again, asking about you," Archer said. "We thought that Commander Evrard might have sent for you."

Edgar gave them both a cool stare.

"But since you're here . . ." Archer tried to smile.

"Since I'm here," Edgar said, "I should be getting on with my work. A pleasure to see you both. And my thanks, again, for coming so quickly to keep the fire from spreading."

He bowed slightly and left them.

Archer's mouth twisted in distaste.

"I don't know which annoys me more," he told Giselbert. "That arrogant lord or his Jew partner."

Giselbert shrugged. "As long as they trade fairly and give me a good price, I don't care."

"That's not enough," Archer insisted. "They don't fit in. In a crisis, who will they side with?"

Giselbert eyed him nervously. "What kind of crisis? Famine? Taxes? Invasion? Do you think the Englishman will side with the Normans if they invade?"

"I wasn't thinking of that," Archer said. "I meant something important. Say, like the Flemings hoarded grain while they bought cheaply from us and then tried to sell it back at exorbitant prices in the time of famine. Would he stand against them and refuse to buy their wool?"

Giselbert scratched at a pimple on his nose.

"I don't know," he concluded.

"You see?" Archer said in triumph. "That's what comes of letting haughty foreigners into the water merchants!"

Both men would have been astonished to see Edgar at that moment, laughing at a ribald joke from the dealer in leather. The two of them had settled on a bench outside the old building and near a tavern.

"But the priest forgot to ask the goat!" the man ended, laughing so hard that he nearly spilled his beer.

Edgar pounded the bench with his left arm in appreciation. "That reminds me of the one about the Saxon sailor and the lovesick seal."

He proceeded to tell it, to the edification of all around him.

By the end of the afternoon, Edgar had made a firm deal with the leather trader and learned a new story to tell Catherine in bed that night. Of course, the last time she had laughed so loudly that James had woken up and come to ask them why they were having fun without him. That had made her laugh even harder, so that he finally had to pull on his tunic and take James back to his own bed, explaining that Mama was inclined to be ticklish and that he'd be more careful in future. Still, Catherine's welcome when he came back to their room had been worth the interruption.

So, after a few bowls of beer and a pleasant afternoon, Edgar set out for home feeling much more content with life than he had been in days. If they made the money they expected to at the *Lendit* they should be set for the whole summer with something put by for winter, as well.

He crossed onto the Île and cut down the street of the drapers to the Grand Pont, not paying attention to passersby as he computed profits in his head. He vaguely heard the harangue from the man on the corner of the *rue des Juifs* but didn't even note if it were to sell goods or save souls. He hoped that, for once, Catherine would be home so he could tell her of his success.

Therefore, when the blow came, he fell facedown into the street, without ever seeing the one who struck.

Eighteen

A street on the *Île de la Cité*. A moment later.

. . . aliud est enim ex intimo et summo causarum cardine condere atque administrare creaturam, quod qui facit solus est creator Deus, aliud autem pro distributis ab illo viribus et facultatibus aliquam operationem forinsecus admovere, ut tunc vel tunc, sic vel sic exeat quod creatur, quod non solum mali angeli sed mali homines possunt . . .

It is one thing to create and care for the creation made through the deepest and highest cause (and the only one who does this is God the creator) and quite another for certain men to use these attributes and faculties to perform actions from the outside so that a created thing appears to be one thing at one time and another at another; it is not only evil angels but evil men who can do this. . . .

—William of Newburgh
History of English Affairs
Book I, Chapter 28

*E*dgar fell facedown into the dirt. He had thrown his arms out to catch his fall and felt the pain in his right palm as he landed on a chunk of old masonry, jutting out of the earth.

Cursing mightily, he pulled himself to his knees and was helped to his feet by a passerby.

"What happened?" he asked, looking around.

For answer, the man pointed to a round rock in the street, still damp, with dirt and moss clinging to it.

"Someone hurled it from the crowd around the preacher," he said. "That's what comes of having all these strangers in town. If he'd hit your head, he could have killed you."

Edgar rubbed his wrist, flexing his fingers. It seemed to be functional. He had felt a momentary terror at losing the use of both hands. The thought of having to be fed and dressed, constantly dependent on others, chilled his blood.

He bent to examine the rock. It was smooth and rounded, like many that one could find along the riverbank. Whoever had thrown it must have picked it up recently; the moss was still fresh.

"Did you see who threw it?" Edgar asked without much hope.

"I just saw it come through the air and strike you," the man said. "But in such a crowd, someone must have marked the thrower."

Edgar looked around. "Probably," he said. "But if he hasn't been cried against and caught by now, he'll have vanished. Those who witnessed his deed don't want to be involved."

His back was throbbing. There would be a bruise he'd have to explain to Catherine. He'd also scraped his hand and torn the leather patch on the other wrist. He scanned the crowd around him for a familiar face. Jehan's came to mind. But he saw no one he knew. Had he simply been the victim of some villein's anger at anyone better dressed and fed than he? Or had someone been following him, waiting for a clear shot? If so, was it a warning or a murder attempt? And, the most difficult question, why?

Yes, even though it would worry her, this was something he had to share with Catherine. It was possible that the person who attacked him wanted to hurt her, as well.

Even though he ached all over, Edgar made it home between the first bell tolling Vespers and the last.

The bruise upset Catherine more than the scrapes. She had known men to die from such a blow, seeming well for a few days, then suddenly collapsing.

"You think it was Jehan?" she asked as she made up a compound to rub on it. "It doesn't seem like him, somehow, but he was by the river earlier today."

She told him about the visit to the wizard on the bank, making sure she mentioned Maurice.

Edgar was still annoyed with her. "Maurice is a cleric. It's already been proven that Jehan doesn't repond to prayers. I would believe him stupid enough to think the wizard could help him."

"You know this wizard?"

"A long time ago. Part of my student days." Edgar quickly returned to speculate on his attacker. "It might have been Jehan, but he's the kind who prefers to gloat at his strikes. He'd want me to know if he hit me."

"Of course it might have been a robber or even some drunk acting on a befuddled urge to do harm," Catherine suggested, still wondering about Edgar and the wizard.

"Only if he was aiming at something else," Edgar answered. "The hit was too hard and accurate to have been thrown by one made witless from wine."

"You were passing near the synagogue then, weren't you?" Catherine asked.

"You think this has something to do with your father?"

"I don't know." Catherine bit her lip. "But everything that happens seems to come back to him. His 'treasure,' his secrets. Why couldn't he have become a good Christian and spared us all this?"

Edgar closed his eyes. He was lying on his stomach on the bed. Catherine had rubbed the oil and herbs onto his back, and the warmth was easing the pain. Her question had no answer, so he gave none. The day had been long, and her hands were soothing. When Catherine continued her musings, his only response was a gentle snore.

She stayed by his side a while, watching his breathing. As she did, her mind kept gnawing at the tangle of recent events. She tried to follow one strand at a time, not sure what it would lead to. She started with the day they returned. The door was barred and shuttered. The lock had been rusty, and yet a body had been brought in recently and the men in the garden had expected to find the door open. The lock on the counting room had been freshly oiled.

How did the body enter the house?

Unlike poorer homes, theirs didn't have ground-floor windows that opened directly onto the street and could be used as counters for business and sales. They had a stone wall that completely surrounded a small courtyard in front. The wall went on either side of the house and down within a few feet of the stream. Hubert had chosen the site because it was so well protected, from both thieves and fire.

Catherine tried to imagine someone hoisting a man's body over the wall in the back from either the neighbor's yard or the street on the opposite side. Perhaps it could be done on a moonless night, but it would be very dangerous. The watch passed here more often because the merchants paid them to. The stream wasn't high enough most of the year to float anything on. No, the most logical way anyone could bring something as large as a body into the house would be through the gate.

She tried to remember the state of the front gate when they'd arrived. The vines were hanging over it, but it wasn't boarded like the back. Could someone have entered through it, bold as a Norman lord, deposited a corpse and sauntered out the same way?

It seemed to Catherine that finding this out was more important than identifying the body. That was the key to the whole thing, and she felt that the answer was hiding in some dusty corner of her mind refusing to show itself. Perhaps it was time for her to do some mental spring cleaning.

She left Edgar sleeping and joined the rest of the family for dinner. Astrolabe was there to say good-bye. He was planning on being at the Paraclete for the feast of the Ascension and was taking Catherine's letter with him to give to his mother, Abbess Heloise.

"I really think you'll like it there," he was telling Margaret. "The countryside is pleasant, and it's not as remote from the world as you might fear."

"That's certainly true," Catherine said. "Mother Heloise felt it inappropriate for nuns, including herself, to be out of the convent for extended times. So what happened? Everyone now comes to the Paraclete. Remember how busy it was when we visited on our way to Trier?"

Margaret still wasn't entirely convinced.

"Will you come visit me?" she asked. "If I decide to go."

"Of course, *bele seur*!" Catherine said. "And I'll bring James and Edana with me. You're not going to be cloistered, only a student."

"And I can come home if I want?" Margaret asked.

"We've told you that many times already," Catherine answered. "Now, we won't wait for Edgar to wake. Samonie! Can you bring the soup now?"

Martin appeared a few moments later, carrying the bowl. Samonie followed with bread and a pitcher of wine.

"Where will you go after the Paraclete?" Catherine asked Astrolabe as they dipped chunks of bread into the communal bowl.

"Back to Brittany, I think," he said. "My cousins always have a place for me there, and I want to find out more about this heretic whom no one seems able to capture."

"He does sound like one of the more bizarre of the malcontents running loose these days," Catherine said. "But there are so many of them that I can't tell one sect from another. They each seem to have some quirk, like those Manichees who won't eat eggs or cheese."

"Why not?" Margaret asked.

Catherine paused. "Well, it seems to have something to do with procreation."

"They don't even think animals should procreate?" Margaret asked. "What difference would it make? They don't have souls to save. Or do these heretics believe that they do?"

"I don't think so." Catherine shook her head. "But what they do believe is no less strange. That's what comes of not educating priests well enough to explain the Faith."

"Catherine," Astrolabe interrupted, "I'll be listening to conversations of this sort soon enough. Could we discuss something less volatile?"

He nodded toward the other side of the table, where James and Edana were listening with interest. Wonderful. She could just hear James explaining to his friends that his aunt Margaret had told him his puppy had a soul. That would fuel the gossip for certain.

"James, we're talking of poor, misguided people," she said firmly. "Your puppy does not have an immortal spirit. That is reserved for humans."

"I know," James said, climbing onto the table to dunk his bread. "But he'll have one when I give him a name."

"Oh dear!" Catherine wondered if she could send James to the Paraclete along with Margaret. Instructing a four-year-old in doctrine was more than she was up to.

Astrolabe laughed. "Don't worry. He'll understand when he's older. I have cousins who would be hard put to deny that their horses won't go to Heaven with them."

The conversation then returned to safer topics.

It was still light out when Astrolabe rose to go.

"You're sure you won't stay?" Catherine asked.

"No, thank you," he answered. "Maurice is good about finding me an empty cot, and it's much less trouble for the canons than for you."

"And you're unlikely to be wakened by small children and animals racing around your bed," Catherine said. "A wise choice."

There were still only a few stars showing when Catherine, the last of the household up, came into her room. She took off her clothes and folded them into the chest, then rinsed her feet in a basin on the floor, put on her sleep cap and crawled over Edgar to her side of the bed.

He grunted in pain as she touched him.

"I'm sorry," she whispered. "Do you need some more oil?"

"Mmmfnnn," he said.

"Oh, well, good night, then." She kissed the back of his head and went to sleep.

Bertulf and Godfrey had gone to Compline and, like most of the Knights of the Temple, had recited a set number of *Nostre Peres* to fulfill the Office. Then they went back to the dormitory with the other guests and men who had not yet taken their vows. They fell into bed fully dressed, only taking off their belts and shoes. Soon the preceptory was still.

Godfrey waited until the rustlings and tossing had stopped, then he slipped out of his cot, grabbed his shoes and tiptoed to the door.

He stood there a moment until he heard the guard pass on his way around the chapel, then he gently pushed the door open and eased out.

Hanging his shoes by the laces around his neck, Godfrey dashed to the wooden fence and squeezed through. Once outside, he put the shoes on, drew his knife in case of attack and set off for the Grève.

In the tavern next to their lodging, Lambert and Jehan were fortifying themselves for the evening's work.

"Don't you think that you should be the one to enter the house?" Lambert asked again. "I'm sure to lose my way and ruin everything."

"Nonsense," Jehan said heartily. "There's nothing to it. Through the hall, up the stairs and in. The counting room is the first door on the right. You'll have no trouble. My job is the dangerous one, watching out for the guards. You're more agile than I. You can slip out the window with no difficulty."

"You'll be there to catch me, won't you?" Lambert asked.

"Of course," Jehan said. "But the drop isn't that bad."

"You're sure the key will work?"

Jehan refilled Lambert's bowl. "Certain. I've had it for years."

Lambert shook his head. "I know I'll drop it or knock something over. I'm not good at this kind of work."

Jehan leaned across the table and grabbed Lambert by the shoulders.

"That's why you have the amulet with you, remember?" he whispered. "No one will even know you're there. I had to pay the wizard dearly for that, but it was worth it. When you put it on this afternoon, you vanished completely."

Lambert nodded. "I know. You walked right into me. But I wish I could have looked in a mirror to see for myself."

"You mean 'not see'!" Jehan laughed. "Between that and the darkness you'll float through the house like a spirit. In and out before you know it."

Lambert sighed and drank his wine.

"And you promise that tomorrow we'll go tell the provost that Clemence is missing?" he said.

"Of course," Jehan answered. "If we don't find her in their clutches. I won't leave you until she's recovered. Even if they've hidden her elsewhere, once they've been denounced, we can force them to tell you where she is."

"But what if they know nothing about her?" Lambert said. "Or what if they do have her and threaten to hurt her."

"Once they're imprisoned, they won't be able to do anything," Jehan said sharply. He was growing weary of Lambert's doubts. "Come. It's time to set out. Don't forget your cloak."

Lambert picked up the cloak and dropped it on the floor, his hands were shaking so much. Jehan retrieved it and made him put it on as soon as they were out in the street. He wrapped his own cloak around his shoulders, pulling the hood down over his face.

"Now we look like men with something to hide," Lambert said.

"Any man out at this hour *has* something to hide," Jehan told him. "Or else he's a fool and will soon be dead."

This explanation did not ease Lambert's trepidation.

They made their way across the Grand Pont and turned right along the river road to the Grève. Lambert started at every sound and once nearly lost control of his bowels when he mistook a rooting pig for a creature from Hell. They passed no one and came to the dark street with no other incident.

"Now, I've watched many a night," Jehan said. "The door to the kitchen will be unlocked. All you need to do is avoid the guards by the creek."

He scanned the street to be sure it was empty, then hoisted Lambert over the wall. He heard a sound of breaking branches and a muffled cry as Lambert landed in a laurel bush. Then silence.

Jehan went around to the other side of the house, where he knew a way into the garden of the grain merchant. Then he made his way along the wall until he reckoned he was under the counting-room window.

There was nothing to do now but hope that idiot boy could manage to follow the plan. Jehan sighed. It was a great risk, but at least if it failed, he could be far away by morning.

Lambert's *brais* and cloak were stuck with laurel now, sending out a pungent aroma. He felt for the amulet and put it around his neck, where it rattled against his cross.

Now he should be totally invisible. He just hoped no one found him by the smell.

He crept around to the back and found, as Jehan had promised, that the door was not only unlocked but ajar. This unnerved him more than if it had been closed. What if someone were waiting for him inside?

After an agonized moment, Lambert pulled the door far enough open to enter. He felt his way around the wall trying not to tip anything over until he found the stairs to the hall.

The empty expanse seemed as wide as the ocean as Lambert started across. There was a small amount of starlight shining through the windows but only enough for every shadow to appear to be an obstacle to avoid.

Was anyone sleeping here? Lambert heard no sound of breathing, but it was hard to make out anything over the pounding of his heart. Every step he made seemed to set the rushes rattling loudly enough to wake the dead.

Finally, he felt his way to the staircase. He groped along the wall and caught a spray of dust as his hand ran into a thick wall hanging. For a moment he was sure he was going to sneeze. Only by wrenching most of the muscles in his throat did he keep it back.

He arrived at the door to the counting room in both physical and spiritual agony. He drew the key from the purse at his belt on the third try and, feeling for the lock with his other hand, managed to insert and turn it.

The door opened smoothly. The hinges didn't even creak. He went in.

The window here was larger, and he could make out the treasure chest Jehan had told him about. Lambert knelt in front of it and, before opening it, said a quick prayer that no one would ever know he had done such a thing, no matter how pure his intentions were. He put his hands on the lid and lifted.

It didn't budge.

Lambert pushed harder. Nothing happened.

Frantically, he felt around the edges. There, just in the

center, was the loop and padlock Jehan had forgotten to tell him about.

He sat back on his haunches. What could he do now? The thought of dropping into Jehan's arms without finding out what was in the chest was more terrifying than his fear of being caught.

In desperation, Lambert tried the key to the door. It turned, and the lock opened.

"It's a miracle," he breathed. "Thank you Saint Omer!"

He felt in the chest but there was no chink of gold or stolen church plate, as Jehan had told him. All he felt were books, each wrapped in cloth.

What if the books contained magic spells? He should take them to Jehan to examine. But there were too many to carry. Would one be enough?

He heard movement on the floor above him. One would have to be enough, he decided. He took the top book from the pile, closed and locked the chest and went to the window. Thank goodness no one had thought to shutter it on this mild night!

Below, he could just make out the figure of Jehan, ghost-like in his cloak. Lambert tapped on the sill to catch his attention. Jehan looked up and held out his arms.

Lambert dropped the book from the window. Jehan caught it, falling backward from the weight. Then Lambert eased himself through the narrow window and dropped.

He landed with a thud on the ground. Before he could decide if he were hurt or not, Jehan grabbed him by the arm, yanked him up and over the wall to the grain merchant's.

Somewhere nearby a dog started barking, setting off all the others in the neighborhood. Jehan pushed Lambert into the cover of the grain shed until it died down. Then the two men crept back to the street and, once out into the open, went as casually as they could down to the bridge and back to their room.

The next morning Catherine came down to find the counting-room door open.

"That's odd," she said to herself. "I was sure I locked it last night."

She looked in. Everything seemed the same. The padlock on the chest was in place. She sniffed. There was a scent of laurel in the room. Strange. The bush was on the other side of the house.

Shaking her head, Catherine took the key from her belt and locked the door.

It wasn't until the afternoon that she went up to work on the accounts and discovered that the book her father had used to keep his records had vanished.

"Edgar!" she called. "What did you do with the account book?"

His voice came back from the storeroom, where he and Solomon were making headway in the inventory.

"Nothing! Why?"

She went into the storeroom. "You must have," she insisted. "It's not in the chest."

Solomon straightened from the box he was searching through.

"Perhaps you left it out," he suggested.

"Solomon, I would have noticed if it had been lying there." But Catherine went back to check.

"No, it's gone," she said when she returned. "And I never take it out of the room."

She then told them about finding the door open.

"But the chest was still locked. How could anyone have gotten in? And why would a thief want a book in the first place?" she said.

Edgar followed her back into the counting room. He moved stiffly, his back still in pain. "We shouldn't assume it's been stolen," he said. "This room is right below ours. We'd hear if someone entered it at night. When did you last use the book?"

"Yesterday," she said. "I wanted to reconcile what I had there with the inventory. Did you make the deal for the leather?"

"*Damedé*!" he said. "I'd forgotten all about it. That stone knocked it out of my head."

"Do you suppose someone hit you to prevent your being able to stop them from breaking into the house?" Solomon asked.

"I don't think I'm that much of a threat," Edgar answered. "We have locks. We have guards. I can't believe anyone could have got in. You must have just misplaced the book."

"Edgar," Catherine said quietly. "Look."

She pointed to the ground under the window. There in the grass was the deep impression of two boots, toes pointed toward the house.

They all stared at the marks. Catherine shivered.

"He must have escaped this way," she said, feeling unnaturally calm. "But how did he get in?"

They all thought the same thing, but no one said it. Finally, Solomon turned back to examine the door.

"No, we aren't dealing with a thief who can fly," he said. "He came in by the door and left it unlocked because he went out by the window and the lock was on the other side."

Edgar let his breath out. "Of course," he said. "Perfectly clear what happened."

"Except," Catherine said, "how did he get into the house in the first place and where did he get keys to the counting room?"

"And," she added, "what possible use to him is Father's book?"

Staring at it in broad daylight, Jehan was thinking much the same thing.

"Where is the treasure box?" he demanded of Lambert. "How could you mistake this for it?"

"There was no treasure," Lambert insisted. "Just books. I thought they might contain evidence of the wickedness of these people."

"Catherine and Edgar are too clever for that," Jehan said. He thought about it a moment longer. "The book was locked up, just like treasure, wasn't it?"

Lambert nodded eagerly.

Jehan sat on the bed and unfolded the cloth cover, revealing wooden boards. The pages between them had been stitched together at different times as more were needed. Cautiously, Jehan opened the cover and looked at the first page.

Lambert watched, ready to run if black smoke or a giant hand suddenly popped out of the parchment.

"Is it in French?" he asked after a moment. "Can you read it?"

"Very interesting," Jehan said, sounding less angry. "Parts are in French, but not all by any means. You see these shapes?"

He held the book up, pointing to a long line of letters.

"That's not Latin," he stated. "That's Hebrew. Sorcerers use it to call on the fallen angels by their true names. That's how you get power over them."

Lambert backed away.

"What does it say?" he asked.

"Don't know," Jehan admitted. "But the wizard might. And there's plenty of clerics who could tell us. I have a bit of old Hubert's writing, with these same characters on one side and French on the other. They wouldn't believe me before, but they'll have to now. Lambert, we have to get this book back into the chest where you found it."

"What!" Lambert cried. "Go there again? I couldn't. No, Jehan, I've done all you asked. Now I must find Clemence! You wouldn't even let me find out if she was there!"

He fell off his stool in his anger and fear and scrambled toward the door on his knees, desperate to get away. Jehan reached over and spun him around. Lambert looked up to see Jehan's knife pointed at his throat.

"I've helped you ever since you got here, you ungrateful *mesel*," Jehan hissed. "We're fighting pure evil here, worse than any Saracen. They could be doing anything to your wife, right this minute."

"I don't believe it anymore!" Lambert said. "You aren't heping me find Clemence. You're just trying to get me to do your work for you."

Jehan gave a snort. "Idiot! It's I who've been helping

you. What use are you to me? I can easily find a bright boy who will do what I ask with no back talk. You're the one who's in trouble. Remember that they may well have killed your wife's father as well as abducting her. Don't you want to see these monsters brought to justice?"

Lambert looked steadily into Jehan's eyes. He was suddenly too worn-out for fear.

"No," he said. "All I want is to find Clemence, safe. After that, I'll think about justice."

The knife shook in Jehan's hand. Lambert looked away. He had thought he had reached the limits of exhaustion and despair. Jehan's face showed him how much farther a man could go and still be this side of Hell.

"What did these people do to you?" he asked Jehan.

The knife was flung across the room, ripping the thin wall hanging and landing on the floor with a clang.

"They stole everything I had," Jehan said. "Even hope. They have taken my life and twisted it like a wet cloth until every drop of happiness was wrung from it. I have nothing left."

"*If* that is so, they must be truly as evil as you say," Lambert said gently. "No wonder you hate them."

Clemence was finding life in Paris a revelation. At home everyone knew she was the castellan's daughter, but they treated her more as a much loved pet than a noblewoman. Here she felt one place removed from the queen. Bodille and her husband were eager to please her, sending out for meat dishes and elegant pastries that she never got at home.

The room she was given had been swept thoroughly before the bedding and other furniture Catherine had loaned her was brought in, but Clemence still found herself sneezing all the time from the wisps of felt that permeated the air in and around the house. She couldn't understand why no one else seemed to notice it.

"I hope you haven't taken cold, my lady," Bodille said when she brought Clemence's midday meal. "It's all these foreign—" She stopped in mid-sentence. "Well, some broth will help, I'm sure. There's good local wine in it, and I sprinkled it with mint and rue."

Clemence thanked her. "Oh, yes," she added. "Is there anyone who can take a message to Catherine LeVendeur and wait for a reply?"

"Of course," Bodille said. "Willa can go. She'd probably like a chance to see her mother."

But when Clemence asked for a tablet and stylus, she was greeted with a blank stare.

"We have no such things. Can't you just tell her the message?" Bodille asked. "Willa can remember whatever you want to say."

So Willa was summoned and Clemence explained to her that she wanted to be allowed to visit Catherine that afternoon if it was quite convenient.

"She may be going to a meeting at one of her neighbor's houses," Willa said. "The wives of the merchants want to form an alms society for the poor of the parish. Catherine said something about having to go."

"Perhaps you could deliver my message and find out for me," Clemence answered. "Tell her I would like to speak with her."

"If they'd found your husband, they'd have told you," Willa coughed deeply, covering her mouth. "You don't need to worry about that."

"Thank you." Clemence said. "I don't doubt it. But I would still like to speak with Catherine."

Willa shrugged. She'd done her best.

"I shouldn't be long," she said.

Clemence was wondering if she'd ever get started.

It was only a little while though, before Willa returned with a note from Catherine inviting her to dine with them that evening.

"She told me she's got to go to the blasted meeting or the other ladies will gossip about her, but she'd much rather have spent the afternoon with you," Willa added. "My brother, Martin, and Lord Edgar will come to escort you after Vespers."

Clemence wondered how much of Catherine's message

had been intended to be repeated. Nevertheless, she thanked Willa again and went to work making the few pieces of clothing she had brought with her into something appropriate for a dinner.

"Chaim, don't be so glum," Abraham told Hubert. "You're lucky to find a party going south in the spring, instead of north to the fairs."

"Thank you, Abraham," Hubert replied listlessly. "It will be good to get back to Arles, where I belong."

Abraham refused to pity him. "If I can't be in *Eretz Israel*, I'd be happy living in the south, with fresh olives, mild winters and dozens of scholars to learn from."

"Yes, I know."

Abraham sat across from him. "Chaim, stop this. Your children are all well. You have grandsons. You've lived to see them. A man can't ask for more."

Hubert bent his head. "I know. It was my choice. Now I regret that none of my grandsons will ever make the covenant of Abraham."

"You don't know that," Abraham answered. "Perhaps it will happen when the Messiah comes. Then men will fight for the chance to become Jews."

That made Hubert laugh, despite himself.

"That's better," Rebecca said. She had come in while they were talking. "Edgar and Solomon are here to see you."

One look at their faces sent Hubert's mood back to gloom.

"Hubert, what was written in your accounts book?" Edgar surprised him by asking.

"Accounts, of course," he told them, bewildered.

"Then why was there so much in Hebrew?" Edgar went on.

"I've tried to explain it to him," Solomon added.

"It's an old practice," Hubert said. "Even my Christian stepfather used it. He learned it from my father. The letters stand for numbers. They indicate the price we paid as opposed to the selling price. That's all."

Edgar glanced at Solomon, who nodded.

"And there are no prayers or incantations to take advantage of competitors?" he asked.

"I wish I'd known some," Hubert said. "I'd be a richer man today. Now what's this all about?"

They told him.

"But no one could have got into the house and the counting room," Hubert said. "Unless someone helped them."

"I know," Edgar said. "Catherine would almost prefer to believe that evil spirits stalk the house. Only Samonie or Martin could have let the thief in."

"But why would they betray you after so many years?" Hubert was incredulous.

"I don't know," Edgar answered. "Catherine made me promise to ask you before I questioned Samonie, in case you had given a key to someone else."

"No, only Catherine and I have had keys since Agnes left to live with my wife's father," Hubert answered.

"Did she leave hers with you?"

Hubert thought. "I think so. I don't remember. You don't think she would have given it to Jehan?"

"Or he might have found the key and copied it," Solomon said.

"I'd prefer that to thinking that our servants were plotting against us," Edgar said. "But I'll still have to ask Samonie about it. If nothing else, she should have heard someone enter."

"Be careful not to accuse her unless you have proof," Hubert said. "Samonie knows far too much about us."

The tightening of Edgar's jaw told Hubert that he already knew this.

"Yes, I know," Hubert concluded. "My fault again."

Abraham had been pretending not to listen to this exchange. Now he had to add his opinion.

"What if the thief were hunting for the Torah, not the accounts book?" he suggested. "Then, if he tried to use it to denounce the family, he'd look like a fool, as well as a housebreaker."

"I think that finding Jehan would answer all our questions," Solomon said. "Everything we've discovered so far leads back to him. We know he's a blustering lunatic. How hard could he be to find?"

"Catherine already saw him," Edgar told them. "For a wonder this time she didn't confront him alone. You may be right. I don't care if the man is a pilgrim festooned with crosses. He has to be stopped."

The city bells began ringing as he spoke, almost to emphasize his vow.

Solomon nudged him. "Edgar, shouldn't you be going?"

"Damn," Edgar said. "Yes, I'm supposed to meet Martin at the felt maker's and see that the girl from Picardy makes it safely to our house for dinner. As if there weren't enough going on."

Edgar and Martin appeared at the appointed time. Edgar's eyebrows rose at the change Clemence had wrought in herself, but when he saw her slippers he frowned.

"Catherine didn't think we needed to order a chair for you," he explained, "But you can't walk through the streets in those."

Bodille offered a pair of her own clogs, but Edgar decided that it would be better to wait while Martin fetched a chair and bearers.

So it was that, as Lambert was crossing the bridge to walk up to Montmartre in his quest for Clemence, he had to wait while some fine lady was carried across in a sedan chair. The curtain was lowered, so he never even saw her face.

Nineteen

Paris, Tuesday evening, 6 kalends June (May 27), 1147; 26 Sivan, 4907. Rogation day, Commemoration of the death of Saint Frederick, bishop of Liège, 1121, believed to have been poisoned by the count of Louvain for the offense of being unbribable.

Et hoc est principale religionis nostrae, ut credeat non solum animas non perire, sed ipsa quoque corpora, quae mortis adventus resolverat, in statum pristinum furtura de beatitudine reparari.

And this is essential to our religion that one believes that not only does the soul not die but that the very bodies, which the coming of death had released, are returned to their pristine condition in the blessed state to come.

—Boethius
"On the Catholic Faith"

Welcome, Clemence," Catherine greeted her in the courtyard as the bearers set down her chair. "Thank you for coming. We plan a quiet dinner tonight. I hope you don't mind."

"I shall enjoy it," Clemence replied. "Your kindness is already more than I can repay."

Catherine made all the proper responses to this and took Clemence into the hall, where the table had been laid and chairs set for four.

First Catherine took Clemence to a side table where the soap pitcher and water had been set out for them, with towels Catherine had embroidered herself back at the convent.

They all stood for the blessing and then sat, while Martin brought in the bread and a fresh fish stuffed with dried fruit and covered in a cinnamon sauce. After it had been admired, he took it back to the kitchen for Samonie to cut up into manageable pieces. Catherine poured the wine. Margaret passed the cup to Clemence.

"Should I?" she asked. "It is a fast day."

"That's why we're having fish," Catherine said. "But if you prefer water, I'll get you another cup."

"No, this is mixed well enough," Clemence said. She didn't wish to appear ignorant of the customs of Paris.

They ate and chatted quietly about things calming to the digestion.

After all the pleasantries custom demanded, Clemence finally could stand it no longer.

"Have you learned anything about where Lambert is, or my father?" she asked.

"We may have located the man Lambert is staying with," Edgar told her. "And we did leave messages for him at all the places I promised. I'm sure you'll be together soon."

"And then what will you do, when you find your husband?" Margaret asked. "It appears that your father may already have left to join the pilgrims."

"I suppose we shall have to return home," Clemence admitted. "And pray that Lord Jordan will respect Father's wish that I hold the castellany with Lambert to manage it until we have a son who's of age."

"It's not unheard of," Catherine said. "Would Lord Jordan be so perverse as to deny the desire of one who has gone to serve God?"

Clemence smiled. "I think he would. And you must admit, that's not unheard of, either."

"Perhaps you could get the king to grant you the castellany before he leaves?" Margaret suggested.

"Louis has little power in Picardy," Edgar said. "Even though he's supposed to be overlord there."

But Catherine thought it a good idea. "If not the king, then why not the pope or the bishop of Amiens? There are so many important people in Paris now. One of them should have some influence with this Jordan."

"And how am I to be given a chance to petition Pope Eugenius?" Clemence asked.

Catherine and Edgar looked at each other, then at Margaret.

"I think we could find someone who will speak on your behalf," Catherine said.

Clemence suddenly remembered who these people were and why she should be more wary of them. They seemed so natural that it was easy to become complacent. She decided that it was time to confront them.

As casually as she could manage, Clemence took out the knife that had been her mother's.

"Oh, is the bread too tough?" Catherine asked. "I'll send it back and get you something else."

"No, not at all," Clemence said. "Just a piece that's a bit hard to tear. I can use this for it."

She held up the knife. The other three smiled and went on with their meal.

Disappointed, Clemence tried again.

"This was carved in our village." She held it closer for them to inspect. "A matching pair for my parents."

"Nice workmanship," Edgar commented.

Clemence was confused. If Lambert's friend, Jehan, were right, they should all have started guiltily. Were they conscienceless or, might they possibly be innocent?

"Hmm . . ." Edgar said. "That looks familiar. May I see it?"

He wiped his hand on the napkin and took the knife from Clemence, holding it up to the light.

"You know," he said, "this looks just like that one that the intruder dropped right after we got here. Remember, Catherine?"

He handed it to her.

"Yes, how very strange," Catherine said. "When Samonie comes in again, I'll ask her what she did with it."

"You admit you have my father's knife?" Clemence was incredulous.

"We'll have to compare them to be sure," Edgar said. "It's your father's? Did you already know we had found it? Why didn't you say something before?"

"I . . . well . . . I . . . tried," Clemence said. She took a breath. "Lambert and I saw it when we came to the house the first time."

"Is that why you ran out?" Margaret asked. "Did you think we'd stolen it?"

"No! I mean, Father was missing," Clemence said. "And there it was."

Catherine got up and went over to her.

"You poor brave girl." She hugged her. "Now don't tell her again that she's been foolish, Edgar. If she'd been a man, you'd expect her to try to find out how we came by this."

"But if it was left here by a stranger, then my only hope of finding my father is gone." Clemence's lips trembled. Catherine handed her a clean napkin.

"I don't suppose we could assume that it was Lord Osto who was our thief?" Edgar said.

"Of course not!" Clemence was aghast. "My father would never behave like a common cutpurse."

No one wanted to utter what they all were thinking. That the intruder had taken the knife from Lord Osto and killed him.

"The knight in the counting room wasn't bald," Catherine said.

"Father has been as long as I can remember," Clemence said. "But that doesn't mean he's still alive. I think it's time I accepted that."

Catherine knelt next to her and spoke to her as if she were Edana.

"You mustn't say that, *ma douz*. All we have in this life is faith, and we must hold to it as long as we can. We'll all pray for Lambert's return and your father's safety. Until then, you mustn't despair."

To her astonishment, Clemence threw herself into Catherine's arms sobbing hysterically.

Catherine held and rocked her while Edgar and Margaret gathered around, patting her now and then in sympathy.

"There now," Edgar said uncomfortably. "It will be fine. There's no need for all this."

"She's just lost her mother and can't find her father," Margaret told Edgar. "She's alone and frightened. I think she should cry all she wants."

The noise brought Samonie from the kitchen, followed by James and Edana, who had been ordered to stay out of sight for the evening.

"Mama! What's wrong?" Edana tried to displace Clemence in Catherine's lap.

"Edana, go to your father," Catherine said sternly.

Clemence lifted her head. "No," she gulped. "I'm sorry, Edana. I didn't mean to frighten you."

Edana wiped her grubby hands on Clemence's cheeks.

"Don't cry," she said. "My papa will make it better."

Edgar rolled his eyes.

"Thank you, Edana" he said. "Now go back to the kitchen with Samonie and wash your hands."

Catherine mopped up the tears and grime from Clemence's face.

"I don't think it's as hopeless as you fear," she said. "Samonie, when you've taken care of Edana, could you bring that knife we found on the floor when Astrolabe scared off the robber?"

"First we'll compare them, to be sure," she told Clemence. "But then, I think we're going to have to ask Samonie a few questions. One person getting into the house at night is possible, but the way we've been invaded, it could only be if someone was leaving the door unlocked for them."

Samonie stood before the four of them, ranged at the table like judges.

"I was never gone long," she said. "And I would never have left at all if I'd known someone was watching for a chance to get in."

"But why didn't you simply tell me," Catherine protested. "I would have given you leave to see your . . . uh . . . friend."

"I had good reason," Samonie insisted. "But I am truly sorry that my stupidity put you in danger."

Now she faced Edgar. "I thought the guards would be enough, but someone must have got past them." She knelt before him. "I swear I didn't know. I owe you everything. I would gladly die to protect you all. Please don't turn me out!"

"And the knife?" Edgar asked. "You had no idea it came from this girl's father?"

"Her father?" Samonie stared at Clemence. She seemed taken aback by the news. "I don't see . . . no, why would he have come . . ."

She turned back to Edgar.

"No," she said. "Why would I have thought a lord would break into our house?"

"Samonie, you know more about this than you're telling us, don't you?" Catherine asked.

"No," Samonie answered too quickly. "There's always such a jumble of people visiting you that it's no wonder I become confused. It was terribly wrong of me to leave the house unprotected just because I wanted to sneak out to see my lover. I'll take any punishment you set, only don't blame Martin. He knows nothing."

Catherine started to speak, but Edgar held up his hand.

"I'm not satisfied with your answer," he said. "But I'm not going to turn you out. Not yet. Catherine and I will discuss the matter. Clemence should have a say, as well, since by your silence you're keeping her from finding out the truth about her father."

"He's not the one!" Samonie blurted.

"One what?" Clemence asked.

"The man I've been seeing," Samonie said.

"Oh," Clemence said. "Of course not."

"We didn't think it was," Edgar said. "Samonie, why won't you tell us the truth? Can't you see how worried Lady Clemence is?"

"I can't tell her anything," Samonie said. "Please, do what you will, but stop badgering me about her father. I don't know how his knife came to be in our house. Ask Master Hubert, Mistress. He's the one who would know."

She stood, untied her apron and threw it on the table.

"I'm going to Willa's," she announced. "If you want to have me charged with burglary, you'll find me there."

"Samonie!" Catherine shouted.

"Let her go," Edgar said. "That's where Clemence is staying, after all. Samonie isn't thinking clearly. Perhaps none of us is."

He laughed without humor.

"I suppose I might as well take you back, if Samonie is going that way. Or would you rather stay here?"

Clemence stared at them.

"I don't know what to do," she said. "My mind is all in disorder. Do you think that woman knows my father?"

"Not carnally, I'm sure," Catherine said. "She was too adamant for me to doubt her. But she may well have met him, if not recently, then when he came to see my father on earlier visits. I can't understand why she won't tell us. What is she afraid of?"

"I don't know, Catherine," Edgar said. "But, until we can come to some sort of understanding in the matter, you and I will have to see that our children are tucked in for the night. Samonie is far too upset. Margaret, will you see to Clemence?"

"I don't mind helping," Clemence spoke up. "I like children."

"Thank you," Catherine said absently. "Edgar, I think you should be sure Samonie does go to Willa's. And stays there."

Edgar thought about this, then nodded. "You may be right. I'll get Solomon on the way. He's had too many good nights' sleep lately."

"I don't need a guard," Samonie said indignantly, when Edgar proposed to go with her.

"I know that," he answered. "We still trust *you*."

"Master, I beg you." She sighed. "I mean no harm to any of you, I swear on the bear-chewed bones of Saint Perpetua. I would slit my own throat before I let anyone hurt you."

Edgar only looked at her, waiting until she had put on her cloak and street shoes. Samonie cringed. His silences were much more frightening than another man's raging.

They said nothing more during the walk to the felt maker's. Just before they entered, Samonie turned to Edgar.

"I've told Martin only that I'm going to spend the night at his sister's," she said. "You won't upset him, will you? Not before you have to."

"I've no quarrel with Martin," Edgar said. "Unless he's helping you."

"He didn't even know about the man," Samonie said.

"He always sleeps like the dead. He never knew I was gone."

Bodille and Willa were still up when they came in. They were surprised to see Samonie instead of Clemence.

"Master Edgar," Willa began, "he didn't come to your house, did he? We wouldn't tell him where she was, even though he threatened to throttle Mistress Bodille."

"Who?" Edgar said, thinking he should return home at once. "No one came to see us."

"Shortly after you left," Bodille told them, "a man came looking for Lady Clemence. He said he was her husband, but he didn't look like a lord to me and you told us not to let anyone know she was here. So we told him he had the wrong house and he finally went off."

"What did he look like?" Edgar said.

"In his early twenties," Willa answered. "Dark hair, Picard accent."

"Lambert," Edgar said. "Damn. Does either of you know where he went?"

The women shook their heads.

"If he should come back, send him to us," Edgar ordered. "Lord or not, he really is her husband, and we have to find him."

Solomon was having a quiet game of chess with his uncle when Edgar arrived.

"Come with me," he said as he threw Solomon his cloak. "We've got to track down Jehan, Lambert and Samonie's lover."

"Her what?" Solomon said as he caught the cloak and swung it over his shoulders, knocking the pieces off the chessboard.

"No demons or ghosts in the house," Edgar said. "Just Samonie sneaking out for a quick tumble."

"You should have her whipped!" Hubert said as he gathered up the chessmen. "Leaving the house open to anyone!"

"I'm taking care of it," Edgar said. "It's nothing to do with you anymore."

"Edgar!" Solomon protested as they went out.

Edgar rounded on him. "Hubert's left us this mess," he told Solomon. "He has no right to tell me what I should do."

"Very well," Solomon answered. "But would you mind telling *me* what we're doing?"

"As soon as I decide," Edgar said, as they stepped into the night.

At the house, Catherine had first made sure all the doors were barred and bolted. Then she told Martin to wait in the entry for Edgar to return. Finally, she, Margaret, and Clemence went up to the third floor, where the children and Margaret slept. James and Edana hopped up in front of them, totally unaware of the tension in their elders.

"I've brought all this trouble on your house," Clemence said. "I'm so sorry."

"My dear, the trouble was here long before you were born," Catherine said wearily. "It's because of us that Jehan took an interest in your husband. It's Samonie I can't believe. She must have bribed the guards to look the other way when she went out and in. But why? Is the man married? A priest? Has she said nothing to you, Margaret?"

"I knew she was worried about something," Margaret said. "But I thought it had to do with Willa."

"What about Willa?" Catherine asked.

"Haven't you noticed? She's not well." Margaret sounded worried, herself. "She's not pregnant, but her fluxes have stopped and she coughs all the time and she's getting thinner and paler."

Catherine stopped in mid-step. "Blessed Mother, forgive me. I saw but didn't realize. Has she seen a leech?"

"Yes. The woman told her it was a wasting sickness and gave her some medicine, but it's not working," Margaret said.

"Poor Willa!" Catherine said. "And poor Samonie! She should have told us. Perhaps a *medicus* would know more. I'll ask Maurice whom to go to."

"I wonder if it's the felt," Clemence said. "I've been

coughing since I got there, but I stopped once I was away from the house."

"Felt?" Catherine said. "I don't know. To be honest, I have no idea how the stuff is made, except that wet wool is pressed to make a thick cloth. Maybe standing in the water all day isn't good for her."

"But I didn't stand in the water," Clemence said. "There must be a foul humor in the air there, like at the tannery or the dyer's."

"I'll go see her tomorrow," Catherine said, "and have a long talk with Samonie. I don't know what's changed her so. She used to tell me everything."

Bertulf waited until he heard Godfrey sneak out before he threw off his covers, revealing that he was not only still in shoes and belt, but also his mail shirt. He picked up his sword and buckler and held them carefully so that they didn't make a sound as he followed his servant.

He thought he was the only one who had noticed Godfrey's nightly peregrinations. However, as he left the preceptory, right behind him followed Brother Baudwin and Master Durand.

"First we're going to question the wizard," Edgar said. "He may know where Jehan lives, and, if not, he can tell us what sort of concoctions he's been selling."

"You mean that crazy old man who lives by the Biévre?" Solomon asked. "I thought only students and girls seeking love potions went to him."

"And fools," Edgar answered. "Do you remember Jehan from your childhood? Was he always so credulous?"

"I don't know," Solomon answered. "He was just another one of those brutes who rode around looking dangerous. He and Catherine's uncle Roger seemed to be the loudest of them, but Aunt Johanna told me that knights skewered bad little Jewish boys at the end of their spears and roasted them, so mostly I just stayed clear of anyone in a mail shirt."

The two men reached the hut mostly by feeling their way

along the pitch-dark path. The sound of flowing water warned them when they had passed it.

"Odd that he doesn't have a lamp," Solomon commented. "You'd think he'd get most of his customers at night."

They slipped over the mossy logs that surrounded the hut and finally found the door. When Edgar knocked, it creaked open.

"I don't like the sound of that," Solomon said.

"Hallo!" Edgar called. "Wizard! *Merda*! I don't even know if he has a name."

"Edgar, if he were here, he'd have answered by now," Solomon said. "This is hardly a five-level keep."

"I wish we had a light," Edgar swore again. "We should have brought a torch."

"I'll go fetch one," Solomon offered. "Even better, let's go together. Just in case he did conjure up a devil after all, and it devoured him."

"Yes." Edgar backed out. "Maybe you're right. Can you find your way back to the main path?"

"Now that we know where the door is, I think so."

Solomon felt for a space between the bushes and, hands out in front of him, started up toward the path.

"I think we're almost to the place where we got lost going down," he said after a moment. "I think the darkness is lighter up there. Just stay close behind . . . Ulp!"

Solomon tripped and fell over an obstacle, with Edgar landing on top of him. They both were immediatly aware that there was a third body present.

"Is that your leg?" Solomon asked.

"No. Is this your arm?"

"No."

They gingerly got to their knees and felt the form of a man. He seemed to be merely very deeply asleep until something clanked against Edgar's ring.

"What's that?" Solomon's voice came from the darkness.

"I'd say a knife," Edgar said.

"Don't cut yourself."

"No fear of that." Edgar grabbed for Solomon's hand and

guided it to the spot. "It seems to be fully sheathed in this man's chest."

Solomon paused to consider this. "How long do you think he's been here?" he asked at last.

They both felt for the man's skin. It was cold and stiffening.

"Get the torch, Solomon," Edgar said. "We need to find out who this is."

"I don't suppose we'd be lucky enough to find it was Jehan," Solomon grumbled as he left.

He was back soon with a lantern he had borrowed from a man using it to light his way to the privy.

"I have to return it by the time he's finished," he told Edgar. "Now."

The light showed a face contorted more in anger than fear.

"The wizard," both men said at once.

"Now what?" Solomon said.

"Well, the one who did it is likely long gone by now," Edgar said. "I wish I could swear this is Jehan's knife, but I don't recognize it."

"What do you think?" Solomon asked after a moment. "Do we go for the watch or head straight home and forget we ever had this little adventure?"

Edgar thought about it briefly. "I suppose the watch will want to know what we were doing down here."

"We got lost on the way to the Blue Boar?" Solomon said. "It sounds feeble even to me."

"Right," Edgar got up. "Home it is."

"You realize," Solomon said, when they were well away, "if Catherine finds out about this, she'll never let us hear the end of it."

"Why, because we didn't investigate further?"

"No," Solomon answered. "Because this time we were the ones to trip over a body."

Catherine got the girls and the little ones settled in for the night. She was amazed at how quickly Clemence fell asleep considering all the uncertainty in her life. It was as if she'd been sharing a bed with Margaret for years. When Catherine checked, the two were nestled together like baby birds sound asleep.

After checking all the doors and windows again and making Martin a mint-and-honey drink to help him stay awake, Catherine was still restless. She knew she couldn't go to bed until Edgar was home again. But why was it taking him so long? Had he and Samonie been attacked? Could she have tried to run from him?

She sat at the top of the steps, her elbows on her knees and her chin resting on her hands. She was prepared to stay there until daybreak, if necessary.

The house was terribly quiet.

She could sense the door of the counting room behind her. It was shut and locked. So why did she keep thinking that she heard something rustling inside?

She was tired, she told herself, and prey to fancy. The ghost of the dead man must know they were doing all they could to find his name and that of his killer. And, if he were a member of the Knights of the Temple, then he must already be in heaven and not likely to haunt the place where he had lain. He hadn't even died there. The sound was only a breeze in the rushes. Except there were no rushes in the counting room. Very well, then it was only her imagination.

"Catherine?"

Catherine's shriek was enough to wake the entire household and topple Martin from the packing barrel where he had been dozing.

Catherine turned at the bottom of the stairs without remembering how she had arrived there. She put one hand over her heart to keep it from jumping out of her breast.

"Margaret!" she said. "Don't ever do that again. Why are you up?"

"I forgot to fill the water pitcher." Margaret held up the earthen jug. "I didn't mean to scare you."

"Go back to bed, Margaret," Catherine took the jug. "I'll bring the water up."

"Is my brother back, yet?" Margaret ignored her suggestion, following her out to the kitchen.

"No," Catherine said as she poured water from the covered ewer on the table into the little pitcher. "I'm sure he'll be soon. Here, take this. I'll wait up. You need your sleep."

Margaret seemed about to object, then yawned and, taking the pitcher, went back up to bed.

Catherine saw that Martin was now sitting alertly on his barrel, although his eyelids were tending to droop.

"It seems that Edgar and Solomon are staying the night somewhere else," she told the boy. "Go on to bed."

Gratefully, he went. That left Catherine the lone soul awake in the house. Determined not to let her fancies dominate her reason, she returned to the top of the stairs.

She heard no more noises from the counting room. As the night wore on and nothing more happened, she began to droop, herself. But something told her that she needed to be watchful.

"What's the matter with me?" she said aloud. "Hours of quiet without interruption and all I can do is sit and stare at the wall?"

She got up and found the key to the counting room. She still hadn't finished reading Master Abelard's treatise. This would be the perfect time for philosophy. It would also be a chance for her to confront her fear.

The door opened onto a still room, empty of ghosts or monsters. Catherine laughed at herself. She went over to the book chest and froze mid-breath.

There on the top of the chest lay her father's account book.

She spun around, her eyes searching every dim corner of the room. Then she bent and gingerly touched the book. It was solid. She lifted it and took it out onto the landing to examine it in the lamplight.

It wasn't exactly as she had left it. The cloth covering it was torn, and there was a stain of wine or blood on one fold. She checked to be sure the book itself wasn't damaged. Then she made sure none of the pages had been torn out. When she was satisfied that it hadn't been ruined, she put it on the floor next to her and stared at it, as if expecting the book to tell her where it had been and how.

"I shouldn't have been such a coward," she berated herself. "When I heard noises in there, I should have gone in to see what it was. Even if it was a demon with scales and burning eyes who took and returned it, at least I'd have known for certain."

She stared at it a while longer.

"Where have you been?" she nearly shouted at it.

"Hunting for Jehan," Edgar answered from the bottom of the stairs. "Why are you still up?"

For the second time that night, Catherine came close to heart failure. Edgar was up the stairs in a moment to lift her from the floor and hold her until she stopped quaking.

"You didn't hear us come in," he surmised. "I didn't see you here then. We went to the kitchen to get a bowl of beer and then I helped Solomon set up his cot."

"I . . . I was in the counting room." Catherine pointed to the book. "Someone must have come through the window. Or maybe it flew. I'm prepared to believe anything at this point."

Edgar patted her head. "My poor little *cicen*," he soothed. "You must have had a dreadful night."

He looked at the book, shaking his head.

"Why steal something only to return it?" he said. "To-morrow we'll go through every page. Something may have been added that will explain everything. Now, both of us are falling over, and dawn comes early this time of year. Come up to bed."

Catherine stood, taking the account book with her. "It's not leaving my side until all this is solved," she said.

"Fine." Edgar yawned. "I only want to sleep tonight, anyway."

They looked into the hall before they went up. Solomon was already sound asleep, one arm hanging over the edge of the cot. Wearily, they made their way to their room. Catherine set the book on the bed while they undressed and then, true to her word, took it with her, wedging it into the space between the mattress and the wall.

Edgar soon joined them, blowing out the little oil lamp once he was under the covers.

The house fell silent.

Edgar rolled over, feeling all his muscles loosen and his various bumps and bruises announce their presence. He wriggled a while until he found a comfortable position and then fell asleep.

The cries from the back garden sent him first bolt upright and then onto the floor in a tangle of covers. He reached for his tunic and knocked over the lamp, spilling oil onto the bedclothes. The shouts were now being echoed up and down the street as dogs took up the call, waking their masters.

As he started down the stairs, he was overtaken by a blond shape in a tunic too small for her and a blanket over her shoulders.

"Clemence!" he shouted, as she raced ahead of him, through the hall and out. "Come back! You don't know what's out there!"

She didn't answer him, but struggled with the bar on the door. Solomon had reached it ahead of her. He was also trying to keep her from leaving.

"Let me go!" she shrieked. "You can't keep me from him! He's out there, and those men are trying to kill him. Papa! Papa! I'm coming!"

Twenty

Very early on a moonless Wednesday morning. 5 kalends June (May 28), 1147; 30 Sivan 4907. Rogation day, Vigil of the Ascension and feast of Saint Germanus, protector of the poor and runaway queens, founder of the monastery of Saint Germain des Près.

. . . ideo rationem singulis datum esse, ut inter verum et falsum ea prima judice discernatur. Nisi enim ratio iudex universalis esse deberet, frustra singulis data esset.

Reason has been given to each person so that they may discern true from false with it as the main judge. If reason were not meant to be the universal judge, there would be no point
in each person being given it.

—Adelard of Bath
Questiones Naturales

$\mathcal{T}$he door opened on the amazing sight of the proud guards marching up to the house, each followed by a pair of men, hands tied together, on a lead.

"Papa!" Clemence cried again as she ran to put her arms around one of the men.

"Clemence!" the man gasped. "What are you doing here? Where are your clothes?"

"Papa, Papa, I thought you were dead!" she cried over and over.

He put his tied hands gently over her mouth. "Hush, darling, hush," he whispered. "I'm Bertulf now. You mustn't call me Father. I'll explain later but don't say anything. Lord Osto is dead."

"But . . ." she started. His hands pressed harder. Clemence nodded acceptance.

Edgar and Solomon had lit oil lamps and were holding them in the faces of the prisoners.

"Master Durand!" Edgar exclaimed. "Brother Baudwin! What are you doing creeping around our garden in the dark?"

Master Durand was furious. When he had announced himself to the guards, ignorant clods that they were, they had not been impressed. They hadn't released their grip or lowered their knives. One had even made a most improper suggestion as to what a priest might be doing out after dark following a pair of men.

"I want these men arrested at once!" His gesture included the guards as well as Bertulf and Godfrey.

Edgar's response was politely puzzled. "Arrest my own guards?" he said. "They seem to have been doing their job very well. I see you found Clemence's father," he told them. "Good work."

"My lord," Bertulf began, "there's been a mistake. My name is Bertulf. I'll be happy to explain it all if you'll tell me why Lord Osto's daughter, whom he left safe at home in Picardy, is at your home in Paris wearing only a *chainse*."

"I was in bed, P . . . p . . . Bertulf," Clemence explained. Behind her Solomon groaned.

"So," Edgar concluded, "Bertulf and his servant were coming to visit us. And what were you and Brother Baudwin planning, Master Durand?"

"We were following the spies," Baudwin said. He stopped. "Why were we doing that again?" he asked Master Durand.

"You imbecile!" Durand shouted. "Because we suspected them of being in league with this pack. And this proves we were right! I'll have you all up before Master Evrard and Bishop Theobald the first thing in the morning! You can answer to them."

"Fine," Edgar said. "Send your men for us. We'll be delighted to tell Master Evrard about your activities. Now, if Bertulf and his servant will come in, I'll have our guards release you, on the condition that you also present yourselves to Master Evrard tomorrow to answer my complaint."

Master Durand's indignant sputters could be heard all the way down to the river, where they were taken up by a flock of ducklings who had been sleeping among the reeds. The point of the guard's knife in the cleric's back left him at a disadvantage, however. A few moments later, the guards returned to report that the men had been shown to the street and had set off in the direction of the preceptory.

Edgar thanked them and ordered that the other prisoners be untied. Then Bertulf and Godfrey entered the house with him, Clemence still clinging to Bertulf. In the hall they found Catherine and Margaret, each holding a child and both wild with anxiety. Between them and the door stood Martin, pale but determined, holding a poker as his only defense.

The sight of the boy melted Edgar's anger at the others. He gave Martin a smile and a pat of approval and led all the others into the room. Catherine and Margaret vacated their chairs for the men.

"Now," Edgar said, "I believe, *Lord Osto*, that you owe us an explanation."

Bertulf stood and bowed to Edgar. "Lord Edgar, I owe you much more than that. My profound apologies for involving you in what has become a labyrinthine disaster. But you must accept that I am no longer Osto. Lord Osto died and was unfortunately left in your house, which was inforgivable. We had no idea you would return before we could move his body."

Catherine wasn't sure if she were confused or simply too exhausted to hear correctly.

"You were Osto, but you're not anymore?" she asked.

"That is correct," Bertulf answered. "When my friend Bertulf was killed, I had to assume his identity. Godfrey and I took advantage of the kindness of Samonie to leave his body here. We had planned to move it closer to the Temple preceptory, where the knights would find it. Then we were going to identify it. But when we discovered that you had come home early and already found poor Bertulf, we didn't know what to do. How could we explain his being in your house?"

"I'm still waiting for that," Edgar said.

"But Papa," Clemence interrupted, "how could you become Bertulf? And Why? Then Lambert's father is dead? How?"

"Yes, my dear," Bertulf answered. "I dread sending word to Lambert of it. And that brings me to you. What, by the blood of the martyrs, are you doing all alone in Paris?"

"I'm not alone," Clemence explained. "Lambert and I came together. We had to find you after Mother died."

"What?" Bertulf—Osto—seemed to have lost his voice.

"That's impossible. She was fine when I left."

Clemence put her arms around him. "I know. It was very sudden. We don't know what caused it. She suddenly fell ill and died within two days. Lambert and I were afraid Lord Jordan would take me into wardship, so we were married at once and came to get you."

Bertulf looked around the room.

"And where is Lambert now?" he asked.

Clemence looked at Edgar, who answered. "We're not sure. But we hope to locate him soon. For the time being, Clemence can stay with us."

Bertulf sat stunned. Catherine ran to get him some wine. He shook his head over and over.

"It seems I owe you even more than I thought," he told Edgar. "All we wanted was for our children to be happy and the castellany to stay in their family. Bertulf hoped that by becoming one of the brethren of the Temple, he could earn the right for his son to marry Clemence. He was prepared to give his life for that. And he did. But too soon. I have taken on his intention. But it must include taking his place completely, down to his name, or my castellany will pass to another."

He closed his eyes. "My poor Edwina. I should have been with you."

Godfrey spoke up, facing Catherine and Edgar. "Please don't be angry with my master. His plans are all awry. Perhaps they were unwise in the first place, but he's given up everything for them. Taking his life wouldn't punish him, but revealing our deception would hurt everyone in our village. Who knows what sort of lord we might be given?"

Edgar ran his hand through his hair, clutching at it for support. This was all too much for a man who couldn't remember his last night's sleep.

"I don't suppose either of you left an account book in the room upstairs earlier?" he asked. "No? Of course not. That would be too simple."

Catherine came back with the wine. "I heated it with some herbs and nutmeg," she said. "I think we should all

have some. Do we dare try to sleep again? Or do you think
we should wait for the horses and elephants to arrive?"

"Elephants?" James said eagerly.

Edgar picked him up. "No, son. Mama was only joking,
I hope."

Solomon gave up his cot to Bertulf.

"I think I should report all this," he said, looking mean-
ingfully at Edgar. "Especially the return of the account
book. I'll be back tomorrow."

After some sorting, everyone was given a place to lie
down for what was left of the night. How many of them
slept is uncertain.

Lambert had spent a fruitless evening waiting outside the
felt maker's for Clemence to return. He had seen Edgar
arrive with a woman, but it wasn't she. But what was Edgar
doing there at all? The portress at Montmartre had only
told him the house where Clemence was staying, not who
had provided it. Why should this enemy of Jehan's be visiting there? Could he be keeping Clemence prisoner?

He knew he couldn't storm the house alone. He had to
go back to Jehan. The wizard had said that the amulet that
made one invisible only worked for one night. They would
have to get another.

Perhaps he should have offered to go along when Jehan
returned the book he had taken from Edgar's house. Jehan
seemed excited about the contents. He said that if it were
found in the house, they could defeat the sorcerers once
and forever, but all this creeping about made Lambert uneasy. All he wanted was to find Lord Osto and his father,
tell them what had happened and let them handle it.

Deep down Lambert didn't really care if he was made
castellan or not, as long as he could stay married to Clemence. From what he had seen, the honor included too much
fighting for others and not enough taking care of one's own.
Between the horses and the mill, Lambert felt sure that he
could give his wife as much as her father had, even if their
children would have no claim to nobility. But the two older

men were so set on the idea that he hadn't the heart to protest.

The night was becoming chill, and lights were few in the windows on the street. Edgar and his friend had left, and the felt maker's windows were all dark. Several people had given him curious stares, and one man had come up to him and whispered a suggestion that didn't sound at all appetizing to Lambert. He decided he should go back to the bridle maker's and wait for Jehan. At least he knew that Clemence had been alive and well earlier in the day. He prayed that tomorrow would bring her back to him.

Master Durand didn't wait until dawn to complain to the commander about his treatment. He confronted Evrard de Barre as he was leaving the chapel after Prime.

"I don't care how well connected this family is," he began without preamble. "They've insulted our Order. I was treated like a common thief! You must have them arrested."

Evrard had finally found an hour of peace with his soul while standing in the chapel, and he wasn't pleased to have it shattered.

"Have you been in the wine vats?" he asked. "You smell like you've been wading in the river. What are you talking about and why weren't you at the Office with the rest of us?"

His glance included Brother Baudwin, cowering a little behind the cleric.

"We have been following your orders regarding the dead knight," Durand reminded him. "Now we find that the men we sent to investigate were spies for that Edgar the Englishman. He threatened us! Told his guard to drive us out."

"What's this? Spies?" Evrard was immediately alert. "Who do they report to? Geoffrey of Anjou? The emperor?"

"The Devil, himself, I'd say," Baudwin said.

Durand pushed him out back. "Much closer to home, Commander," he said. "There's some conspiracy surrounding the deceased knight. I don't believe he was a member

of the Order at all. I think it's part of a plot by the English
or the Jews."

"Or both," Baudwin added.

"To discredit the Temple," Durand finished.

"I've not heard that either group has anything against the
brethren of the Temple," Evrard said mildly. "Unlike others, we haven't persecuted Jews either here or in Jerusalem,
and there have only been a few incidents involving the
English."

Durand began to sputter again. Evrard held up his hand.

"Bring me a full report after Sext, and I'll decide what
is to be done."

"You must send men to apprehend them now, before
they escape," Durand insisted.

"After Sext," Evrard repeated. "And be sure you bring
proof of your accusations."

The two men walked away dispiritedly.

"Proof?" Baudwin said. "What more is there than that
those two Picards went into the house while we were driven
away?"

"It would be enough for any reasonable man," Durand
agreed. "But Master Evrard is too caught up with his duties
in the Holy Land to understand the danger at his very door.
It's up to us to find something that will awaken him to it."

"Before Sext?" Baudwin's shoulders slumped. "But I've
not slept at all tonight."

"Offer up your wakefulness as a sacrifice," Durand suggested. "Like the desert saints."

Muttering that the heart of Paris was hardly a desert,
Baudwin followed after Master Durand, wondering what
damning evidence could possible be found in so short a
time. Once again, he was thankful that thinking wasn't required of him, only obedience.

Samonie returned the next morning, summoned by Martin,
who gave a garbled account of what had happened the previous night. It was intriguing enough to have her set off at
once with him for home.

Their way was hampered by the number of Rogation

processions in the streets. They were larger this year because of all the pilgrims and poor, who followed the priests and monks from church to church, begging God to save their bodies as well as their souls.

Samonie fell in behind one that was crossing the bridge, adding her prayer for Willa's recovery. A night listening to her daughter's coughing had only increased her worry.

The first thing she saw when she entered the house was Godfrey, sitting in her kitchen, dipping bread in a bowl of gruel.

"What are you doing here?" she gasped.

He looked at her in anger, gruel dripping down his chin.

"Where were you last night?" he countered. "I waited in the garden until all hell broke loose."

"And then invited yourself to breakfast?" Samonie came in and snatched the bowl from under his fingers. "Martin told me that there were trespassers in the garden and that they'd been let into the house. How could you do that after all I've done for you?"

"I had no choice!" Godfrey reached for the bowl again. "If you'd been there, then Master Bertulf and those men from the Temple would have just found us thumping each other and gone quietly away. Instead . . ."

"What, you brought friends to watch us?" Samonie was furious. "My family has been harrassed and threatened because of you and your 'Master Bertulf.' How dare you sit there eating their food?"

"Mother, Mistress Catherine wants to see you," Martin tugged at her arm.

"I'll not protect you anymore, Godfrey," Samonie said as she went out.

"You won't have to," Godfrey said sadly. "There's nothing left to protect."

The air was full of voices as Samonie came into the hall. Catherine and Edgar were there, along with Godfrey's friend, Bertulf. But the rest of the street seemed to have congregated there, as well. What had happened?

"First the body, then a fire, then thieves and all sorts of

commotion," Archer was complaining to Edgar. "You scandalize the whole community!"

"And someone dumped a ladder over my wall last night," Pagan, the grain merchant added. "It smashed my vegetable plants!"

At that Edgar raised his eyebrows at Catherine. "Ghosts don't need ladders," he mouthed at her.

"What's that?" Pagan said. "Are you going to pay for the damage or not?"

"Of course, Pagan." Edgar smiled at him. "And you may keep the ladder, as well. Now, Archer, I understand your concern, but I think we've sorted out the problem."

"Not that I've heard," Archer answered. "I'm not impressed with your station, *Lord* Edgar. You gave up any right to respect when you left your own land."

"This is my own land," Edgar said, indicating the house around them.

Catherine looked up quickly. His voice was soft. She needed to intervene before Archer felt the full fury of Edgar's anger.

"Well it's not your private kingdom, my lord," Archer said. "What you do affects all of us, and I'm not having my business soured or my family threatened because of your doings. Old Hubert wouldn't have stood for it, either."

Edgar nodded very slowly. "I'm sure he wouldn't have," he said. "And neither shall I."

Before Archer knew what was happening, Edgar spun him around and was propelling him toward the door.

"Edgar, no!" Catherine and Archer's wife, Richilde, came from opposite sides of the room to stop Edgar from throwing the miller into the street. Pagan and Giselbert reached him first. One man grabbed Edgar, the other caught Archer before he fell.

"Edgar, don't let passion rule you," Pagan said. "Archer is an ass, but he's right this time. We all need each other to survive."

Giselbert kept a tight grip on Archer as he feigned dusting him off. "What are you thinking of?" he chastised the miller. "Insulting a man in his own house! He may have been born to the nobility, but he's trying to be one of us. Do you want him to believe we're all as arrogant and selfish as they are?"

"He laid hands on me," Archer protested.

"One hand, Archer," Giselbert pointed out. "Do you want people to know that you picked a fight with a maimed man, and lost?"

This calmed Archer more quickly than any appeal to reason.

Pagan and Catherine had managed to soothe Edgar's anger, as well.

"Edgar," Catherine said sadly, "you're acting just like your father."

That comment had an instantaneous effect. Edgar settled down at once. With great effort, he then went over to Archer and held out his hand.

"I ask your pardon," he said. "Your fears are understandable. I can only assure you that all these disturbances don't involve anyone else. Your family is in no danger from these men."

He indicated Bertulf and Godfrey.

"There has been an unfortunate occurrence here," he continued. "But I believe that it will soon be resolved."

"I should hope so," Archer said grumpily. But he shook Edgar's hand.

Behind them, Bertulf had been observing Archer's behavior, first with amusement and then with a growing horror. Slowly, he rose, pointing a finger at Archer.

"That's the one!" he cried. "I knew I could mark his voice if I heard it again! That's the man who killed Lord Osto!"

Archer gaped at him. "What? Killed? What are you talking about? Who's Lord Osto?"

"Take him!" Bertulf ordered. "Don't let him escape. I heard them that night. This man fought with my lord in the tavern, and then came back and drove a spear through his back when the poor man went out to relieve himself."

Archer's jaw dropped. "That's nonsense! How can you . . ."

He turned on Edgar. "This is your doing, isn't it? You paid this man to accuse me!"

"Archer, I swear," Edgar said. "I know nothing about this. But it seems that you do."

"Pagan, Giselbert! Stand up for me!" Archer pled. "How can you stand silent? You know I never killed anyone."

"Of course he didn't." Richilde went to stand beside her husband. "This man is a foreigner and a stranger. How can anyone take his accusation seriously?"

Giselbert joined her. "I'll stand with you, old friend. Archer has a terrible temper, we all know. But if he struck a man, it would be in anger and to his face, not when his *brais* were down and his tunic up."

"How certain are you of this accusation?" Edgar asked Bertulf.

"I'll stake my life on it," Bertulf answered. "It was our second night in Paris. The Sunday after Easter. We'd found Hubert's house empty, but that afternoon his servant, that woman there"—he pointed to Samonie—"was in the garden. She remembered us, and my servant, Godfrey, had apparently come to know her quite well on an earlier visit."

They all looked at Samonie, who stared back in defiance.

"Anyway," Bertulf continued, "later that night, Lord Osto went down for a pitcher of wine while I stayed up in the loft, resting. But I heard this man clearly." He nodded at Archer. "He began by taunting my lord for his accent and the cut of his boots. Lord Osto took offense, as any man would, but one doesn't charge a bull in his own field. He endured the gibes with saintly patience."

Pagan was listening with interest. "Wait now, I remember that night," he said. "Archer was much the worse for drink. He never liked Lowlands men. But as I recall it this man, Lord Osto, took him by the throat and threatened to make him eat his words with a sauce of horse dung."

"One can only be saintly for so long," Bertulf admitted. "After that, this Archer left. Soon after that, Lord Osto must have gone out. When I came down and saw he wasn't there, I sent Godfrey to look for him. He found Lord Osto dead in a ditch across the road."

"I didn't do it!" Archer insisted. "I couldn't have. I'd been long gone by then. You remember, Pagan."

"I remember that you backed down when the knight threatened you," Pagan said. "You were very angry, but I'd have said too drunk to do any harm. You left soon after."

"And waited outside for Lord Osto," Bertulf repeated.

"No!" Archer shrieked.

"You should have waited and come home with us," Pagan said to him. "Then we could be sure."

"What I don't understand, My l . . . Bertulf," Catherine broke in, "is why you didn't start the cry when you found your lord dead."

"For the same reason Lord Osto shouldn't have let himself be drawn into a quarrel," Bertulf explained. "We were strangers. I didn't know who had been involved in the murder. It might have been everyone in the tavern. I had no one to stand with me in the accusation."

"Where was your servant?" Edgar asked. "Did he hear nothing?"

Godfrey stared at the floor. "I was tending to the horses," he muttered. "And was delayed. I should have been there with him."

"You can't take any blame," Bertulf assured him. "We were careless of danger, when we should have been watchful. But now I do cry out, and against this man."

He pointed again at Archer.

Edgar wanted nothing more at the moment than to get all these people out of his home.

"Bertulf," he said, "your accusation will have to be investigated and other witnesses found. Then the matter will have to be taken to the authorities. Who will swear to Archer's compliance when summoned?"

"I will," Pagan said.

"And I," Giselbert agreed.

The other neighbors in the room added their voices.

"Very well," Edgar said. "Tomorrow is a feast day, but on Friday, we'll bring the matter to the provost. Archer, you might spend the time finding someone besides your wife who saw you at home before Lord Osto was killed."

"My doorkeeper can vouch for me, too," Archer muttered, as the neighbors led him out.

Slowly the room emptied. Even though Archer feared for his life, Edgar was sure that he wouldn't try to flee. If he did, his property and that of all the friends who stood with him would be forfeit.

When they were alone Bertulf apologized once more to Edgar.

"I should never have brought you into this mess," he said.

"It was my fault, Master Edgar," Samonie said.

Edgar turned to her in astonishment. He hadn't even seen her enter. "You let them into the counting room, didn't you?"

Samonie nodded. "They didn't know anyone else," she explained. "When they came to me, I first told them to take their problem elsewhere. But then they told me why the body must seem to be Lord Osto's and how they needed time to prepare the deception."

She appealed to Catherine.

"Mistress, I know how good you've been to me," she said. "But if Willa had come to you and said that she wanted to marry a lord, you would have told her she was mad."

"Only because I know a lord's family wouldn't have permitted it," Catherine said.

"And I know it all too well," Samonie agreed. "And yet Willa's father is better born than any of you. Her blood is noble, only her birth was base. Her father doesn't even know she exists, and wouldn't admit to her if he did. After all, I was only a kitchen maid."

Catherine was beginning to understand.

"So you helped them for the sake of Bertulf's son," she said.

"Lord Osto was willing to pretend to be less than he was," Samonie answered. "I've only known one other man in my life who would do that. He was also willing to see his fief governed by a man who had once been his dependent, one who wasn't even a knight. I've never known any man who would do that. Of course I helped. My fondness for Godfrey had nothing to do with it, whatever he may think."

"And that's why you wouldn't tell us?" Catherine asked.

"There are some things, Mistress, I can't expect you to understand," Samonie said. "Even you, Master Edgar. You were willing to give up your birthright because you carry your belief in your own nobilty inside your soul. It can't be removed. But would you stand by to see your patrimony taken by one of your serfs and him set up in your place?"

She could see by his face that Edgar found the idea preposterous.

"As Christians we're taught to believe that the last shall be first and that all souls are equal," Bertulf reminded him.

"In the eyes of God, of course," Edgar said. "Even within the Church to some extent. Our friend Maurice is the son of peasants. But for those who must rule others, blood is essential."

"Nobility of spirit can transcend breeding," Bertulf answered. "My friend was willing to earn a place for his son. Should that be denied because death intervened?"

"It won't matter to Archer's punishment if he killed a knight or a miller," Catherine said. "He can only hang once. I think we should accept the word of Bertulf that the body we found was that of Lord Osto. But you two must go to Commander Evrard and explain to him that we had nothing to do with his death."

"I agree with Catherine," Margaret said. "Edgar, do you want Clemence forced to renounce Lambert and marry someone she doesn't know, just because you wouldn't keep silent?"

"Of course not," Edgar said. "I won't interfere with your plans, Bertulf, although I'm not sure I agree with them. As long as the matter of Lord Osto's body is cleared up, I consider the rest of your business none of mine."

"Thank you!" Bertulf smiled. "Thank all of you for your help and consideration. Clemence, isn't that wonderful?"

There was no answer. They all looked around.

"Clemence?"

Twenty-one

At the same time, in the house of Abraham the vintner.

Quod luctus dabat impotens
Quod luctum geminans amor
Deflet Taenara commovens
Et dulci veniam prece
Umbrarum dominos rogat.

That which his unchecked sorrow gave,
and his love, doubling sorrow,
Moved Taenara to tears
And through his sweet supplication
Begs mercy from the lord of shadows.

—Boethius
Consolation of Philosophy
Poem XII, on Orpheus

*I*t's a relief to know that my accounts have been returned," Hubert said to Solomon. "But I'd feel better knowing why they were taken in the first place and by whom. By the way, you should go through the book with Catherine soon, after things have settled and I've gone. The names of all our contacts are in it, along with what they trade in and how trustworthy they are."

"Once this business of the dead knight is completed, I will," Solomon promised. "Now that we know who he was and how the body got there, it should soon be resolved. At least it should alleviate any suspicion on Edgar and Catherine."

"So Jehan had nothing to do with the man's death?" Hubert asked.

"I'm afraid not, Uncle," Solomon said. "I wish I could say that he had. Which reminds me, did you ever see that daughter of Lord Osto's?"

"No, I only met him at the fairs. Why?" Hubert asked.

"It's amazing. She's extremely pretty and, at first glance, she looks very much like your daughter Agnes."

On the Grève, a thorough search had been made in the house and down to the river. There was no sign of Clemence.

"Would she have gone off on her own to look for Lambert?" Edgar asked.

"She might have," Bertulf answered. "She was always a

willful child. But she knew she'd have more luck finding
him if she stayed with us. Has your boy returned from
asking at his sister's, yet?"

"Yes," Catherine said. "Willa hasn't seen Clemence.
Have we tried Montmartre?"

"She wouldn't go back to the nuns," Margaret said. "It's
too far, and she knows Lambert already asked there."

"Then the only other possibility is that she's been abducted," Bertulf said. "All of those people in the house,
any one of them could have waited outside for Clemence
and spirited her away for ransom."

"With no one noticing?" Catherine spoke firmly. "I'm
sure she's fine. It's broad daylight, and the streets are
crowded with penitents. Perhaps she joined one of the processions."

"Without telling us?" Bertulf asked.

Catherine admitted that it was unlikely. "But she might
have stopped to watch and been swept up in the crowd."

In the midst of their worry there came a pounding on the
door. Martin went to open it, followed by everyone else.
All of them were hoping that Clemence had returned.

Instead they found a group of soldiers in the black cloaks
of the Temple sergeants.

"We've come to arrest *dom* Bertulf and Godfrey on the
charge of abandoning their post and of insinuating themselves into the preceptory of the Temple with the intent to
do evil," their leader announced. "By orders of the marshal,
they're to come with us to answer the charges."

Bertulf shook his head, backing away.

"I can't come now," he said. "I have to search for my
. . . Lord Osto's daughter."

"That's not our concern," the sergeant told him. "Our
orders are to take you by force, if necessary."

"These men are guests in my house," Edgar said.

The sergeant looked at him. "Then perhaps you had better come with us, too."

Bertulf stepped forward, "No. We've caused these good
people too much trouble already. Leave Lord Edgar be. I'll
go with you. Come, Godfrey."

"We'll find her and bring her to you," Edgar promised.

"Just swear not to betray us," Bertulf whispered.

Edgar nodded his promise as the men were led away.

"Will they be harmed?" Catherine asked.

"They've done many foolish things," Edgar said, "but nothing truly wrong, I hope. I believe that Bertulf can clear his name."

"And Archer?" Catherine asked.

"That I don't know," Edgar said. "It looks bad for him. But our first duty is to find Clemence. If only I knew where to begin."

"I think you should see what you can do to help Bertulf," Catherine said. "The rest of us will continue the search for Clemence."

A suspicion was growing in her mind that she knew what had happened to Bertulf's daughter. If she were correct, it was imperative that Edgar not be nearby when Clemence was found.

Clemence was terrified. She had only stepped out for a moment to clear her head. The closeness of the hall full of people was making her dizzy. The next thing she knew she'd been trussed up and covered with a bag smelling of mushrooms, then thrown in a narrow, deep cart. She'd wiggled and screamed as best she could through her bonds, but there had been too much noise in the street for anyone to hear. At least no one had come.

Finally, she'd been taken out of the cart and carried for a while in a man's arms before being dumped onto what felt like a lumpy mattress. To make things worse, the man seemed confused as to who she was. He kept calling her Agnes.

"There, my darling," he said as he swung her off his shoulder and onto the mattress. "You're safe now. No one saw you leave your house. They'll never guess where to look for you."

The sack came off, but the light was too dim for Clemence to see her abductor clearly. A finger stroked her cheek, and she shrank from it.

"I knew you'd come back to me," the man said. "You were never like the rest of them. You don't even look like them. My sweet, pure girl. You've made me so happy."

Clemence struggled to spit out the gag and tell him that he'd got it wrong.

"No, my dear, I can't untie you yet." He continued to stroke her cheek. To Clemence it felt like a file rasping her skin. "I know you've come back to me, but I must be sure of your change of heart. Don't fret; I know it won't be long."

Clemence opened her eyes wide, trying to make out the man's features. It was no one she knew, she was certain. The cloth in her mouth was chafing her lips. The rope around her wrists burned, and the sound of water flowing nearby made her realize that she really had to go to the privy.

As though he had sensed her thoughts, the man took another length of rope and tied one end to a post holding up the roof and the other to the bonds around Clemence's hands. Then he untied her feet and set a chamber pot on the floor next to her.

"I have to go for a while," he said, patting her on the head. "I'm sorry about the ropes, but it's only until you regain your right reason. Don't worry. I'll return as soon as I can."

After he left, Clemence kicked and pounded and made what noise she could with her mouth closed, but no one came.

"I need to see Commander Evrard," Edgar announced to the porter at the Temple preceptory. "It's about the men from Picardy who were brought in a short time ago as prisoners."

"They don't need an advocate," the porter told him. "Lord Evrard is a fair judge."

"I'm sure he is," Edgar said. "But unless I can talk with the prisoners, he won't be able to get to the truth of the matter."

"Think a lot of yourself, don't you?" The porter spat next to Edgar's boot.

"And I may well be justified," Edgar said. "Why don't you let the commander decide?"

Shortly thereafter, Edgar was taken into a small room and told to wait while the prisoners were brought to him.

At first, Bertulf wasn't inclined to talk to anyone. Godfrey simply folded his arms on the table and buried his head in them, asking them to wake him when it was time for the trial.

Edgar looked at Bertulf in annoyance.

"You know, your accusation of Archer would be attended to more seriously if you admitted your real name," he said.

"That would defeat all I've done so far," Bertulf answered. "If the judge is honest, then I'll be believed. You saw how even his fellow tradesmen had to allow that this Archer had infuriated my friend."

Edgar crossed his arms on the table and leaned across it. "They didn't have to allow anything, Bertulf," he said. "They did it because they're honorable men."

"All the more reason to feel confident that the murderer will be punished," Bertulf answered. "But I can't worry about that when Clemence is missing. Has no one reported seeing her?"

"There are a thousand girls with brown eyes and blond hair in Paris," Edgar said. "I didn't know how many until we began searching for one."

Bertulf buried his face in his hands. "Nothing has gone right since I left Picardy. Perhaps it's true that God is angry with both of us for trying to change our station in life. The priest did tell me that we should be content with what we were given. But I believe Lambert would make a fine castellan."

"Then you'll tell the judge and the Temple commander that you're really Lord Osto?" Edgar asked.

"I've come this far," he answered. "I don't know if I can. Right now all I can think of is Clemence. If she's been killed, then nothing else will matter, ever again."

∞

Jehan returned to his room to pack up his things. Agnes was his at last! He would take her with him, far away, where none of her family could ever find her again. He was so filled with plans and joy that he had forgotten all about Lambert, who was waiting for him, sitting miserably on the bed in the little room.

"Did you find her?" He jumped up from the bed, his heart leaping at the satisfaction on Jehan's face.

"Yes," he answered. "Finally she came to me! I have to leave at once before her sister and father find her and try to pollute her heart against me once more. Returning the book made them understand that I was serious. I knew they'd let her go if I threatened them with exposure. I'm sorry, Lambert, I have no more time for your search. I have to buy provisions for the journey and hurry back to my love."

"Found her? How? Clemence has no sister," Lambert said. "Where is she?"

"Clemence? Oh, your wife. No, I know nothing about her." Jehan was stuffing his clothes into a leather bag. "She's probably gone back to the nuns."

"She hasn't." Lambert tried to make Jehan stop long enough to pay attention to him. "At Montmartre they said she'd gone to a felt maker's house on the Île, but when I got there they said she wasn't there anymore. Later, I saw that Edgar visiting the felt maker. Why would my Clemence be with him? Do you think they've stolen her?"

Jehan finally focused on him.

"I'm sure they did," he said. "Just as they did my Agnes. You'll have to be crafty to rescue her. I'm sorry I can't help, but I must rush before they find out where Agnes is hiding and try to steal her back from me."

"Wait!" Lambert tried to keep Jehan from going. "You can't abandon me. I have no one else!"

Jehan's expression changed. "Then you're no worse off than I was. I would stay if I could. At least you know what you're up against. I hope you find your wife. Good-bye."

Lambert flung himself at Jehan. "No! I've done everything you asked. You must help me!"

The young man was no match for Jehan. The knight left him sprawled on the floor, weeping in anger and fear for Clemence. At last he pulled himself up and wiped his face on his sleeve.

"Very well," he told himself. "If I must face the demons alone, it's time I started."

His first thought was to go to the wizard for another amulet of protection. Then he remembered the man's insistence on payment. He had nothing left. His hand went to the iron cross at his neck. Christ would protect him, wouldn't he? Lambert's faith wavered. Perhaps he could sell his good boots for enough to get another invisibility charm.

Lambert had never sold any of his possessions before, but Lord Osto had once mentioned that Jews took pledges in exchange for small loans. Jehan had gone on about the book they had taken being full of Jewish magic. That meant there must be some in Paris that he could take his boots to.

In her determination to prove Archer innocent, Richilde had persuaded Genta to come with her to see Catherine. The two women were now seated in the garden, sipping beer and ignoring the tray of cakes.

"Surely you don't believe this preposterous accusation against Archer," Genta was saying. "We've all known him for years. The mere fact that your husband could intimidate him is proof that he's not dangerous."

"The man who died was hit from behind," Catherine said. "It takes little courage to do that."

"My husband would never do such a thing," Richilde stated. "He's a member of the water merchants and takes his position seriously. He's not some common *ribaud* to attack a man in the dark for such a petty reason!"

Catherine put down her bowl. "I'm inclined to agree with you, Richilde. Archer isn't the sort of man who murders. But a sergeant of the Temple has accused him. We can't ignore that."

Genta put a hand on Richilde's arm. "I've been making some inquiries about this Bertulf," she said. "He hasn't yet become a member of the Temple, and there is some question now if he'll be permitted to take the vows at all. Who is he? Just some stranger. You say he's a friend of your father's?"

Catherine sighed. "He has done business with my father," she explained. "I'd never met him before, but Solomon remembers the horse Father sold him."

"And on his word you let the man be a guest in your house?" Genta's eyebrows rose.

"Not precisely," Catherine said. Obviously Genta hadn't heard that Bertulf had been taken back to the preceptory under guard. "However, I can see no reason for him to accuse Archer without some reason."

"To turn suspicion from himself, perhaps?" Genta suggested.

"Possibly," Catherine said. "But I doubt it. No suspicion ever rested on Bertulf. He didn't need to tell us who the man in the counting room was."

"But if the information were discovered, wouldn't it have been wise for him to have someone else to fix the blame on?"

Catherine agreed. "But, as I don't believe Archer could lie in wait for a man and drive a spear through his heart, I don't think Bertulf would, either. If he had wanted to murder his lord, he would have had many chances along the journey. He could have waited until they reached the Holy Land and say they had been ambushed by Saracens."

"Still," Genta said, "I think it far more likely that he did it than Archer. I've already spoken to Commander Evrard about this, and I will to Queen Adelaide, if necessary."

"I wish you would," Catherine surprised both women by saying. "Their authority may be able to get to the truth of the matter in ways we can't. Despite Edgar's anger, he has a high regard for Archer. Neither of us would be pleased to see him hang for something he didn't do."

∞

Abraham was puzzled by the young man standing before him.

"I don't know who sent you to me," he told Lambert, "but I don't give loans on boots. And I don't know anyone who would take a cross as security, except from a bishop or abbot. But if you're hungry . . ."

"No, I need money for something else." Lambert knelt before Abraham and raised his hands in supplication. "My wife is being held prisoner. I must save her."

"You want ransom money?" Abraham asked. "Have you no family to help you raise it?"

Lambert sank down on his haunches. "Actually, no one has asked for ransom. But she's missing, and I think she was taken by the family of a merchant here in Paris. If not for money, I don't know why. My friend, Jehan, says it's because they're wicked and no one can comprehend what evil has in its mind."

"Jehan!" said a man seated at a table on the other side of the room. "You can't mean the knight from Blois, can you?"

"He is from Blois, I believe," Lambert said. "Do you know him? I understood that he had no business with your people."

Hubert felt a strange thrill at being accepted as a Jew by this young man. He wasn't sure whether or not he liked it.

"The one I know hates us all passionately," Hubert described him as Lambert nodded. "Yes, that's Jehan. You can't believe anything he says. He's totally mad."

"What do you know of it?" Lambert challenged him. "Everything he's told me so far has proved true."

"Then why haven't you gone to him for help?" Abraham asked.

Lambert started to explain, then stopped. These men were infidels and clearly Jehan's enemies.

"He's leaving Paris tonight and can't help me further," he told them.

Hubert sighed in relief. "I'm glad of that. I was afraid he'd never go until he took his revenge on us for not letting him marry Agnes. Thank goodness she's safe from him in Germany."

Lambert looked at him. "Agnes? The merchant Hubert's daughter? You mean she doesn't live here in Paris?" he asked.

"No, she married last year, to a German lord," Hubert said. "Jehan was an embarrassment to everyone then insisting that she marry him. His actions might have caused her serious harm."

"She's not in Paris," Lambert repeated. "Then whom did he rescue?"

"Young man, what are you talking about?" Abraham asked.

In confusion, Lambert explained. Hubert and Abraham gave each other a worried look.

"Your wife," Hubert asked. "She isn't the daughter of Lord Osto, is she?"

Lambert was too bewildered to prevaricate.

"Yes," he admitted. "Clemence."

"Heaven save us!" Abraham said. "Young man, I want you to go directly to the house of Catherine LeVendeur and her husband and tell them everything!"

"The thought of that poor child in Jehan's clutches!" Hubert exclaimed.

"Chaim!" Abraham said. "The boy is frightened enough already. Will you go there at once?" he continued to Lambert. "Do you know the way?"

"Yes, I do," Lambert put on his cap and turned to go. Then he stopped, the new information finally penetrating.

"Do you mean Jehan is the one holding my wife?" he asked. "Are you sure?"

"Yes," Hubert said. "Now hurry, before he gets away." Lambert did.

When he had gone, Abraham called Solomon to come up. He explained what had happened.

"I think you should go along after the boy to be sure he finds his way to Edgar's house and is able to tell his story in such a way that they'll understand the urgency."

"Of course I will," Solomon told the two men. "But I have no doubt that they'll understand."

At the Temple preceptory Evrard de Barre had been informed of the situation regarding Bertulf and Godfrey.

"Their story doesn't have the ring of truth," he said. "If their lord had been killed by a citizen of Paris, why not start the cry at once?"

"They say it's because they were strangers and worried that they would meet the same fate as Lord Osto," Durand replied. "But I agree that there's something not right here. For instance, the man Bertulf says that the destrier they brought with them is his. But it's not the horse of a miller turned soldier. What nobleman would let one of his villagers take his best horse?"

"A Christian one?" Evrard suggested. He brushed aside Master Durand's expostulations. "Yes, it does sound odd. Even worse, *Domna* Genta has asked me to judge the matter, myself. It seems she's a friend of the accused man's wife. She hinted that if I don't, she'll ask the king why the Temple is taking in men without a complete examination of their character. As if we had time these days! That means another day borrowed from the work I have to do before I leave. I pray I'm never called upon to pay them all back."

Lambert ran to the Grève, heedless of people and things in his way. Solomon was glad he didn't have to keep track of him. He had enough to do helping people to their feet and picking up objects Lambert had knocked down in his hurry.

However, as he approached the door, Lambert's pace slowed. After the rude way he'd behaved, why would they let him in or pay attention to his tale? Then he thought of Clemence. He realized that it hadn't only been that there wasn't any place suitable for her that had kept him from taking her with him to Jehan. It had been the man himself. Lambert had sensed the madness but had been too preoccupied to recognize it.

He lifted the dragon's nose and sounded the bell.

Martin showed him in. Catherine was still trying to

soothe and entertain Richilde and Genta. Lambert barely noted the other women present. He went straight to Catherine.

"Please help me," he begged. "Do you remember me? My name is Lambert, son of Bertulf the miller. Master Abraham told me that my wife has been abducted by Jehan. He said you'd know what to do."

Catherine tried to take all of this in. Quickly Richilde and Genta stood to go.

"Young man," Richilde said, "your father has just accused my husband of murder. I see no need to stay in the same house with you."

"My father?" Lambert gaped at her. "Murder?"

Genta put an arm around Richilde.

"Catherine," she said, "if this is an example of the things that happen in your household, I'm not sure we'll be seeing much of one another in the future."

In the back of her mind, Catherine sent up a prayer of thanksgiving.

"I should be very sorry if that happened," she told Genta. "Take care of Richilde. I'm sure this will all turn out well. The true killer will be uncovered and Archer exonerated, I'm sure. Now, Lambert. Why do you think Jehan has Clemence?"

"I don't know," Lambert replied. "But Master Abraham and his friend said you would understand."

Solomon had entered as the women left.

"Clemence looks like your sister," he explained. "I suspect that Jehan took her to replace Agnes."

"Saint Radegunde's pristine privies!" Catherine exclaimed. "I felt he must be in this somehow, but couldn't find a reason or an opportunity. How did he know Clemence was even here?"

"She was? Why didn't you tell me?" Lambert exclaimed.

"Jehan must have been spying on the house," Solomon said. "You say he's your friend?" he added to Lambert. "You poor fool! And you have no idea where he could have taken her?"

"No. He came to our room, said he was buying provisions and then leaving with 'Agnes,' " Lambert said. "If only I had known!"

"Then he may not have gone, yet. Think! Where could he have left her?" Solomon insisted.

Lambert pressed his fingers to his forehead. "If not with the nuns on Montmartre, I don't know."

"He wouldn't have done that," Catherine said. "She'd have told them immediately that she was being abducted. It would have to be a secret place, where she wouldn't be easily discovered."

Solomon put his hands on Lambert's shoulders.

"Now, I know this will be difficult," he said, "but you have to try to remember every place you went with Jehan since you met him."

"Every place?" Lambert thought of the midnight visit to the counting room.

"Yes," both Solomon and Catherine answered.

"Very well," Lambert closed his eyes to think better. He opened them again. "What was that about my father? Have you seen him?"

"Not now," Catherine said. "First we must find Clemence before Jehan leaves the city with her."

Edgar was relieved that the question of the body had been resolved, but annoyed with Bertulf for refusing to admit that he was really Osto. Still, it would be easier to convince Commander Evrard that the accusation against Archer was weak if it came from a miller. But if not Archer, then who? Edgar passed through the Rogation processions without even noticing them. His mind was on the things he needed to do once all this was ended. He hadn't yet admitted it to himself but, deep down, he didn't think he would mind being a merchant, as long as he could be a wealthy one.

Solomon met him at the door.

"Don't take your cap off," he greeted Edgar. "Do you know if the cry has been raised for the death of the wizard?"

"I've heard nothing," Edgar said.

"Neither have I," Solomon said. "But I think Jehan has stowed Clemence in the old man's hut."

"Jehan!" Edgar blinked. "What has he to do with her?"

"Everything," Solomon said. "We have to get there at once. And, if that's where she is, then it's because Jehan knew that the wizard wouldn't be there. Do you know what that means?"

Edgar's eyes began to light. Slowly, he smiled.

"We've got him!"

Catherine wondered if she should have told Lambert that his father was dead. He'd have to know soon. She hoped that Lord Osto's faith in him was warranted. Lambert didn't seem capable of the steady hand needed to maintain a castellany. Catherine had observed her brother at it many times. Even though a merchant's son, Guillaume had been raised at their uncle's keep and knew how to fight as well as administer a fief. Unlike Picardy, France allowed for noble blood on one side only, if the other side was at least respectable.

She told herself that it wasn't her problem. She should be worrying about what would happen if Solomon and Edgar found Jehan with Clemence. She was glad they were there to protect Lambert. But she was afraid that they had confused Jehan's weak mind with a weak body. Even though Jehan was much older than either of them, she had no doubt that he would defend himself fiercely if cornered.

Catherine had told Margaret about Lambert's visit when she came down, hearing Solomon's voice. Now she realized that the girl was fretting, as well.

"Jehan won't beat Clemence, will he?" she asked, her hand rubbing the scar on her cheek.

"Of course not," Catherine said. "He thinks she's Agnes. He would never hurt her. Edgar and Solomon will find him before he realizes his mistake."

The next question surprised her.

"What if Solomon kills Jehan?" Margaret asked. "He could get in trouble for the death of a Christian."

Catherine remembered an earlier time when this had happened. Solomon had killed to save her life, but Edgar had taken credit for it rather than risk Solomon's safety.

"Jehan isn't much of a Christian," Catherine answered. "And there will be three of them. I'm sure they can take him without serious harm to anyone."

Margaret nodded doubtfully. Catherine decided that Margaret needed distracting.

"Why don't you take Martin and go over to Willa's," she suggested. "You can collect anything Clemence might have left there. Take Willa some honey and cakes, as well."

"Yes, I will," Margaret answered. "But I fear they won't help her. She seems weaker every day. I think it will take a miracle to make her well."

"Then we'll all pray for one." Catherine kissed her and sent her on her way.

"You think Jehan killed the wizard?" Lambert asked as he trotted after Solomon and Edgar. "Shouldn't we call out the watch?"

"It would take too long," Edgar answered not wanting to mention his lapse in informing the watch. "You want to get to Clemence before Jehan comes back, don't you?"

Lambert trotted more quickly.

"What if he's in there with her?" he asked.

"We're sending you in first," Solomon answered, his breath coming in pants as they all sped up. "He doesn't know you suspect him."

"Me?" Lambert squeaked. "Face Jehan?"

"It's your wife in there, isn't it?" Edgar said.

Lambert's fists clenched.

"Yes," he answered, his face suddenly older. "And I'm going to get her out."

Twenty-two

Still Wednesday, early in the evening. Vespers is sounding.

Filz Loois, a celer ne te quier,
Quant Deus fist reis por peuple justicier,
Il nel fist mie por false lei jugier,
Faire luxure, ne alever pechié.
Ne orfe enfant por retolir son fié . . .

"My son Louis, never seek to hide the fact
That God made the king to give justice to the people,
He never made him to judge the law falsely
to be debaucherous, nor to promote wickedness,
nor to steal the orphan child's fief. . . .

—Le Couronnement de Louis
Laisse 13

I still don't understand how you decided this was the only place he could have taken her," Lambert said when they stopped at the head of the path down to the wizard's hut.

"Not the only, but the most likely. If no one else has been here, you'll find out soon enough," Solomon answered. "Now, quietly."

He and Lambert started down the path. Edgar stayed at the top to watch for Jehan.

"If he's down there, you'll hear from us," Solomon assured him.

They were halfway down when Solomon stopped and looked around, peering into the undergrowth.

"Did you lose something?" Lambert whispered.

"The wizard," Solomon whispered back. "Jehan must have dumped him in the river. Damn."

He held up a finger to remind Lambert not to say any more as they approached the hut.

The door was shut. The only sound that came above the running water was a rhythmic thumping from inside, interspersed by an occasional muffled squeak.

Lambert gave a shout, "Sweet Jesus, he's raping her!" and broke the door open with one blow of his body.

They saw nothing at first in the dim light. Then there was a scrape from one corner and the squeaking rose to a muffled wail.

"Clemence!" Lambert cried. "What has he done to you?"

He pulled off the gag. Clemence took a long breath and then began coughing.

"My dearest!" Lambert cried. "Are you all right? Did he hurt you?"

He felt her all over for signs of injury. While he did, Solomon took out his knife and cut the ropes around her wrists.

"*Fi!*" She cried. "Oh, that hurts. My hands, Lambert, rub them."

"Anything, my love!"

Clemence tried to hold back her tears, but pain and relief were too much for her.

"I feared no one would ever come." She sniffed. "That man! He kept calling me Agnes. He was so sure of it that I began to wonder if it weren't my name after all. Oh, Lambert! I'm so sorry about your father. What are we going to do now?"

"My father?" Lambert stopped his rubbing to stare at her.

Solomon thought it would be better if he were elsewhere. He went back up the path to find Edgar.

"She's in there," he said. "Unharmed as far as I could tell. Jehan seems to have only tied her up."

"That means he hasn't come back, yet," Edgar said. "He must be getting his horse and provisions."

They both thought about that.

"We should take Clemence and Lambert and hurry home before he returns," Solomon said.

"Then he would get away," Edgar objected. "How can we prove he killed the wizard if we don't have the body?"

"He still abducted Clemence," Solomon reminded him.

"And if he finds her gone, don't you think he'll get out of Paris as quickly as he can?" Edgar asked.

"No." Solomon ran his fingertip along the blade of his knife. "I think he'll come back to your house, hunting for her. He thinks she's Agnes, and you're the ones keeping her imprisoned."

Edgar looked at him. "That's insane! After what he's done, I don't want to risk him near my family, ever again."

"I agree," Solomon said. "That's why one of us should

see that those two naive children get safely back to the house, while the other goes back to the wizard's hut and waits for Jehan."

"Then you take them back," Edgar announced. "I have more scores to settle with him than you ever will. No, don't use my hand as an excuse. I'll have surprise on my side."

"You mustn't kill him that way," Solomon told him. "Not lying in wait for him like a thief."

"Why not?" Edgar asked. "He deserves no better."

"Edgar"—Solomon put a hand on his shoulder—"I'm not thinking of Jehan. There's no death too vile for me to pity him enduring it. But you can't have that kind of revenge on your soul."

"How can you lecture me on my soul?" Edgar was too amazed to be angry.

"Because I know it," Solomon said. "If you killed him in secret, in the dark, it would haunt you forever. And Jehan would have won after all."

"So, what do you propose?" Edgar asked, irritated at his accuracy. "Do you intend to kill him in order to save me the guilt? I won't have it."

"No." Solomon gave a humorless laugh. "Jehan would have joy in Hell knowing that I, and perhaps other Jews of Paris, as well, had been hanged for his death. On consideration, I think all of us should wait here for him and take him alive to the authorities. His crimes should be known to everyone."

"And what of his accusations against us?" Edgar said. "How do we keep him from denouncing the family as secret Jews?"

"Now that the Torah is no longer in your house, what can he prove?" Solomon said. "Let him rant. It will only increase the perception of his madness."

Edgar had to admit that Solomon's argument made sense. But how he ached to drive a knife deep into Jehan's heart and know that it had stopped beating forever. Then it struck him that his father had never hesitated to kill an enemy. But instead of ridding himself of them, from the blood of each man had arisen a thousand more.

"If you insist; we'll do it your way," he said. "But remember, I'm only agreeing with you because you're right."

"I understand." Solomon grinned.

Willa wasn't working when Margaret and Martin arrived. Her husband was stamping down the wool in the trough in her place, but jerkily, as if his legs weren't well attached to his body.

"Thank God you're here," he said when he saw them. "I wanted to send for your mother, Martin, but my master wouldn't let me go until the work was done. The king's leaving within the week, and we must finish supplying his men with the hats we promised."

"Is Willa worse?" Margaret asked.

"She was too weak to stand this afternoon," Belot said. "And she's coughing blood. Lady Margaret, you shouldn't get too close."

"Nonsense," Margaret said. "Martin, run back home. Ask Catherine to send a stretcher for Willa. She should be where she can be cared for. Belot, when you've finished, come see her at once. I know she'll improve if she can have rest and the right medicine."

Belot gave a wan smile. "I believe you, my lady."

But when Margaret went in to sit with her friend, she wasn't so hopeful. Willa was pale as death already, with a feverish flush on her cheeks the only spots of color. Margaret started to say something cheerful but the words froze on her tongue. She simply put her arms around Willa and cried.

"It's all right, dear," Willa told her between coughing spasms. "I've guessed for some time. But I didn't want to upset Belot. It will be good to be rid of the pain."

Margaret managed to control herself.

"Nonsense," she said. "We're taking you home, away from the noise and fluff in the air. We'll let you lie on a bed like a grand lady with hundreds of servants. Then you'll get well."

Willa only smiled. Margaret took her hands.

"I'm selfish, Willa," she whispered. "I've lost too many people I love. You can't leave me, too."

Willa coughed again, for several minutes, crying in between at the pain. When it finally subsided she lay back on her thin pillow.

"I'd like to die in a garden," she said.

When Solomon and Edgar returned to the hut, Lambert and Clemence were both sitting on the bed. Lambert obviously knew that his father had died.

"I should have guessed when they described him," he said. "But they told me at the Temple that the man was wearing the garb of a knight. Why would my father have a white cloak?"

"Perhaps my father can explain it," Clemence said.

"But that means we have no hope," Lambert continued. "If Father can't earn a place of honor among the brethren of the Temple, then how can we convince Lord Jordan to let us keep the castellany?"

"It seems my father has taken his place," Clemence told him. "When we see him next, you must remember to call him 'Father' and not 'my lord.' "

Lambert didn't look capable of remembering that or much of anything else. Edgar decided to distract him with the matter at hand.

"We need your help," he told the young man.

He explained to them both what they had to do.

"Solomon and I will be hiding just inside the door," he assured them. "You can tell Jehan you were waiting for him or that you were just leaving because the wizard didn't seem to be home. But you must think of something to get him to go inside. Can you?"

Lambert nodded. "The state he was in when I last saw him, he wouldn't note a word I said."

"What do we do now?" Clemence asked.

"We wait," Solomon said. "Are you well enough? It shouldn't be long."

Clemence thought she could endure a bit longer. "But I would so like something to drink," she sighed.

Lambert saw a pitcher on a shelf and started to pour a cup for her.

"I wouldn't drink anything I found in this place," Solomon said.

"I'll go up to the tavern," Lambert said. "It won't take a minute."

"No, there isn't time." Edgar said. "Jehan could come back any moment."

"Clemence can't wait," Lambert said. He started out, then turned back.

"Umm, I forgot," Lambert added. "I have no money."

"If you must," Solomon tossed him a couple of coins and he ran off at once.

"It might be well if he weren't here," Edgar commented when he had gone. "Clemence, we want you out of harm's way. Can you curl up in the far corner of the bed, just as you might be if you were still tied?"

"I won't put that gag on again," she said. "You can't imagine how vile it is."

"I doubt he'll be able to see you well enough," Edgar said. "Sunlight never seems to enter this place."

They all waited in silence, trying to think of something that might improve their chances of capturing Jehan alive without being slashed to ribbons themselves. Clemence wished she'd never mentioned how thirsty she was. What if these two men attacked Lambert by accident? What if Jehan found him first?

Solomon realized that the sound of the water running nearly under the hut would mask the sound of footsteps approaching. He wondered how long he could stand like this, poised to strike. His muscles were already aching.

It seemed forever before they were all jolted by the creak as the door was slowly pushed open.

"Agnes, my love," Jehan said. "I'm—*Guai!* What—?"

Solomon and Edgar had caught him from either side, causing Jehan to drop his bundles. Solomon had drawn his knife, but in the dark didn't dare slash out for fear of cutting Edgar. He tried to find Jehan's neck from the direction of the sputtering and cursing.

"Thieves! Help!" Jehan roared. "Let go of me, you *gloton*!"

Edgar was trying to wrestle Jehan's left hand behind his back and discovered that it was hard to do one-handed, even with his opponent befuddled by surprise and the darkness.

"Do you have him?" he shouted at Solomon.

"Is there a knife point in your gut?" Solomon answered.

"No!"

"Then I have him. Don't move, you bastard," Solomon told Jehan.

"You!" Jehan yelled, realizing who held him. "Infidel! *Mesel!* And you, filthy English coward! I should have known. Agnes! what did they do to you?"

He lunged toward the bed. Solomon felt the point of his knife bend on the rings of a mail shirt. The scrape as it ran down the metal set his teeth on edge. Unable to do more, he stuck out his leg as Jehan moved forward, and sent him tumbling onto the bed. Clemence screamed.

"Clemence!" Lambert was standing in the doorway. "I'll save you!" He stepped in and smashed a full pitcher of beer down on the back of Jehan's head.

The clay shattered and beer went flying. Jehan's body slumped, half on the bed and half on the floor. Clemence quickly climbed over him and into Lambert's arms. Edgar wiped the beer from his eyes and tried to see what had happened.

"Edgar." Solomon was kneeling by Jehan. "He's still alive. Help me tie him up before he wakes."

They used the ropes that Clemence had been bound with. When they had finished, they dragged Jehan out into the dying light.

"How will we get him to the provost?" Solomon asked. "He's too heavy to carry."

Edgar stared down on the recumbent form. He would have enjoyed kicking and rolling him the whole way, but too much of it was uphill.

"Clemence and I will go fetch someone with a cart," Lambert offered.

"Yes. Go to my house. Ask Pagan, who lives next to us," Edgar said. "He has a cart small enough to make it down the road as far as the path to this hut."

After they had left, Solomon and Edgar mopped up the spilled beer from their faces and hands. Solomon licked his fingers sadly.

"It was Blue Boar Ascension Feast Special," he mourned.

"We can drown ourselves in it after we get Jehan safely locked up," Edgar promised him.

"He won't slip away this time, will he?" Solomon worried. "Even if no one ever finds the wizard's body, he still abducted Clemence."

"My only fear is that he'll be considered too witless to hang," Edgar said.

"Mine is that some ignorant priest will set him a pilgrimage as a penance instead of punishing him now," Solomon said. "I don't suppose we can prove he also killed 'Lord Osto.' "

"I don't see how," Edgar said. "Although I'd like to try, for Archer's sake."

By the time Pagan and Lambert came back with the cart, Jehan was beginning to stir.

"Quickly!" Edgar said. "We forgot to gag him. Where's that rag he used on Clemence?"

Solomon managed to tie the cloth over Jehan's mouth before he came fully awake. It took all four men to get him into the cart and then, even trussed up, he shook it so that Pagan was afraid it would upset.

"Keep still!" Edgar ordered. "Or we'll make you crawl all the way to the provost."

Jehan subsided.

The sun had set by the time they had made it to the watch house on the *Grand Chastelet* and convinced the guard to lock Jehan up until the provost could arrange a trial for him. The strong aroma of Blue Boar Ascension Feast Special made it harder for them to convince the guard that the matter was serious. When they left Edgar felt as if a load had been taken from him.

"At least we know he can't do anything to us from there," Solomon said.

"And nothing will be done about him tomorrow," Edgar reminded him. "Everyone will be celebrating the Ascension."

"Not everyone," Solomon said. "But I wouldn't mind a bucket or two of that beer. I'll celebrate *Rosh Hodesh*."

"What's that?" Lambert asked.

"The new moon," said Solomon. "And the start of a new month."

"A better one, I hope," Lambert said.

"If it finally sees the departure of all these so-called pilgrims," Solomon said. "And the end of our troubles with Jehan, it will be."

Clemence was greeted with joy by Catherine.

"We'll send word to your father at once," she promised. "He was frantic about you."

"Can you have your maid fill a bath for me?" Clemence asked. "I'm not hurt, but dirty and sore from the ropes, and the touch of that horrible man."

"Oh dear, Samonie can't now," Catherine said. "Her daughter is very ill. Willa, you remember."

"Yes, I noticed when I was there that she didn't seem well," Clemence said. "I'm sorry she's worse. Is it very bad?"

Catherine's eyes filled. "We're doing what we can, but I don't believe she'll last the night. She's in Samonie's bed here."

"Then I'll just get a basin and wash my face and hands," Clemence said. "Can I help with Willa?"

"Margaret and Samonie are taking care of her," Catherine said. "I'll run over and ask if Hersende can spare her maid to go to the bathhouse with you. The baths are often busy the night before a feast day, but the one here on the Grève isn't usually as full as the one on the Île, and you won't have to worry so much about the students playing jokes. You're sure Jehan is unconscious and tied up?"

"Oh, yes," Clemence said. "Or I wouldn't have let Lambert go back to help transport him."

Thus reassured; Catherine arranged for Clemence's bath and then returned to the little room off the kitchen where Willa lay, drifting in and out of awareness.

"I've made a drink for her," Catherine said. "It's heating now."

Catherine had rummaged in her medicine box, well stocked thanks to Hubert's travels. From it she had concocted a syrup from pear wine, honey, balsam, myrrh, pepper, ginger, cinnamon, and iris. It was supposed to fortify the body and stop coughs. Even as she poured the medicine into a cup, she was afraid it was too late.

Samonie took the cup and tried to get Willa to drink a bit. Margaret knelt at the end of the bed, trying to rub some warmth into her friend's feet.

"There, precious, a little more." Samonie caught the bit that had dribbled from the side of Willa's mouth and tried to get her to swallow.

"She's burning with fever, but she complains that her feet are cold," Margaret said, panic in her voice. "What more can I do?"

"We'll sponge her with vinegar," Catherine said. "And we'll pray."

"I haven't stopped praying since I realized she was sick," Samonie snapped. "Do you think God will pay more heed because you petition Him in Latin?"

"I'm praying directly from my heart." Catherine laid a hand on Samonie's shoulder. "Just as I did when the baby was sick."

Samonie winced. "In that case, try Latin, Hebrew, anything! I'd pray to Satan if I thought he'd save my child."

"Samonie, don't talk like that," Margaret said. "Willa wouldn't want you to."

Catherine watched them for a few moments. She could almost see the life ebbing from Willa. There had been talk of going to Genta for help since her father had been a doctor. But it was clear to them now that it was time to bring in the priest.

∞

Edgar and Solomon came back with Lambert to find a house in which the lamps hadn't been lit nor dinner prepared. Catherine met them in the entry.

"James and Edana are asleep in the hall so I can hear if they wake," she said quietly. "Clemence is at the bathhouse, perfectly safe. Why don't the three of you go to the tavern across from the baths and bring her home, after you've eaten?"

"And you?" Edgar asked.

"I can't eat tonight," Catherine answered. "I keep choking on my tears."

She laid her head on Edgar's shoulder. He held her close and promised that they would take care of themselves until morning.

"What can we do?" he asked.

"Could you go for the priest at Saint Merri?" Catherine asked. "Father Menhard. He knows Willa. I can't think that she would have anything to confess, but I know she'd want to receive the rites from a friend."

"There's no hope?" Edgar asked.

"Perhaps if she had rested more and had the medicine sooner," Catherine said. "I don't know. But now, she has no strength to fight the fever."

The three men went, as instructed, first to the church and then to the tavern. They all still smelled of beer, but it wasn't particularly noticeable there.

"Is it just that we're almost to Saint John's Eve or has this been an especially long day?" Lambert said. He put his head on the table while waiting for his fish soup and beer.

A moment later he lifted it up carefully. His hair stuck to the wood.

"Maybe I'll see how Clemence is coming with her bath," he said. "I am her husband, after all."

"The attendant won't believe you," Solomon said with certainty. "I've tried it."

"She'll be out soon," Edgar said. "I think the three of us need some time to decide what we need to do next. I am sorry that it was your father we found, Lambert. I realize that the shock is still new to you."

"I don't think I believe yet. So much . . . and Jehan, what a fool I was."

"You helped him?" Edgar was aghast.

"I thought you were holding Clemence," Lambert explained. "From the outside, everything Jehan told me seemed perfectly logical. You had Lord Osto's knife. You consort with . . . ah . . ."

He looked at Solomon in embarrassment.

"You *are* known for consorting, Edgar," Solomon said. "I've often meant to speak to you about it."

"I apologize," Lambert told Solomon. "I didn't understand the nature of your business."

"Very well, now you do," Edgar said. "The question is what are we to do with Jehan?"

"But the provost has him now, doesn't he?" Lambert asked. "Clemence will testify that he took her from outside your home. What more do we need to worry about?"

"That he'll convince the provost of Paris he should be tried by someone else," Edgar suggested. "His ultimate lord is the count of Champagne, not King Louis."

"What would happen then?" Lambert asked.

Edgar waited while the barmaid brought their bread, and a bowl of thin fish soup as it was a fast day, and poured more beer for all of them.

"I know Count Thibault," Solomon said as he tore off a piece of bread and dipped it in the soup. "He won't hang a man who shows repentance or one, like Jehan, who is obviously insane."

"Then he'll go free?" Lambert was indignant.

"Not exactly," Edgar said. "He may be told to leave the country and never return. He was already supposed to be going to fight in Spain, so that wouldn't be so bad. But we can't count on him dying there."

"A pity, but true," Solomon said. "And you and I may well be in Spain some year and run across him again. I confess I'd like this problem taken care of once and for all time."

"It's our own fault," Edgar said. "We should have called the watch when we found the dead wizard. There are reasons for laws like that."

He and Solomon sat staring glumly into the soup, occasionally pushing a fish head back under the broth. Lambert tried to share their worry. But he was too busy grappling with the idea that his father had died. In some ways, he had anticipated Bertulf's death when the men had set out for the Holy Land. He'd borne his worst sorrow then. To his shame, what was uppermost in his mind was the fact that Clemence was standing naked in a warm soapy tub just across the road.

"Is there a section for men at this bathhouse?" he asked suddenly.

Edgar and Solomon looked at him in surprise. Then they both looked down, trying to hide their grins.

"I believe so," Edgar said. "Here are a couple of sous. You'll have to hurry. She's been there quite a while."

They managed to contain their laughter until Lambert was out the door.

"It would be a *mitzvah* if you and Catherine donated your bed to them tonight." Solomon chuckled. "Although I'm sure they'd make do with a blanket in the corner."

"Catherine probably won't mind," Edgar said, thinking of Willa. "I doubt she was planning to sleep tonight anyway."

Solomon nodded. "Margaret will be devastated. Willa is her friend." He stared into his beer a moment. "I didn't want to speak of it in front of the boy," Solomon said, changing the subject, "but what about the accusation against Archer? He could be convicted solely on the evidence that he had fought with Bertulf. I wouldn't mind if he had done it. The man avoids Jews like lepers. But I can't see it somehow."

"Neither can I," Edgar said. "Richilde says he was home before Compline, but a wife will lie to protect her husband. No one else saw him after he left the inn. If we could just place Jehan there."

"It was Godfrey who discovered the body," Solomon

said. "Perhaps he saw some clue that was ruined when the body was moved. Something he didn't recognize as important. I wish I'd seen the wound."

"No, you don't," Edgar said, picking up a fish head and popping the eye into his mouth. "It was disgusting. Even after a week or so, it was clear that whatever ran him through wasn't a sword or knife. It could have been a spear, which would make Archer even more unlikely. I thought of a tent peg, myself. Something wooden, metal tipped at best."

"Does Archer have a walking stick?" Solomon asked.

"Not that I've ever seen," Edgar said. "Who, apart from cripples, would use one in the city?"

"Right," Solomon said. "So, what does that leave? A beanpole? Too blunt. The same for a stick for driving cattle. Archer would hardly bring a fishing spear when he went out to drink with his friends."

"But, if Bertulf went out to the stream to relieve himself, he may have surprised someone poaching fish."

"Maybe," Solomon agreed. "You'll have to ask Godfrey, but I had the impression that the body was found not far from the road. There's no stream that close."

"Another soldier or pilgrim?" Edgar suggested.

"Doing a little robbery on the way to the Holy Land?" Solomon liked that idea. "That wouldn't leave out Jehan. Did they say anything was taken?"

"I don't remember, but he was still wearing his mail and boots." Edgar ripped off another hunk of bread. "Archer does seem the most likely culprit, after all."

"I wonder if Richilde will keep the mill going," Solomon said.

Catherine heard their footsteps in the hall and came to meet them. She hugged Lambert and Clemence, asked if they needed anything, then mentioned that she had just changed their bedding that morning. She didn't wait for their reply but turned to Edgar.

"I wish you'd sleep down here," she told him. "To make sure the children are all right."

Edgar pushed away a stray curl on her forehead and kissed it.

"It would be a shame to waste freshly cleaned sheets," he said. "Would you two mind taking our room for the night?"

Lambert looked as if he'd just been given the keys to Heaven, but Clemence protested that they couldn't possibly take such an honor.

"Yes, you can," Catherine told her firmly. "After what you've been through in the past few days, you need some spoiling. Only, Lambert, I'd like you to help us for a moment first."

"Anything you wish," Lambert said instantly.

"We need to carry Willa's bed out into the garden," Catherine said. "I know the night air is harmful, but she can't seem to breathe very well in the house. The air is warm, and we'll bundle her up. Will you take a corner? We don't want to jar her."

"Of course." Lambert took Clemence's hand. It seemed selfish to be looking forward to carnal joy while another woman, no older than they, lay dying.

Catherine read their thoughts.

"What could be a better tribute to a life lost," she said, "than a new one made?"

Only the children slept that night. Just before dawn, Willa's wrenching breaths finally stopped. A breeze blew through the garden, dislodging the apple blossoms above her and the first light of the sun found her, her body covered in drifting petals.

Twenty-three

Sunday, kalends June (June 1), 1147; 1 Tammuz, 4907.
The feast of no one special.

Par communal consel de trestout le chaspitre nos contredisons et commandons a estre detrenchié si come familier vice, ice que sans descretion estroit en la maison de Dieu et des chevaliers dou Temple que les sergans et les escuiers non aient blanches robes.

By common consent of all the chapters, we forbid and command, in order that he be separated by a known emblem which without doubt marks him as of the house of God and the knights of the Temple, that the sergents and the squires may not have the white cloak.

—Rule of the Temple, 28

*C*atherine would have preferred Samonie's grief to be more spectacular, as hers had been when baby Heloisa died. Instead, Samonie had bundled all the pain inside and released it through scrubbing anything within reach. Margaret and Catherine stitched Willa's shroud, weeping as they sewed. Clemence contributed a length of embroidery she had made.

The funeral was the Sunday after the Ascension. Edgar paid for Masses at the local church and, when Maurice learned about it, he arranged for one to be said by Bishop Theobald at Nôtre Dame.

Word had been sent from Commander Evrard for Archer to present himself at the Temple preceptory that afternoon to answer the accusation of murder made by one Bertulf, soon to be a sergeant of the Knights of the Temple of Solomon. Edgar and Catherine and their family also were told to come to give testimony.

Catherine and Edgar were finishing their breakfast. By mutual consent they had hired a woman to take care of the cooking and the children until Samonie had scrubbed out her grief.

"Clemence and Lambert went back up to bed after Mass," Edgar noted. "They didn't seem interested in their breakfast."

"Neither were we, when we were first married," Catherine said. "Even now most of the time we don't go to Mass at all."

"I worship at another shrine," Edgar replied.

"Edgar, that's blasphemy!" Catherine was half-scandalized and half-pleased. The latter won.

"If they don't get up soon," Edgar said, "we'll let James and that puppy of his play outside their door for a while."

"Is he ever going to name it?"

"So far it answers to 'puppy,' " Edgar said. "It may progress to 'dog.' "

"At least I don't have to deal with him wanting to baptize it for a while." Catherine sighed. "I don't know why we have to be at the Temple this afternoon. Our witness won't make a bit of difference to the outcome."

"Aren't you at all curious?" Edgar was surprised. "I would have thought you'd want to hear every argument."

"I think I've already heard them all," Catherine said. "I wish Commander Evrard could also judge Jehan. Every day he stays in the *Chastelet*, I worry that somehow he'll escape."

"He has no tricks to melt locks, *carissima*," Edgar said. "His trial will wait. I still have hopes that the body of the wizard will turn up."

"With Jehan's knife still in it?" Catherine was doubtful.

"I think it was stuck in the breastbone," Edgar said. "It didn't budge when Solomon and I touched it. And Jehan isn't the type to panic and leave a weapon unless he couldn't free it."

"I know," Catherine said. "Edgar, how much force do you think it took to drive the weapon that killed 'Lord Osto'?"

"His attacker was either very strong or perhaps on horseback," Edgar said, considering. "But the angle wasn't right for that."

"Edgar," Catherine asked, "could a stick, spear, bean-pole, whatever, have been damaged in making a blow of that force?"

"Perhaps," Edgar answered, calculating in his head. "Depending on what it hit, the kind of wood, if it were iron-tipped, things like that. Why?"

"Bertulf and Godfrey moved the body here," Catherine

said. "They've told us as much. We couldn't look for a weapon because we didn't know where the man was murdered. Now we do."

"But that was over a month ago," Edgar said. "There won't be any evidence left by now."

"No bloodstains or dropped gloves," Catherine said. "They would have been washed away or taken. But who would notice a broken piece of wood? And, if the wood were soft enough, mightn't there still be stains on it, even with all the rain?"

Edgar put down his spoon.

"You have an idea, don't you?" he said. "Someone other than Archer."

"The glimmer of one," Catherine admitted. "It came to me while listening to Samonie at Willa's bedside. There was someone with far greater reason to kill Bertulf than poor hot-tempered Archer."

Edgar tried to follow her logic. Sometimes Catherine's thinking was more convoluted than that of the bishop of Poitiers. Slowly, he began to see.

"It will be hard to prove," he said. "Harder than convincing a judge that Archer did it."

"I know," Catherine said. "That's why we have to find the weapon. No, not us. We should have nothing to do with finding it. We need someone completely trustworthy and unbiased."

"It's too bad Astrolabe has gone," Edgar said. "Who else do we know . . ."

"Maurice!" They said it together.

"I'll go ask him at once," Edgar said, getting up. "I'll tell him to bring anything he finds directly to the preceptory."

"Do you think he'll think such a task beneath him?" Catherine asked.

"Maurice? You know him better than that," Edgar said. "Especially when I tell him his work may save an innocent man."

He noticed that Catherine was putting on her street shoes and getting the children ready to go out with her.

"We don't all have to see Maurice," Edgar said.

"I know," Catherine answered. "You go ahead. I have an errand to run. We'll be back soon."

At the preceptory, Lord Osto felt as if he were the one about to be tried. The grand gesture of taking on his friend's identity seemed much more ridiculous now. Bertulf wanted to make a place for himself and Lambert by becoming a hero in the battle against the Saracens. That was fine for Bertulf. He might have been born a miller, but he had the spirit of a warrior. And he knew horses better than any knight Osto had ever met.

Bertulf would have been a hero. But Osto wasn't one, and calling himself Bertulf didn't change his nature. He was only a caretaker, seeing to the needs of the people in his village, protecting them from the worst of the tithes and taxes the higher nobility would place on them. He loved horses but was happiest just watching them, raising them. Other men could ride them into battle. He was content with his lot. He'd even been happy with the wife his father had chosen for him. Poor Edwina! How he would miss her!

Nothing had gone right since Bertulf died. He had been the true leader of the group. Osto was beginning to doubt that Godfrey would hold firm to his pledge to go with him, now that there was no reason to send him home. He was even starting to be unsure of his accusation of the man in the tavern. The voice, yes, that was the same, he'd wager his life on that. But was the man a murderer? Could it have been a passing stranger instead? Some drunken knight eager to test his lance. He didn't know anymore. He wanted so much to go home.

But what would happen to Clemence if he failed? Jordan might well take her inheritance and give it, with her, to one of his landless friends. She would have to give her consent to the marriage, of course, but Osto knew what kind of pressure could be brought upon her to do so. When she had been missing, all he had cared about was finding her alive and whole. Now that he knew she was safe, her future was once more his concern. Even more, he admitted, he wanted a grandson of his to hold his land, not some stranger. He wanted that man to be Bertulf's grandson, too.

"Godfrey!" he called. "Aren't they ready for us, yet?"

"I can't see, Master," Godfrey called back from the window on the floor above. "There are too many people milling about."

Osto got up and joined him.

"I can't believe Commander Evrard is taking the time to decide this, himself," he said. "I thought he was leaving tomorrow."

"I don't think he's happy about it," Godfrey said. "But that will be all to the good. He'll hear our testimony and make his judgment quickly. The matter of your true name may not even arise."

"Let's hope not." Osto put on his black cloak and was Bertulf again.

"Chaim, the men are here," Abraham said. "It's time to go."

Hubert sat on a bench, his few clothes packed in a bag wrapped around the Torah. He looked up sadly.

"Did you tell Catherine I was leaving?" he asked.

"Solomon did."

"I had hoped she would come to say good-bye." He got up slowly and slung the bag over his shoulder. "I'm ready."

The weight of it bowed him over. He was grateful that one of the other traders had offered to let his mule carry Hubert's pack. Now, if someone would just offer to bear the weight in his heart.

They loaded up the pack animals in Abraham's courtyard and then went out the gate, single file. Hubert was almost at the end, walking beside the mule. He kept his face down, to avoid being recognized. Behind him, Joel gave him a nudge. He looked up.

There, across the street stood Catherine, holding the hands of James and Edana. Hubert lifted his hands to her and would have crossed but for Joel's hand on his arm. Catherine shook her head.

The children were admiring the animals and paid no attention to the bearded man who was staring at them, marveling at how much they had changed in only a few months. He tried to imprint every line of their faces in his mind, knowing this was the last time he would ever see them.

"We must be going," Joel said, leading him into the line of men and beasts.

Catherine stood there watching, until they turned the corner, Hubert turning to gaze at them one final time before he vanished.

When she and the children arrived home, it was time to go to the preceptory.

"Will you be all right, Margaret?" Edgar asked. "I don't think Samonie is well enough to care for the children."

"I don't mind staying home," Margaret said. "I never liked trials when Father presided. I don't think I'd like this one, either."

"I wish I didn't have to go," Lambert said. "I can't get used to knowing my father's dead and that it will never be known."

"It's what he would have wanted," Clemence reminded him. "I also find it difficult to have my father addressed as 'Bertulf.' "

When they reached the Temple preceptory they were told that Commander Evrard was holding the proceedings in the chapter room. A number of people were headed that way, including Archer, supported by Richilde and his fellow water merchants.

"I don't know what you and that Picard have in mind," one of them shouted at Edgar. "But we stand with Archer!"

"Do you think you'll be heard?" Catherine asked Edgar.

"Of course," Edgar answered. "I only hope Maurice finds the weapon."

"Our case is good without it."

"But with it, there would be little room for doubt."

The room was already crowded when they got there. There were two chairs set up in one corner, one for Evrard de Barre. Catherine wondered who the other one was for. Another judge?

She was astonished when the commander did not enter the room first. Instead she saw a man in episcopal regalia. But it wasn't the bishop of Paris but Pope Eugenius. Catherine wasn't the only one surprised; there were murmurs all around her.

They were followed by kights and chaplains of the Temple, including Master Durand. The sergeant accompanying the commander and pope called for silence. The voices all rose for a moment, then the room was still. Commander Evrard stood in front of his chair and adressed them.

"While this is a trial for the crime of murder," he began, "I have been advised that there are other issues involved here that I have no power to decide. Therefore I have asked our revered Father, Eugenius, Bishop of Rome, to listen to the arguments and give his judgment along with mine."

He sat. Everyone began talking again, asking each other what could be meant by this. It took the sergeant several minutes to restore order.

Archer was brought in from one side, Bertulf and Godfrey from the other. The charge was read and loudly denied by Archer.

"Do you have any who will swear to your innocence?" Evrard asked.

Giselbert Trickster stepped forward. "Archer is a member of the water merchants of Paris. We pledge our surety that he has done no murder."

"And you, *dant* Bertulf." Evrard turned to him. "Are you prepared to swear to this man's guilt?"

Bertulf hesitated. Godfrey nudged him.

"I am."

"Then let us hear arguments from both sides," Evrard said. "If no decision can be made then, Archer, will you or a designate submit to the ordeal to prove your innocence?"

Archer, pale at the thought of hot iron, nodded. Richilde took his hand.

"Then Bertulf of Picardy, step forward and repeat your accusation, giving your reasons for it in front of all."

Bertulf told the events of the evening, explaining that he had only heard Archer's voice, but that even his own friends admitted that the miller had taunted Lord Osto.

"When my lord didn't return I sent our servant, Godfrey, to see what had become of him," Bertulf concluded. "We found him across the road, dead."

"The fact that you moved the body without permission doesn't speak well for you," Evrard said.

"We were strangers," Bertulf explained. "Our lord had been killed. We were afraid we would be next."

Edgar started to move forward in the audience.

"But you brought the Temple into danger of scandal by wrapping your lord in the white cloak, even though he hadn't earned the right to wear it." Evrard was stern.

"I know, my lord Commander," Bertulf said. "I apologize. My friend set out to become a Knight of the Temple. Only death thwarted his plan. We felt he had earned the right to wear the cloak he had brought with him. Did you bury him in it?"

Evrard nodded. Then he called Archer to give his side of the story. Nervously, Archer told everyone that he had been drinking a bit much and let his anger at all the foreigners spill out on Lord Osto and his servant.

"But I forgot all about it before I was halfway home!" he protested. "I didn't even know he had been killed until this man, whom I never saw before," he said, pointing at Bertulf, "accused me of murder."

Catherine had been waiting by the door in the hope that Maurice would soon arrive. Now she turned over the task to Lambert and edged through to where Edgar was standing, waiting for a chance to speak.

"There's something wrong here," she whispered. "We may not need Maurice's evidence."

She stood on tiptoe to explain everything to him. The pope noticed her and asked Evrard who they were.

"Lord Edgar," Eugenius said suddenly.

Edgar started. "My lord Pope." He bowed.

"Didn't I meet you in Trier last November?"

Edgar bowed again. "I'm flattered Your Lordship remembers me."

"My friend, the abbot of Cîteaux, told me about you then, and your wife. Not many laymen there spoke both French and Latin."

Behind Edgar, Catherine blushed and gave a bow, as well.

At a prompting from the pope, Evrard beckoned Edgar forward.

"I hope you and your wife weren't having a domestic conversation?" he asked, amidst titters from the crowd.

"No, my lord," Edgar answered. "As you know, my wife and I were as insulted as you by the deposit of the body in our home. We have spent the time since then defending ourselves from the charge of complicity in his death."

Edgar looked pointedly at Master Durand, who glared back.

"Because of that, I believe I have a stake in seeing the matter resolved," he continued. "Particularly since because of this we also became responsible for the children of *dom* Bertulf and Lord Osto."

"Edgar . . ." Bertulf warned. "You promised."

"I'm sorry," Edgar said. "But I can't stand by for the sake of an oath and see my fellow water merchant hanged for a crime he didn't do."

"What do you mean?" Godfrey cried out. "Of course he did it! My master heard him!"

"Godfrey," Edgar said, "where were you when Archer was belittling Lord Osto and all those of Picardy?"

"I was out tending to the horses," Godfrey answered.

Bertulf nodded agreement. "He didn't come in until after Archer had left."

"I see," Edgar said. "May I question Godfrey further?"

Pope Eugenius nodded and Evrard lifted his hands in resignation. Who was he to contradict the pope?

"Godfrey, you, Lord Osto and Bertulf had three horses, is that correct?" Edgar asked.

"That's right," Godfrey said. "And a pack mule."

"So that was one for each of you to ride?" Edgar went on.

Godfrey snorted. "Of course not. You haven't seen

Vrieit. No one would use a fine destrier like that for ordinary travel. He was on a lead."

"So, Bertulf the miller and Lord Osto rode their horses," Edgar said. "And you the mule?"

Godfrey gave him a disgusted look. "You can't be much of a lord if you'd let a mule be overloaded like that. I told you, it was for the baggage."

"Lord Edgar?" Evrard said. "This doesn't interest me."

"Don't you see?" Catherine blurted out.

Instantly, she clapped her hand over her mouth.

Anger and amusement warred in Evrard. Fortunately for Catherine, he was a charitable man.

"Lord Edgar is going to tedious lengths to show that the servant, Godfrey, must have walked while his masters rode. What's so unusual about that?"

Catherine opened her mouth to answer, but Edgar was faster.

"Two things," he said. "One, Lord Osto was certainly Godfrey's master, but what was Bertulf to him? He's a miller, a horse breeder, much wealthier than the average man of his village, but what gave him the right to ride when Godfrey walked?"

"Nothing!" Godfrey said loudly. "His father and mine were first cousins. He had no business ordering me about just because he'd picked up a few coins. And then he wanted his son to be our castellan! I told him, 'You're either born noble or like the rest of us. You can't change it.'"

Evrard spoke from behind Godfrey. "But that's what Bertulf wanted, didn't he? To change his place in the order of things, by earning the right to a white cloak. Bertulf, I could have told you that it wouldn't have happened. We've expelled better-born men than you for lying about their status."

Bertulf shook the tears from his eyes. "It was a dream Lord Osto and I had. It started with the horses. We found that it was good to bring in some common stock from time to time to breed in strength and endurance. Then, when our children fell in love, we thought, why not? My line was sadly lacking in stamina."

Evrard sighed. "Lord Osto, isn't it time you stopped this game, however worthy you might think it?"

Bertulf started at being addressed by his true name. Then slowly, he nodded. "I told Godfrey I couldn't do it. I should have been the one to die. Bertulf could have been a great lord."

"And that's why he was the one who had to die," Edgar said. "Isn't that right, Godfrey?"

"No!" Godfrey backed away. "I'm devoted to my master. Ask anyone!"

"I know you are," Edgar continued. "And that's why you had to save him from throwing his life away in the Holy Land for such an ignominious reason. But it didn't work, after all. Lord Osto believed in the plan so strongly that he was willing to pretend to be less than he was. You didn't expect that, did you?"

"You're mad," Godfrey said. "Master, tell them!"

Lord Osto/Bertulf was staring at him as at a stranger.

"Godfrey, were you in the tavern when that man was making fun of Bertulf?"

"No!"

"Yes!" Half a dozen voices spoke.

"We all saw him there," Giselbert said. "He came in just before the fight and stayed. Helped clean up his friend and took him out to wash."

Godfrey licked his lips. "Perhaps I did. I don't remember. What difference does it make?"

"You told me you wouldn't know the face of the man I only heard," Lord Osto said. "You didn't want him found, did you?"

"Master!" Godfrey pled.

"Godfrey, what happened to your walking staff?"

Bertulf was gone for good now. Lord Osto stood before his villein and demanded the truth.

There was a mild voice from the back of the room.

"I think this might be it," Maurice said.

∞

In the end Godfrey had to be dragged away, screaming epithets at Osto, Bertulf and anyone who came near him. Most of the people left, delighted at having been given a good show.

Lambert knelt on the floor, looking at the pieces of wood.

"I can see where the iron was blunted," he said. "But Godfrey might have done that at any time along the road. What I don't understand is how the blow that killed my father could have caused this wood to snap. It's old chestnut."

"Godfrey broke it himself," Catherine said. "While sitting with Samonie waiting for Willa to die, she told me that she'd been attracted to Godfrey in the first place because he understood how she felt. Her position in life meant that Willa became the wife of a felt maker and worked herself to death within a year. But Willa's father is a great lord, one we all know, Samonie says. By blood, Willa could have been a fine lady. And there was Lambert, with no noble ancestors at all, being put over Godfrey as lord, as Bertulf had treated his cousin as a servant."

"So why did he break his own staff?" Lambert asked.

Catherine shrugged. It was hard to explain. "I think he hated it. He walked, and Bertulf rode. That was the only difference he could see between them."

Pope Eugenius had been silent since he had recognized Edgar. Now he spoke, more to himself than to the others.

"How much wickedness comes from not accepting the place God has assigned us." He sighed. "We're all equal in the eyes of Heaven. Rome is overrun with people like that poor man. They drove me out and what do they have now? Chaos."

"Then you believe that the children of Lambert and Clemence should not be allowed to inherit my fief?" Osto asked.

Eugenius called his thoughts back from Rome. "That is not my decision. You'll have to convince your lord of that. What I can say, and the reason I suspect Master Evrard asked me to be here, is that if you, Lambert, and you, Clemence, entered into the sacrament of marriage in good faith and with the consent of your families, I will oppose anyone who tries to have it annuled."

Both Lambert and Clemence went down on their knees to thank him. A bit stiffly, Osto did, too.

"And I?" he asked. "I tried to deceive the Knights of the Temple and came to join them for the basest of motives, the future of my own family. What penance would you place on me?"

The pope looked at him for some time. "I shall have to confer with Commander Evrard on that this evening. Perhaps you should also take counsel with your own soul."

When they left the chapter house they were amazed to find it was still afternoon. The sun shone warmly on soft grass and budding flowers. They found the other water merchants waiting outside. Archer came up to Edgar, who took a step back. Archer took his hand.

"Thank you! Thank you!" he said. "I knew you wouldn't desert your fellows. I said that, didn't I?"

"After the fact, yes," Pagan said. "But we all thank you, Edgar, for saving Archer from the ordeal and for naming yourself as one of us and not a lord of Scotland."

"It's just been pointed out to me that I can't change what I was born," Edgar said. "But I can decide whom I stand with."

Only Catherine heard the ambiguity in that statement.

Catherine wasn't sure that Samonie understood when she told her that Godfrey had killed the man in the counting room.

"Did you hear me?" she asked as Samonie went back to cleaning the cupboard in the kitchen.

"Yes, I guessed as much," Samonie said.

"Why didn't you tell us?" Catherine asked.

"What difference did it make?" Samonie said. "If it would have saved your life, I'd have spoken up. But you were in no danger, except from that Jehan."

Jehan. Catherine had been trying not to think of him.

∞

"Edgar, what will they do with him?" she asked one night a few days later, when no trial had been called for Jehan.

"I've been talking with the provost and Lord Osto," Edgar told her. "You're not going to like this."

"They couldn't set him free!" Catherine protested.

"There's been word from Count Thibault and Abbot Suger, as well," Edgar went on. "They feel that Jehan served them well and his action against Clemence was a temporary madness, a lovesickness. Since she wasn't harmed, they begged Lord Osto to forgive him."

"Lord Osto! What about us? He broke into our house. Lambert said he was going to denounce us."

Edgar scratched his newly shaved chin. "Oh, that. That was interesting."

He paused, mainly to tease Catherine.

"The meeting this afternoon at the water merchants?" she asked, her fingers in his ribs. "Did that have something to do with Jehan?"

"Yes," he admitted. "Stop tickling! Apparently Jehan has been telling everyone that we're secretly Jews and plotting with the Saracens to take over France."

"Sweet Virgin!" Catherine commented. "And his proof?"

"The account book," Edgar said. "With the 'magic' Hebrew writing. I didn't even have to produce it. Archer said he'd been doing the same thing for years. He doesn't like Jews, but he's not above learning a good trick from them. The water merchants told the provost that such an accusation was nonsense."

"Archer!" Catherine said. "Imagine that. I suppose it's a good thing that we didn't let him hang."

"Are you sorry we couldn't convict Jehan?" Edgar asked.

"Not as much as you and Solomon might be," Catherine said. "I suppose I can't help but believe in the possibility of redemption."

"Of Jehan!" Edgar gave a whoop and began tickling her. "Woman, you can't be serious. See, you're laughing right now!"

"Edgar!" she shrieked. "Stop it or I'll . . ."

One thing led to another, although they continued laughing. They didn't hear the door creak open. Edgar rolled over, Catherine on top of him when both were startled by a pair of grey eyes peering over the mattress and an indignant voice saying, "Mama, Papa, why are you having fun without me?"

Epilogue

The first Wednesday after Pentecost, 3 ides July (June 11), 1147; The first feast of Saint Barnabas, Apostle, and the beginning of the fair at Lendit, north of Paris.

Illo anno in quarta feria Pentecostes edictum accidit; sic regi celebria cuncta succedunt. Dum igitur a beato Dionysio vexillum et abeundi licentiam petiit . . . visus ab omnibus planctum maximum extavit et intimi affectus omnium benedictionem accepit.

That year the fair took place on the Wednesday after Pentecost. So great numbers came there, lingering to see the king. At that time he asked for the oriflamme banner from Saint Denis and also permission to leave. In the sight of all he caused great sorrow and accepted the blessing of everyone and their deep affection.

—Odo of Deuil
de Profectione Ludovico VII in Orientum
Book I

By Sharan Newman
from Tom Doherty Associates

CATHERINE LEVENDEUR MYSTERIES

Death Comes as Epiphany
The Devil's Door
The Wandering Arm
Strong as Death
Cursed in the Blood
The Difficult Saint
To Wear the White Cloak
Heresy

GUINEVERE

Guinevere
The Chessboard Queen
Guinevere Evermore